"How long will you ... **u will have finished thinking by Wednesday afternoon?"**
Izzy asked.

"I don't know," Sophie said. "I'm not sure."

"But you will come back? To live forever and be our . . ." Izzy started, then stalled.

"What sweetheart?" Sophie asked her.

"Be our sort of mummy," Izzy finished, looking anxious, as if she'd just asked for something she knew she was not allowed.

Sophie pressed Izzy's small body into hers and held her close. "I will always be there to look after you in every way that your mummy would have, I promise."

Yes, but . . . if you don't marry daddy, then there won't be any rings and I won't be able to say it, will I?"

"Say what, sweetheart?" Sophie asked.

"Say Mummy to you," Izzy said, unable to look her in the eye.

Praise for *The Accidental Mother* by Rowan Coleman

"An exceptional and touching read about love and loss."
—*Booklist*

"A funny, touching story—and another unputdownable read."
—*Company* magazine

"Fun, poignant."
—*OK* magazine

Also by Rowan Coleman

Mommy By Mistake

Another Mother's Life

The Accidental Mother

Rowan Coleman

The Accidental Family

Pocket Books

New York   London   Toronto   Sydney

Pocket Books
A Division of Simon & Schuster, Inc.
1230 Avenue of the Americas
New York, NY 10020

First Pocket Books trade paperback edition September 2009

POCKET and colophon are registered trademarks of Simon & Schuster, Inc.

For information about special discounts for bulk purchases, please contact Simon & Schuster Special Sales at 1-866-506-1949 or business@simonandschuster.com.

The Simon & Schuster Speakers Bureau can bring authors to your live event. For more information or to book an event contact the Simon & Schuster Speakers Bureau at 1-866-248-3049 or visit our website at www.simonspeakers.com.

Manufactured in the United States of America

10 9 8 7 6 5 4 3 2 1

Library of Congress Cataloging-in-Publication Data

Coleman, Rowan.
   The accidental family / by Rowan Coleman.—1st Pocket Books trade pbk. ed.
      p.   cm.
   1. Stepmothers—Fiction.   2. Country life—England—Fiction.   3. Cornwall (England : County)—Fiction.   4. Chick lit.   I. Title.
   PR6103.04426A63   2009
   823'.92—dc22   2009011114

ISBN 978-1-4391-5528-8
ISBN 978-1-4391-6505-8 (ebook)

The
Accidental
Family

A Bedtime Story

"Right . . . um, well—once upon a time, not that long ago, there lived an exceptionally beautiful princess who had long, golden hair and was a size ten as long as she stayed off white bread and cake.

"Princess Sophie lived in a very nice one-bedroom turret in an up-and-coming part of the kingdom, and she owned an extensive and extremely stylish collection of shoes and one cat named Artemis. Actually, she didn't exactly own the cat; the cat just lived in the flat with her. More like a flatmate really, or a flatcat . . . *anyway,* Princess Sophie thought she was very happy because she had a very nice home, a lot of nice clothes and shoes, and a particularly nice white sofa that she and Artemis were very fond of, although they hardly ever sat on it at the same time because Artemis liked her space.

"The princess even had a very serious and important job that she was very, very good at. She was a career princess, one who knew that events management wasn't just planning a lot of big parties. In fact, Princess Sophie was very good at most things except being close to other people. She didn't realize it at the time, but the princess was actually quite lonely.

"Then one day a very badly dressed fairy godmother came to visit her from the land of Social Services. She told the princess that a very sad thing had happened. The princess's oldest and best friend, Lady Carrie, had died. And she had left behind two daughters who needed to be looked after. The fairy godmother reminded Princess Sophie that once, long ago, she had made a promise to Lady Carrie that if anything ever happened to her, Princess Sophie would look after her two little girls.

"Well, Princess Sophie didn't exactly know what to think. She was very, very sad about losing her friend, but also she was scared. When she had made that promise, she never dreamed that one day she would have to keep it, and she wasn't sure she knew how to look after two small girls—okay, one small girl and one big girl . . . fine, two big girls—because the only thing she had ever looked after before was herself and her cat. And she wasn't sure that leaving out food and water constituted actual caring for a living creature.

"But when she thought about her lovely friend, Princess Sophie knew she couldn't let them down. And so the two small—I mean big—girls came to stay. Their names were Bella and Izzy. Bella was an artist and pony expert who could fly as long as no one was looking, and Izzy was a true fairy, which was easy to see because she always dressed as a fairy even when she went to bed, *even* when she had a bath.

"At first Princess Sophie and Artemis weren't sure at all about Bella and Izzy, especially when they turned her lovely white sofa into a green curry-scented one, ruined her makeup collection, and got stuck down the loo. Princess Sophie thought there was no way she would be able to cope. But the two big girls needed a friend to look after them, and Princess Sophie was the only friend they had, so she stuck it out.

"And gradually, day by day, Princess Sophie got to like Izzy and Bella a bit more, and they got to like her a bit more too. And even though all three of them felt sad, they were all sort of glad they had each other.

"Then one day a handsome stranger called Prince Louis arrived at Princess Sophie's door. He was Bella and Izzy's daddy. He had been in a faraway land for three years, and as soon as he found out what had happened, he came back to look after his daughters. But no one had seen him in all that time and Princess Sophie didn't know if he was a nice man or not. Pony expert Bella wasn't sure if, after all that time, she still wanted him to be her daddy. Only fairy Izzy, who had never met her daddy before, decided to like him right away—and you know what they say: first impressions are always right. Apart from Princess Sophie's first impression of Prince Louis, because she thought he was a tramp with mental-health issues.

"Ever so slowly the two big girls and Princess Sophie got to know Prince Louis. Izzy first, because she was the best at making friends, and then Bella and Princess Sophie, although Princess Sophie found Prince Louis quite irritating because he was so handsome and mysterious, and he made her heart beat faster whenever he was near her, which was highly inconvenient.

"One day it was time for Prince Louis to take Bella and Izzy back home to the Land of Mermaids, by the sea. Princess Sophie felt very, very sad, but she knew they had to go. She knew they'd be happy there, in the place Lady Carrie had loved best. And so she drove all of them there in her magic chariot, Phoebe the car.

"And when they got there Sophie realized something wonderful and scary too. She realized that she loved Bella and Izzy, that she loved them with all her heart—and even more scarily she realized that she loved Prince Louis too.

"Well, Princess Sophie didn't know what to do about that, because she wasn't used to loving anyone apart from her cat, who she wasn't at all sure loved her back. She didn't know how to show or tell the people she loved how much she cared about them. She didn't know if they would want her to love them. So when she saw how happy Prince Louis, Bella, and Izzy were, she decided to leave and go back to her turret, even though it broke her heart.

"Once she got back home, she felt sad every day. She felt sad even though she was crowned queen at her office and became the boss of everything, which was really only what she deserved because she was so very good at her job. At night she lay on her slightly green and smelly sofa missing the three people she loved.

"Then Princess Sophie's friend Cal, who isn't a fairy exactly but who does have magic fashion powers, told her that if she stayed in her turret pining away, she would never be happy. He told her she had to be brave, she had to go on a quest to the Land of Mermaids and find Prince Louis and Bella and Izzy and tell them she loved them, and that, come what may, she wanted to be near them.

"Princess Sophie wasn't sure she could be that brave, but magic Cal told her to pull herself together and get going. And so she did.

"She traveled down to the Land of Mermaids, and when she got there she told Prince Louis and Bella and Izzy how very much she loved them, and the best thing—the happiest thing of all—was that they told her they loved her back.

"And Princess Sophie decided to stay in the Land of Mermaids forever and ever.

"The end.

"Or perhaps it's just the beginning."

Prologue

The room was dark except for the artificial orange glow cast by the fake coals of Louis's 1970s electric fire.

Sophie stared into the dusty coals, her head on Louis's chest, listening to the rhythmic beat of his heart. His fingers had been gently smoothing her hair away from her face for the last twenty minutes or so and neither of them had said a word to the other, principally because there had been far too much kissing for small talk.

"You've been here for six hours and eleven minutes," Louis said quietly, almost to himself. "You've actually, physically, really been here, and not just in my imagination, for over six hours."

"Have I?" Sophie lifted her head from his chest to look at him, finding two tiny golden reflections of the fire glinting in his dark eyes. The trouble was, whenever Sophie looked at Louis she wanted to kiss him, and so for the last twenty minutes she had tried not to look at him. She felt, particularly given the circumstances of her arrival earlier that afternoon, that they should probably be doing less kissing and at least *some* talking about what was going to happen next now that she'd left her entire life in London to be with him and his daughters in Cornwall. Only kissing was so much nicer, and it didn't involve her having to talk about all the things she was thinking and feeling, which was always a plus where Sophie was concerned.

Still, there was something unseemly about the fact that the last six hours and eleven minutes had been largely comprised of kissing, with a break for tea and putting Louis's very overexcited daughters to bed. She was sure there should be more speeches, more declarations of intent. Sophie found herself worrying, wondering if Louis minded all the kissing, and then she wondered how she would ever go about asking him such a question. Perhaps it was better just to kiss him and think about the consequences later; after all, it was that kind of rationale that had brought her here in the first place.

Sophie Mills was being uncharacteristically impulsive.

Just as Sophie was caving in to her desire to kiss Louis, he spoke.

"I think six hours and eleven minutes is the longest time we have ever spent together, in one go," Louis said. "Apart from that night when—"

"Do you think I'm crazy, Louis?" Sophie asked.

"You probably are a *bit* mad," Louis said, smiling fondly in the artificial light. "I don't know many women who'd give up their job, their *career*, their home, and their life in London to come and be with a single dad and his two unruly children in St. Ives, Cornwall."

"I am mad!" Sophie sat bolt upright, feeling a chill rush along the parts of her body that were no longer welded to Louis's. "You hardly even know me, and I've just landed on your doorstep telling you I'm here to stay! You must be horrified."

Louis tapped one long finger on his thigh three times. "Yes, yes I am," he said, nodding. "I'm totally horrified. Hence all this kissing, that's me in turmoil, that is. Look—getting to know you is one of the most wonderful things I have ever done, and I feel as if you know me better than anyone else ever has. I don't know what Bella and Izzy would have done these past few months if it hadn't been for you. You were there for them when no one else was, and they need you in their lives. I think you need them too, and hopefully, you need me a bit too. At least for one thing."

"Do you mind all this kissing, by the way?" Sophie asked him intently, silently cursing herself for her apparently boundless capacity to ask stupid and inappropriate questions that were far more likely to make a man fall out of love with a woman than in.

Louis laughed. "Like I said, I'm horrified. It's dreadful kissing an incredibly beautiful woman for hours on end."

"Are you being sarcastic?" Sophie thought it was best to double-check.

"Of course I'm being sarcastic! Good god, woman, I *love* kissing you!"

Sophie found herself smiling, her shoulders relaxing again as she let her torso lean into his, her thigh resting against the length of his.

"I do love the girls," she said thoughtfully. The realization of that fundamental truth still shocked her, but it was inescapable. Two small, lost children had inspired emotions in her she had never believed possible—and the girls weren't even hers. "I do love them. And I'd do anything for them but . . ." Sophie's mouth went dry. Declarations weren't really her thing and she'd already made one today, which was one more than she had ever made in her entire life, but still, now that she was here, she felt she had to say something important and *momentous*. "I came here for you, because I, you know, love you and stuff."

"And stuff?" Louis repeated, his voice full of warmth.

"Yes, and stuff," Sophie said, holding his gaze defiantly.

"Sophie." Louis picked up her hand and stroked the back of it with his forefinger. "Thank you. Thank you for leaving your life in London to come down here for me. And I really mean that because I am stupidly, wholly, utterly grateful to you because I *love* you. I love you *and* stuff, if stuff is a requirement. I haven't said it before now because for the last six hours and—" he checked his watch— "twenty-two minutes I've been wondering if you're really here or if this is all some illusion I've conjured up for myself, because god knows, all I've done since we parted is daydream about having you near me." Louis kissed the back of her hand. "But now that you've told me you love me 'and stuff,' I know it's really you. Only the real Sophie Mills would say that. So maybe it is impossible for two people to fall in love after only a few months, and maybe we are crazy, but you being here has made me the happiest man this side of Plymouth and probably beyond. I love you, Sophie Mills."

Sophie put her hand over his and felt tears in her eyes.

"I'm glad," she said. "Because I would have looked like an awful idiot if you didn't."

"And look," Louis told her earnestly, "I want you to know that I'm here for you all the time. The second you have a worry or a doubt or feel like freaking out because you've realized that no one wears high heels on a weekday round here, all you have to do is come to me and I'll talk you down, because—"

"Louis." Sophie stopped his mouth with her finger.

"Yes," Louis said against her skin.

"Shut up and kiss me."

One
Six months later

"Scones and clotted cream are the devil's work," Sophie said out loud as she inspected herself in her latest pair of jeans. Technically she was still a size ten, but if she was honest, the almost daily trips to Carmen Velasquez's Ye Olde Tea Shoppe had pushed her hips to the size's upper limit, something she'd have to sort out eventually, particularly if she really was going to wear quite so much denim.

Once, before Bella, Izzy, and their father had come into her life, Sophie had owned only one pair of jeans, which she hardly ever wore. She had been an occasion dresser, with a fondness for silk blouses on workdays and a rule that a heel should never dwindle below three inches. But since she'd come to stay in St. Ives, not only had she not bought a single pair of high heels, she'd collected four pairs of jeans, two denim skirts, an assortment of casual tops, and an anorak. Sophie loved her double-zipped weatherproof red and navy blue anorak, but it was a love that dare not speak its name, at least not when she was on the phone talking to her erstwhile secretary and good friend Cal about her outlandish new life in Cornwall.

"Have you got any wellies yet?" Cal would ask her without fail during their weekly chats.

"Me, wellies, are you joking? I have some standards," Sophie would tell him breezily. And then, hoping to change the subject, she'd try to engage him in some work talk. "Tell me what's new, do you have new accounts—are things as bad in the city as they say they are?"

Cal, who was never that fond of bad news, would ignore her. "Wellies mean you aren't coming back," Cal took pleasure in telling her. "Wellies are a sign of commitment to your new way of life. Wellington boots are the nearest that you, Sophie Mills, will ever get to an engagement ring."

"Thanks, Cal, thanks very much for boiling my entire romantic happiness down to rubber boots," Sophie would reply. "Besides, what would you, the king of commitment phobia, know anyway? I might get married one day—anyway, I was thinking that if the big corporations are cutting back on parties to show how sorry they are, why don't you target smaller firms? I know what you're thinking. You're thinking that if the big guys haven't got any money, then the little guys certainly don't, but—bear with me—smaller events at discounted rates mean less work and less outlay—more accounts and only marginally reduced revenue. You should run that by Eve—you can tell her it's your idea if you like."

"Sophie, have you forgotten that you traded in the life of a corporate junkie to breathe in sea air and be fulfilled? I don't need your ideas, I have ideas. I'm going after the pink pound. I'm much more interested in the idea of *you* getting married—you!"

Trying not to feel hurt that Cal had rejected her idea so entirely, Sophie gazed out her bedroom window at the gray and stormy sea beyond the harbor below. Before she'd left London to come here, she had never once daydreamed about getting married or being a bride. But during the last six months she'd spent with Louis, she felt like a different person, no, a different version of herself, the self she might be if she were living in a novel or a film. The happy-ending self. And if you were the sort of person who believed in happy endings, then you knew they always came about with a wedding.

"To Louis?" Cal persisted.

"Potentially." Sophie's mouth curled into a smile meant only for herself. "One day, you know . . . when the time is right."

"Wellies first." Cal was adamant. "Once you've bought the wellies, then he'll finally know you're committed and he'll ask you. That's what he's waiting for."

But as of yet there were no Wellington boots in the wardrobe in Sophie's room at the Avalon B & B, and at six months she was the second-longest-staying guest, second only to Mrs. Tregowan, who had been there for nearly a year since her husband died and she had decided she couldn't bear to go back to her bungalow without him.

Sophie had arrived in the Cornish town of St. Ives in the spring. Fully experiencing the burgeoning season and embracing the renewal of life, she'd felt herself awaken to the unknown possibilities that the future might hold. On weekend mornings she and Louis had waded in the freezing waters of the harbor with the girls until her soft city toes turned blue, collecting interesting shells and bits of pottery. Sophie had let the cool, crisp sea breeze ruddy her cheeks and whip her fine blond hair into a tangle. As they climbed over the rocks and stones to the harbor wall, Louis would hold her hand in his, reviving her numb fingers with his body heat until she felt the blood tingle and throb in the tips.

She had stayed for the whole fickle summer, which had been a stretch of warm, rainy days occasionally studded with jewel-like ones bathed in sunshine. During the summer holidays, when Louis was working on building up his fledgling photography business, the girls gave her their own personal tour of the town they'd grown up in. Picnicking among the clover and daisies in the meadow above the whitewashed town that seemed to be perched so haphazardly on the rocky cliffs that tumbled to the sea, dodging the tourists for the roller disco that took place at midday in the guildhall, which Sophie found both exhilarating and humiliating in turn. They took her to the Tate Gallery and showed her the paintings that had been their mother's favorites, Bella lecturing her confidently about light and perspective. They led her in and out of the maze of tiny cobbled streets, showing her their favorite houses, their window boxes laden with geraniums. And in the evenings before bed, after Louis had got home from that day's assignment, they'd walk along the harbor wall until they found the family of seals that was always there, lounging on the rocks just out to sea as if they rather enjoyed their celebrity. Izzy would give the seals a new name every day and Bella would tell Izzy stories about them.

For most of that time, Sophie hadn't thought about the career she'd left behind. It was as if she had finally put her foot on the brake of her life, which had been careering recklessly toward a final goal that she had never been sure of, and taken a moment to look around and feel what it meant to be alive in the world. And then in the last couple of months she'd started to feel restless and irritable. For a while she'd worried that she wasn't madly in love with Louis after all, and that the whole escapade had been a terrible mistake. But then one evening as they'd strolled along the seafront, the girls bounding along ahead of them, Louis had turned to her and said, "You're not happy, Soph, and I know why."

"I am so happy," Sophie had replied, panicking. "Look at me. I'm delirious!"

"You're bored," Louis said, smiling while squeezing her fingers.

"Bored? How could I be bored with this, with you and those two?" She nodded at the girls, who were screaming in delight as the seagulls dive-bombed them, trying to steal their chips.

"Look, it's okay, you know. I mean I know that I am endlessly fascinating and deeply sexually satisfying and that holding a conversation with either of my daughters is just as intellectually rewarding as reading Shakespeare—but if you need something more in your life, that's cool. Something just for you. It doesn't mean you don't love us or want to be here. It just means you want to be you, and as it's you I love, I'm all for it."

"Something just for me," Sophie mused. "You mean something apart from cakes."

"Sophie, you're a doer—a woman with ideas who makes things happen. And I don't think that includes making beans on toast for the girls' tea. Look, there's no high-finance or six-figure jobs around here—but you should look for something to get your teeth into, like Carmen did with the tea shop. Think about it. I guarantee there is something in this town that needs Sophie Mills's magic touch. And I'm not just talking about my—"

"You're right!" Sophie had exclaimed in relief. "That's what's missing. I need a thing. A thing to do, that's it! Oh, but what?"

"I can't answer that, but I'm sure you'll figure something out," Louis told her.

"You really know me, don't you?" Sophie turned to him, tugging at his fingers to bring him a little closer. "I think you might be the first person ever to really get me."

Louis had smiled at her and kissed the tip of her nose.

"Well, someone's got to," he'd said.

Now it was late September and things had stayed more or less the same since the week she'd arrived, a charming mixture of novelty and routine combined with the kind of happiness she had never felt before and the sense that this wasn't really her life she was living after all. It couldn't be. She felt as if she were walking through the pages of a romance novel or had suddenly been given the lead role in a movie, because real life was never this easy.

She saw Louis and the girls every day. Since the new term had started, she'd been taking the children to school now that Izzy had turned four and joined the kindergarten at Bella's school. And every other afternoon she would pick Izzy up at 1:00 P.M. and they would go to Carmen Velasquez's Ye Olde Tea Shoppe for a snack before returning to school to fetch Bella at 3:15. Then they'd go for a walk on the beach, making sand castles and chasing each other with lumps of slimy seaweed if it was sunny enough, or hang out making things from dried pasta at Louis's house if it was rainy. And just occasionally they'd partake of a second snack at Ye Olde Tea Shoppe, as it didn't seem fair that Bella had missed out.

In the evenings, after the girls were in bed, Sophie and Louis would sit in front of the electric fire he kept swearing he was going to replace with a period fireplace to match the house's Victorian exterior and laugh and talk and share news and hold hands and do a great deal of kissing. And most nights the kissing would lead to touching and the touching would lead to the most wonderful and dazzling sex Sophie Mills had ever known. Louis's sofa had seen a lot of action over the last six months, and his rug had seen a great deal more. But to date, Sophie had never stayed the night.

"I am fairly sure you could sleep over if you wanted to," Louis had said one night as the two of them lay sprawled in front of the fire, which they had switched on for old times' sake even though it was August and one of those rare swelteringly hot nights. He traced a finger along the curve of her breast, which shimmered in the firelight. "I'd love to go to sleep with you, Sophie," he murmured. "And wake up with you. I'd like to see you in the morning with your hair all tangled and sleep creases in your cheeks. I'd like to have sex with you in the morning, while you're still half dreaming and biddable."

"Well, you'd be unlucky," Sophie told him as she stretched, wriggling because the rug was a nylon mix and a bit itchy on her skin. "Because I sleep like a princess and I never get tousled or creased. Besides, I am only ever biddable when I want to be, which might be right now if you play your cards right."

"Stay over," Louis asked her gently, kissing her shoulder. "Please."

"I can't, Louis. What would they think?" Sophie said, pointing at the ceiling. Bella and Izzy were fast asleep upstairs.

"They'd think you stayed the night and then, seeing Daddy in such a good mood, they'd wonder if they could score Coco Pops for breakfast two days in a row even though they're only supposed to have them twice a week," Louis said. "They wouldn't care, Sophie, I think they'd be happy about it."

"I can't," Sophie replied uncertainly. "It wouldn't be right. They aren't ready for that."

"They do know we're going out together, you know," Louis said wryly. "All the hand holding and 'I love yous' have given it away. I think you're the one who's not ready."

Sophie dropped her gaze momentarily. Perhaps Louis was right. Everything seemed so perfect, so wonderful now, that she sometimes felt as if her happiness was balanced on a high wire. She was afraid of changing anything lest the perfect peace she'd found here teetered and crashed. And staying the night, living here, meant letting real life creep in and she wasn't ready for that quite yet. Sophie eyed Louis from beneath her lashes. It was odd that she could lie here, naked, with him but wasn't sure she could tell him her fears about moving ahead with their relationship. She wasn't sure he'd understand.

"So we are going out together then?" Sophie teased him instead. "Only you've never formally asked me, so I did wonder. Look, it's just that the children are only seven and four. I can't possibly stay over—not when we're not . . ."

"What?" Louis had propped himself up on one elbow and looked at Sophie, his gaze traveling slowly up from the tops of her thighs, over her breasts, and finally meeting her eyes with the kind of look that made her blood fizz.

"We're not, you know . . . ," Sophie said, her mouth curling into a smile as she wound her arms around Louis's neck and drew him down to kiss her. But his lips stopped short of hers by a hairsbreadth.

"Marry me then," Louis had whispered.

Instead of answering, Sophie kissed him hard, pushing him onto his back on the carpet and climbing on top of him with the kind of unbridled abandon that, had she stopped to think about it, she would have found rather embarrassing. But she didn't stop to think, because one of the best things about being in love with Louis Gregory was that when she made love to him, she didn't think about anything apart from how very wonderful it made her feel.

Still, as delightful a distraction as that had been, Sophie had not answered or even acknowledged Louis's question. And while it had not gone unnoticed, neither of them mentioned it because Sophie and Louis did not talk about much besides the children and that day's events. Sometimes the thought would creep into Sophie's mind that all she and Louis knew about each other, apart from the history they had shared through Carrie and her children, was how to make each other laugh and their bodies sing, but Sophie didn't dwell on it.

Then, as on most evenings, after spending a few minutes talking to her cat, Artemis, who had moved in with Louis on the very first day they arrived from London and lorded it over the resident ginger cat, Tango, with the ferocity and splendor of a feline Boadicea,

Sophie would get in her car if she hadn't been drinking, or take the local taxi if she had, and go back to the B & B to sleep alone.

It wasn't that she didn't long to wake up with Louis's arms around her, because she did. It was just that before she moved any further along that precarious high wire, she wanted to be absolutely sure that what she was doing was the right thing and that she wasn't making a terrible, terrible mistake.

Sometimes she worried about how her relationship with Louis looked to people on the outside. She and Louis, essentially strangers to each other, had been thrown together by circumstance. People might think that, as fond as he was of her, Sophie was little more to Louis than a rather convenient replacement for his children's lost mother, one who'd come ready-made with his children's trust and love already assured. And because she was a person who had always been desperate for other people's approval, it was hard for her to throw caution to the wind and decide that she didn't care two hoots about what other people might think.

Although the general feeling of contentment and joy that had pervaded her daily life since she had come down to Cornwall supported a favorable outcome, Sophie was waiting for something, some tiny, indefinable piece of information to fall into place before she could know for sure she was meant to be here permanently. The problem was, Sophie wasn't sure exactly what it was she was waiting for.

A knock at the door interrupted her thoughts and she ran to hide in the closet.

"Aunty Sophie?" Bella called out as she pushed open the bedroom door. *"We're coming to get you!"*

"You is going to get got!" Izzy giggled as she galloped into the room with Bella, the two of them sounding like a herd of small elephants.

Sophie remained silent in the wardrobe, secreted between business suits and party dresses that hadn't seen the light of day since she'd arrived in St. Ives. Her job on the days Louis picked the children up from school and brought them round was to wait to be found. And even though she knew the girls knew exactly where she was hiding, she had to wait nevertheless. Sometimes Izzy wouldn't be able to stand the excitement and she'd open the closet door in less than a minute. On other days though, the game could take quite a long time and by the time she had been discovered, Sophie would have quite a crick in her neck and pins and needles in her calves.

"Is she . . . under the bed?" Bella's muffled voice suggested that she had crawled under there to check.

"Is she in the toilet?" Izzy's giggle bounced off the walls in the tiny bathroom and Sophie smiled to herself. Izzy had changed a lot in the last six months, but her devotion to toilet humor had never wavered.

"Is she up the chimney?" Bella called out.

"Or on the lamp shade?" Izzy suggested.

"Of course she's not on the lamp shade, Iz," Bella said matter-of-factly. "The lamp shade is tiny and small and made of paper and Aunty Sophie is *huge!*"

Sophie pursed her lips and silently swore off clotted cream and scones for about the seventh time that week.

"I think . . . ," Bella said in the tone of voice that meant Sophie had to prepare to be discovered, "that she might be . . . in . . . the . . . closet!"

In the second that Bella flung open the door, Sophie leaped out yelling, "BOO!" at the top of her voice, an event that never failed to make both girls scream and giggle, and jump on Sophie and propel her in one very girlish heap onto one of the room's twin beds.

"You got me," Sophie said when she had got her breath back. "Where's Daddy?"

"Downstairs talking to Mrs. Alexander about sandwiches," Bella said, sitting up, pushing her bangs out of her eyes. Sophie brushed the child's dark hair off her forehead and, sitting up, kissed her on the cheek.

"You need a haircut again," she said. "Your hair grows faster than anything else I know."

"What about me, do I need a haircut?" Izzy wound her arms around Sophie's neck and rested her cheek against Sophie's.

Sophie wound one of Izzy's caramel curls around her finger. "You have hair just like your mother's," she told the younger girl, knowing how much Izzy liked to talk about Carrie. "You can cut it and brush it and wash it all you like but it will do exactly what it wants to do . . . which reminds me of the little person it's attached to!"

"I'm not little anymore," Izzy protested. "I go to school now, and anyway, are you coming for a cream tea?"

"Of course she is," Bella said. "Aunty Sophie always comes for cream teas."

"I can't deny it," Sophie said. "But today is absolutely my last one."

"You said that yesterday," Bella reminded her.

"I know something," Izzy said with big, round eyes and in a typically dramatic tone of voice. "A really, really specially secret thing that Daddy says I'm not to tell you!"

"Do you?" Sophie said, mildly anxious. The last major secret Izzy had had involved Artemis and an entire packet of smoked salmon that she had fed the cat under her bed in a bid to make Artemis love her more than Bella. What Izzy had failed to understand was that Artemis would never turn down food, not even from her worst enemy, and it was a miracle that she actively liked any human at all. Artemis had lived with Sophie for years in her flat in London and had barely ever spoken two words to her, so to speak. For some reason Bella was the only human Artemis loved, whether it was because the once mistreated cat saw something in Bella she recognized or because Bella was the only person on the planet who knew how to tickle Artemis behind her ears the way she liked it, Sophie didn't know. But she did know that all copious amounts of smoked salmon would achieve was piles of orange fishy vomit deposited all around the house.

"Have you been trying to make friends with Artemis again?" Sophie asked.

"No, it's even better than that!" Izzy said, giggling gleefully.

"It's not really," Bella said firmly. "It's not anything at all. It's really best forgotten about."

"Yes, we are not to tell because Daddy says he has something very important to ask you but we mustn't say what it is," Izzy said, wiping her nose on the back of her hand and then her hand on Sophie's fuchsia candlewick bedspread.

"Izzy!" Bella hissed, digging her little sister in the ribs. "Shush."

She smiled at Sophie, a wide, toothy grin that Sophie had seen once before, when Bella denied using Sophie's steak knives as tent pegs to make a den out of her best and, for that matter, only leather coat.

"Oh come on, girls, what are you two hiding? Is your dad finally going to strip that hideous wallpaper in the living room?"

"It's much more exciting than that," Izzy told her. "It's the excitingest, biggest thing *ever*!"

"No it is not!" Bella tried to urge her little sister into discretion by waggling her eyebrows, which might have worked if her bangs hadn't been so long that they obscured them. "Daddy has nothing to say to you whatsoever." She pronounced the new, unfamiliar word with great care. "I expect he won't want to talk to you about anything of consequence at all."

"Except that don't forget he's going to ask her to . . . ," Izzy began.

"Pay for the cake because he's lost his . . . money," Bella interrupted her.

"Or at least he hasn't got any monies left because he's spent them on this most beautifulest—"

"Hat," Bella finished for Izzy. "He's bought a completely *enormous* hat."

Sophie looked from girl to girl. It could never be said that she was the world's most intuitive woman. It had taken her a rather long time to realize, for example, that Louis loved her back and that the feelings she had for him weren't just an unrequited, slightly psychotic, and rather ill-advised crush. Yet here was Izzy seething with secrets, talking about something exciting and big that Louis wanted to ask her, and there was Bella gamely trying to cover up with a tale of lost money and an enormous hat. A few months ago Sophie would have been wondering what on earth Louis wanted with an enormous hat, but she had changed from that blunt black-and-white woman, and these children had helped her do it. That and the fact that they were dreadful at keeping secrets led her to believe that unless she was very much mistaken, what the girls were trying not to tell her was that their father was going to ask her to marry him. Again.

Only this time she wouldn't be able to pretend she hadn't heard him, and there would be no opportunity for distraction sex right in the middle of Ye Olde Tea Shoppe.

Two

Carmen Velasquez looked exactly like her name. A few years older than Sophie, at thirty-seven she had olive skin, dark pool-like eyes, and shiny black hair that fell in a neat cut to her shoulders. She looked, Sophie remembered thinking the first time she had met her, like a Spanish rose. Which was interesting because she sounded exactly like what she was—an Essex girl through and through.

The story of how Carmen had come to be running a tea shop in St. Ives was nearly as far-fetched as the one that made Sophie the second-longest-staying guest at the Avalon B & B. Carmen had fallen for a strapping young man, twelve years her junior, at a nightclub in Chelmsford. She had been dancing on a podium when she'd been literally whisked off her feet by a decidedly Nordic-looking young man who hadn't bothered to ask her name or inquire about her marital status. He'd pressed her up against a wall and kissed her until the fluorescent lights finally flickered on at 2:00 A.M. They had spent a night of unbridled passion together whereupon it became clear that the young man's name was James, he was on a stag night out with his best mate from school, and he was currently employed as a long-line fisherman off the coast of Cornwall. Carmen Velasquez, who at that point in her life had been called Carmen Higgins, had kissed James good-bye as the sun came up and sadly supposed that that brief but joyful intermission in her life was over and she would never see him again. But she had been wrong.

Less than two weeks later, James appeared at the office where Carmen worked, in human resources for a small children's charity, and told her he hadn't been able to stop thinking about her. After giving the matter some thought, Carmen took the afternoon off and booked a hotel room in which they discussed the matter further. She'd told Sophie on the very first afternoon that the two women met that she would probably have felt guiltier about betraying her marriage if it hadn't been for the fact that she didn't have any children and her husband was a jerk, to quote Carmen directly. From that fateful afternoon onward, Carmen and James shared various hotel rooms located around the southern half of the country for over a year, Carmen all the while expecting the younger man to tire of her at any moment, and bracing herself to get on with her loveless marriage, but with the knowledge that she had at least tasted happiness for a short while.

Only, James didn't tire of her. James fell in love with her and begged her to run away to Cornwall to live with him. Finally, after eighteen months of minibars and shredded credit card statements, Carmen had taken the plunge, left her husband, and reclaimed her much more impressive maiden name.

Never one to sit about on her arse, as Carmen put it most succinctly, she had decided to channel her passion for pastries and baking into a career and turn the local tourist-reliant tea shop into a thriving year-round concern. She'd succeeded within her first year of owning the shop. And she and James were still going strong, something that Sophie would have found heartening if she didn't believe in the law of averages. Surely the chances of there being two happy whirlwind romances blooming into two successful long-term relationships in the same Cornish town seemed rather remote. But even if Carmen had dibs on the fairy-tale ending coming true, it didn't stop Sophie from liking her enormously. It wasn't only the quality of Carmen's jam that led her back to the Ye Olde Tea Shoppe so regularly. It was that she could really talk to Carmen and Carmen could certainly talk back. Carmen had stepped into the void that leaving Cal in London had left in Sophie's life, and Sophie found her forthright friendliness a port in the storm as she settled into a new town.

"He's gonna what?" Carmen asked her, her thickly mascaraed eyes widening as Sophie whispered her fears over the lace-doilied counter as Louis and the girls sat at the table only a few feet away. "Never! What, here?"

"I think so," Sophie said. "Although to be fair I'm not one hundred percent sure. It's just that Izzy said he had a big question to ask me and that he'd spent a lot of money on something really special."

"Right, well, I love that child, but isn't she the one who made a mouse out of cheese and kept it in a matchbox under the bed until it grew actual fur?" Carmen asked. "I'm not especially sure you should base your assumptions on what she has to say, bless her. What about Bella? Bella's the one who normally knows what's going on from here to Land's End. That girl loves information."

"Bella tried to cover it up, going on about hats and stuff. Bella was *definitely* trying to keep something a secret—it has to be a proposal, it fits the facts, and it wouldn't be the first time—"

"Wouldn't it?" Carmen's eyes widened. "Don't say you've turned him down before?"

"Not exactly," Sophie said, experiencing a rather wonderful flashback of exactly what had happened after Louis had proposed the first time. "*Anyway,* that's not important at the moment. What's important is—*what am I going to do?*"

Sophie glanced back at Louis, who was letting Izzy dress him with a hat she'd fashioned out of paper napkins and some secret bubble gum. It was a good thing he wasn't fussy about his hair, Sophie thought fondly.

"Say yes, you idiot," Carmen told her in hushed tones. "That feller's pure class, love. If I didn't love my James, I would, let me tell you."

"Would you?" Sophie watched Louis, trying to see him through fresh eyes. To her he was the most beautiful creature who had ever walked the earth in the form of a man, but it always interested her to know how other women saw him.

"Look at him," Carmen all but growled. "He's sex on legs, that one."

"Sex on . . . ? Oh, never mind. The point is, any moment now he's going to ask me to marry him and I'm going to have to say no, Carmen. I'm going to have to turn him down."

"Excuse me? Turn him down? But why?" Carmen fired the questions at her in quick succession, each one gilded with incredulity.

"Because this is too much, too soon, too fast . . . ," Sophie said, faltering. "We've only been together six months. And it's not much longer than that since his wife died and he came back to look after his estranged children and found me as their guardian. How's it going to look to the outside world? It will look like Louis is getting himself a free nanny with added sex benefits. Everything is so perfect now, we're so happy. I'm so happy, and if we're that happy, then why change anything? Why not just stay as we are . . . ?"

"Forever?" Carmen asked her. "Well, I can think of a few reasons, one of them being that if you keep doing it on his sofa you're going to slip a disk, and the other possibly more pertinent one is that if he makes you happy, and you love him, then you are *supposed* to marry him. That's traditionally how it goes, otherwise what's the point?"

"The point is that there is no need to rush things. He's not ready to get married."

"*He's* not ready you say?" Carmen said, twisting her mouth into a tightly skeptical expression.

"Of course he's not!" Sophie said. "Look at him, he's confused!"

Just at that moment Louis was surrendering while both his daughters held him in a headlock and tickled him until his laughter filled the entire café.

"He does look miserable, now you come to mention it," Carmen said drily. "Look, sweetheart. You don't know that he's going to ask you anything yet. This is probably just you imposing your own fears and obsessions on something those two little lovelies said . . . in fact . . . ," Carmen gasped and clutched her hand to her chest. "Stone me, I know what it is they were on about!"

"Does anyone really still say 'stone me'?" Sophie asked her. "Go on then, what's your theory?"

"It's not a theory, it's definitely what Izzy and Bella were trying not to tell you—him and James and some of the other lads have been talking about a boys' surfing trip to Hawaii for ages, haven't they? Well, James has got together the cash to go now, and he's trying to get the others to put deposits down so he can book early and get a good deal. He asked Louis about it last night. I bet that's what Louis wants to ask you, to look after the kids and cats while he's away living it up in the sun and ogling fit young women in bikinis."

"Really? That would be brilliant!" Sophie said, seizing on the thought.

"I'm not so keen on the young women in bikinis myself," Carmen said, pursing her lips. "But if you find that preferable to a proposal, then who am I to disagree?"

"It *could* just be that, couldn't it?" Sophie mused aloud. "His photography business is pretty much established now, and he's always wanted to go to Hawaii. Plus, it fits the facts. It *is* a big question to ask and it *would* cost him a lot of money and he'd definitely ask the girls if they minded before he'd go."

"Yes," Carmen said. "And he'd probably be a bit worried about telling you in case you scamper back to London while he's not looking."

"I reckon it's that," Sophie said with more than a little relief as Carmen piled a cake stand high with scones, pots of clotted cream, and jam. "That's what it is, oh god, I'm such an idiot."

"I'm not going to try and fight you on that one," Carmen said. "Now is there anything else?"

Sophie looked at the cake stand.

"Well, as it's my last cream tea ever, how about another pot of jam?"

"What were you two talking about all cloak and daggers?" Louis asked her as she set the tray down on the red-and-white gingham tablecloth.

"Oh, nothing," Sophie said, trying her best to look unconcerned and exactly like the sort of girlfriend who was very relaxed about her boyfriend taking a holiday without her. "Girl talk, you know Carmen."

For a good half hour the table was largely silent as cream and jam and scones and cake were liberally passed around in a delectable feast, one Sophie was ashamed to say she was just as involved in as the girls. And then finally two replete and not to mention hyperactive children climbed off their chairs and went to look for entertainment.

"So anyway—good news," Louis said a little nervously. They sipped tea in relative peace while the girls helped Carmen clear the tables of place mats and menus, as the café was about to close.

"Oh yes, what's that?" Sophie asked, trying to sound casual.

"Mrs. Alexander's coming over to babysit tonight. I'm taking you out to dinner at Alba." Louis had made a reservation at the best fish restaurant in town, the one that looked out over the harbor from which the fish it served were caught, and where, if you were lucky enough to get a window seat, you could see the town's collection of rather dashing lifeboat men (including James) take the boat out for practice runs.

"You're taking me out to *dinner*? I mean, just you and me?" Sophie asked him. In the last six months, not only had she never stayed the night at Louis's house, they had never been on a date with just each other. They had spent more time together than Sophie had ever spent with anyone else, but there had always been two other delightful little people tagging along—unless you counted the evenings in front of the electric fire after the girls had gone to bed, which were wonderful but not exactly dates. It wasn't something Sophie had wondered or worried about, it was just the fact of their situation.

"Yep, you can put on a dress if you like and maybe some of those high heels you carted down here with you," Louis said, raising a brow hopefully, which made Sophie blush.

It was clear to Sophie that Louis was buttering her up for news of his departure, but she didn't mind. She thought it was sweet that he was so worried about how she would take the news of his impending holiday, and she wanted to dress up. She wanted to dress up because he clearly wanted her to and that made her feel kind of sexy. Louis was probably the first man she had ever known who made her feel sexy. Other men had found her attractive. Jake Flynn, for example, the New York businessman she'd had a near miss with around the same time Louis and the girls had come into her life. Jake looked at her and she could feel his desire for her, but for some reason it didn't penetrate through her outer layer despite his square jaw and strong arms. For a long time Sophie had thought that her inability to feel passion had to be because of something lacking in herself, and then one night, on her first visit to the Avalon B & B, back when they still barely knew each other, Louis had kissed her good night on the cheek. It was nothing, his lips barely grazed her skin, but she could not sleep for the rest of that night because of the way his touch had made her feel. Suddenly she'd felt frighteningly, viscerally alive.

"Mrs. Alexander said she'll stay over the night at my place if you don't mind locking the B and B doors at midnight and making sure Mrs. Tregowan gets her cocoa. Nancy will let herself in in the morning to start the breakfasts," Louis said, directing his gaze out to sea. "I thought I could stay over with you."

"Stay over the night with me?" Sophie asked him.

Louis laughed. "Yes, I don't know why we haven't thought of this before; you don't have to worry about the girls being freaked out and I can finally wake up with you and see if it's true that you sleep like a princess." He leaned a little closer to her. "And you and I can make sleepy early-morning love." Louis saw the hesitation in her face. "Come on, Sophie, don't tell me you don't want me staying over with you? That's what serious couples do, you know, they sleep together, by which I mean actually sleep, overnight and in a bed and everything."

"I know, I know." Sophie covered his hand with her own, suddenly yearning for the warmth of his bare skin against hers. "And it will be great; I suppose I'm just surprised that we haven't thought of it before."

"I don't know," Louis said, looking back at her, the promise of what was to come lighting his eyes. "We haven't really done a lot of thinking about just us, have we? We've got into a bit of a routine I suppose. A lovely, brilliant routine that I adore, but it doesn't hurt to have a night just for us once in a while, does it? The girls are stoked about it, they reckon they're going to have a midnight feast."

"They can try," Sophie joked. "But I don't fancy their chances much. Beware the fool who tries to come down for breakfast any earlier than seven fifty-nine A.M. Mrs. Alexander takes no prisoners."

"So I'll pick you up at eight then," Louis said. "Be ready?"

"I will be so ready," Sophie said.

"I love you, Sophie Mills," Louis told her. He must have told her the same thing many, many times now, but every single time she heard those words, Sophie still could not quite believe her luck. She was too happy, everything was too perfect. Sooner or later something would have to go wrong.

Three

As it turned out, Sophie was ready by 7:29, so she went downstairs to sit with Mrs. Tregowan, who was the only guest who ever made use of the sitting room. Grace Tregowan would sit in the floral Windsor armchair opposite the TV and the true crime channel for up to eighteen hours a day. She didn't watch any of the other channels. The other channels, she had told Sophie once, were full of muck and doom and gloom and not in a good way.

"Give me a paternity test any day of the week, or a nice grisly murder," Grace had told her.

Sophie had been mildly shocked. She had forgotten that little old ladies were once young women, and she supposed that just because she would one day be old, it wouldn't mean she would suddenly stop thinking or feeling the way she did now.

Over the last six months, though, she had gotten to know the eighty-nine-year-old well, and now nothing Mrs. Tregowan said could shock her anymore. Grace had had a colorful life to say the least, a life full of lovers, danger, and husbands, four of them. So perhaps it was because of that passion-filled life that Grace was so content to finish her days in the Avalon guest house watching TV while her motley collection of cash-grabbing relatives who never bothered to visit or even call clamored desperately for their inheritance. Grace had told Sophie in one of their very first conversations that she was now mainly staying alive just to annoy them.

"What do you think of my outfit?" Sophie said, walking into the sitting room. She twirled in a soft pink beaded chiffon dress with a dropped waist and a fringe of beads all around the bottom. She'd been wearing it the first night she met Louis.

"You look lovely, darling," Grace said, looking Sophie up and down. "I had a dress similar to that, you know, before the war. If I recall correctly, 1938—I was living in Paris, in Montparnasse with this painter Jacques Bellaconti, lovely man, but so serious. He was a Communist—never yet met a Communist with a sense of humor. Still . . ." Grace trailed off for a second and Sophie got the distinct impression that the old lady was fondly remembering a past love. "Anyway, I had a dress just like that, only I was as thin as a whip— there was nothing to me. That was the way they liked it back then. That was the way Jacques liked it anyway, and he always preferred me with my clothes off. I expect your young man's the same."

Sophie blinked and caught her reflection in Mrs. Alexander's gilt-framed mirror.

"He does rather, but given that we're going out for dinner, do you think this will do? This is our first proper date in . . . well, since I came down here really."

Grace smiled at Sophie, her blue eyes still bright and clear. "You look lovely, darling. So much better than when you first arrived, with all those dark shadows and anxious looks. The sea air must agree with you, and of course . . . sex is a marvelous restorative tonic."

"That must be it," Sophie said as Grace's attention drifted back to the TV. Sophie went to the window, and after some riffling through Mrs. Alexander's various layers of lace curtains, she tweaked back enough diaphanous material to be able to see out. It was dark outside and Sophie felt the skin on her arms prickle with goose bumps as she imagined the chill of the night air cutting through the thin material of her dress. There was something else too, prickling at the back of her neck.

It was fear. Sophie realized that she was having first-date jitters. She hadn't felt this tense and high on adrenaline since that day she'd turned up at Louis's house and told him she wanted to be with him. Everything that had happened since had been something of a roller coaster and she had been speeding along up every incline and down every descent, caught up in the euphoria of love. They talked, of course, but never really about anything, never about their pasts, their fears or dreams, and much of the time the girls were there, twin suns for their conversation and attention to revolve around. And obviously they had fabulous sex, but they had never been alone together in *this* way. There was something frighteningly formal about the two of them going on a date even if it was just Louis's way of buttering her up to tell her he was going away surfing. What if they didn't have anything to say once they were dressed up and staring at each other over a flower arrangement and a tea light? What if, when it came to it, their relationship was based entirely on their shared love for the girls and really excellent sex?

Soon she would seriously have to start thinking about what she was doing. She'd have to start planning again. In another six months her savings would run out, and if she was going to stay in Cornwall, she'd need to think about finding a way to earn money down here. Soon the short-term lease on her flat in London would come to an end and she'd need to decide whether to rent it out again or even put it on the market. Soon the demands of daily life would come crashing in and she'd need to know if the life she was leading now could be permanent or if it was just a castle of dreams that could be blown away at any moment by a passing gust of reality. But not yet, Sophie told herself as she watched the path. Not quite yet.

When the B & B security lights blinked on, they revealed that Louis was wearing a suit, causing Sophie to think two things. First, that her boyfriend looked really good in a suit and second, that she hadn't even known he owned one.

"Well," Louis said, looking around him at the chic modern interior of Alba as the waiter poured their wine. "This is nice."

They had been given the best table in the house, on the first floor, in front of the floor-to-ceiling plate-glass window that looked out over the harbor and across the sea. It was dark and blustery outside, of course, but somehow even through the insulated glass Sophie could hear and sense the movement of the ocean only a few feet away, and all that fathomless power churning just on the other side of the centimeter-thick glass made her feel a little as if she were perched on the uppermost arc of a roller coaster that was about to plummet. Or perhaps it was something else that was giving her that feeling; she decided not to dwell on it.

"Yes, this is nice," Sophie said, picking up her glass and sipping as she looked out the window. For a second she stared at her ghostly reflection, a pale imitation of herself in the glass, and then looked away. She appeared very tense for a woman on a date.

The pair of them examined the menus in silence as Sophie listened to the noise of other people's conversations. It seemed as if the whole of St. Ives was on a date tonight and they all had something hilarious and fascinating to say.

Say something, Sophie urged herself. *Go on, say something witty and charming and romantic that will make him smile and look at you through his lashes like he does when he's thinking about how to get you naked.*

"Mrs. Tregowan says that sex is a tonic," Sophie blurted out, seemingly at exactly the same moment that everybody else in the busy restaurant took a break from talking.

Louis looked at his menu for one beat more and then glanced up at her. "No wonder I'm so fit then," he said. Sophie could tell he was trying not to smile, which made her want to smile.

"Sorry," Sophie said, lowering her voice as she leaned toward him. "I was trying to think of something witty and flirty to say and that's what came out."

The two of them sat there watching each other over the tops of the menus for a moment longer.

He should say something now, Sophie thought as she looked into his black eyes. *It's his turn.*

But Louis didn't say anything, he just watched her face closely, as if he were trying to decipher something that lay somewhere in her eyes. Finally Sophie broke the moment by glancing down at her menu. When she looked back up, she saw that Louis was staring intently at the menu, but she was almost certain that he wasn't really reading it. *What was he thinking? Surely breaking the news of a lads' holiday to her could not be this intimidating, unless . . . unless.*

"Are you okay?" Sophie asked him despite Cal having reliably informed her that this was the second-worst-possible question to ever ask a reticent man, beaten only by, "What are you thinking?"

Louis looked up quickly, as if she'd startled him, his skin flushing red across the bridge of his nose.

"It's just, you look a bit tense," Sophie prompted, deciding she couldn't bear the tension for much longer.

"Do I?" Louis said, polishing off his glass of wine in three long gulps and then topping it up before the wine waiter could get near.

"That's funny, because I'm not tense at all. I'm really, really happy." He leaned over the table and picked up her hand. "Actually, the thing is, I'm the happiest I have ever been in my whole life and it's all because of you. I really love you, Sophie. I hope you realize that. I hope you know that I love you and that I am committed one hundred percent to making this work between us. I know that I haven't been the most . . . mature man in the past. I know I walked out on my children because I couldn't handle Carrie's affair. I know that I rushed into marrying Carrie because I didn't really know what I wanted or needed back then. But I don't regret it. I don't regret anything because I'd never regret having known Carrie or having my two beautiful daughters in my life. And now I have you too . . . or at least I hope I have you. Look, I want to ask you something, and I was actually going to wait until dessert, but it seems that I can't behave like a normal person until I've actually said the words, so here goes—"

"Louis," Sophie said, panicking. Suddenly she wanted very much for Carmen to be right. She wanted the conversation they were about to have to be about a surfing holiday. "Look, relax. This is not as big a deal as you think it is . . ."

"What isn't?" Louis asked her uncertainly.

"Carmen told me what you were going to ask," Sophie said, pressing on, still hopeful that she could somehow wrangle this moment into the one she was prepared for and go on to enjoy two fish courses and then Alba's sticky toffee pudding, which was famous for miles around, without having to have made a decision that was any more life changing than whether to have clotted cream or ice cream to accompany it.

"Carmen told you?" Louis looked horrified. "I can't believe she'd do that!"

"Well, you know Carmen," Sophie said breezily, her anxiety exacerbated by how dismayed Louis was. "She can't keep a secret, and anyway . . . it's fine. I don't mind at all. I'm not in the least bit bothered."

"You're not *bothered*?" Louis's face froze and Sophie plowed on, sure she could somehow blunder her way out of this.

"No, of course I'm not. I know that what you want to ask me might seem a bit nervy after our being together officially for only six months, but we're both adults—we can take it!" She grinned at him. "So come on, out with it then. Ask me!"

"I'm not sure I want to now," Louis said, his ruddy face now blanched of color.

"Oh, don't be so silly!" Sophie said carefully. "I know what you want to ask me, and I'm totally relaxed about it. Fully chilled out and calm."

" 'Fully chilled out and calm,' " Louis repeated, topping up his wine again. "I don't really know how I feel about that."

"Well, what did you want me to be like?" Sophie asked, a thin edge of hysteria sharpening her tone. "All stressy and clingy and needy and freaked out, acting like a headless chicken caught in the headlights? I'm not like that. I'm not that kind of girlfriend. I can totally handle it. I mean, look at me."

Louis looked stricken as he chewed on his lip. "I am, and you look a bit like you'd rather be anywhere else than here right now," he said slowly.

"Fine, don't ask me," Sophie said, crossing her arms and leaning back in her chair. "In fact, let's not talk about this now, let's just have dinner and forget about it, shall we?"

"No," Louis said, looking adamant. "I made arrangements and got prepared and took my suit to the dry cleaner's . . . I mean, I still want to . . . it's just that this isn't how I pictured it going . . ."

"Okay, let's sort this out right now," Sophie said, as if she were chairing a board meeting back in London. "Let's cut to the chase and then maybe we can order some food, because I'm starving. You don't have to ask me because the answer is yes, okay?" Sophie smiled at a shocked Louis. "Yes, yes, yes. I'm totally fine with it. I'm more than fine, I'm happy. So it's a yes to the question you were going to ask me. Now can we move on?"

"Yes?" Louis's expression was caught halfway between confusion and a smile. "I mean, that's great, but this is a bit weird. This isn't at all how I thought I would feel when you said yes."

"How did you think you'd feel?" Sophie asked him, a touch impatiently, shaking her head.

"I thought there'd be crying and surprise and joy and . . . hugging," Louis said.

"Louis, all you're doing is asking me to look after the girls and Tango and Artemis while you go on a lads' surfing holiday to Hawaii!" Sophie exclaimed so loudly that more than a few pairs of eyes swiveled in her direction. "That's all you're asking me, isn't it? That's what Carmen said. So why would I cry?"

"What?" Louis's eyes widened and his jaw dropped. "That's what Carmen told you?"

"Yes!" Sophie said desperately. "Now can we please move on? I think the kitchen closes at ten!"

"Er, yes, you see—that's not exactly the question I wanted to ask you," Louis said, catching Sophie's gaze and holding it until her racing heart gradually began to slow and she found that she couldn't look away. "That might be what Carmen told you and that might be what you think you'd rather hear, but *I* think that you and I both know that isn't the question I am going to ask you."

"It's not?" Sophie's voice trembled.

"It's not, and I've never seen a more terrified and panic-stricken woman in my life, but I'm getting to know you and I know that sometimes you need to feel the fear and do it anyway—so here goes." Louis stood up and patted his pockets before producing a small dark blue leather box, opening it to reveal a diamond ring nestled in midnight blue velvet.

Sophie leaned back as far in her chair as its rigid back would allow and felt her heart cease to beat as he dropped to one knee in front of her.

"Sophie Mills," Louis said, commanding the attention of the whole restaurant. "I love you and I want to be with you for the rest of my life. Please will you marry me?"

About fifty people held their breath as Sophie looked first at Louis and then at the ring. She knew she had to say something, that now was the appropriate time to say *something*, but for what seemed like an eternity nothing would come out, not even an exhalation of breath.

"Um, right," Louis said, looking around at the other diners. "You might not like the ring, and if you don't, we can change it. Only I thought you would. It's from the 1930s and it's a Deco platinum setting. It's not huge, it's a half carat, but it's good quality and it took me ages to choose it. I thought it was classy and stylish and timeless and . . . silent—like you. Say something, Soph, my knee's gone numb and everyone's looking at us."

Abruptly Sophie felt her heart start to beat again and a rush of blood to her cheeks. She exhaled, and when she took another breath, she felt tears brimming in her eyes.

"Oh, Louis," she said, her voice husky and taut.

"What?" Louis asked her with a hopeful smile. "Is there going to be tears and joy and hugging, or just tears? Still feeling calm and chilled?"

"Not exactly," Sophie half-sobbed and half-laughed. "You've frightened me nearly to death!"

"Not the textbook response when it comes to proposals," Louis said, smiling. "But it beats the dumbstruck horror I was getting."

Sophie laughed and took Louis's hand, hauling him to his feet so they were standing opposite each other.

"I feel frightened and nervous and a bit sick and quite giddy," Sophie said. "And a lot like a huge semipsychotic idiot. Are you sure you want to marry me?"

"Despite your rather casual acquaintance with sanity, I still want you to be my wife, Sophie," Louis told her, his voice low and serious. "So? Do you want to marry me?"

Sophie nodded her head. "Yes," she said. "Yes, I think I do."

Sophie sat bolt upright in bed, her heart pounding. It took a while for her eyes to adjust to the half-light and she took a couple of deep breaths as she waited for whatever dream had woken her, frightened and full of panic, to fade away. And then she realized. It wasn't a dream. Louis had actually asked her to marry him and she had said yes. She'd made a decision about the rest of her life. She'd said *yes*.

"Morning," Louis mumbled sleepily. Sophie felt his finger drift up her bare back and gently wind a hank of her hair around his wrist, tugging her back down onto the bed. After several attempts and one incident that could have sent the pair of them to the emergency room with an awful lot of explaining to do, they'd given up on sleeping in the twin beds, which they'd pushed together, and had ended curled up tightly together in a single instead. Exactly as they had done on the very first night they'd slept together, Sophie remembered. The night after they'd brought the girls back to St. Ives for the first time since they'd lost their mother here. It had been a difficult and dark day, a day full of pain and breakthroughs and some joy. It had been the day when Sophie had finally said good-bye to her old friend, the day she really believed Carrie was dead. That night her jumble of attraction, anger, mistrust, and longing for Louis had boiled over and she'd gone to bed with him, uncertain of what it meant or where it would lead, because for at least a few hours she hadn't cared as long as he had his arms around her. The next morning she had woken with her heart pounding, just as she had this morning. She'd run away from him and the girls and she'd tried her best to go back to her normal life as if none of this had happened. She'd tried and she'd failed. Now on this second and so different morning in a single bed with Louis, Sophie recalled all the angst and anxiety, the guilt she'd been plagued with that night, wondering if any trace of it tainted this morning, but there was nothing, so why was her heart beating like a drum?

She had never been happier, more filled to the brim with joy, and yet at exactly the same moment she had never been more afraid.

Louis reached across her and picked up her left hand, looking at the ring that glinted faintly on her finger in the morning light.

"I always thought I liked you best when you were totally naked, but now I realize I like you to leave a little something on." He brought the ring, and her hand, to his lips and kissed it. "Don't ever take this off."

"Really?" Sophie asked him. "Only I was thinking, we probably don't want the whole world to know right away, so it might be best if—"

"The whole world does know." Louis smiled as he kissed her fingertips. "After the performance we put on last night, it would be impossible for the whole world not to."

"Well yes, that *is* true. All those people know, but I mean Bella and Izzy. Mrs. Alexander. The school mums, the school mums will have a field day, and Carmen! Carmen won't shut up about it. Not to mention my mother and Cal! Cal will never believe it. Then there's Christina and the other girls back home. And Carrie's mum, we have to tell Carrie's mum. There are a lot of people we need to tell, so perhaps until we have I shouldn't wear the ring. Not until we're officially official—"

"Rubbish," Louis said. "Just tell everyone. That's what you do, you get engaged and then you tell everyone and everyone is excited and pleased for you."

"Yes, I know." Sophie stretched out her fingers to look at the ring. "It's just that it's such a public thing, isn't it, an engagement ring. People look at it and they know everything about you."

"Well, they know that you are engaged," Louis said, twisting the ring full circle on her finger. "It is a little bit loose though," Louis said. "I'd hate for you to lose it. I know, we'll take it into Newquay today and get it resized. We can take the girls. They will be so excited. They've been trying really hard not to talk about bridesmaids' dresses in front of you for two whole days, but I must warn you, there is a fight breaking out between pink and lilac and there has been some mention of wings."

"Wings," Sophie said absently as she studied the ring that suddenly said so much about her. "That sounds nice."

Louis leaned up on his elbow and looked in her face.

"Sophie, if there's *anything,* any worry or uncertainty that you have, then please, tell me now," he said, a lazy smile on his lips that told Sophie he didn't for a second think that she had a single one.

"It's only that the rest of our lives is a long time," Sophie said slowly. She watched a slight frown form between Louis's brows and instantly she wanted to make it disappear again.

"I don't mean I don't want to marry you, I'm just saying, are you sure, Louis? Are you sure you know me well enough? After all, we haven't been together very long and we're still in that first flush of sex-fueled love. Maybe we should wait a bit—"

"What, until we start getting bored and stop making love?" Louis laughed.

"No, it's just . . . I never want you to regret me," Sophie said, suddenly serious. "I want you to be certain, because I couldn't ever bear for you to regret me."

"Sophie." Louis traced a finger along the curve of her cheek. "Life goes by in a flash, in the blink of an eye, and then it is gone. I am certain that I love you and that I need you and that for as long as I'm here on earth, I want you to be with me. I couldn't be more certain. I certainly couldn't be more certain that I am going to kiss you right now."

It was hard to concentrate as Louis kissed her, his hands rediscovering her skin under the covers as he pulled her body hard against his, and indeed as she felt his lips on her breasts and his fingers between her thighs, Sophie found it hard to think about anything at all other than how much she wanted him. But there was still one question, just an ember of a query, flickering dimly in the corner of her mind. An ember that blinked out the moment she felt Louis move inside her.

The question she had asked herself and had forgotten in a second was: was *she* certain? There hadn't been time for an answer.

Four

It was a busy Saturday morning in Newquay. The tourists had fallen away but the students were back in town, and even after a summer spent largely in a small town rammed up to its eyeteeth with holidaymakers, Sophie found the bustle of the vibrant town hard to adjust to, which was foolish because she was a city girl, a Londoner born and bred and used to elbowing her way through crowds along with the best of them. But something in her had changed since Bella and Izzy burst into her life. For the first time she felt vulnerable, as if the merest glancing blow would bruise her badly. The world outside the four of them seemed like a much more frightening place, with danger lurking in every corner, which Sophie had been mercifully unaware of before she had two children to worry about. Carrie's sudden and pointless death had given her a sense of her own mortality, but more than that, it had made her see how fragile the lives of those around her were too. How easy, if improbable, it would be to lose the people she loved.

Apart from that new nagging anxiety, she was also finding it hard to adjust to her new persona. Sophie was aware that she wasn't Sophie Mills career-girl-about-town anymore. She wasn't even former-career-girl-about—St. Ives, at least until she found a new professional niche for herself, which so far hadn't progressed much further than her ruling herself out of a career as an artist, largely because Bella was constantly telling her she was the only adult in the world who couldn't even draw a stick figure, or marketing her culinary skills as Carmen had. Culinary skills, Carmen told her, had to extend beyond heating things up in order to constitute a career. You had to know how to chop and mix and have a basic knowledge of ingredients. And although Sophie was becoming a pro at grilling, that was where her kitchen prowess ended. Whatever it was she was destined to do down here in Cornwall, apart from be happy and in love, she hadn't found it yet and in the meantime struggled to accept the identity she did have— Sophie Mills, official engage-ée. Or fiancée, Louis reminded her once he'd pointed out that the word "engage-ée" didn't actually exist.

"You are my fiancée and I am yours," Louis had told her happily as they walked up the garden path to his house earlier that morning.

"I know, I know," Sophie said. "It's just going to take me a while to get my head around that word being associated with *me*. I mean, for starters, it's awfully *French*."

"Okay, if you don't like 'fiancée,' how about 'betrothed'? How about I call you my betrothed?"

"Mmmm." Sophie sounded skeptical.

"What—too medieval?" Louis asked her.

"No, it's just that it's a very formal word," Sophie said. "It's not very fun."

"I see where you're coming from. It's just that I think getting engaged slash betrothed is supposed to be a tiny bit formal," Louis pointed out.

"I know, I'm just saying there should be a third word, a fun word. A word that isn't quite so loaded."

"Loaded?" Louis raised his brow. "Okay, I'll give it some thought."

"Well?" Mrs. Alexander had opened Louis's front door before he could fit the key into the lock. She'd obviously been waiting for them by the living room window.

"The Avalon has not burned down and Grace is absolutely fine," Sophie reassured her. "How are the girls? Did they run you ragged?"

"They did no such thing," Mrs. Alexander said. "It takes a lot more than a couple of sweet little poppets like those two to get the better of me. That cat of yours, on the other hand, nearly had my eye out when I tried to pet her."

"That's because she doesn't like people. I did mention it," Sophie said, wondering if Mrs. Alexander might consider letting them in anytime soon. "She likes her space and she's very protective of her privacy. She takes her time forming relationships . . . she's a rescue cat, you know. I've had her for years now and she still doesn't like me. I try not to take it personally."

"Good job, by the sound of it," Mrs. Alexander told her. She appraised Sophie with a cool blue-eyed gaze. "So, are you going to marry him?"

Sophie's jaw dropped and she looked at Louis. "Did the whole world know what you were planning?" she asked.

"More or less," Louis said, shrugging apologetically.

"And are you?" Mrs. Alexander pressed her, still barring the doorway as if somehow their entry was dependent on Sophie's answer.

"It seems that I am," Sophie affirmed, feeling Louis's arm

around her waist. Worrying that she hadn't seemed sufficiently happy, she added, "Louis and I are officially to be married. It's very exciting."

Mrs. Alexander beamed quite unexpectedly, which turned her habitually sour expression into one of pure delight. "I'm thrilled for you, darling," she said, hugging Sophie with uncharacteristic fervor and releasing her just as swiftly. "I'll need a month's notice on the room if you're going to want your deposit back."

"Oh, I don't expect I'll be moving out for ages yet," Sophie said, avoiding Louis's gaze.

"Anyway, the girls have been waiting all morning for you. They've got a little show." Mrs. Alexander stepped aside to allow them into the house, smiling at Louis. "I wanted to make sure everything was okay before I unleashed them just in case Sophie turned you down, love." She fluttered her lashes at Louis, casting him her best come-hither glance, which if they hadn't known Mrs. Alexander, most people would find quite intimidating.

"Okay, girls," Mrs. Alexander shouted up the stairs. "Take it away!"

There was a burst of excited laughter from upstairs, the yowl of a very angry gray cat that whizzed past and out the front door with what looked suspiciously like a pink bow tied around its neck, then followed, in a much more sedate fashion, Bella and Izzy parading down the stairs humming a passable version of "Here Comes the Bride," Bella hefting the much more submissive and lace-laden Tango under one arm.

The shower curtain had been detached with more force than care, as far as Sophie could tell by looking at the ripped holes where the rings should have fit through, and turned into a white-plastic shiny cape. Bella's pink flowery bedroom curtain had been fashioned into a skirt worn over two or three fairy and Disney princess costumes, and what blooms of late summer that had been left in the garden had been savagely hacked down and stuck into hair and behind ears. The girls had finished off their bridal look with a generous helping of Sophie's second-best makeup. (She had learned long ago never to leave her best stuff lying around.)

"We are your bridesmaids, Aunty Sophie!" Izzy shrieked as they finally reached the bottom of the stairs in one piece, which was a minor miracle in itself given that their trains contravened most health and safety laws. "We are, aren't we? We ARE your bridesmaids?"

"Aren't we?" Bella reiterated, her expression a good deal more solemn and just a bit more threatening than Izzy's despite the two rosy dots she had lipsticked onto either cheek. Sophie knelt down and put an arm around each of them, glancing over her shoulder at Louis, who was leaning on the banister at the bottom of the stairs.

"Do you think it's a good idea for me to marry your daddy?" Sophie asked them, aware a beat too late that she didn't really have a contingency plan if either of them said no.

"I do," Izzy said, nodding as she spoke. "Because there will be a *big* party and a wedding cake and I've seen a picture of a wedding cake and it was *big*. And you love cake, Aunty Sophie, so getting married will make you really, really . . ."

"Massive?" Mrs. Alexander offered.

"No, happy, silly!" Izzy giggled and kissed Sophie on the cheek. "You will be happy."

"Excellent," Sophie said, looking at Bella and raising a hopeful eyebrow.

Bella twisted her mouth into the sideways knot Sophie had come to learn often preceded a difficult question. She braced herself.

"I do think it is a good idea for you to marry Daddy," she said slowly, as if she were working out her thoughts as she spoke. "Mostly."

"Mostly?" Sophie asked her gently. "What do you mean, Bella?"

Bella shrugged. "I just mean mostly," she said. "I want you and Daddy to be married, mostly."

"Okay," Sophie said briefly, pressing the palm of her hand against Bella's cheek. "Well, if you think of what the mostly bit means, then you will tell me, won't you? Because how you feel is more important to me than anything; and anyway, as if I could ever possibly have any bridesmaids other than you even if I wanted to. Although I think we might have to work on your look a bit."

"I was thinking wings," Izzy said. "Glittery ones."

"And I was thinking of ponies," Bella said, catching Izzy's enthusiasm and making her momentary reticence seem like a passing whim. "I thought we could ride ponies down the aisle. That would be really cool!"

The word "aisle" made Sophie think of a million different things at once. But principally churches, dresses, guests, an actual wedding that would result in an actual marriage that would mean she had made a real and life-changing decision that would be finally finalized in about the most final way that a decision possibly could be. With a legally binding contract. Suddenly she found that she was the one who was "mostly" glad she had agreed to marry Louis Gregory.

"Well, we can sort out all the details later," Louis said, catching the look in Sophie's eyes and peeling himself off the banister to help her to her feet. "For now we're going to Newquay to get Sophie's engagement ring resized."

"Can we wear this?" Bella asked him, gesturing at her bridesmaid-meets-Vegas outfit.

It would have been churlish to refuse.

• • •

It wasn't a long journey to Newquay, but it had been a very loud one.

"Aunty Sophie," Izzy had asked. "Who will you be once you and Daddy are married?"

"Who will I be?" Sophie had glanced at Louis, who was driving. "I'll be me, of course."

"Mrs. Sophie Gregory," Louis said proudly.

"I'm not changing my name," Sophie said without thinking. She glanced at Louis, unable to read his expression from his profile. "I mean, no one changes their name these days, plus I've got my professional reputation to think of. Sophie Mills has a reputation in the events industry. No one will have heard of Sophie Gregory."

"But, Sophie, you don't have a job anymore," Bella pointed out with her usual clarity. "No one cares what you're called."

"Don't have a new job *yet*, Bella," Sophie corrected her, noticing how Louis kept his eyes on the road, his expression set in neutral. "But I will have one and, well, I've been me for a long time now. I'm used to it."

"Could I change my name to Princess Izzy, Queen of Ice?" Izzy piped up. "I'm not used to my name at all!"

"The second you turn eighteen," Louis told her, soliciting an extended "not fair" moan from the rear of the car.

Sophie did not mention the other niggling anxiety that had popped into her head the second Louis mentioned her potential name. She'd already taken Carrie's children, admittedly according to the wishes of her friend, and now she also had her dead friend's husband. To take her name seemed to be going too far, as if she were really trying to step into the shoes of that mythic first wife, just like a latter-day second Mrs. de Winter obsessing over Rebecca.

"How about Mrs. Aunty Sophie?" Izzy hazarded.

"I like 'Sophie Mills,'" Bella said, providing Sophie with an unexpected ally. "And just because her and Daddy will be married doesn't mean she won't be our aunty Sophie anymore."

"Exactly," Sophie said.

"But what if I want to call her—" Izzy began.

"GIRLS!" Louis had raised his voice to cut across whatever Izzy had been about to say. "That's enough questions, you're giving Sophie a headache! Look, we're here now. Stop shouting and show me how pretty and ladylike and bridesmaidsey you can be. Because only quiet, respectable, ladylike girls can be bridesmaids."

"With wings," Izzy muttered under her breath.

"At all," Louis said.

"Except," Bella had told him, looking at him from beneath her bangs, "that we are your daughters and so we are definitely going to be bridesmaids *at all cost*."

Sophie followed the Gregorys through the shopping crowds from a slight distance. She knew Louis had guessed she was a bit overwhelmed by the maelstrom of feelings, opinions, and questions the girls had thrown at her, and she loved the fact that he knew her well enough to give her this small distance from them while she adjusted to everything that was happening. The very fact that he had discovered that about her gave her joy in itself. It was evidence of how their relationship had deepened since they'd first met. And she had discovered that she wanted to make him happy, and that she'd do more or less anything to do that. That had to be love.

What she needed to do, Sophie decided, was to take baby steps. First step: she *was* in love with Louis Gregory. The wild leaping of her heart whenever she stood next to him proved that conclusively—she had already taken that step and she thought she'd adjusted to the news rather well, what with all the sex and happiness it entailed. Second step: she had very recently agreed to marry him,

which would take a bit of getting used to, but she was confident
that she would get used to it because, after all, she had got very
used to step one alarmingly quickly. Third step: she'd have to think
about some sort of wedding eventually, although she'd read in an
old edition of the *Tatler* she'd found in the doctor's surgery when
Izzy had a chest infection that long engagements were the latest
trend, so perhaps it didn't have to be that soon. Fourth step: that
would be the actual being-married-to-Louis step, the part where
she moved out of the Avalon and in with him and the girls. Then
there was the fifth and final step: the whole rest of her life with
Louis and the girls, the rest of her natural life being fully married.

As her heart was gripped by a sudden vision of eternity, Sophie
decided then and there not to dwell on any of the steps past one
and two. One and two really were the only pertinent steps right
now. After all, she hadn't even told her mother yet that she was engaged, and everybody knows that nothing is really ever true or real
until you've told your mother.

As long as she had a little more time simply to enjoy being in
love with him and getting her head around being engaged to him,
then Sophie was certain she'd be able to deal with the other issues
eventually. After all, now that she'd said yes, there was no going
back.

The ring would be ready and perfectly sized within a couple of
hours, so Louis suggested lunch. Bella suggested bridesmaid shopping and Sophie suggested the pub. In the end they compromised
by going to the Bell, which was located next to a bridal shop and
served food all day. As Sophie sipped her gin and tonic, she watched
Louis and the girls talking, planning, laughing. They, the Gregorys, were a family now. A proper unit, something they had not
been until very recently. And Sophie was proud that in some small
way, she had helped make that happen. Or in a rather large way,
actually, she admitted to herself, quietly blowing her own trumpet.

After all, it was Sophie who had taken Bella and Izzy in when all she had to offer them was microwavable frozen dinners and a one-bedroom flat with a neurotic cat. And it was Sophie who had employed a private detective to track down the girls' father after Carrie died. Sophie had stood guard over Bella and Izzy while she tried to work out if the wildly handsome stranger who happened to be their father was friend or foe, and it was she who had done her best to reconcile the three of them even when Bella insisted that she hated the father who had once abandoned her. Sophie had bonded them back together and she had done it for Carrie, for her dear friend who for so many years had always been the best, most free, and wildest part of her.

Sophie looked at Louis, brushing a lock of dark hair from his eyes as he laughed at something Bella said.

On many of the nights she spent alone in the B & B, Sophie sometimes wondered if she would ever have fallen for Louis if she hadn't met him in that way and at that time. If he hadn't been a confused man, a jilted husband suffering from guilt and loss? If she hadn't loved the woman he'd once loved or fallen for his strange, lost daughters so hard, would she have felt the same way about him?

"Hey, Wendy? Wendy Churchill, it is you!"

Sophie was snapped out of her thoughts as Louis called after a woman who had walked past their table. "Don't try and pretend you don't know who I am!" Louis teased her jovially.

Sophie studied the woman's face as she slowly turned to face Louis. Perhaps a couple of years older than Sophie, she had reddish hair pulled back into a ponytail.

"Louis Gregory," the woman said slowly. "Last I heard you'd moved away."

"I came back." Louis grinned as he stood up. "And so did you by the looks of things! Last time I saw you . . . well, it was over twenty years ago."

Sophie blinked as her betrothed stepped away from their table and engulfed the woman in a huge bear hug. She was smaller than Sophie, qualifying as petite, with slender hips and narrow shoulders, and the sort of pretty elfin looks that Sophie hadn't realized until that very second she despised.

"How long since you lived up north?" Louis asked, glancing at his girls. Izzy was doing her best to get the entire contents of one mini-sachet of ketchup onto a single French fry. Bella, though, was staring hard at this Wendy woman from underneath her bangs and listening intently to every word being said. Bella liked to know everything that was going on, she spent much of her young life trying to ensure that no piece of information, no matter how trivial it might seem, ever got past her.

"Moved back down here about a year ago. I've got my own business—running costs are lower here and I missed it, it's always been home." Wendy smiled. "What about you? Where did you go and why did you come back?"

"Well, it's a long story, but basically I lost my wife in a car accident. I came back to look after my two daughters, Bella and Izzy." Louis gestured at his daughters.

"Good afternoon," Bella said gravely.

"They're yours?" Wendy Churchill said, glancing briefly at the two girls without returning Bella's greeting. "You're a *dad*?"

"Yes." Louis laughed. "No need to sound so shocked, Wend! Bella is nearly seven, Izzy is four. I'm a dad twice over, and after a serious false start, I'm not doing too bad a job of it now. In fact, things are going really great and this . . ." Finally Louis gestured toward where Sophie was waiting to be introduced, but Wendy Churchill did not look at her. She looked back at Bella who, after a second wrinkled her nose and then wrested the pot of ketchup sachets from Izzy, choosing to ignore the stranger.

"They look like you," Wendy said slowly, as if she were processing some other hidden piece of information.

"Do they?" Louis looked pleased. "I can see it with Bella, but Izzy is the image of her mum."

"No, they both look exactly like . . . you." Wendy stopped, glanced over her shoulder, and then seemed to collect herself. Suddenly she beamed at Louis.

"God, I'm sorry, it's just been such a long time since I last saw you. I still think of you as sixteen, the great, tall, lanky lad you were. Bumping into you now—a real grown-up man with kids—is a bit of a shock."

"*You* don't look any different," Louis told Wendy, which made Sophie purse her lips a little because if this woman was about Louis's age, some old school friend or something, then there was no way she could look the same as she had at sixteen. Not unless she'd had wrinkles and dark roots back then too.

"Daddy, who is this lady and what does she want with us?" Bella returned her attention to the stranger. "And why is she staring at us as if we are animals in a zoo?"

Sophie beamed at her; she could always rely on Bella to ask the pertinent questions.

"This," Louis said, finally tearing his eyes off Wendy's face, "is my old friend Wendy Churchill. We used to go to school together."

"And we were a little bit more than friends," Wendy said, smiling coyly, which made Sophie want to slap Wendy Churchill quite hard.

"Oh well," Louis chuckled, and Sophie was dismayed to see him flush. "You never wrote, you never called. You broke my heart, Wendy Churchill!"

"You never tried to find me," Wendy added, her tone a touch more serious than Louis's.

"Hey, you were the chucker, I was the chuckee," Louis said. "And that reminds me, this is my fiancée, Sophie Mills."

Finally Wendy removed her gaze from Louis's face and looked at Sophie.

"Wow, you don't let the grass grow, do you? I thought you said your wife only just died." Sophie found it rather hard to maintain her fake smile.

Louis laughed awkwardly. "Carrie and I had been apart for three years when she died," he explained, his smile faltering. "Sophie was there for me and the children when it happened. She saved all of us."

"I, oh, *see,*" Wendy said, nodding, as if the mysteries of the universe had suddenly all become clear.

"Well anyway, Wendy." Louis's smile vanished. "It was nice to see you again. Take care of yourself."

"I've always had to." Her reply implied something that Sophie could not fathom, except that it was barbed with just a hint of resentment. "Good-bye, Louis."

She stood there looking at Louis for a second longer than Sophie deemed appropriate and then made her way out through the crowds.

"What a charming lady," Sophie said, exchanging a knowing look with Bella.

"Who *was* that funny lady?" Izzy asked, emerging from her food and slinging an arm around Sophie's neck to kiss her, leaving a tomato-ketchup kiss on her cheek.

"She was a rude lady," Bella said. "I didn't like her."

"She's just someone I used to know," Louis said as he watched her go, but there was a look in his eyes that belied his casual dismissal of her, a look that reminded Sophie of the fact that she knew hardly anything about Louis's life before Carrie. He never talked about it. There were years, decades, of his life that were a mystery to her.

"When I knew her, she never used to be quite that intense."

Louis leaned over and wiped away the smear of ketchup from Sophie's cheek with the ball of his thumb. "I'm sorry, Soph. She was pretty rude to you, ignoring you like that."

"Was she? I didn't notice," Sophie lied, more interested in finding out about this relic from Louis's past. "Childhood sweetheart, was she? She's probably been pining for you all these years and is put out that you're with me. Pure jealousy, and who can blame her, hey, bridesmaids?"

As Sophie expected, the word sent the girls into paroxysms of hysteria and the Wendy interlude was soon forgotten as Louis had to catch Izzy as she raced around the pub in excitement, her loo paper bridal train fluttering behind her.

That afternoon back at Louis's house, the electric fire on and the lights blazing against the driving rain that pelted the house's white-washed pebbled exterior, Sophie sat near her cat Artemis and waited for Louis to come back from the kitchen with a cup of tea for her. She would have liked to sit next to Artemis, but she'd learned, after many claw-related injuries, that you never approached the cat, you waited for the cat to approach you, and this afternoon Artemis was clearly not in the mood. So Sophie sat near her and missed her because she loved her cat even if she knew her cat could mostly take her or leave her.

The girls had gone upstairs to draw some designs for Sophie's wedding dress, dragging poor old Tango with them just in case they needed a mannequin to model dresses on, and Sophie was glad of a few moments' peace even though she wasn't sure about being considered the same body type as a blatantly tubby ginger tom.

"I'm glad you're happy here without me," she told Artemis, who tucked her two gray paws neatly beneath her and blinked in response. "I mean, I wouldn't want you to miss me, or pine for me, or go off your food just because I gave you a home when no one else wanted a psychotic, antisocial cat and we shared a flat for years and years. I'm glad you're emotionally independent."

Artemis regarded her with a long, flat stare that Sophie was reasonably sure said "If you haven't got any food with you, you might as well leave."

"What do you think about this Wendy woman then?" Sophie asked Artemis. "She fluttered all over Louis today, acting all weird and mysterious, and she *was* acting that way, I didn't imagine it. And *he* . . . he gave her this funny little look. This wistful look, what was that all about? Who was she to him? I have no idea. That's the trouble. I haven't got a clue. I mean, what do I really know about him or his life before he met Carrie? He never talks about it."

"About what?" Louis said as he came in carefully carrying two mugs of hot tea. "And why are you talking to that cat?"

"She understands every word," Sophie protested weakly.

"Yes, but she doesn't give a toss. If you want to talk to a dumb animal, you should try me. I hang on your every word." He sat on the carpet and leaned his back against the sofa, his shoulder brushing Sophie's knee. The glow of the fire tinted his complexion a ruddy orange as he passed her her drink.

"Okay then," Sophie said, taking a sip of her tea. "I asked Artemis, what do I know about you? I mean, I know that you're lovely and an excellent kisser and fabulous in bed or on the sofa or whatever and that I love you, but what do I know about you? I know hardly anything about your family—"

"Because I don't really have one," Louis said, exchanging glances with Artemis.

"Or your past. I mean that Wendy from today, who was she?"

Louis sipped his tea. "I told you. A girl I used to know at school."

"You were more than just friends she said while ignoring me," Sophie added rather pointedly.

"Oh god, I was sixteen, she was fifteen—it was that time when you're going out with one girl at morning registration and she's chucked you by afternoon break. Technically I was 'more than just friends' with half my class. The female half."

Louis laughed, but Sophie did not.

"Come on, Soph," Louis said, setting his tea down on the coffee table and kneeling to face her. "It's just someone I used to know, it's no big deal. I want to kiss you, I haven't kissed you in at least two hours; I'm going through withdrawal."

One hand slid up her thigh as he took her drink from her and moved in to kiss her.

"No . . . Louis, wait," Sophie said. Louis waited, looking mildly surprised.

"What, you don't want the cat watching? I have to admit, she's putting me off a bit too," Louis said, glancing over his shoulder at Artemis who, if she'd had lips, would have been pursing them in matronly disapproval.

"No, listen." Sophie put her palms on either side of his cheeks and made him look at her. "You and I are engaged. To be married and stuff."

"Yes." Louis smiled. "It's great, isn't it? Especially the stuff bit."

"Yes, it's lovely, but I don't know anything about you. Your life before you met Carrie is a complete mystery to me. And I want to know, I want to know all about you, every little thing, from your first memory onward, because it's all part of what makes you you and I love you and I think if I know more about you, I'll feel more . . . secure."

"Secure? I've just asked you to marry me. How secure do you need to feel?" Louis asked her, perplexed.

"All right, not secure then—closer to you. The more I know about you, the closer I feel to you."

"I've often found that naked kissing and stuff is the best way to achieve that." Louis's lips curled into a smile, but Sophie was adamant.

"No, no kissing. I want to know, tell me about her. Tell me about Wendy, please."

Louis sat back on his heels and sighed.

"Fine," he said with a shrug. "You want to know about Wendy. Well, Wendy was my first proper girlfriend, my first love, I suppose. I'd had this crush on her from the minute I set eyes on her when she first arrived at our school. I was thirteen and she was twelve. This gingery hair and . . . well, she was the first girl in her year to have curves, put it that way. I saw her and I thought, that's her, that's the girl I'm going to marry one day."

"Oh." Sophie was taken aback by the sudden flare of jealousy in her chest. "And?"

"And?" Louis shrugged. "And that's it. Wendy was my first love. Who was your first love?"

Sophie thought for a moment, but just then she didn't want to tell Louis that it was him. "That can't be it, you met her when you were thirteen, but you knew her for at least three more years. What happened next?"

"Do you want a daily or monthly account?" Louis's tone was sardonic. "Only it was a long time ago and I might have forgotten some of the details. How many sugars she had in her tea—that sort of thing."

"Louis, I'm serious!" Sophie told him, trying to wrestle the frustrated tone out of her voice. "You went out with her, for how long and when?"

Louis sighed and stood up, crossing over to the armchair where Artemis was perched. The two of them regarded each other for a second like gunfighters in a spaghetti western and then, realizing who was by far the more superior animal, Louis sat down on the floor in front of the fire, crossing his legs like a schoolboy on a camping trip.

"So I carried a torch for her." Louis smiled to himself. "God, I loved her. She never talked to me, never looked at me. We weren't in any of the same classes or anything, so I had to try and bump into her in places where I thought she might be. I remember once walking round and round this park near her house, until it got dark, on the off chance she might turn up, but she never showed."

"Which park?" Sophie asked him, hungry for details so she could more clearly picture the lovesick thirteen-year-old Louis. "The one near the guildhall?"

"What? No, no, this was in Newquay. Wendy and I grew up in Newquay."

"Did you?" Sophie asked him. "I never knew that about you."

"It's not that important, is it?" Louis asked her. "It's just a place. I don't think about it as home, this place is home. Wherever you are is home, which is why it would be so much better if you moved in here with me."

"Tell me what happened next. How did you get together?" Sophie pressed him, even though her heart shied away from knowing. Louis's answering smile was fond and full of warmth.

"We were both at the end-of-year party; I knew she was going to be there and I knew that might be the last chance I'd have to talk to her. I was leaving school and it was the summer holidays. I gave myself a deadline—I'd either tell her I loved her that night or never at all, typical teen dramatics. It sounds silly now, but when I think about it, I can still feel it, that tight band around my chest whenever I thought about her or looked at her. Wendy and those red curls and the way that—" Louis caught the look on Sophie's face that matched the thunderous skies outside the window and caught himself. "Anyway, I was very nervous—this was my moment of truth. I decided to have a drink for Dutch courage, and another one and another one. Four pints of cider on an empty stomach while I was waiting for the right moment, the moment when I felt brave and handsome enough to talk to her. Only, if it ever came, it was lost somewhere between being petrified and incoherent and utterly drunk. I passed out on a bench. When I woke up the party was over, my head was banging like a drum, and I hadn't said two words to the girl I loved." Sophie watched as Louis's gaze slipped from her face, looking instead into his past. "God, I was gutted, I missed my moment, I'd blown it. I realized I'd have to live the rest of my life without her. Eventually I decided to walk home, and out of habit I suppose I took a detour past her house, probably to get one last look at her window. Only, when I turned down her road, she was there sitting on the wall outside her house, smoking a cigarette.

" 'You took your time,' she said as I walked up to her, really, really hoping I wasn't going to throw up again. 'I've been waiting here all night, I was just about to go in before my mum and dad realize there are pillows under my quilt and not me.' "

Louis grinned to himself. "I was all over the place, not entirely sure I wasn't still on that bench and dreaming. So I asked her, 'How did you know I was going to come?' And she goes all cool as a cucumber. 'You always walk home past my house, I didn't suppose tonight would be any different. Never once knocked on my door though, so I thought I'd better sit out here waiting for you or else you'd never get round to asking me out.'

" 'You could always have asked me out,' I said, because I was a kid and a bit of an idiot.

"And she hopped off the wall and wound her arm around my neck and said, 'I'm the girl, girls don't make the first move.' And then she kissed me, and we stayed like that, necking on her front wall, until the sun came up."

Sophie steeled herself against the disappointment she felt at knowing that Louis had ever spent hours kissing anyone but her, but it was useless, the jealousy swept through like a fire through kindling. She knew he had a past, of course he did, he'd been married to Carrie, but the idea of him ever loving anyone else the way he loved her, even some fifteen-year-old decades ago, hurt her almost more than she could bear.

"For that whole summer we were inseparable," Louis went on. "We spent every day together, just us two. I didn't see my mates for weeks. It was an amazing time, it was like . . . it was like . . ."

"A wonderful dream you didn't want to wake up from?" Sophie asked him.

Louis nodded. "Yes, except that I had to. She left, or rather her family left, almost overnight. I couldn't believe it. I didn't know a thing about it."

"Even though you saw her every day."

"Toward the end of the holiday she didn't want to see me as much, lost interest in me, I suppose. When I phoned her she was never in. And I never saw her in town anymore. None of her friends seemed to know what she was up to. Then I walked past her house one morning, hoping she'd come out, and it had a Sold sign outside it. It was already empty, they'd gone. I knocked on a neighbor's door and she told me Wendy's dad had got a new job up north. He'd moved them all in one weekend, just like that. I never heard from her again."

"Never?" Sophie asked him.

"Nope." Louis shook his head. "I was heartbroken, destroyed, it took me ages to get over her, I suppose because I really thought we were soul mates . . ."

"Soul mates?" Sophie asked. She hoped that Louis was her soul mate, but if he'd already had one in his lifetime she wasn't sure. She wasn't sure exactly how many soul mates a person could encounter in one life, but she got the feeling that if it was more than one, then the whole concept was rather less special than she'd been led to believe.

"Yes, silly teen love, you know—plus she was the first girl I had sex with, that was a big deal." Louis dropped that bombshell casually, as if it were the least important detail.

"You slept with her!" Sophie couldn't stop the betrayal in her voice.

"Sophie, come on, it was years ago. At our age we're bound to have a past, you can't be jealous, can you? After all, you weren't a virgin when I met you."

Sophie wanted to say "only technically" but didn't.

"No," she lied instead. "No, of course I'm not jealous."

"We've got it!" Bella ran in clutching several pieces of paper, closely followed by Izzy, whose arrival caused Artemis to discreetly retreat to the top of the bookshelf where she was far less likely to have to ward off unwanted advances from a small girl who just wouldn't believe the cat didn't love her.

"We've designed the perfect dress for you, Aunty Sophie," Bella told her, delivering the sheets of paper into her lap. "Only on here we've written the 'purrrrfect' dress because we've drawn it on a cat. It's a joke that is funny, do you see?"

"Yes, I do see." Sophie took the piece of paper, smiling at the confection of glitter glue and felt-tip that Bella and Izzy had presented her with. "It's marvelous and I shall certainly bear it in mind when I select a dress."

Sophie half-listened as the girls began to chatter, filling her in on all the dress's design points, like its secret going-to-the-toilet skirt-lifting device and refrigerated pocket for perishable items.

What was the point, she wondered as she listened to Bella's plans for a pony-themed wedding, of telling Louis that everything about Wendy Churchill made her feel uncomfortable, tense, and as if she was in exactly the wrong place, with the wrong man, at the wrong time? That for a second Wendy made her feel like the inter-loper she sometimes suspected she might be in Louis's life. That was nothing more than her usual paranoia and neuroses manifesting themselves in new, cruel, and unusual ways. Other than a woman she didn't know being slightly rude to her, and Louis doing exactly what she had asked him to do, recounting an incident from his past, long ago, nothing had really happened. And besides, it wasn't as if she would ever have to see Wendy Churchill again.

Later that night as Sophie lay in her single bed in the B & B, gazing at the roses that circled the floral ceiling fixture, she found herself going over and over Louis's story, adding details and embellishments of her own, images of Louis and Wendy walking hand in hand in unknown sun-drenched cornfields. She closed her eyes and tried her best to think about something else, anything else, fingering her engagement ring, which still felt odd on her finger. Still, thoughts of Louis and Wendy crowded her muddled, foolish head. Eventually she sat up, switching on the lamp next to her bed. Wearily she climbed out of bed to make use of the tea- and coffee-making facilities that Mrs. Alexander so kindly provided in every room and made herself a hot chocolate, then climbed back into bed to look once again at the wedding-dress designs the girls had made her promise she would pin up above her bed. And as she looked closely at the drawings, reading all the labels that Bella had so carefully spelled out in her best handwriting, picking up the more outrageous details that Izzy had added, Sophie felt the tension in her chest subside and a slow-spreading warmth take its place.

Louis, her first love, her soul mate, had asked her to marry him, she realized, as if his proposal had only truly just sunk in. He'd asked her to be with him and his daughters for the rest of her life, and she couldn't imagine anything more wonderful. It was everything she wanted. He was everything she wanted and she was going to marry him. All at once Sophie realized with a rush of adrenaline that the time to sit on the fence and wonder about her future was over. Now was the time to leap into tomorrow and embrace and enjoy the one thing she knew was going to complete her. She was going to be Louis Gregory's wife and she could not wait.

Five

Sophie arrived on Louis's doorstep at the crack of dawn, surprised to find him and the girls already up.

"Hello," she said, kissing him warmly on the lips. "I was coming over extra early to make you all a surprise breakfast."

"Ah well, you'd have had to sleep over for that," Louis said, his arms encircling Sophie as the girls watched, nudging each other and giggling. "I've got to get my gear ready for that fiftieth-anniversary lunch in Penzance tomorrow. I'm re-creating the wedding photos of the happy couple outside the church they were married in. It's seriously sweet. You should see them, Sophie, Mr. and Mrs. Harris, met and fell in love when they were fifteen, married before they were twenty, and still as happy and as crazy about each other now as they were then. Who says young love doesn't last, hey?"

"Me," Sophie told him happily as she sat down at the kitchen table with the girls, who were making their way through their customary Sunday-morning piles of toast and jam. "I woke up this morning and realized that hardly anybody knows we are all getting married. And I thought, we need to tell everyone we possibly can. We need to start making calls!"

"We do?" Louis said, sitting down next to her. "You really want to tell everyone?"

"Yes, of course I do," Sophie said. "I can't wait for the whole world to know that I'm marrying you."

Despite her enthusiasm, it was Louis who got to work making calls as soon as he cleared the breakfast dishes and settled the girls down with a box of Legos in the front room. He trawled through his old address books and rang his friends. Sophie, on the other hand, paced in the kitchen, her joy battling a barrage of nerves. She wondered why she found it so much harder than Louis to break the news. Perhaps it was because he didn't have a mother to tell, Sophie thought. If he had a mother to tell, he would be feeling much more nervous. Of course he did have an ex–mother-in-law to tell, but as of yet they had not discussed whose list that particular name should be on, although Sophie guessed from Louis's carefree and joyous demeanor that he wasn't expecting it to be on his.

What she was really afraid of, Sophie realized as she ran the ball of her thumb over her phone's keypad, was of the people she loved and cared about not taking her seriously. She needed them to understand exactly how happy she was, how serious she was about marrying Louis, and, more than anything, she needed them to be happy for her.

Deciding she needed to be alone to make her calls, Sophie took herself out into Louis's garden and sat on the bench that the girls had nicknamed the fairy bower because it was located under a trellis smothered with a creeping rosebush that, at the merest gust of wind, scattered soft, silky pink petals on whoever was sitting beneath it. On this thankfully warm and dry Sunday morning, with the last remnants of the summer's heat just detectable in the air, the remaining roses had already shattered during an earlier shower, littering the seat, a faded pink confetti of petals.

As she scrolled through the names in her phone, she made a mental list of who to call and in which order she would tell them. Then she crossed off the names she least wanted to tell until there was nobody left on her list and she had to start again. Finally she decided the only fair way was to do it alphabetically. Taking a deep breath Sophie found Cal's name and pressed Call.

"What now? Sick of sharing your lover with a sheep?" was Cal's friendly greeting.

"Oh, how very professional," Sophie said. "You can tell that McCarthy Hughes is going to hell in a handbasket—you were never that rude when I worked there."

"That's because you were always a rudeness-free zone—in all senses," Cal said. "Besides, it's Sunday morning and I'm still in bed. In fact, you're lucky not to be interrupting anything. So come on then, tell me, which crisis of confidence are you having this week? Have you discovered you're allergic to clotted cream? Are you afraid the locals might try and burn you in a wicker man? Only you're going to have to hurry up if you want me to dispense my usual pearls of wit and wisdom, as I have to prepare for a breakfast meeting with your old friend Jake Flynn tomorrow morning. He wants us to do the Christmas party again this year, and it's got to be bigger and better than the last one, and so far no one has had any ideas to top the cruise ship so . . . have you got any ideas?"

"You're meeting Jake?" When Sophie heard Jake Flynn's name, she forgot completely about her news, and Cal's question, which normally she would have pounced on in delight as tangible proof that McCarthy Hughes did miss her among its ranks even if Cal swore that her absence from the office went entirely unnoticed.

Jake Flynn, a handsome New Yorker, was the man Sophie had been endeavoring to fall in love with when Louis walked into her life. At the time, Jake had been her most important client, as she had been planning for his organization a huge Christmas party on an ocean liner that regularly docked at Tower Bridge. She'd been mildly attracted to him from the start but had been using their professional relationship as an excuse not to have to do anything about it. Once, before Bella and Izzy, Sophie had been the queen of not acting on her feelings, of living her life at arm's length. The old Sophie would have been quite content to have conducted her own particular brand of long-distance romance with Jake indefinitely—one that involved him not knowing about it at all.

When Cal had told Sophie Jake liked her, she refused to believe him, but when Jake himself told her he was interested in her, it became hard to ignore. He'd been sweet and patient and so understanding when Sophie had decided to take time off from work to look after the girls. He'd even kissed her with all the charm and expertise that any woman could ask of any man. Except that by then Sophie had already met Louis, and even if she didn't consciously know it, it was Louis who was constantly occupying her thoughts. She would never know what could have happened between her and Jake if she hadn't met Louis, if a more quiet and conventional romance might not have developed over time. If perhaps now, nearly a year from their first meeting, there might have been an engagement announcement posted in the *New York Times*. Probably not, Sophie reasoned. There had been nothing between her and Jake except a sort of long-distance attraction. There had never been any heat, and with Louis heat was a constant, simmering presence, on the point of boiling over the second he walked into a room. A heat that she could look forward to basking in until their own fiftieth anniversary and beyond. In a blink Sophie forgot Jake and remembered what she was so desperate to tell Cal.

"Yes," Cal said, interrupting her thoughts. "Jake couldn't have been that brokenhearted when you legged it, because we didn't lose their account—thank god—it's practically the only thing keeping us afloat right now. Anyway, for their transatlantic offices the Madison Corporation are having a big hands-across-the-ocean Christmas bash that we're organizing. So far it's the only big event we've got booked. You know how important this account is, especially now with everyone's head potentially on the chopping block. And your ex-nemesis and my new boss Eve's given it to *me*. I can't afford to screw this up, Soph, so I need you to tell me exactly what you would have done in this situation, even though I'm certain that it would be exactly what I'm going to do, I'm just double-checking, that's all, as you were once quite good at your job."

"Let me get this straight," Sophie said, happily distracted from the purpose of her call. "You are asking me for professional advice. You are admitting that you miss me and that you still need my considerable knowledge and expertise. Is that right?"

"No." Cal was adamant. "Well, maybe a little. I'll be honest, I'm terrified, I just want to get this right. No one wants to get on the wrong side of Eve. Marshal from accounts got on the wrong side of Eve; two weeks later he turned up temping as a waiter at one of Eve's events. She put a cigarette out on his tray of canapés. Rumor has it that she ruined his professional reputation from here to New York and now all he can get is a job washing up. I can't be a part-time waiter, Sophie, I can't. Besides, I have the hands of an eighteen-year-old milkmaid—they must never know the horrors of detergent. Say you'll help me and then never speak of it again, please. That's what a real friend would do."

"Well, I'm guessing your budgets have been cut . . ."

"Like you wouldn't believe," Cal moaned.

"So think outside the box, Cal. All the obvious venues will cost too much, and the last thing you want is a cut-price version in some awful low-rent convention center."

"I know! But what? Where? I've wracked my brain, Sophie."

Sophie thought of the Tate Gallery in St. Ives, a wonderful modernist building made up of white concentric circles, angles, and other shapes. It would be the perfect place for a party.

"Start ringing places that don't cater for events. Everyone needs extra revenue right now, so try museums, galleries—even empty buildings awaiting redevelopment will have someone who owns them desperate to get some return. Look for anywhere that's a bit different and see if you can get the space for less, perhaps with some sort of cross marketing as an incentive. You know, hold it in a gallery with the opportunity for guests to purchase art. Or in a beautiful house that's on the market. Promise them the kind of guests who might buy. If you cut your venue fees, then you won't have to skimp on the catering or entertainment."

There was a short silence.

"I'm only going to say this once and then you and I are both going to forget that these words ever left my mouth. You are a genius, Sophie, and I love you. I think you might have saved the day."

"Of course I have—you can take the girl out of the city but you can't take the city out of the girl." Sophie smiled, enjoying feeling that buzz once again. "And when you see Jake, give him my love, I mean my best wishes, won't you?"

"I will, but he won't care," Cal replied breezily. "He's got this über-sexy girlfriend he brought with him when he was meeting with Eve, some New York chick, groomed to within an inch of her life—stunning and slightly scary. You know the type."

"Really, that's great," Sophie said, more than a little surprised, considering the reason for her call, that she felt rather peeved. "I'm happy for him."

"Great, everybody's happy for everybody—so tell me what you've got to tell me, and we can get on with our lives."

Sophie's mind went blank for a moment and then she remembered.

"LouisaskedmetomarryhimandIsaidyes," she gushed, keen to get the sentence out of her head and into the ether before she lost her nerve.

Sophie braced herself, but nothing happened except for a long and highly uncharacteristic silence on the other end of the line.

"And I didn't even have to buy any Wellingtons," Sophie added with a touch of childish triumph that she supposed wasn't all that becoming for a blushing bride-to-be.

She waited for a response from Cal, but he was silent.

"Cal? Are you still there?" Sophie said impatiently.

"Louis. Asked. You. To. Marry. Him?" Cal said each word slowly and heavily, each one weighted with disbelief. "Bloody unbelievable!"

"Yes, it's great, isn't it?" Sophie prompted him. "Isn't it?"

"But *why?*" Cal asked her.

Sophie had been expecting many things from Cal, sarcasm, of course, a pretense that he had seen this coming from several miles off despite all his declarations that Sophie would never get near an altar, and, finally, she had been looking forward to the kind of warm goodwill that characterized the real friendship beneath the thin veneer of cattiness and sarcasm. But she had not expected that question at all.

"*Why?* Because I love him and he makes me happy—Cal, I've honestly never been happier in my life than when I'm with him. He was so sweet and nervous about proposing, and you should see the ring he picked out for me. Vintage 1930s—it is perfect—"

"No, I don't mean why did you say yes," Cal interrupted her.

"Of course *you* said yes. And of course he asked you, he's crazy about you. I mean, why did he ask you to marry him *now*? You've only been there for six months. You don't even have any wellies. Are you pregnant?"

"Cal! No, I'm not pregnant! And I don't need any wellies to know that I want to marry him, and he obviously doesn't need me to have any to want to marry him," Sophie said. "It's not as if either of us is a feckless teen. I'm thirty-three nearly, and he'll be thirty-six in . . ." Sophie trailed off, realizing she wasn't 100 percent certain of the birth month of her betrothed, let alone the actual date. "A few months."

"Well, I have always thought that impending death is a good enough reason for a proposal," Cal said drily.

"Oh, for god's sake, Cal!" Sophie snapped at him. "You're the one who persuaded me to leave London and come down here. You're the one who said I should be spontaneous and grab happiness and all of that. Well, I've done that and I'm still doing it—why aren't you happy for me?"

When Cal spoke it was with the warmth that Sophie had been hoping for. "Of course I am. Of course I am happy for you, Sophie," Cal said. "It was just a bit of a shock that you, Sophie Mills, are getting married to a man who actually exists in reality and not just in your head. Oh, Sophie, my little girl, finally all grown up . . . ," Cal trailed off, and Sophie couldn't be certain but she thought she heard the faintest sniff.

"What?" Sophie urged him.

"It's just you, happy and in love and getting married. It's just brilliant and I'm delighted for you, which is odd for me because I hardly ever care about anyone else's happiness. And who cares if it's quick. I've conducted whole relationships between breakfast and dinner on the same day!"

"And you are really, really pleased for me? Because, Cal—I'm so happy and I'm so sure and you know that I've never been terribly good at being either of those things before."

"Sophie Mills, you've done what so many people never have the guts to do," Cal told her. "You've chased down happiness, rugby-tackled it to the floor, and pinned it there until it had no choice but to submit to your will or suffocate under your substantial weight. And frankly, as it was mainly me who persuaded you to move down there and go after Louis in the first place, making me entirely responsible for all of your newfound happiness, then I demand that you make me your chief bridesmaid."

"Ah," Sophie told him. "I think there might be some stiff competition for that role, although I will accept bribes."

Christina, Sophie's last remaining single friend, actually cried when Sophie broke the news. And they weren't tears of joy either. They were wet, rattling sobs that required deep, rasping, inward breaths to sustain them, which Christina seemed to manage to be able to do indefinitely.

"Don't cry, Christina," Sophie begged her. "At least not in a bad way. You're kind of bringing the overjoyed and happy vibe down a bit."

"I'm sorry, I'm not crying *really*, if I was crying really, then what sort of sad clichéd single woman in her thirties would that make me?" Christina wailed. "I'm premenstrual. They are irrational premenstrual tears. It's my hormones that are making me cry . . . and really, that should make me feel happy—at least I still have hormones—see, there's always a bright side."

"Yes, it's a little different from the bright side I was thinking of, but still . . ."

"Now I really am the last one, aren't I?" Christina asked. "I really am the final aged single friend, the one who'll turn up in a BBC Two documentary about women who can't find love and need a specialist's advice . . . I didn't think I would be the last one to find someone. I really thought it would be you."

"It's so touching that everyone had such high hopes for me," Sophie muttered.

"I suppose there's always Alison," Christina said, referring to a woman Sophie had met briefly. "I mean, she's been married and had kids but now she's getting a divorce, so *she's* single, and maybe it's worse being single and divorced than just single, but at least she's been married even if it was to a total jerk—what do you think?"

"I think you'll probably meet someone at my wedding," Sophie said to cheer Christina up, suddenly thrilling at the thought of being able to set an actual date when she would be able to make Louis her husband. "There'll be loads of fishermen and surfers and just men in general, hundreds of them."

"Really?" Christina perked up considerably. "When is it going to be, is it going to be soon? I know this designer who will make you bespoke personalized invites . . . He's single, well, when I say single I mean he's not married yet, which I think counts as single, I think men are fair game until they've got that wedding ring on, don't you?"

Briefly Sophie thought of the way Wendy had looked at her fiancé.

"No, I certainly do not," Sophie said, a little more firmly than she'd meant to.

"Oh sorry, forgot," Christina said. "You're on the other side now."

Sophie thought for a long time before ringing her mother. She was aware that not only should her mother have been first on her list of calls to make, no matter where *m* came in the alphabet, she should also probably have gone home, along with her betrothed, to tell her mother face-to-face that she was getting married. Iris Mills barely knew her future son-in-law, and although she had taken Sophie's sudden departure to Cornwall with good grace and was even pleased for her, Sophie wasn't sure how she'd feel about her making the move permanent. Her relationship with her mother hadn't been an easy one since her father died suddenly when she was a teenager. There had been distance between them ever since, a sort of nameless and entirely unfounded blame. Sophie was always cross and impatient with her mother, and after the only man in either of their lives had gone, Iris seemed detached from her daughter, more caught up with the various waif and stray dogs she collected from the streets of North London than with Sophie.

It was only when Sophie had taken on Bella and Izzy that she turned to Iris for help, the first help of any kind that she had ever asked for since she was fifteen years old. Gradually their relationship had changed and Sophie had found a way to relate to her mother again. It had been Iris who convinced Sophie that a small amount of cat food probably wasn't fatal for a three-year-old, Iris who had babysat the girls even though she knew that wherever the two children were, the risk of fire and flood damage increased at an alarming rate. And it was Iris who had assured Sophie that Sophie would be able to cope with whatever situation was thrown at her because, if anyone could cope with two small, bereaved children, then it was her strong and capable daughter. For the first time in decades, Sophie began to see that her mother admired her, and they had slowly drawn closer together. Sophie had spoken to her about twice a week since she'd come down to St. Ives, but they'd never spoken about anything serious. Her mum would always say how lovely it was to hear her sounding so happy and relaxed and then they'd talk about fleas, ticks, or dicky-doggy tummy for the next half hour.

But there was no getting away from it; a conversation about ear mites was not going to cut it this time. Sophie had to tell her mother that she was engaged in the business of getting married.

As ever, Sophie had to wait for a cacophony of barking dogs to die down as her mother rescued the handset from the jaws of Scooby, her Great Dane, and clambered over a pack of hounds to the kitchen, where she would shut most of them out so that she could talk in relative peace.

"Hello, love," Iris said. "It's not your normal day to call."

"Isn't it?" Sophie had not been aware that she had a normal day to call, but she wasn't surprised, her life had slipped into a soothing lullaby of a routine since she had arrived here. "Well, that's because it's not a normal day!" she added brightly.

"You're telling me," Iris sighed. "You remember Skippers, that little Jack Russell cross that was left tied up in a plastic bag in that Dumpster on Balls Pond Road? Well, he got hold of the neighbor's trash cans yesterday, had them out all over the street, so you can imagine how popular that made me with the neighbors again."

"Mum . . ." Sophie paused and took a breath. "Mum, I can't talk to you about the dogs today. I have some *news*."

Sophie paused to let the weight of the word sink into her mother's dog-filled consciousness.

"News?" Iris asked. "Oh, are you pregnant?"

"No!" Sophie was scandalized. "No, I am not pregnant, but . . . oh honestly, Mum—you've totally stolen my thunder. Louis and I are getting married!" Sophie paused for a beat, but when Iris didn't immediately react she rushed on. "And I have the happiest and most content and most alive feeling that I have ever had and you should feel really, really happy for me!"

"I'm thrilled for you, darling," Iris said, a little hesitantly, as soon as Sophie let her get a word in.

"Are you?" Sophie asked uncertainly.

"Of course I am. If you're happy, I'm happy. I'm honor bound to say the sorts of things that mothers say, like isn't it a bit soon and are you sure you know him well enough to marry him?"

Sophie paused; after all, these were the doubts she herself had had.

"Yes, Mum, it is technically a bit soon and no, I don't know every single thing about him. But I love him and want him and need him now—and isn't it better to find out about the person you love as you go along together? Wouldn't life be boring if you knew everything about your partner right from the start? And I want this, I want it really badly. I didn't realize how badly I wanted it until now that I've almost got it. I couldn't bear to lose him."

"Well, I can't think of any reason why you would," Iris said. "But believe it or not, darling, I do remember how that feels and I understand. You love him and he loves you and you want to grab happiness and cling to it with both hands. Okay, so you're breaking boundaries and stretching taboos . . . but who cares what other people say if you're happy?"

"Am I stretching a taboo?" Sophie asked her. "What? Because he's already been married to my dead best friend?"

"Did I say taboos?" Iris paused as she gathered her thoughts. "I don't think you realize how proud I am of you. I so much admired you for picking up and going off to Cornwall the way you did to be with Louis and the girls. It's so easy to sit behind your net curtains, watch your favorite TV shows all day, and just let life slip past you without any passion or promise. But you took a stand. You were determined not to let that be you, leading a half existence until you die, and I don't think I ever told you how much you inspired me. I've wasted too much time since your father passed away, and seeing you take that chance with Louis made me really think about my own life, Sophie, I—"

"Oh, Mum, you don't know how much it means to hear you

say that." Tears sprang into Sophie's eyes and she realized exactly how much she had wanted Iris to be pleased for her.

"That man, those children, have made you so happy and so content," Iris went on. "I couldn't be more delighted for you. And listen, I know that how you got together was a little unconventional, but none of that matters, and don't you worry, I know just the person to look after the dogs while I'm down there helping you organize the wedding—oh! That reminds me—did I tell you about Scooby?"

"No, has he got another hernia?" Sophie asked resignedly. Sophie knew that her mother loved her more than any other person alive. Whether or not she loved any person more than she loved her dogs was a moot point.

There was one other person Sophie had to tell, only this time she could not call. She had to find the right place to relay the news; after some reflection she decided that she had to go alone. Louis was still on the phone when she pulled her sneakers and rainproof anorak on.

"I'm going for a bit of a walk, get my head together," she whispered to him. He nodded and smiled, crossing the room in two easy strides to plant a warm kiss on her lips and hug her tightly before saying into the phone, "Yes, mate, I'm a condemned man and I couldn't be happier about it."

It was blustery and cold on the cliffs that rose above St. Ives. The sea was gray and foreboding, merging with a dark sky that threatened rain. The shortening autumn day was already darkening and Sophie found herself alone on the cliff top, the season's last remaining tourists chased away by the bite of the wind and the warm promise of the tearooms.

Sophie had thought long and hard about where to tell Carrie that she was marrying Louis. Carrie didn't have a grave. She had never wanted anything so sober or depressing to be left behind for people to stand over, or, worse, forget. There were really only two places that Sophie could think of to find her friend. There was Carrie's little house on Virgin Street, where she had started her married life, lived as a family with Bella and Louis at first and then raised her two children alone after he'd found out about her affair. Or there was here, the spot where Carrie had loved to walk and paint and gaze out to sea daydreaming, planning her future. The spot where Carrie had first met Louis.

Carrie's house was occupied now. A sweet young couple had bought it. Louis was determined to sell it to local people who would make a home of it and not a holiday rental and had let it go for much less than it was worth.

Sophie remembered talking to the woman, Emily, while she and her boyfriend had looked around the tiny house. Emily told Sophie that she'd met Steve in a nightclub in Newquay two years ago. They'd dated on and off and Steve had left her briefly when he thought that everything was getting too heavy. But a few months later, he had found her again and told her he realized that he loved her, and now they were buying their first home. On that sunny afternoon in the tiny living room where Carrie used to sit and sing Manic Street Preacher's songs to her daughters, Sophie found herself envying the couple. Theirs had been a slow and gentle romance, an easy approach to commitment that seemed full of assurance and certainty. They had a benign confidence in the future that, even as happy as she was, Sophie had lost a long time ago and thought she would probably never regain.

While Sophie thought the couple would probably let her come in now for a moment or two, it didn't seem like the right place to find Carrie, especially now that her things would not be there. Carrie was never the kind of person to hang around in the past, she was always moving on.

It was here on the cliff top, overlooking the wild wind- and rain-whipped sea, that Sophie knew she would be able to find Carrie, where she'd be able to picture her and remember her most clearly. Carrie, who always seemed to have the wind in her hair, even indoors. Who always had a certain light in her eyes and a kind of restless grace that made you feel she was constantly on the verge of leaving. It was only when she was with her children that Sophie ever saw her friend become completely still, her lips pressed against their hair, her eyes closed as she held them. Carrie was like the sea she had always been drawn to. Always moving, always changing, often dangerous and sometimes perfectly serene. Yes, it was here that Sophie would find her.

"Hello, Carrie." Sophie spoke into the wind, which snatched her words away with urgent, greedy gusts. She felt her stomach contract and realized how nervous she was. "I'm going to marry Louis. I'm going to marry your husband. There—I've said it, and no matter how many times I say it out loud, it still sounds like a reader's true story in a gossip magazine. But there it is; it's happening . . . it really is happening. You know, ever since I met Bella and Izzy and Louis, I've wondered what you'd think, how you'd feel about it if you were here. I tried to love your girls because I loved you, and that was a lot easier than I thought. And I tried not to love Louis because I loved you, and I'm sorry, Carrie . . . but that was impossible."

Sophie pushed her windswept hair off her face and took a deep breath. "The hardest thing is that I know I would never have met them if you hadn't died. I would probably have gone on having my secretary send them gifts and cards every birthday and Christmas. Louis might have stayed in Peru, and who knows if I would have seen you again. It breaks my heart that I had to lose you to find them . . . but, Carrie, you knew that I would fight for your daughters, that's why you made me their guardian, and you knew that after quite a lot of stupidity and a serious number of epiphanies I would love them as much as I do. And I'll never let them down, I promise you.

"I don't suppose you expected me to fall in love with Louis. I don't suppose that *I* expected it. How could I, uptight, repressed me, ever be attracted to the man *you* once loved? He took me by surprise, Carrie. But I do love him, I love him an incredibly frightening heart-stopping amount, and I do . . . I do want to marry him. I do. So I've come to ask you . . . to tell you, that this is what I am going to do . . . one day, after we've set a date and saved up a bit, because these things take ages to organize, so it might be months or even years yet . . ."

Suddenly Sophie had a picture of her friend laughing, her eyes sparkling, her hair tossed in the wind. "Yes, you're right, I am terrified about it. I am scared stiff, but I can't see into the future. I can't know what's going to happen, how can I? You and I know that better than anyone. All I can know is that at this moment, this hour, this day I love him and I want to be with him. And right now I can't imagine that's going to change, and that's all I can know, isn't it?" Sophie smiled and closed her eyes, spreading her arms wide to embrace the full force of the wind that battered and rippled her coat. "We made each other a promise when we were girls—*always, forever, whatever*. You made that promise to your daughters, so have I, and now I'm making that promise to Louis." Sophie opened her eyes and looked into the silver-streaked sky. "And I don't know where you are, my dear, dear friend, but wherever you are I hope you'll be happy for us."

Sophie held her breath, hoping for something, a beam of sunlight cutting through the gray sky, a sudden cessation of the wind— some sign that Carrie was happy, but of course there was none. There was never going to be anything so concrete. Sophie had known that before she'd come to the cliff top. Still, even in the midst of the building storm, Sophie felt better and calmer. She didn't feel alone.

Which wasn't all that surprising because at exactly that second, a small but fast creature decked out from head to foot in a red waterproof suit careered into her legs and hugged her hard around her hips.

"Izzy! What are you doing here?" Sophie exclaimed; she wouldn't have put it past the often adventurous child to have somehow come up here on her own, so when she glanced over her shoulder and saw Louis hanging back as Bella ran toward her, Sophie was relieved and touched.

"What are you all doing out here in this weather?" Sophie laughed, pleased to see them.

"Daddy said he thought he knew where you'd gone," Bella explained, her face clenched against the rain. "He said he thought you wanted to come and tell Mummy about the wedding and he was worried for you on your own. And he asked us if we'd like to come, because it's our wedding too and our news as well. And we wanted to come."

"Yes, because we are bridesmaids," Izzy said. "And Mummy would be awfully interested in that."

"She would be," Sophie agreed, crouching down so that her body shielded their smaller ones from the worst of the elements. "Your mummy loved to dress up and put flowers in her hair and find something sparkly in her ballerina jewelry box to put on."

"We are bridesmaids, Mummy!" Izzy ducked under Sophie's arms and hollered into the wind and rain. "It's ex-ter-reem-ly exciting!"

Her sister, looking briefly into Sophie's eyes, gave her a small smile and then followed, leaving Sophie to watch, her heart in her mouth, as Carrie's daughters spoke to their mother across the sea.

"And we are going to wear wings!" Bella shouted at the top of her voice.

"And there will be ponies, I expect!" Izzy added. "And cake, chocolate, hopefully."

"And, Mummy, we are very happy," Bella yelled. "Me and Izzy and Daddy are very, very happy, so you don't have to worry, because Sophie loves us and she'll take care of us."

"Although she doesn't like to tidy up much," Izzy added. "Or cook. But we still love her."

"Also," Bella called out, "could you please make it so it doesn't rain? I'm not sure what day it will be, but I can confirm at a later date."

"And we love you, Mummy," Izzy said.

Bella put her hand in Izzy's and they glanced at each other before shouting as loudly as their young voices would allow, "We love you—always, forever, whatever!"

Finally they turned back to Sophie and ran into her outstretched arms, knocking her backward so that she tumbled with a full thud into the cold wet grass.

"There," Bella said, kissing Sophie on the cheek. "Mummy knows properly now."

"Can we have toasted tea cakes?" Izzy said thoughtfully. "I'm starving."

Sophie put her hand on Louis's chilled cheek as they reached him, his hands thrust deep in his pockets as he waited.

"Thank you," she said, placing her lips next to his ear. "You never stop amazing me with how well you know me."

"It's only because you're not that mysterious," Louis teased her gently. "No, that's not true. You are quite often unfathomable. But I knew you'd never let anything this big happen without wanting to tell your best friend, and the girls felt the same way. It was a brilliant idea, Sophie."

"Shall we go home and have some toasted tea cakes?" Sophie asked him. "I am cutting down, but I thought that as it's the weekend, I might as well wait till Monday . . ."

"I'll catch up," Louis said, looking at the cliff top. "I've got one or two things to say myself."

Sophie looked into his eyes. She wanted to ask him what he was going to say, but she knew that whatever it was, it was just between him and his memory of Carrie.

"We'll be waiting for you." She kissed him lightly on the lips.

"And knowing that is what makes me the happiest man on earth," Louis told her.

As Sophie walked back down the cliff-top path with the girls just in front of her, she turned a few times to look at Louis as he stood, gazing out to sea, talking to the wife he'd left and lost and probably had barely ever known. She paused for a second to watch his solitary figure, feeling the icy wind rip through the insulation of her coat, and a shiver that had nothing to do with the weather raised goose bumps that ran down her back. She felt as if, as Carrie's mother was fond of saying, someone had just walked over her grave. And all at once Sophie was overwhelmed by the impulse that she had to marry Louis, and soon, before something or someone took him away from her for good, just as Carrie had been taken so suddenly from all of them.

Six

What Sophie had not been prepared for when she accepted Louis's proposal was just how keen she would be to end her engagement to him and become his wife. Within twenty-four hours she realized that rather than having agreed to a vague if beautiful declaration of love, she had committed to an actual event that she urgently wanted to make happen at the earliest possible convenience.

As Sophie began to think of all the things that needed to be done in order to bring the wedding to fruition, she felt a little as if she were having an out-of-body experience, as if she were floating just above the top of her own head watching this other woman, this alien, excited, joyous being who spent in excess of twenty pounds on bridal magazines and hours trawling the Internet for wedding locations, while she, the old Sophie, the Sophie who did not commit and wasn't especially fond of feelings, kept well out of it. But that was only now and then, when she'd catch sight of her flushed face in a mirror or realize she'd spent twenty minutes reading an article on the best tear-proof mascara. She'd laugh and be amazed by how unlike her old self she'd become since she'd allowed herself to love Louis and how wonderful it was to feel so alive. For the most part though, she was there in the moment, fretting over panda eyes on her big day even though she did not yet own a dress, have a venue, or had even set a date.

On Sunday evening after the girls had gone to bed, she had been kissing Louis in the doorway of the living room. This often happened; she'd be going somewhere in the house, from the kitchen to the living room or from the living room out into the garden, their paths would cross, and suddenly Sophie would find herself pinned against a wall, a kitchen counter, or, as in this case, the doorway, Louis firmly gripping the tops of her arms as he pushed her back against whatever surface happened to be available and kissed her.

Sophie had been breathless and expectant when he broke the kiss and looked at her.

"I still can't believe it's you," he said softly.

"Why, who are you expecting?" Sophie asked with the hint of a smile.

"I mean I still can't believe that's it *you*," Louis whispered, scanning her face with his eyes. "I still can't believe that *you* are here with *me,* that you are going to marry me."

"I'm fine with that, check away," Sophie told him happily. She closed her eyes for a second, breathing in Louis's proximity. "Sometimes I can't believe it's me either, or that you are you or that we go so well together—but we do, don't we?"

She opened her eyes and searched his for affirmation.

"I seriously suspect that we are the two most compatible people in human history," Louis told her seriously. He glanced up the stairs that were partially lit by the landing light he left on for Izzy, who maintained that, after dark, monsters lived in every shadow, despite Bella assuring her quite firmly that they did not, they lived under beds and in wardrobes.

"I was thinking." Louis spoke slowly, lowering his lids. "Now that you and I are officially engaged, you could stay over for the night? Because although being with you on the floor or the sofa or your single bed at the B and B or the kitchen or anywhere is *amazing*, it would be great to go out-and-out kinky and make love to you in a full-size adult double bed. I might even wake up without a sex-related back injury or friction burns for once."

Sophie laughed, but when he pulled her hand to follow him, she hesitated.

"They're asleep up there," she said.

"I know, it's great—they're flat out, come on," Louis urged her.

"But what if they wake up, what if they hear us? What if—god forbid—they walk in on us?" Louis stood perfectly still, looking at her for what seemed like a long time.

"Well, other couples with children must do it," he reasoned eventually. "Otherwise the world would be full of only children."

"Look, I know, and I want to stay over too, but if I have anything to do with it, we'll be married really soon and I just think it will be easier for them to understand."

Louis thought for a moment and then nodded.

"Okay—you're probably right and I love you for caring about them so much, but promise me this—once we're married you must promise to come to bed with me every night in our bed and not worry about anything except that you won't be getting very much sleep. I love you, Sophie, but I'm going to have to put my foot down about having sex in the bedroom once I've got that wedding ring on your finger."

"It will be different when we're married," Sophie assured him, on a sharp intake of breath as he pressed the weight of his hips into hers against the doorway. "I can't wait to be married to you."

"I have a question for you," Louis said as he kissed her neck. "Sofa or rug?"

"Rug," Sophie said, lifting her chin as he nuzzled her jawline. "But first I have a question for you."

"How about we get married on New Year's Eve?"

Sophie couldn't wait to invite Carmen to go to a wedding show with her. Well, the word "invited" wasn't exactly accurate— "pressganged," "co-opted," or "drafted" would all have been more appropriate. After dropping the girls off at school the following morning, Sophie swanned into Ye Olde Tea Shoppe on the pretext of fancying an éclair for breakfast and showing off her ring. But the very second Carmen turned her back to froth a cappuccino, Sophie whipped out her pile of wedding magazines and fanned them out on the counter.

"We're getting married on New Year's Eve!" she exclaimed as Carmen turned back, nearly sloshing a jug of hot milk over herself when she saw the literature Sophie had brought to accompany breakfast.

"New Year's Eve—that's like practically next week!" Carmen said.

"I know!" Sophie said. "Well, less than three months anyway. There's loads to do between now and then, so we've got to get started. I've bought us these mags to go through to get some ideas and I printed out all this . . ." She slapped a ream of printer paper down on top of the magazines that represented at least half a small Amazonian rain forest. "It's information on venues I found on the Net. First I just went Cornwall wide, and then I thought, no, let's go crazy, so I did Devon too. There's traditional churchy type stuff, manor houses, modern venues, hotels, and even one parachuting wedding, because I mean Louis is a surfer, isn't he? He might like an extreme wedding, mightn't he? What do you think?"

"I'm thinking I should make this coffee a decaf," Carmen said, pressing her lips together. "Slow down, darling, you've only had the ring on your finger for five minutes. Last time I saw you, you were all 'oh no I can't possibly marry him.' And now it's 'I've got to get him down the aisle quick before he changes his mind!' What's changed? Are you pregnant?"

"No, I am not pregnant; why does everybody think I'm pregnant!" Sophie said loudly enough to make two hikers look up at her from their full English breakfasts. "Which reminds me, thanks very much for feeding me a false line about Louis and the bloody surfing holiday."

"I know, I'm sorry," Carmen apologized. "It's just that you looked nervous and I wanted to help calm you down, get you to the restaurant so the poor bloke could ask you at least. I had no idea you'd be so . . ."

"So what?" Sophie asked.

"Enthusiastic." Carmen shrugged, crossing her arms. "I was fully expecting you to say no."

"Me too," Sophie said. "I really did right up until the moment he asked me. I was thinking, oh please, god, don't ask me, and then he did and then I said yes and then . . ."

"What?" Carmen asked her on bated breath.

"Then I realized how I'd feel if I ever lost him, and worrying and waiting and wondering didn't seem important anymore. Carmen, I'm getting married, of course I'm enthusiastic! Enthusiastic is the watchword of brides everywhere. Do you want to see my engagement ring?"

Sophie thrust her hand under Carmen's nose and wiggled her fingers.

"Of course I want to see the ring!" Carmen took Sophie's fingers in hers and peered at them.

"Babe, it's perfect. Not huge, mind you, but who wants a huge one anyway? They're simply vulgar. My husband bought me a massive rock when we got engaged and it didn't make us any happier. Plus, it's very you. Louis really thought about it. You can tell." She met Sophie's eyes as she smiled and then, without warning, she flung open the hatch that divided her from her public and engulfed Sophie in an icing-sugar–scented hug, sending the weighty, glossy wedding magazines slipping and slapping onto the floor in slow motion.

"I'm so happy that you're so happy . . . you two, you're just perfect together."

Sophie was touched and a little surprised to see tears in Carmen's eyes.

"And so are you and James," Sophie reminded her. "You and James are one of the loveliest, happiest couples I know."

"I know . . . ," Carmen said, tears beading on her waterproof mascara. It seemed as if she might be about to add a "but" but none came. "And you and Louis will be too—which is why your wedding needs to be perfect."

"It will be," Sophie said confidently, bending to scoop up an armful of magazines. "We just need to get some venue ideas; maybe we'll find one when we go to the wedding fair."

"A wedding fair?" Carmen asked, as if Sophie had just suggested they hop on a bus to the moon.

"Yes, it's in Plymouth all this week—how lucky is that?" Sophie told her. "The West Country Wedding Fair. We're going tomorrow, I've just bought the tickets. Louis is on a half-day assignment taking photos for a local produce magazine, so he can pick the girls up from school, plus they give away champagne by the truckload at those places, so we'll be laughing."

Carmen shook her head and smiled. "You really want this, don't you?"

"Of course I do," Sophie answered. "Which is lucky because we are getting married in *three . . . months' . . . time.*" She spoke the last words slowly because she found that she was enjoying the fear coursing through her body at the very idea. "Just think, in less than ninety days from today, I could officially be married at my own wedding!"

"Well, why wait?" Carmen said as she sat down at the table with Sophie and leafed through a magazine. "Where did waiting ever get anyone? If you're sure, you're sure, and let's face it, if you've said yes, then you ought to be sure. Besides, the quicker it is the better it will be for those girls. If you wait much longer, for one thing they will explode from excitement, and for another they won't be *quite* as cute anymore—no offense, they are lovely kids—I'm just saying, for the photos, younger is cuter . . . ooooh, look at that dress! We're going to try on wedding dresses, I bloody love that."

"We?"

"You, I mean you," Carmen said quickly. "Just think, Sophie, and remember this moment, because this is it—this is the beginning of the rest of your life."

Sophie tried really hard to stop everything, even the beat of her heart, so that she could think with a clear head. One second of total clarity was all she craved, one moment of stillness so that she might advance confidently into a million moments of mayhem from this point on, this moment where she finally left her old life behind for good.

"Give me a cake," Sophie said, pointing at a particularly fat éclair that glistened plumply in the fresh-cream chiller.

"A cake?" Carmen quizzed her, obliging nonetheless and putting the éclair on a plate in front of Sophie. "What's a cake got to do with it?"

"Well, if I'm getting married in ninety days, then I've definitely got to give up cakes and I want that one to be my very last."

Carmen gave her a side of clotted cream for luck.

"So you're getting married?" Grace Tregowan asked Sophie as she waited, skittish as a young colt on a spring morning, for Carmen to come and pick her up in her shiny black BMW SUV. "It's a lovely thing, marriage, I should know, I've done it four times."

"Four times, Grace?" Sophie said, dropping the net curtains and perching on the edge of the sofa in the B & B's sitting room as Grace awaited the paternity-test results on one of the characters in the television show she was watching. "Four husbands, that's an impressive tally!"

"Well, some women would call me greedy," Grace said, shrugging her frail shoulders.

"Tell me," Sophie asked her. "Did you love them all, or were three of them mistakes while you were waiting for the fourth one?"

"I loved them all, in different ways," Grace said, drawing her arms around her middle as if she'd just felt the chill of the past. "Take my Vincent, my first husband. I met him in France during the war. Special Ops got hold of me after I got back from Paris, and they sent me back out there because I could speak the lingo like a Frenchy. Three months' training, then they drop you in a field in the middle of bloody nowhere and tell you to remember that your name is Claudette. I was a wireless operator, sending messages back home. Vincent was running the local resistance, he was only twenty-two. These days that's nothing, you all still act like kids well into your forties, moaning about responsibility and mortgages . . ."

Grace sighed. "Vincent was just a boy fighting for his country's freedom, fighting for his life. He was so young . . . so serious and so handsome; Sophie, you should have seen him. Dark hair, so thick and curly you couldn't run your fingers through it, never mind a comb, and eyes as violet as the lavender in the lane. You have to try and imagine that we were frightened *all* the time, death was always just a heartbeat away. We saw it, smelled it all around us. We saw our friends, people we loved, killed or taken from us. It's easy to love when you live that way—it's hard not to love because when you love, you know you are still alive. And I loved Vincent with all my heart. We didn't plan to get married, but then I got pregnant. And he was a good French Catholic boy. We had a secret midnight wedding in a chapel in the town, but it wasn't legal. I never knew his real name and he didn't know mine."

"You married a man whose name you didn't know—but wasn't it sort of important to know that about him? Sometimes I think I don't know nearly enough about Louis, but at least I know his real name. Or I think I do."

"It wasn't important," Grace told her. "All I needed to know about him was that he was there, his heart beating for me. At first I used to beg him to tell me his real name, but he wouldn't and he never asked me for mine. At first I was angry with him, but then I realized he was only trying to protect me. He didn't ask me because he loved me. So the local priest risked his life to conduct a sham marriage, because to us it was real . . . it was . . . what's the word? Sacred. We always said that after the war, we'd do it properly, but I think even then we knew that wouldn't happen, we knew that one of us wouldn't make it. I tried to keep my pregnancy a secret, but my controller found out and pulled me out. That was in 1944. I didn't want to leave him. I was desperate to stay, even with the baby." Grace dropped her head, her eyes traveling over her blue-veined hands. "I knew the night I said good-bye to him that it would be the last time I saw him alive. We clung to each other for the longest time in the darkness in the field where the plane landed to pick me up, and he promised he'd be there when the baby was born . . ."

She trailed off, looking up into the distance.

"But he didn't make it?" Sophie asked her, breathless.

"Killed the next week. Shot by the Nazis," Grace said. "They always used to say, it's when you've got something to live for, when you are afraid of dying, that you were in trouble, because you'd hesitate and make mistakes. They were right."

"And the baby, is that Frank?" Sophie referred to Mrs. Tregowan's eldest son, who she had never met but who, from Grace's description of him, sounded frankly awful.

"No, that was my poppet, my little girl Claudette," Grace said. "Pneumonia took her before she was three months old." She smiled at Sophie and patted her chest where her heart was. "I keep her here now with her dad. I loved Vincent. I loved him with all of my heart. Would I have loved him if I'd met him on a normal day at a normal time when there weren't bombs falling out of the sky and death squads on the march? To be honest, I don't know." She smiled at Sophie, showing her slender yellowed teeth. "The trick is, Sophie, to love while love has you. Enjoy it, savor it, revel in it. So what if you're rushing into marriage with a man you hardly know? Marry him while you love him. What's the point in waiting till he bores you?"

"Grace," Sophie said as she heard Carmen's car pull up, "did anyone ever tell you how amazing and brave you were, and did anyone ever say thank you to you?"

"What for?" Grace sniffed, looking at the TV. "I did my bit, that's all."

"Bloody hell," Sophie said as she and Carmen walked into Plymouth Pavilions, where the wedding fair was being held. The huge space had been decked out with white and gold balloons and there was stall after stall of wedding paraphernalia, from dresses to table favors to romantic doves and helium-balloon sculptures. The vast room was crowded with women of all ages, mothers and daughters, sisters and best friends, all of them with that faintly manic glint in their eyes, that special glow that said "I'm going to have a great big massive party that's all about me and there's nothing you can do about it."

As she scanned the crowd, Sophie spotted the odd beleaguered-looking man, mostly fathers, but sometimes a groom trailing along after his woman like a relic from a former age, when more was required of the groom than standing at the altar and saying, "I do."

"Look at all this wedding stuff and look at all the people here looking at all the wedding stuff. Who knew that so many people got married?" Sophie said.

"I know, and they all look a bit scary to me," Carmen said, hooking her arm through Sophie's. "What is it about weddings that makes women go all feral?"

"I don't know, but what if one of them gets to my dress before I do?" Sophie asked, that manic glint lighting her eyes. "We need to get in there now."

"We can do this," Carmen said, as if they were about to go over the top of some trenches. "I'm a pastry chef, and you, you were the premier corporate-event organizer in London, Europe, and North America. You know everything there is to know about planning parties."

"You're right," Sophie affirmed. "I'm the woman who once organized a book launch in a hot-air balloon, and two years ago I did a satellite linkup with the Russian space station for a Russian energy company. I'm Sophie Mills, none of these other chicks stands a chance."

"Dress stands twelve o'clock," Carmen said, pointing across the vast hall.

"Marvelous," Sophie said. "Cover me, I'm going in."

• • •

"I need cake," Sophie said, emerging from the dress section of the exhibition with her hair tousled. Her lipstick was smudged and her shirt buttoned up wrong, as if she'd just had secret sex, except that what she had been doing was a million times better than that. She'd tried on every single style of wedding dress that had ever been brought into existence. From the giant puffy meringue to a white lace thigh-length miniskirt with a detachable train, Sophie had tried them all on and then for good measure so had Carmen. "Look, there's the wedding-cake section. Let's go over there and score some cake."

"I thought you were giving up cake, because you need to if you want to wear that minidress," Carmen said as she followed her.

"I am giving up cake. I'm just exhausted from all the lace and sequins. I can feel my blood sugar level dropping and we haven't even started yet. I need emergency cake. It's medicinal."

"I like the last dress with the bustle and the sleeves," Carmen offered as she hurried after Sophie, struggling to keep up with her friend's sensible heels as she tottered beside her in her high-heeled ankle boots.

"God no! That one made me look like a sheep carcass dressed as mutton!" Sophie said.

"Okay, well, that gold one with the bows and the glitter effect was really something."

"Yes, it was something. It was something that a lady does not repeat. I loved trying on all of the dresses, especially the one with the butterflies and the diamanté—"

"And the one with the neckline that was so plunging the vicar could get a good look at your navel—"

"But none of those dresses was right, Carmen. I need the right dress and I need it today or tomorrow. What am I going to do? I've just tried on every single wedding dress in the history of wedding dresses and I haven't found the right one and . . . I really need cake. Now.

"Look over there," Sophie said, pointing at a stall with a sign hanging over it that read CELESTIAL CAKES—BLISS IN A BITE. "That's what I'm talking about."

"The main thing is that you looked stunning," Carmen said, trotting along trying to keep up with her. "Truly you did. In every single gown, even the hideous ones . . . you glowed. You're so lucky you're getting to marry the man you love."

"You could marry James if you wanted to, couldn't you?" Sophie asked her, stopping so suddenly by the Celestial Cakes stand that Carmen bumped into Sophie's back.

"Not really—I'm still married," Carmen said with a shrug.

"Then why not divorce your ex?" Sophie asked her.

"I don't know," Carmen said, sighing as she looked over the cake samples that were on display. "I'm waiting, I suppose . . ."

"Waiting for what?" Sophie asked her. "You've moved down here, you live with James. St. Ives is your home now. What is there to wait for?"

Carmen thought for a moment and looked as if she were about to say something more. Then her eyes slid past Sophie to something behind her and widened.

"That's your dress," she breathed. "That's the perfect dress for you."

Sophie turned round to see a model walk past serenely in an ivory satin dress, simply cut so that it skimmed the model's hips and swished around her feet, like the froth of an incoming tide, as she walked. The scoop neckline and low back were edged simply with seed pearls, and the light reflecting off the material seemed to make the girl's skin shine.

"Want that dress," Sophie said, suddenly monosyllabic. "I really need to follow that dress and get that dress. I wonder what size that model is, because that's the dress for me, maybe I could have her dress and take it home today. What do you think? Do you think they'd do alterations on it now, you know, stick material in where her hips and thighs should have been, because I need that dress and I've got only ninety days—"

Carmen picked up a square of iced fruit cake from the Celestial Cakes table and shoved it in Sophie's mouth. "Calm down, woman."

Sophie was appalled by Carmen's silencing tactic, but the cake really was delicious.

"Eat the cake, love the cake, think only of the cake, and relax. In a minute we'll go over to where they are having the catwalk, and we'll find out who makes the dress, and you can try it on. Everything will be fine." Carmen talked as Sophie munched. "Now I don't know what your policy on hats is going to be, but I'm thinking of a fascinator for me as your head bridesmaid. What do you think? You can swallow before you answer that."

The two women stared at each other for several seconds, long enough for Sophie to have a stunning idea.

"That's it!" she exclaimed, clutching Carmen's arm. "I've got it!"

"Got what? Is it catching? I'm only thinking of Louis."

"Everything I've got to do for this wedding is practically giving me a nervous breakdown, right?"

"Well, I didn't like to say so, but I was thinking of lacing your tea with Prozac, yes."

"And okay, there are wedding planners here, but none I'd entrust my own wedding to."

"Okay, well, good—you've worked out that you're too controlling to hire a wedding planner. I have to say that's not a surprise to me."

"No, silly—I'm going to start my own business. I'm going to be a wedding planner. You said it yourself, I've got years of experience in events and more than that, I've got ideas. Money's tight right now, but people still get married, and what they want for their money is originality and something unique—special. I had this brilliant idea for Cal about unusual party venues in London. Well, I can do that here. I can find venues—castles, private houses, galleries, cliff tops, beaches, tin mines—who knows? I can approach the owners directly and then persuade them to get licensed to hold weddings—but only through my company. I'll have exclusivity. And bolted on to that I can choose local dress designers who will work only through me, amazing bespoke caterers—like you—and wonderful and original photographers like Louis! Everything I offer will be unique and exclusive. Like clotted cream and scone canapés or fish and chips for your wedding breakfast! I can choose all the best things to make a truly special day and bring them all together under my company; people will love it. Think about it, Carmen—second marriages, stepfamilies being brought together, gay couples—the last thing couples like that want is a stuffy old hotel or church. Even funky first-timers. They want a day that reflects them and their love. I'm telling you, people will actually flock to Cornwall to be married by me!"

"Are you a secret vicar then—or a ship's captain?" Carmen repressed a smile, delighted by the enthusiasm in her friend's eyes.

"Stop joking and admit it—it's a genius idea, right?"

"It does seem a bit mad that no one else has done it before . . ." Carmen looked around the vast hall. They'd been here for hours and hadn't seen anything that came close to Sophie's vision.

"Everyone knows that the best ideas are the most obvious ones!" Sophie said and beamed. "Look around you. If I see one more hotel wedding brochure or balloon sculpture, I'll kill myself. This industry's crying out for me!" Sophie flung her arms around Carmen and hugged her tightly.

"You know what?" Carmen said, managing to squeeze out a breath. "I think it is—it is a good idea, it's a great idea. It's just that starting a new business while getting married might be a bridge too far for your mental health."

"I know that!" Sophie laughed, her eyes bright as her idea caught fire and spread. "Which is why I'm going to treat my wedding like my first commission. You know, use the experience to start my empire."

"Romantic." Carmen nodded. "Well, all the more important then that you have the kind of head bridesmaid you can rely on."

"Ah yes, well you see, the issue over head bridesmaid isn't fully resolved yet," Sophie said, thinking of the three adults and two children who so far were vying for the post. "Not because I don't love you or anything but more owing to the fact that due to the principal reason of the fact that . . . oh thank god, there's Louis! What's he doing here?"

She felt a rush of relief as she saw the back of Louis's head and shoulders a few stalls away, at the wedding underwear stand. For some reason he seemed to be riffling through a box of frilly knickers.

"Louis!" she called out, but he did not turn round.

"Are you sure that's him?" Carmen asked her, momentarily diverted from her bridesmaid pitch. "What on earth would he be doing here unless he's got a thong habit that he wasn't planning to share with you until the wedding night? Why's he got his head in a box full of knickers?"

Sophie began to hurry over to where he was standing.

"Well, he said if it wasn't for the shoot, he'd have popped down with us to do some industrial spying on the wedding photographer, find out his rates and things. Maybe the shoot finished early and he's come to find me. Come on, let's get him and show him that dress—"

"Over my dead body," Carmen gasped, stopping Sophie with a hand on her shoulder. "You do not show the prospective groom the prospective wedding dress! Do you know nothing about basic wedding etiquette? You know, stuff like asking your only adult female friend who goes with you to wedding fairs to be head bridesmaid, for example. Besides, that's not Louis, since when has Louis worn low-rise tight black jeans and a studded leather belt?"

Sophie stopped and looked again at the figure. Carmen was right. It wasn't Louis.

"But he really bloody looks like him, doesn't he?" Sophie said. "His hair, his shoulders, even the way he's standing there. It could be . . ." Her sentence ground to a halt as the subject in question turned round. "Louis."

He was a young man, perhaps twenty or twenty-one; he still had a bit of acne around his chin, but he stood with the confidence and self-assurance of a much older man. He had none of the awkward posture that characterizes young men who haven't yet worked out how to get all their limbs moving at once. And he looked almost exactly like Louis.

"He *does* look like him," Carmen said, digging Sophie in the ribs. "Here, take a photo on your phone, we can tease Louis about having a secret love child when we get home."

"He must be a relation," Sophie said, watching the young man as he hung bits of frilly underwear on a stand without even a hint of self-consciousness. "A cousin or something. He has to be. Look at his mouth . . . those lips are just like Louis's. He must be related. I have to ask him, because Louis has no family that I know of. I bet he'd be really excited if I found him a cousin or something. A long-lost relative—it would be the perfect wedding present."

"I wouldn't mind him for Christmas," Carmen breathed as they watched the young man effortlessly flirt with a bride and her mother over blue and cream frilly garters.

"Hands off, Carmen," Sophie said, feeling unexpectedly territorial. "Your younger-man quota is filled. This one's mine." Brushing cake crumbs from around her mouth and briefly running her fingers through her hair, Sophie approached the young man, feeling a bit as if she had stepped back in time and was getting the chance to meet the love of her life when he was younger and hadn't yet acquired any baggage.

"Hello," she said, smiling at him. His returning smile was confident and attractive. Sophie struggled to contain the confusion of butterflies that went off in her chest and found herself coloring.

"You really are a blushing bride." He smiled, holding her gaze. "Come on, you can tell me what you're after—I'm unshockable."

"Actually, it's you I'm interested in, not your thongs," Sophie said, surprised to find herself flirting with him, not least because she never flirted with anyone. She wasn't even sure if she'd ever flirted with Louis. It just wasn't something that came naturally to her.

"Best news I've had all day." The boy grinned at her.

"Do you mind if I ask you your name?" Sophie asked him.

"Probably best if we're going to be going on a date," the boy said. Sophie found herself giggling, but Carmen's raised eyebrows brought her back to her senses.

"Seth," he told her, holding out a hand. "And you?"

"Seth," Sophie said, repeating his name. "I'm Sophie Mills and I'm not asking you out on a date—it's just that you look an awful lot like my boyfriend . . . fiancé . . . betrothed. Still not really sure what to call him."

"So we've established I'm your type, and hey—I like an older blonde, especially one with curves," Seth told her. Sophie was ashamed to feel heat rising in her belly. Standing here with Louis from the past, a past before he'd met Carrie or run off to Peru, was really very confusing. She glanced sheepishly at a very sour-looking Carmen and made an effort to pull herself back together.

"You are very confident, aren't you?" Sophie remarked. "How old are you?"

"Twenty," Seth told her, tipping his head to one side to appraise her figure. "Too young for you?"

"No, I mean yes, I mean you really do look like him." Sophie frowned. "Do you know anyone called Louis Gregory?"

"Nope," Seth said. "Should I? Is he likely to want to fight me for you?"

"I thought you might be related, cousins or something—he doesn't have much family."

"Neither do I," Seth told her with a shrug. "It's just me and Mum; Gran and Granddad live up north. I don't know about cousins or uncles. Look, if that's all you're really interested in, you're better off talking to Mum when she gets back."

"Seth!"

The young man looked up and sighed. "Here's the boss now; she's going to want to know why I'm flirting with the bride again instead of selling her theme hen-night knickers." He treated Sophie to a slow grin. "The things a student will do for cash. Come back at five and I'll take you for a drink."

"Seth, I thought I told you to get all the stock out; it's not going to sell if it's in a box, is it . . ."

Sophie turned around at the sound of the oddly familiar voice and came face-to-face with Wendy Churchill.

"It's you," Sophie said bluntly. "You work on the stall?"

"Seth, go and get the rest of the stock from the van." She turned to Sophie. "It's my business—and you are?" Wendy raised an eyebrow, which let Sophie realize that she knew exactly who she was but was choosing to pretend not to.

"Louis's fiancée, Sophie Mills," Sophie told her with her best corporate smile. "We met the other day . . . I was just chatting to Seth because I wondered if he might be related to Louis in some way. He told me to ask his mum—do you know where she is?"

There was a beat of silence between the two of them while everything slotted slowly into place and Sophie felt her stomach plummet through her toes.

Wendy held her gaze for a moment longer, and then the tension in her mouth and eyes relaxed just a fraction, revealing a hint of a smile, and what she told Sophie, Sophie suddenly already knew.

"I'm his mum," Wendy said, holding Sophie's gaze, keeping her voice low so that it couldn't be heard above the hum of the chatter-filled hall. "I had him when I was fifteen."

Sophie looked over to Seth, who was looking at his watch as he was expertly flirting with Carmen over a lacy cream basque. "He works for me part-time while he's finishing his degree." Wendy paused and eyed Sophie with her cold gray eyes. "And yes. Yes, Louis is his father. But he doesn't know that. And Louis has never known anything—he didn't even know I was pregnant, let alone about Seth. I haven't seen Louis in over twenty years—until I bumped into him the other day. Look—Sophie, Seth and I are fine. We are happy without him. We are doing really well. And if you and Louis are getting married, then I guess you must be happy too. Nothing has to change, does it?"

Sophie looked into Wendy's eyes. About ten thousand thoughts were chasing each other around in her head, each one screaming to be heard, not a single one making sense in the melee. But she knew one thing. Wendy was asking her to keep quiet about Seth.

"Wendy . . . you've just told me that the man I'm going to marry has a son he knew nothing about. Are you seriously suggesting I shouldn't tell Louis that he's got a child—a grown man of a son walking around less than fifty miles from where he lives?"

"I am," Wendy said, her eyes glassy and reflective. "What would it hurt?"

"You must realize that I can't possibly do that," Sophie replied. "I can't keep something that huge from the man I love, the man

I'm going to marry. Besides, he has a right to know about his son!" Sophie fought to keep her voice down, reeling from the weight of knowledge that she was suddenly burdened with.

"No he doesn't." Wendy's face was dark with fury. "I didn't tell him then for a good reason and I'm not going to tell him now. Seth is *my* son, I've brought him up alone for all of these years, and I have done bloody well for myself by working my guts out. He has *nothing* to do with Louis."

"But why?" Sophie asked her. "Why didn't you tell Louis about him, if not back then, then at some point in the last twenty years?"

Wendy shook her head bitterly. "I had my reasons," she warned. "And they are none of your business."

"Mum, I've got that gig," Seth said, coming over again and grinning at Sophie with that same easy smile his father had. "If I don't go now, I'll miss the sound check and I'll get fired. Again."

"Go on then." Wendy smiled indulgently, taking some money out of her back pocket and pressing it into his palm. "See you tomorrow, same time, okay? Don't drink too much and don't—"

"Mother, I am a grown man," Seth said, winking at Sophie and stooping to kiss his mother on the cheek. "It's the ladies who have to watch out."

The two women watched him leave and Sophie's heart was in her mouth as she watched his familiar gait and the Louis-like flick of his hair as he left the room.

"Look," Wendy said, her face softening a little, which for some reason Sophie found even more intimidating. "All I'm saying is that nothing has to change. And if you give yourself a second to think about it, you'll realize that is the best option. You can go your way, have your wedding and your life, and I'll go mine. No one will ever know."

Sophie shook her head. In the space of twenty minutes, everything she thought she knew had changed, and there was no way to put things back where they had been before she knew what she did now.

"Wendy, I'm sorry, but I love him, we've gone through a lot to be together, what kind of person, what kind of wife, would I be if I kept this from him?" she said.

"You'll regret it," Wendy told her quietly. "I can promise you that. This cozy little life you think you've got for yourself will be over for good."

Seven

Sophie stood in the playground waiting for Louis and Izzy to arrive to pick up Bella. She and Carmen were supposed to have been gone for the whole day, so Louis had made sure he had the afternoon free to collect Izzy at one and Bella at three fifteen. She knew he'd be here soon, and she knew she had to see him as soon as possible so she could tell him about Wendy and Seth. So she could tell him about his son. She had no idea how she was going to tell him, how the necessary words would form a coherent sentence and emerge from her mouth, but she knew she had to tell him at the first opportunity or otherwise lose her nerve, and the consequences of that happening were unimaginable. For whatever reason, Wendy had tried to intimidate her and warn her off telling Louis the truth. But really, there was no alternative—she had to tell him no matter what happened next—even though it seemed certain that whatever it was, it was going to change everything.

She had been driving back with Carmen toward St. Ives when

she came to the realization that her knowledge of Seth and Wendy was simply not something she could keep to herself. No matter how much she might want to.

"Who was she?" Carmen had asked her as soon as they were out of the car park. "You looked like you wanted to deck her, and I've never seen you want to get out of a place so quickly."

Sophie thought for a moment. It wouldn't be right to tell Carmen about Seth before she told Louis, but she knew if she told her one piece of information about Wendy and Seth, then Carmen's busy female brain would have assimilated the rest in a nanosecond and worked it all out herself.

"That woman was Louis's ex-girlfriend," Sophie told Carmen. "I met her when we bumped into her a few days ago. They went out together one summer, back when they were teenagers. She was his first big love, his first . . . everything."

"Was she really? So what's she got to do with . . . oh my god! Louis is Seth's dad, isn't he?" Carmen asked, taking her eyes off the road for a second to stare at Sophie.

"And he doesn't know a thing about it," Sophie said.

"And now you've got to tell him?" Carmen asked.

"Yes I do, don't I?" Sophie glanced at Carmen, whose eyes were fixed firmly on the road ahead, a frown slotted between her brows. Fear clutched Sophie's stomach and her conviction wavered. "I mean, I do, don't I? Have to tell him."

After a second Carmen pulled the car over and turned off the engine. She twisted in her seat to look at Sophie.

"Let's think about this," Carmen said, tapping the leather-covered steering wheel with one long, enameled nail. "Do you have to tell him? Because, after all, if you hadn't bumped into Wendy or if she hadn't happened to have a wedding-lingerie business that her son was helping out with, then you would never have known any of this. You'd have gone and ordered your dream dress instead of running out, and we'd have come home tonight none the wiser."

"I know, but I *did* bump into Wendy and I *did* see Seth and I *do* know," Sophie said, twisting her fingers in knots. "I do know, and how can I know something as profound about Louis as the existence of his own flesh and blood when he doesn't? How can I possibly?"

"I don't know." Carmen shrugged. "Does he know everything about you? Do you know everything about him? Look, that Wendy woman and her kid must have been living around here for months at least, only a few miles from where Louis lives, and nothing has happened. Maybe nothing needs to happen now. Maybe you don't have to do this."

Sophie shook her head. "Would you tell James if another woman had had his child and he didn't know about it?"

Carmen's face dropped and she dipped her head. "No, I wouldn't," she said. "I'd be too afraid of losing him."

"Really? You really think there's the risk that I'll lose Louis if he finds out about Seth? But how, why?"

"Children change things," Carmen said. "Kids—big ones, little ones—they change things, especially if they belong to someone else. I mean, it wouldn't be just you and Louis and the girls anymore. It wouldn't be just you and Louis and the girls and Seth. There'd be that Wendy woman, she'd be in your life for the rest of it too. Think about that."

"Bella and Izzy haven't come between us, so why would Seth?" Sophie asked her.

"I don't know . . . I don't know anything about him or his mother, I just know that this is a massive thing, Sophie. You have to think about this before you go through with it."

Sophie stared out at the road ahead as she tried to imagine having a conversation with Louis about his unknown son.

"The thing is," she said slowly, "I can't marry a man I'm keeping such a huge secret from. I might want to, I might want to carry on and pretend I didn't see Wendy or Seth, but I can't. Because what if Louis finds out about Seth another way, maybe even bumps into him and Wendy the way I did? Cornwall is not a huge place and they both work in the wedding industry—it's only a matter of time. What if he finds out that I knew and I didn't tell him? No one can get married on that big a lie, Carmen, it just wouldn't be right. So I've got to tell him—haven't I?"

Slowly Carmen nodded once, gently placing her palms on either side of Sophie's head and turning her face to look at her.

"Mate, you're right—you've got to," Carmen said. "There's no way out of this one."

Izzy spotted Sophie first. The little girl was still in her uniform from morning nursery school, only now it was bejeweled with splotches of paint, and possibly jam, and what Sophie hoped was chocolate spread.

"Aunty Sophie!" she cried out happily, running up to Sophie who picked her up and hugged the child's sticky cheek against her own, noting Louis caught at the gate by one of the mothers who was no doubt arranging a play date. Louis was very popular with the mothers, a lone father carrying on with his children. They all loved him. Oddly, they hardly ever spoke more than two words to Sophie, but she supposed it was because she wasn't a proper mother, not officially in the club, as she hadn't ever given birth. She could be wrong, of course, but sometimes, standing on the playground waiting for the girls to either go in or leave school, it was far more intimidating and clique-ridden than being at school had ever been before.

"Hello, poppet. How was school today?" Sophie asked her, careful to keep her voice cheerful. Woe betide anyone who referred to Izzy's half day at nursery school as anything less than school.

The four-year-old took it very seriously and considered herself to be just as much a schoolgirl as her big sister.

"We learned letters and did role playing," Izzy told her. "And for show and tell I did 'I am going to be a bridesmaid with wings and a big skirt.' But mostly I had to tell as I didn't have anything to show." She tipped her head to one side, her cascade of curls tumbling across her face. "When exactly can we get my wings and how often can I wear them? Do you remember my fairy dress, Aunty Sophie? I miss my fairy dress. What happened to it?"

Sophie did indeed remember the garment that the then three-year-old Izzy had been wearing when she'd arrived at Sophie's flat more than a year ago to stay with the guardian aunt she barely knew. It was an item of clothing she refused to take off. At one point Sophie had even resorted to bathing her in the outfit in a bid to get it clean. Izzy had clung to the dress with the determination and willfulness that only a small child can have, and it took Sophie a long time to realize that it was her comfort blanket, her familiar thing in a world full of strange faces and places. In a world where one moment she had been sitting in her mummy's car singing along to the radio and in the next her mother was dead and she was all alone. When the dress could take no more abuse, Sophie had replaced it, but since they had come back to St. Ives, she'd thought Izzy had grown out of her obsession with it. Should she worry that the little girl mentioned it now? Could it be a sign that she wasn't as happy and secure as Sophie hoped?

"It's in your wardrobe, sweetie," Sophie told her. "Do you want to put it on when we get home?"

"I was just thinking that I could use the wings to practice with," Izzy said. "Until you get me my real wings. Will I be able to fly . . . ?"

"Hello?" Louis caught up and kissed Sophie on the cheek. "I didn't expect to see you here. Wedding fair a washout?"

"It was . . ." Sophie hesitated. "It was unexpected. It made me think that we have a lot of things to talk about, Louis." Which was true, but the knowledge of Seth must have given her voice a heavier edge because Louis's face dropped.

"I don't like the sound of that," he said. "I don't like the whole 'we have a lot of things to talk about' line. What does that mean?"

Sophie bit her bottom lip as she looked at him, unable to find the right words to reassure him.

"Soph!" Louis's laugh was uncertain. "Don't tell me you're getting cold feet," he asked her anxiously.

"No . . . no, not at all. But you and I do need to talk." Sophie looked into Louis's eyes and decided that now was not the moment to bring up Seth. So she released her other concerns, which had been building before Seth eclipsed them all. "Especially before my mother gets involved and Cal sticks his oar in, otherwise we'll end up having a three-ring circus instead of a wedding, and that's not what I want. Besides, I've got this idea for a business that I think could really take off, and the best thing is that it will help your business too. The wedding fair gave me so much to think about, and not just our wedding, but all the money that's to be made out there. Louis, I want to marry you on New Year's Eve, but it's so near and we'll never find a nice place—"

"Ah, but I have found a nice place." Louis cut her off with a grin that reminded her of standing opposite Seth less than two hours ago, and made her feel guilty for changing the subject as if nothing at all had changed.

"Really?" Sophie asked him, hopeful that this was a sign that everything was going to be okay.

"Yes, subject to your approval of course," Louis said. "Fineston Manor, up on the moor. It was where I was doing the magazine shoot, believe it or not. Homemade mince-filled pastries on a big, dark oak sixteenth-century trestle table—all very historical, you know. Anyway, it's an amazing place. They have just got licensed to hold weddings, because the upkeep of the place is so expensive, and ours would be the first."

"That's fantastic, it sounds perfect—exactly what I'm looking for for my business."

"Your business?" Louis was momentarily thrown. "Anyway, they said that in the winter there would be log fires and little candles everywhere. It could be really magical. I was talking to the owner while the food was getting fluffed. I've done some sums in my head and I think we can do it as long as we keep the guest list down . . . I'll show you photos when we get back—"

"Louis, that's brilliant news," Sophie said, hugging him so hard she winded him. "You don't know how brilliant!"

"Blimey, I was wrong about the cold feet, wasn't I?" Louis said, wrapping his arms around her. "I'm glad you're pleased—you see? It's a sign. It's a sign that everything is going to be brilliant. I promise you."

"I know . . ." Sophie thought of those words rattling around in her head that she'd have to spit out sometime. "I know. Whatever happens, everything between you and me will be fine. Nothing can come between us."

Louis's smile faded into a frown, but before he could press her further, Bella arrived carrying her book bag and a rather elaborate cardboard hat, with feathers and sequins glued onto it. She examined Sophie closely. "Why is everyone here? It is very unusual. Are we going to Ye Olde Tea Shoppe for tea? Is that why everyone is here? That would be acceptable."

"That is a lovely hat, and normally we would go out for tea," Sophie began, glancing at Louis. "But Daddy and I have lots of things to discuss, so probably we'd better go home—"

"But please, please, *please*!" Izzy begged. "I am starving, I *neeeeeed* a scone!"

"You *neeeeed* some vegetables and fruit and stuff," Sophie

pointed out, hoping that the real mothers still in the playground would overhear and realize that even though she had never given birth, she knew how important it was to get five portions of fruit and vegetables into a child—even if she had no idea how to actually do it.

"Strawberries are fruit," Bella pointed out. "Strawberry jam is fruit."

"We can go for cake, can't we?" Louis said, smiling coaxingly as he tucked a strand of Sophie's hair behind her ear. "I'm glad you're keen to see Fineston, but the photos can wait awhile. It's nice us all being together."

Sophie tried to picture another hour or two pretending everything was fine, telling Louis about her plans to start her own business, discussing their wedding. She tried to imagine it as it would have been if only she hadn't bumped into Wendy. But she couldn't.

"No, Louis." Sophie hesitated for one second, not wanting to say the words that would start the chain of events for which she could not predict a conclusion. "I have to talk to you about something else." Her serious tone caught him off guard.

"What?" he asked her warily.

"Not here," Sophie began, glancing around at the now nearly empty playground, and uncomfortably conscious of Bella's gaze.

"Sophie." Louis's tone darkened, his coaxing smile evaporating in an instant. "If it's not the wedding you're worried about—then what? Just tell me now please, I'm not in the mood for games."

Sophie looked at the girls. Mercifully Izzy had jammed Bella's hat onto her head and was shrieking with laughter as she tore away from a furious Bella, who raced after her. Perhaps in the middle of a school playground wasn't the best place, but then, where was the best place to tell Louis that for over twenty years he'd had a child he didn't know about?

"I saw Wendy Churchill at the wedding fair," Sophie said, leaning close to him so that her voice was barely more than a whisper. She paused, breathing in his scent and the heat of his proximity. For some reason she felt it would be harder to be so close to him after she'd told him what she knew. "She was there with her son. She has a twenty-year-old son, Louis."

Sophie waited, but Louis's male brain was not making any connections.

"She must have got pregnant when she was fifteen." Sophie looked into Louis's eyes before pressing her lips against his ear and whispering, "He looks just like you. Louis, he's your son."

Back at home, after Louis had stalked out of the playground, making it clear that a visit to Ye Olde Tea Shoppe was most definitely not in the cards, Sophie made the girls tea while Louis stood in the garden staring very hard at his decaying flower beds. Her culinary skills had come a long way since the first tea she'd made them, which had been two microwavable meals mixed together to avoid argument. Now she was able to grill sausages and mash potatoes without having to concentrate much at all, although admittedly that was because the girls rather obligingly liked her lumpy, or as Sophie preferred to call them "textured," mashed potatoes.

Louis had not said a word to her since the playground, leaving Izzy to fill in the gaps with her usual endless stream of consciousness punctuated occasionally by Bella's sage asides like "Fairies live in dells not groves, idiot" and "No, the tooth fairy doesn't collect toenail clippings. The toenail-clipping fairy does that, obviously." Sophie had not pressed Louis to talk. She had no idea what he was thinking or feeling or if he'd really understood what she had just told him. Now she watched him through her own reflection in the kitchen window as he stood in the twilight, perfectly still, just standing there, staring into the soil as the sky dimmed.

"Sophie, when you and Daddy are married, where will you sleep?" Bella asked her suddenly, dragging Sophie's attention away from the window.

"In a bed, hopefully!" she said brightly even though she knew Bella would never be satisfied with such a straightforward answer. For a seven-year-old Bella had a particularly effective questioning technique and the dogged determination to gather as much information as she could about whatever might touch her life in some way. Sophie had been expecting these questions, but she had rather hoped not to have to answer them today.

"And where will the bed be?" Bella asked her intently.

"Well, I'll sleep here, in this house with you," Sophie hedged, suddenly wishing she'd delayed her bombshell until after the girls were in bed so that Louis might be here to help her field these questions.

"Which room will you sleep in?" Bella asked her slowly. "Because I don't want to share with Izzy again, she is a very restless sleeper."

"I am not," Izzy said through a mouthful of sausage. "That's not me, that's Tango. He is a very restless sleeper, especially when you cuddle him up."

"No, I'll sleep with . . . I mean, I'll sleep in the same room as your daddy when we're married. That's what normal married people do. They sleep together in the same room," Sophie said. She withstood Bella's searching gaze for a second more before springing up to cool her cheeks in the freezer while she looked for the blackcurrant sorbet the girls had recently become obsessed with.

"Will you do kissing when you're married?" Izzy asked her, giggling through her gravy-stained fingers. Bella rolled her eyes.

"They already do kissing," she told her little sister. "That's allowed because they are in love." Sophie paused as she took two bowls off the drain. Louis was still there, still in exactly the same spot. She had gone about this in the wrong way. She shouldn't have just blurted it out on the playground like that. What was she thinking? Yes, Seth did look remarkably like Louis, but she didn't have any proof that he was Louis's son, only her own expectations and Wendy's word. And there was something about Wendy that Sophie didn't trust. She was self-aware enough to know she didn't like her because she was yet another part of Louis's past she would never have access to, a part so clearly precious and important to him. But it wasn't just that that made her mistrust Wendy. Something about the way she'd looked at Louis that first time they'd met in the pub had made her uneasy. There was something destructive about her.

"Sophie?" Bella said again, that same persistent tone Sophie had learned signaled that the child had something on her mind and wouldn't rest until she'd resolved it.

"Yes?" Sophie steeled herself, scooping the sorbet out into bowls, one eye still on the garden.

"Will you and Daddy have babies?" Bella asked her. "Will we have a brother or a sister? Well, really a *half* brother or a *half* sister."

Sophie sat down and slid the bowls to each girl.

"Well . . ." She and Louis had never discussed having their own children. Sophie supposed in the back of her mind that perhaps one day they would have a baby, although, rather like being properly married to Louis, until recently she hadn't been able to picture it as a concrete event. But whether or not he wanted more children was another matter. Especially as he was just getting used to the idea of his twenty-year-old son. "I don't really know, Bella."

"Because if you had a baby with Daddy, it would call you Mummy, wouldn't it?" Bella asked her carefully, taking the smallest spoonful of her sorbet so as to make it last longer.

"Well yes, if I did have a baby with your daddy, when it was big enough to talk it would call me Mummy."

"And it would call Daddy Daddy?"

"Yes," Sophie said.

"But we'd still call you Aunty Sophie," Bella said. "Because even though you'd be married to our daddy and living here and we'd have a half sister or a half brother who called you Mummy you'd still be our aunty Sophie and not our mummy."

"That's right. . . . ," Sophie said slowly, trying to work out exactly what it was that Bella was worrying about. "You know that I would never ever try to take the place of your mummy. I couldn't do that and I don't want to."

Bella looked at her for a long time with her dark, grave eyes. She had come a long way from the quiet, self-contained child Sophie had met less than a year ago, the little girl who was struggling to grow up because she felt there was nobody left in the world to look after her or her baby sister. Before Sophie's eyes Bella had blossomed into an inquisitive child, funny, with an infectious giggle and a surprisingly dry wit for one so young. According to her father and her grandmother, she was almost the same as she had been before her mother was suddenly taken from her. But sometimes Bella would still get that look in her eyes that told Sophie she knew the world could hurt you when you least expected it. That was a lost innocence that could not be recovered.

"Bella, darling." Sophie picked up her hand. "Do you mind me marrying your dad and living here?"

"No," Bella said, shaking her head. "I want you to marry Daddy and live here. I'm just not sure about what will happen when you've got a baby who calls you Mummy and we aren't calling you Mummy . . . will we be split in two? Will you prefer your baby to us?"

"Will you?" asked Izzy, who up until that point had been rather physically involved with her sorbet, to the point that she was wearing most of it like a beard. She paused, mid-spoonful, her eyes suddenly brimming with tears.

"No . . . no, of course not. That could *never ever* happen, I'll always love you exactly the same amount that I do now, which is gigantic," Sophie told her, trying not to be distracted by the sound of Louis coming in the back door.

"Is that as much as a proper baby?" Izzy asked her.

"She means your own baby," Bella said.

"I think it would be impossible for me to love anyone alive on this planet more than I love you two," Sophie said. "I mean, yes, I love your dad, but you two—you made me happy again when I didn't even realize I was sad."

"Will you love the baby as much as you love us then?" Bella asked.

"Baby?" Louis snapped as he sat down at the table. "Good god, please tell me there's nothing else you want to tell me, is there, Sophie?"

Sophie could see by the angles of his shoulders that he was tightly wound. When he was angry he almost seemed to fold in on himself, armored against any assault of reason or affection. She took a breath before she spoke, concentrating on keeping her tone light, as if it were a perfectly normal day and she hadn't just told Louis about his secret love child, hopeful that if she kept on acting as if everything was okay soon he would relax and unfurl and again be the man she could talk to.

"We're just talking about what would happen if we had a baby after we're married," Sophie said lightly, keen for him to tune in to how sensitive the girls were feeling.

"Oh, you don't have to worry about that." Louis's laugh was harsh. "I think I've got more than enough children to last me a lifetime. We won't be having any more kids."

Sophie dropped her gaze to the tabletop, aware that Bella was watching her closely, surprised by the sting of tears in her eyes. She felt as if Louis had physically hit her, the pain of his bombshell was so sudden and unexpected. He was angry and confused about Seth, and his instinct was to shock and hurt her as much as she had him, but she still found discovering his opinion on any future children hard to brush off. They had never talked about having children. It was one of the many things she didn't know about the man she wanted to marry, one of the things she had so confidently told her mother and Cal and anyone else who would listen that she'd find out about him after they were married, part of the big adventure of life with him. But if he was serious? If he really didn't want more children, what then? Sophie didn't even know if she wanted children, but the thought of someone telling her she wasn't going to have any made her feel cornered.

"Sophie?" Izzy piped up, her face sodden with sorbet. "I would call you Mummy if it wasn't for Mummy, because I do love you a lot."

Sophie blinked back the threat of tears and made herself smile before she looked up, resting the back of her hand against Izzy's fruity, wet cheek.

"That's a lovely thing to say," Sophie said gently. "Thank you, Izzy."

"And now," Louis said, picking Izzy up out of her chair and hoisting her under his arm, "it's bath time. Bella, run upstairs and get out your jammies and find some towels, we need to get this monster scrubbed clean!"

Izzy shrieked with giggles as Louis tickled her and Sophie worried about the imminent reemergence of the sorbet as he dangled her upside down by her ankles and swung her like a pendulum before setting her down and letting her scramble off upstairs.

"Are you okay?" Sophie asked him.

He looked at her for a long moment in the unrelenting glare of the kitchen's strip lighting.

"No," he said. "I don't think I am."

• • •

Sophie watched Louis pace up and down the living room, stepping over Tango, who was stretched out on his back in front of the fire, warming his belly after making off with two sausages that had been left on the grill. Artemis, who was perched on top of the bookshelf, watched Louis fixedly, her head following his journey back and forth as if at any minute she might pounce on him and attempt to wrestle him to the ground, something Sophie wouldn't entirely put past a cat that still hadn't gotten over missing out on sausages.

The girls had been silent for twenty minutes or so, which usually meant they were properly asleep and not engaged in some impromptu late-night craft activity or staging of a musical. Normally by now Louis would have shooed Tango upstairs where he'd find the warmest spot to cuddle up in and sleep off his food, Artemis would be out in the cool night air disemboweling small mammals with abandon, and Sophie would be in Louis's arms. They'd be discussing their day in the short punctuation marks between long kisses. But that wasn't the normal part, Sophie realized as she watched him—this was. Trouble and trauma and working through things together. They had met under stressful circumstances, that was certainly true. It had been grief and loss that had brought them together. But for the last few months, everything had been perfect, absolutely perfect, and it could have stayed that way if she hadn't bumped into Seth and Wendy at the wedding fair. But she had. This was happening, and now she had to find a way for Louis and herself to work through it together. The trouble was, it seemed like the last thing he wanted to talk to her about. It even felt as if he would prefer it if she wasn't here at all.

"Please, Louis, don't shut me out. Tell me what you're feeling," Sophie said, wincing as she said the words.

"What I'm feeling?" Louis's laugh was mirthless as he stomped over his prone cat once again. "What am I feeling? Do you know, Sophie, I have no idea. No . . . no, that's wrong. I know exactly how I'm feeling. I'm angry, I'm really bloody angry . . . Sophie, why did you have to tell me then, like that?"

It came as a shock to Sophie to discover that Louis was angry with her.

"First of all, keep your voice down, we don't want to wake the girls. Second, I didn't want to tell you like that—but you said you wanted to know and . . . you made it pretty hard for me not to tell you right then, Louis." Sophie was reproachful.

"It's just . . . I can't get my head around what you're telling me. You're telling me I have a twenty-year-old son? How? I mean how can that be?" Louis asked.

"Well, presumably when you and Wendy—"

"Once." Louis laughed fretfully. "We had sex only once. It was at this kid's birthday party. Me and Wendy had been going out for a while. I was so, so in love with her. I think I would have married her then and there if we'd been old enough. We decided that the party was going to be 'the night.' We were both terrified, so we got really drunk on cider and ended up under the coats, in the parents' bedroom. I barely remember anything about it except that I wasn't one hundred percent sure where everything went and it was over very quickly. Wendy cried. It was pretty awful, to be honest, but afterwards . . . I'd never felt so close to anyone before in my life. I really felt like I'd connected to another human being. We stayed there under the coats holding each other. I stroked her hair until she stopped crying."

"But you didn't use any protection?" Sophie asked him, desperate to block out the image of him ever being sweet and tender with another woman.

Louis looked at her and shrugged. "I can't remember, but I was barely sixteen and I was drunk. I'm guessing not."

"And then what?" Sophie forced herself to ask him.

"Then? We saw each other a few more times and then she disappeared." Louis scowled at Sophie. "I told you all of this. Back then I didn't think I'd ever love another girl again. But I've hardly thought about her in years . . . not until we bumped into her in the pub, and now I find out she had my kid at the age of fifteen and I never knew anything about it? And she's been living less than fifty miles away for god knows how long and I've never bumped into her before."

"If you think about it, you've only been back in the country for a little while," Sophie said, trying hard not to have heard the "hardly" part of what Louis had just said. "And I think she's only been back in Cornwall for a few months."

"Maybe he's not mine," Louis said. "Chances are he's not—aren't they?"

"Except that you haven't seen him," Sophie said, shaking her head. "Louis, he looks just like you. I mean he has your same mannerisms, your smile—he's pretty cute actually." Sophie attempted a smile, but the black look she received in return soon quelled it.

"Sorry, Soph, I just don't think this is a joking matter," Louis said, entirely distant, making Sophie feel as if it would be impossible to reach out and touch him.

"I know, I'm sorry," she said. "So what's next?"

"What is next?" Louis asked her. She wished that he would sit down so they could talk properly, looking into each other's eyes, holding hands—between kisses, the way they normally did when they were alone. But he persisted in standing, his hands on his hips, looking as if he wanted someone to blame. Looking at her.

"Well, I suppose the next thing is to get in touch with Wendy, to arrange a time to talk to her . . . ," Sophie suggested tentatively. "Meet this head-on and deal with it."

"Yeah, I suppose. Did she say when would be a good time to call?" Louis asked her, running his fingers through his hair.

"Well, not exactly," Sophie said, slowly finding that she was twisting her engagement ring around and around her finger.

"What did she say, exactly?" Louis asked her darkly.

"She tried not to tell me and then when it was obvious that Seth was yours, she told me not to tell you. She said she'd gotten by for the last twenty years without anyone knowing and she was doing just fine. She said she was happy and she didn't want anything to change. She said if I told you, I'd regret it."

"She said that?" Louis was perfectly still for a moment. And then he exploded. "Then why the hell did you tell me, Sophie? Why the hell did you do this to us?"

Propelled to her feet by shock and anger, Sophie stood up to face him, aware that she was trembling.

"Louis, for god's sake, keep your voice down," she hissed at him. "What did you expect me to do? Did you expect me to not tell you? Did you expect me to marry you knowing about your son and not mention it? Is that the kind of relationship you want with me, Louis? If you want to do this, you have to realize it's about more than snogging in doorways and holding hands."

"If *I* want to do this . . . ?" Louis trailed off.

"I'm the one who gave up my whole life to be with you," Sophie snapped back.

"Yes, and you're the one who still lives in a B and B."

"Because I'm trying to make things easy for your daughters," Sophie protested, not sure how this conversation had turned so savagely on her. "I want to marry you. I really, really want to marry you, but when you're like this . . ."

"Like what?" Louis asked her darkly.

"So angry and shut off and—I don't know how to handle you when you're like this, Louis. Because I don't know you when you're like this. Right now, you're like a stranger to me."

"You don't know how to handle me? Hell, Sophie, I'm a man,

not an animal in a circus. Or maybe that's what you want me to be. Your performing poodle."

"All I want is for you to be you, to be the man I love and the man I want to marry and the man I can talk to about anything and who can talk to me. The man who must know I didn't have any choice about this. Think about it, Louis. How could you trust me, how could you marry me if I kept this from you?"

They stood there staring at each other for a second and Sophie could hear all the unspoken words threatening to fly between them. Suddenly everything she had with Louis felt impossibly fragile, a beautiful web of silk that might be shattered at any second by the glancing blow of a casual breeze.

"I'm sorry," Louis said suddenly, his shoulders drooping. "This isn't about you. It's just that I'm shocked and angry, and you're right, I'm taking it out on you. I'm sorry."

Tentatively he reached out and picked up her hand. "Of course you had to tell me about him. You didn't have any choice, and I'm glad and grateful that you were brave enough to do it. Honestly I am."

Sophie nodded and took a step closer to him and searched his face, which was still stricken with remnants of anger. "You do believe that I want to marry you, don't you?" she asked him. "You do know how much I love you and how scared I am that all of this could be ripped away in a matter of seconds?"

"Scared?" Louis asked her, winding his fingers in her hair and pulling her lips toward his. Sophie resisted even though she was desperate for him to kiss her, desperate to be back in that familiar place with him once again.

"Things change, people change. You left Carrie once when things got tough . . . what if you leave me?"

"I left because Carrie was in love with another man, I didn't leave her—I know I shouldn't have gone, I know I shouldn't have walked out on my girls, but I'm a different man from the one I was then. All I've done tonight is shout and blame you, no wonder you're scared. Maybe I've been waiting for something to ruin this for us, maybe I don't really believe I can get this right. I haven't got much else right in the past . . ."

"You have," Sophie told him. "You're doing so well with the girls, and building up the business from scratch . . ."

"Only because of you. Because I love you. And I can't lose you, Sophie."

"You're not going to lose me," Sophie said, willfully snuffing out the small cold part of her that was still frightened because she might lose him. All she wanted now was the closeness between them restored, the safe little bubble they lived in re-formed around them like a shield, even if only for a few more hours, until the sun came up and reality rose with it. "It's just that kissing can't be our main form of communication. We have to talk sometimes too."

"I know, I know," Louis told her. "And I promise you that nothing is going to stop us from getting married on New Year's Eve. I promise you." He pulled her to him, winding his arms around her as he held her.

"I really don't want you to go back to the B and B tonight," he whispered. "I really don't want to be parted from you. I need you, I need to be able to hold you tonight, all night."

Sophie pulled back from him and looked into his eyes. She wanted to give him something, something to salve the anxiety and worry he was feeling, and more than that—she didn't want to leave him.

"I'll stay," she whispered with a smile. "I'll get up early, before the girls, so they won't even know. I don't want to leave you tonight either."

Sophie surrendered to Louis's kiss and felt her body burn up at his touch.

"And I'll help you get things sorted with Wendy and Seth," Sophie breathed as Louis kissed her neck and pulled her T-shirt up over her head.

"I know, I know you will," Louis said, running his hands down her bare back and unhooking her bra strap.

"And, Louis." Sophie forced herself to still his hand and made him look her in the eye. "I love you so much."

"I believe you," Louis said, smiling at her. "And I want you, right now."

Eight

I think Eve is planning to lace my coffee with arsenic," Cal told Sophie breathlessly as she sat in the guest sitting room with Mrs. Tregowan, her cell phone to her ear.

"Well, that would be totally in character, but why on earth do you think that? You just got one of London's most prestigious private houses to open for functions exclusively for McCarthy Hughes. If anything, she should be promoting you."

"Yes, if she wasn't sociopathic, not to mention just plain evil, she would. But when I did my big reveal in the boardroom it made her idea about reinventing the toga party look utterly pathetic and inept. Ever since then she's been giving me snake eyes."

"Oh, you are going to die," Sophie assured him. "Still, at least when you're dead life becomes a whole lot less complicated. I should imagine there are practically zero love children coming out of the closet, for example, when you're dead. Or mothers. Mothers who want to come and plan your wedding when you've just found out about all of the above."

"She wants to come and visit just when you've found out about the love child and the slutty ex?" Cal gasped, momentarily distracted from his own impending doom.

"Exactly. I love her and everything, but the last thing I need right now is her down here making my already complicated life two hundred times more difficult to manage, plus I haven't exactly told her about her future son-in-law's unexpected offspring yet . . ."

"I don't believe this." Cal sounded for once genuinely aghast.

"I know, I know I should tell her, but it was only five minutes ago I was announcing my engagement and telling her how happy I was. Telling her about Seth would just be so . . . so . . . embarrassing."

"That's not what I can't believe. You not sharing vital information with the people you love, that's a given as far as you're concerned. What I can't believe is that your life is so much more interesting than mine! That's got to mean Armageddon. Pass me a Bible, I'm checking Revelations, because the day Sophie Mills's life gets interesting, the end of the world is surely nigh."

"I'm talking about my life here, Cal, my fiancé, my wedding, my so-called happiness, my boyfriend's love child," Sophie complained. "Besides, your life is interesting. You're finally getting somewhere with your career, you're outgunning Eve. This is the first time your life's been about more than your paycheck and who you're dating. You're growing up, Cal."

"Oh god," Cal sighed. "I'm not entirely sure I want to do that."

"Cal," Sophie said. "You're becoming a man, a real one. That's sexy."

"Well, there's always a bright side," Cal said. "But actually, Sophie, I'm sort of past that . . . casual sex with strapping young men. I'm ready for something more."

"How many times have I heard that before?" Sophie laughed. "When you say something more you mean a one-night stand plus breakfast. Come on, Cal, you're not the settling-down type."

"I don't know," Cal said a little sadly. "I've got this sudden urge to share custody of some bed linen and maybe a Gaggia espresso machine. I'm broody for a washer and dryer."

"Okay, I promise that once I've sorted out the hell that is currently my life, you and I will settle down and plan how best you can become a blushing bride. But in the meantime let's talk about me," Sophie demanded, something she could get away with only with Cal. "I've found out that Louis has a fully grown love child on the loose. And more important, he's just found out—and he's all weird about it and angry and tense."

"I can see where he's coming from," Cal said. "I'd be angry and weird and tense if one of the little buggers who have surely been sired from my donated sperm ever turned up on my doorstep."

"You donated sperm? When?" Sophie asked, aghast.

"Oh, a few years back. I thought it was wrong to deprive the world of my superlative DNA just because the idea of impregnating a woman makes me want to heave. So I cut out the middleman, or rather, put one in . . . anyway, if a child suddenly turned up *I'd* be angry and resentful and confused and desperate to make sure they'd inherited my fashion sense. So god knows what Louis must be feeling."

"No one knows what Louis is feeling, that's the problem," Sophie said. "He won't talk to me, not properly. And let's face it, he hasn't exactly got a good track record on dealing with difficult issues. The last time he had a major problem in his life, he ran away to Peru."

"True, but he came back when it counted," Cal reminded her.

"And then there's this Wendy woman," Sophie mumbled, picking at the hem of her sleeve. "His first love and all that nonsense. You should see his face light up when he's talking about her. I think he still has feelings for her."

"He still has memories of feelings for her," Cal said. "That's a different thing entirely, that's nostalgia, not love. Anyway, tell me more about the love child. He looks just like Louis, you say?" Cal mused. "Is he straight?"

"I'm not dignifying that with an answer," Sophie said tartly, smiling at Grace, whose attention had briefly wandered from the TV. "The point is, I'm already marrying my dead best friend's husband who I've known for barely a year. And now it turns out the countryside is littered with his progeny. Cal—what am I thinking?"

"'Littered' is a bit of an exaggeration—at least as far as we know," Cal told her. "And what do you mean, what are you thinking? Are you getting cold feet, Miss Mills? Has the love child put you off?"

"No!" Sophie protested. "Well, not exactly but . . . Cal, what *do* I think about it? Why do I feel as if things have changed between Louis and me? Why do I feel that I've somehow ruined everything for us?"

"Things have changed between you and Louis," Cal said simply. "The honest truth is, you don't know that much about him . . . which doesn't mean you don't love him. I'm just saying, you haven't known him for long. You've found out something about him, a part of him you hadn't seen before, and it's bound to change your perception of him slightly."

"But it's not as if this was last year or even five years ago, this happened when he was a kid," Sophie said. "He made a mistake, so why should that bother me?"

"Everything else shouldn't bother you, not if you're sure about Louis. All you should be worrying about is helping him get through this and getting on with marrying him. And you are sure about him, aren't you? You said so."

Sophie paused for a long moment. She knew what Cal was waiting for her to say. She knew that as soon as she uttered even one word of uncertainty, he'd pounce on it like Artemis on an injured bird. She glanced sideways at Mrs. Tregowan, who seemed immersed in the story of a mother who sold her daughter's baby to pay for drugs.

"I am sure," she whispered. "I couldn't wait to marry him before all this happened, and I still can't. I'm just worried, worried that somehow this is going to ruin things between us."

"You know what you need to help take your mind off things, don't you?"

"Vodka?" Sophie asked hopefully.

"A hen night. A massive full-on London-based hen night organized by the nearest thing you've got to a best friend."

"And how on earth will your taking me to a string of gay clubs help take my mind off things in a way that won't mean I will require psychiatric help?"

"Because we won't go to only gay clubs and because once you're back in the Big Smoke, you'll feel like yourself again. You'll have perspective, distance, decent shoes on, and, most important, vodka on tap. You could be here by the weekend."

"Bizarrely enough, that does sound quite tempting, but we're going to confront Wendy today," Sophie informed him. "Louis is coming by to pick me up any minute. I can't just say, 'By the way, darling, I'm clearing off up to London for a drinking binge because the skeletons in your closet are freaking me out.' "

"Well, you could, but since you won't . . . I'll bring the hen night to you. Well, I'll bring me to you anyway, you drum up some hens. I'm coming down and I won't take no for an answer. Line me up some fishermen! I'll see you Friday night."

"Cal, I'm just not sure that now is the time—"

"Oh come on, Sophie, I need to get away from London and forget that the woman I depend on for an income hates me. I want to be with you, miserable, bitter, dysfunctional, and doomed-to-romantic-failure you, because you always make me feel better."

"It's tempting when you put it like that but—"

"Book me a room with Mrs. A., I'm on my way, darling!" Cal said and hung up.

Sophie stared at her silent handset and wondered why her life was populated by a whole lot of people who thought they knew more about what she needed than she did herself. She concluded that it was probably a statistical inevitability given that most of the time she felt as if she knew nothing at all.

"So today's the big day with the love child then?" Grace asked her.

"Well, the love child's mother," Sophie said. She should have known that nothing got past her fellow guest. Besides, Mrs. Alexander had been polishing the occasional table on the landing outside her room for quite some time while she'd been making arrangements with Louis about going to see Wendy.

"All set?" Mrs. Alexander asked Louis as she opened the door for him. He looked tense, his face tight and drawn, an expression Sophie was not familiar with. He hadn't even looked that way when he'd first come to claim his daughters. Her own stomach was in a tangle of knots, but she was determined not to let her anxiety feed Louis's. She was going to be the calm one, the one who was strong for him even if she did feel like running a million miles in the opposite direction.

"I guess," Louis said, looking at Sophie.

"I looked her up on the Internet and I've printed off the address of her workshop," Sophie said. "All we do is go there and hope she's in."

"Right." Louis nodded. Sophie was surprised by exactly how much the prospect of seeing Wendy again terrified him, even considering the circumstances. She had seen him in adversity and he had never been like this. No matter how hard it had been for him to come back and find that Bella hated him and Izzy didn't know him, he never lost his optimism or his confidence that he would work things out. It had been one of the things about him that had infuriated and impressed Sophie the most. Sophie wondered if it was the prospect of meeting his son that was making Louis so nervous or if it was seeing the girl he'd once been so in love with.

"I'm sure it will be fine," Mrs. Alexander said, rubbing Louis briskly on the back as if he had no more than a bad case of dyspepsia. "You just tell her you want to meet your son and there's nothing she can do about it."

"Right," Louis said, pecking Mrs. Alexander on the cheek.

"Do I?" he asked Sophie as he was about to get into her car.

"Do you what?" she replied.

"Do I want to meet my son?"

The workshop was on an industrial estate outside Torquay, one of thirty or so identical-looking units.

"It's unit thirty-seven," Sophie said as she drove slowly down the concrete-covered road that ran between the tentlike buildings. "Can you see the number? Louis?"

She braked and looked over at him. He was sitting stock-still, staring straight ahead, his fingers twisted in his lap.

"Is this really that bad?" she asked him, regretting the impatience in her tone immediately, working hard to curb her own misgivings about what they were to do. "I mean yes, yes, it is bad, I know, and it's a shock. But we'll face it together and we'll work out how best to handle it. If this is what you want, then I'm here for you. Or we could always just turn around and go back—"

"No, you're right," Louis said, looking at her and reaching over to take her hand. He squeezed her fingers hard. "This is something I have to face. I'm so glad you're here with me, Sophie. I haven't had anyone in my corner since . . . well, since Carrie."

"So," Sophie said, trying not to feel regretful that Louis didn't want to turn around and leave. "It's not that bad, is it?"

"It's just . . . what if Wendy hates me? I wouldn't blame her. I got her pregnant and abandoned her when she was fifteen."

"You didn't abandon her, you didn't know until a couple of days ago! She never gave you a chance to do the right thing, whatever that would have been at sixteen. But now you have a chance to do *something* at least. She won't hate you, none of this is your fault."

"You're right," Louis said. "I don't know why I'm so nervous about seeing her again . . ." Louis trailed off and Sophie knew that in that moment he was thinking about the summer he had spent with Wendy all those years ago. She dragged him back into the present, where he belonged to her.

"Look, that's unit thirty-three, so it must be . . ." Sophie put the car into first and crawled along a few more units. She turned to look at Louis. "We're here."

The radio had been playing when Sophie and Louis pushed open the door. There were a couple of girls in their late teens packing underwear into boxes, probably to fulfill online orders, after all, it was at bridebodybeautiful.com that Sophie had finally tracked down Wendy Churchill. She saw that Wendy guaranteed delivery within three to four working days for all orders made online. These girls must be in charge of delivering on that promise.

"Yeah?" one of the girls asked them as they came in.

"You can't buy the stuff here," another one said. "You have to go to a fair or buy online."

"We're not here to buy," Sophie said. "We're here to see Wendy."

"Oh, right, out back," the first girl said, nodding in the direction of a small office. "WENDY, VISITORS!" she yelled.

"We'll go through," Sophie said, pulling at Louis's hand and then pulling again when she realized that he didn't seem to be moving his feet.

Wendy's smile froze on her face the second she saw who her visitors were.

"You told him," she said to Sophie.

"I had to," Sophie said calmly. "Surely you must see that."

Wendy sat back in her chair and looked at Louis. Sophie waited for the hate and thinly veiled anger she had experienced from Wendy at the wedding fair to be unleashed on her fiancé, but instead Wendy smiled. It was a rueful, regretful smile. A pretty flirtatious smile.

"You poor bastard, you must have been going through hell," she said warmly.

"It's been a bit of a shock, I'll admit," Louis said, tentatively smiling back at her.

"Look, I'm sorry I got all stressy with your girlfriend at the fair." Wendy gestured at the one empty chair in the room and Louis sat in it. "It was a bit of a shock for me too, having my deep, dark secret outed like that by some strange woman. I probably didn't handle it as well as I should have."

"We understand, don't we, Soph?" Louis said, reaching up over his shoulder and taking Sophie's hand.

"Yes we do," Sophie said, trying, largely unsuccessfully, to repress the violent feelings of hate that Wendy effortlessly seemed to inspire in her.

"So—what do you want to do?" Wendy asked him pleasantly. Sophie wondered where her evil twin had gone, where the vicious threats and anger from the fair had gone and, more important, why? She told herself it was just childish jealousy and resentment that made her feel so negatively about the woman. After all, she had thrown a twenty-year-old, six-foot-two spanner in the works of what was supposed to be Sophie's fairy-tale ending, but it wasn't just that. There was something about Wendy that troubled her.

"I don't know what I want to do, really," Louis said, shifting uncomfortably in his chair. "I mean, first of all I want to say I'm sorry. I'm sorry I got you pregnant when we were kids. I was dumb, and drunk. I didn't know what I was doing."

"Oh, I don't know," Wendy said, raising a suggestive eyebrow; Sophie had to work hard to stop her mouth from dropping open in horror. "I have fond memories of that night, and besides, it wasn't just your fault. I went to the same sex-education classes as you. We were both young and drunk . . ." Wendy shrugged in a way that suggested the last twenty years of single motherhood had been no trouble at all. "We both wanted each other so much."

"But why didn't you tell me?" Louis asked her. "I don't know what I would have done about it. I was a bloody stupid kid with no parents to help me out. But I don't know—I'd have done something, got a job maybe . . ."

"I didn't tell you because I didn't know, not straightaway," Wendy said. "When you made it clear you didn't want to go out with me anymore—"

"When *I* made it clear?" Louis looked surprised. "You were the one who ignored *me*! I was heartbroken!"

"You were?" Wendy laughed. "No, you've got that wrong. After that party I was so excited about seeing you again, now that we were lovers—but you couldn't even look at me."

"No, you've got that wrong—*you* ignored *me*. I thought I'd disappointed you so much that you'd decided to chuck me on the spot."

"Far from it!" Wendy actually fluttered her lashes, which made Sophie want to shove her fingers down her throat and vomit. This was not going at all the way she'd expected. For starters, the opportunities for her to be a supportive and understanding fiancée seemed to be negligible, particularly since Louis had carelessly let go of her hand. Plus, there was a distinct lack of shouting or angst. Instead there was flirting. *Flirting.*

"I can't believe that . . . ," Louis said, shaking his head as he smiled at Wendy. "I pined for you for weeks."

"Same!" Wendy exclaimed. "Anyway, I didn't notice I'd missed my first period. Mum and Dad announced that we were moving for Dad's job, and I thought, why not? The only boy I'll ever love has chucked me—I might as well move on. I was a skinny little thing back then, really petite—"

"You still are," Louis assured her chivalrously.

"Oh, I don't know about that," Wendy said coyly. "But when I started to get a bit of a tummy, Mum said it was my hormones. Puppy fat! We'd been in Oldham for a couple of months when I felt it kick. Of course I didn't know it was a kick. I thought I had an alien life form inside me. He must have been moving around before then but I'd put it down to indigestion. But this—this was a really proper kick. I went running to my mum in tears, thinking it was cancer or worse. She put her hand on my belly and felt it and suddenly *she* was crying.

" 'You silly stupid bloody foolish girl,' that's what she said to me. I'll never forget it. Or what she said next. 'You've gone and got yourself pregnant.' "

Wendy shook her head, looking over Sophie's shoulder and through the venetian blind. "But they were brilliant about it in the end."

"Didn't they want to know who the dad was?" Louis asked her.

"Yes," Wendy said. "And I told them."

"And your dad didn't come down here to kick my head in? Why not?" Louis asked her.

"My dad said what bloody use would a kid of barely sixteen be? He said we'd take care of it ourselves. And as for me, I thought you'd gone right off me. I didn't see the point in telling you either. I must admit that when we moved back down a year or so back, I wondered what would happen if we bumped into you. But we never did."

Wendy and Louis looked at each other across the desk with a kind of familiar fascination and wonder that made Sophie feel very uncomfortable. They looked as if they had just rediscovered a long-lost treasure that had once been very dear to them.

"And did he . . . did Seth ever ask about who his dad might be?"

"We lived with my mum and dad till he was eight," Wendy told him. "My dad was still young enough and fit enough to play football with him, run in the fathers' race. The subject never came up, I think because he'd never had a dad, so he didn't miss one. Actually," she said, pausing and looking pensive for a moment, "he did ask me when I met someone and got married. He wanted to know if Ted was his dad."

"Wait, you're married?" Louis asked her.

"Not anymore." Wendy shrugged. "It didn't work out. I tried to love him, but in the end there was always something holding me back . . ." She looked up through her lashes at Louis. "Or maybe someone."

To his credit Louis broke Wendy's gaze first, clearly feeling a little awkward by the implication of her last comment.

"So what did you tell him?" he asked her.

"I told him Ted wasn't his dad, but that his dad was someone I'd once loved very much."

"And he has no idea about me now?" Louis asked her.

"None," Wendy said.

"And are you going to tell him?"

Wendy hesitated and Sophie waited for the same angry denial she had experienced.

"No," Wendy said, reaching across the desk to take Louis's hand. "I think you and I should tell him together."

Nine

As Sophie paced the single and largely empty platform at the St. Ives station waiting for her guest to arrive on the 4:46, she wondered about two things. First, why Cal had never learned to drive and was forcing her to meet him at the station on this chilly and gloomy afternoon, and second, why Louis had arranged one of the most important and momentous events of his life without discussing it with her at all.

After Wendy had dropped her bombshell, Louis had just sat there for a moment. Sophie hadn't been sure exactly how he would react. She'd expected something radical though—some kind of drama that seemed befitting of the occasion. But instead Louis had merely sat back in his chair, his whole body relaxing as he ran his fingers through his hair, shrugged, and said, "Okay then, when?"

He'd looked relieved, Sophie thought, glad that someone else was taking charge of the situation, telling him what to do. She couldn't blame him, she supposed, but she also couldn't help the feeling of unease that blossomed in the pit of her stomach. No matter how reasonable and sensible Wendy seemed now, Sophie found it hard to trust her and she was sure it was due to more than mild jealousy over Louis's past love. But as Sophie stood in the tiny cramped office at Wendy's workshop, she realized that regardless of whether she liked Wendy, Wendy was the mother of Louis's son, and when Sophie married Louis this woman would be in her life forever.

Wendy had smiled, watching Louis's face closely. "You two are so alike, you know. Of course I've known Seth for twenty years, he's my boy. I did my best to forget what you were like, and I don't just mean how you look, but your mannerisms . . . your smile." Sophie looked on as Louis and Wendy watched each other closely. "Now I look at you sitting in that chair and it's amazing. He's the spitting image of you."

"Sophie mentioned that." Louis's laugh was easy and relaxed, as if suddenly he'd decided that discovering a child wasn't that big a deal after all. "It's pretty crazy to think that's he out there, this son I've never met . . . so when shall we go and see him?"

"I need to pick the right time," Wendy said, glancing at Sophie briefly, as if she was irritated by an eavesdropper. "How about Friday? He's coming over to my house for dinner, he often does on Fridays, says he needs to get a good feed in before the onslaught of the weekend. How about you come too?"

"We could make Friday, couldn't we, love?" Louis asked Sophie, looking up at her. Sophie had been momentarily thrown by the fact that he'd called her "love"—a term of endearment he had never previously used and one she'd always thought more fitting for either couples who had been together for more than a hundred years or bartenders.

"Well, Cal is supposed to be coming on Friday afternoon, but this is much more important. I'll get out of it, he'll understand and—"

"Actually, I think it would be better if it's just us, I mean just you and me, Louis," Wendy said, cutting across Sophie. "It'll be enough of a shock for the poor kid without strangers trooping in too."

"Except that Seth's already met me," Sophie retorted before she could bite her tongue. "I'm not the stranger, Louis is."

"No, and you're not his father either," Wendy said, directly addressing Sophie for the first time. "Look, I'm sorry, you might have been the one to work out who Seth was, but as far as I'm concerned, for now Louis is the only one who gets to be there when we tell Seth who his dad is."

Sophie had waited for Louis to object and to insist that Sophie should come with him, but he hadn't. He'd just twisted in his chair and looking up at her said, "I think Wendy's right, love."

Sophie checked her watch. Louis was there now, at Wendy's house in Newquay. She'd invited him over for four thirty, giving them time to work out how they were going to handle things before Seth arrived around six.

Sophie had been looking for the spare key in Louis's hall table drawer to give to Mrs. Alexander, who'd agreed to babysit, when she'd come across the brochure for Fineston Manor. It had been only a couple of days since she'd found out about Seth and since Louis had told her he'd found the perfect place to get married. They still hadn't looked at the brochure together, and as far as she knew he hadn't booked the place for any date, let alone New Year's Eve. She held the glossy folder in her hands for a few seconds, counting backward from ten, trying to snuff out all the irrational and childish feelings that surfaced in her when she considered that all of their plans had been so suddenly and carelessly shelved. Of course discovering Seth was more important than booking their wedding day, but even so, as Sophie looked at the brochure tucked away in the drawer where Louis put credit card bills, bank statements, and everything else he didn't want to think about, she couldn't help feeling jealous and neglected.

Only a few days ago the whole world had been about them and the girls, about how she felt about Louis and how he felt about her and the new family they were endeavoring to put together in the best possible way. It had been about kissing in doorways and the awe and delight they felt in each other. Now all of that was gone, and despite herself Sophie discovered she was angry.

"What about this?" Sophie asked Louis as he came down the stairs. He'd dressed carefully in a blue shirt and jeans, a shirt to appear smart and dadlike, Sophie guessed, and jeans to show he was still young and cool. His hair was brushed off his face and tucked behind his ears and he'd shaved too, which oddly made him look younger and undermined the responsible-adult image Sophie thought he was trying to achieve. He didn't look like himself. The tension, nerves, and fear of the unexpected had altered his face somehow in small, subtle ways so that his features were all slightly out of kilter.

More than that, he hadn't looked at her in the way he usually did in several days. Instead he looked at her as if he didn't really see her. It felt like suddenly finding yourself standing in the shadows when you had become accustomed only to basking in the sun.

"What about what?" Louis asked her.

"This." Sophie held the brochure under her chin, peering up at him over it, like a child peeping over a tabletop. It seemed to take Louis a second or two to register what it was.

"Oh . . . that," he said. "I haven't booked it."

"I guessed as much," Sophie replied, putting the brochure back in the drawer. "And I understand why . . . it's just—do you still want to get married on New Year's Eve? Because if you do, then we should probably sort it out, that's all." Her voice was edged with an unreasonable anger that Louis registered with a sigh.

He picked up his keys and looked first at his watch and then at the front door. Sophie knew that he didn't want to discuss it now. She knew that he wanted to drive to Newquay and be on time to meet Wendy and then eventually his son. She knew all of that and yet still she asked him. She discovered she couldn't stop herself.

"Of course I still want to get married . . . ," Louis said, frowning at the front door as if he could somehow will it to open.

"Still on New Year's Eve?" Sophie pressed him uncomfortably.

"Well yes, why would that change?" Finally Louis focused his attention on her and looked her in the eyes, reaching out to cup her cheek in the palm of his hand. "I love you, Sophie," he told her, with just a shade of impatience. "All this secret-son stuff is doing my head in, but it doesn't mean I don't love you or don't want to marry you anymore . . ."

"Really?" Sophie heard herself sounding insecure and needy and felt the muscle in her gut wince. She rested her hand on Louis's chest, feeling the beat of his heart against her palm. "I'm sorry—I know this is a really important day for you and that you have to go now and that the last thing you need is me asking you if you still feel the same but I can't help it, I can't . . ."

Louis engulfed her in a hug, the kind of all-encompassing embrace that had been absent for the last few days.

"You nut," he said gently, kissing the top of her head. "How I feel about you hasn't changed, *nothing* can change how I feel about you. I really want to marry you more than anything and preferably before they chime in the New Year. I promise you I'll ring them tomorrow, because I'd be gutted if we lost out on our New Year's Eve wedding for any reason. But right now I have to go and meet my adult son who I knew nothing about and who has no idea I exist."

Louis sucked a thin breath in through his teeth.

"I'm so sorry." Sophie looked up at him, nipping her bottom lip. "I've behaved like a selfish brat . . . and I feel like an idiot. Of course nothing is more important than getting to Wendy's on time."

"I actually kind of like it that you care enough about the wedding to bring it up now, just at the very second I'm going out to meet Seth." Louis's smile was wry. "I like the irrational, vulnerable bit of you. I *love* all of you and I am going to marry you as soon as I have sorted this, okay?"

"Okay," Sophie said, allowing a small smile to insinuate its way into the corners of her mouth. "But at no point did I openly admit to being irrational."

"And remember," Louis said, keeping his voice low as he kissed her temple. "If the girls ask, I'm going to meet a cousin and you're out with Cal."

"You're sure you don't want to tell them about Seth right away?" Sophie asked, risking starting another conversation, but only because she wasn't at all sure about Louis's decision to keep the news of a half brother from the girls. However difficult it might be to tell them now, Sophie was worried that with all the people who already knew, including Wendy, Carmen, Grace, Cal, and even Mrs. Alexander, they'd find out some other way, and if they did she wasn't sure how it would affect them, especially Bella, who had struggled so hard to trust her father again.

"I am sure." Louis nodded. "It's too much for them to take in right now. I'll tell them in my own way when the time is right."

"Okay then," Sophie said.

"Okay then," Louis repeated. He kissed her on the cheek, smiling briefly. "Wish me luck."

"Good luck, and Louis . . ." Sophie hesitated, unsure if she should risk skewing the equilibrium that had been so delicately restored between them. "Just be careful of Wendy. I know she seems great and friendly and open but . . . she was a whole different person when I spoke to her at the wedding fair. She didn't seem very . . . nice."

The description was something of an understatement but Sophie thought that calling her a "threatening, vicious, hatchet-faced old harridan" might not be terribly tactful at that precise moment.

"Don't worry about Wend," Louis said, shortening her name with familiarity. "I know her—she's great, and more important, she's handling all of this amazingly well. I expect she was probably shocked when you found out about Seth and that probably made her act all angry and protective. I know she's not great around you, but that's probably just because she's a bit jealous . . ."

"Jealous?" Sophie snapped. "Of what?"

"Of you." Louis shrugged, his hand on the door latch. "But you don't have to worry, because it's you I love . . ."

"I wasn't worrying until then!" Sophie lied, wondering if Louis had spotted her silently seething whenever Wendy came up in conversation. "It never crossed my mind she might be after you, but it's crossed yours, I see."

"It hasn't!" Louis insisted. He looked at his watch. "Look, I'm sorry, but I haven't got time for this now, it's just stupid! I've really got to go."

"I know," Sophie said miserably, feeling the peace between them wash away again.

"There is nothing to worry about," Louis told her firmly as he opened the door.

Sophie knew she should just have smiled and nodded and hugged him and sent him on his way feeling that everything was okay between them before he faced his son. But she felt confused, angry, and anxious, so instead she simply looked him in the eyes and said, "Isn't there?"

He'd slammed the door on his way out.

• • •

Finally the train pulled slowly into the station, a total of eleven minutes late. Sophie hugged her arms around her torso, waiting for Cal's tall, elegant frame to emerge from one of the carriages. On this cool late-September evening he was easy to spot among the five or six passengers who reeled off the train, because he was the only man wearing a gray cashmere overcoat over a tailored suit finished off with black patent-leather shoes, but even if he had arrived in the heat and turmoil of the summer season, he would have stood out a mile. Cal was one of those people other people looked at. At some point in his life, as part of his evolution into an adult being, he had made a decision to stand out from the crowd. It had nothing to do with his looks, although he certainly was striking, or even that he was gay; it was something more fundamental than that. Cal had decided that life was too short to blend in, and that he'd been put on this earth to be seen, regardless of the consequences. And no matter how much they argued and bickered, it was the part of Cal that Sophie had always admired and aspired to the most.

That part of her, the part that had loved clothes and worn high heels religiously, had faded since she'd come to St. Ives. She still had all her glamorous clothes in her B & B closet (barring the red patent-leather Jimmy Choos she had loaned Bella with uncharacteristic largesse when Bella was playing *Wizard of Oz*, and had never seen again, except during the girl's renditions of "Somewhere Over the Rainbow"), but she'd only had one occasion to wear any of them, and that was the night Louis had proposed.

First she blamed her newly sensible look on the fact that she was living literally at the very end of the British Isles now, where fashion was irrelevant, except that alongside its history of fishing, artists, and tiny working-class cottages, St. Ives was an utterly stylish place, chockful of designer shops and as many well-dressed and well-heeled people as you could hope to see anywhere on the streets of London. Sophie could easily have worn heeled boots and a pencil skirt to do the school run and not looked out of place, but she didn't. She'd frequently told Cal that there was no point in wearing anything nice when you had two girls hell-bent on literally painting the town red, and she had evidence of many a ruined item and irretrievably stained garment to back that up from their time living in Sophie's one-bedroom flat, but that wasn't it either. Since the incident when Izzy had rather helpfully tried to jazz up Sophie's best little black Chanel dress by gluing sequins and pom-poms onto it as a surprise, and Sophie had actually cried over the loss of one of her best and oldest friends, the girls had desisted from raiding Sophie's closets.

Sophie had always believed, although she hadn't told Cal because he'd laugh in her face, that when she came to Cornwall to be with Louis, she had shed everything about her life that was inconsequential and unimportant. That she had pared herself down to her bare minimum, unless you counted the extra cream-tea pounds, and shown Louis the essence of herself, because that was the kind of courage that truly loving someone required. The fact that he still loved and desired her when she wasn't tottering about in beautiful heels or trussed up in a tight top only affirmed how right and how liberating her decision to come here had been. But as she watched Cal walking down the platform toward her, Sophie considered, for the first time, another reason she had let her devotion to glamour and shoes slip so easily away. Had she lost herself here? Had she lost herself in Louis and the girls and let her identity slip and bleed into theirs? All at once Sophie missed the hours of preparation it had taken simply to leave the flat every morning in London, she lamented her former dedication to shaping her brows on a daily basis and shaving her legs. She missed the fact that her nails used to be long and were never chipped and that the balls of her feet always burned with the gratifying pain that said "these shoes are gorgeous."

As soon as Sophie saw Cal striding toward her she felt better, a little more like her old self again. She felt as if he'd brought more than just himself and a cerise Yves Saint Laurent suitcase on wheels. He'd brought a little bit of her back with him too. The little bit of her that wanted the world to sit up and take notice.

"Good god, where am I, and why?" Cal asked as she hugged him. "Because I know we are friends and everything, but I can't possibly like you *this* much."

"Gucci?" Carmen asked Cal with a raised eyebrow, nodding at his shoes.

The first place Sophie had taken him was for after-hours cakes at Ye Old Tea Shoppe to meet her best St. Ives friend.

It had been a mutual-appreciation society between Sophie's two friends from the start. Carmen had handed him a slice of baked custard and nutmeg tart and admired the tailoring in his suit and he'd told her he'd never expected anyone so classically styled to be anywhere so far from civilization, particularly not behind the refrigerated display counter in a cake-shop–cum-café.

"Now she," he said, nodding in Sophie's direction with a cursory glance, "was always going to throw everything away for a slim chance at happiness, that's desperation for you, and as I've always said, desperation is Sophie's middle name. But you, Miss Carmen Velasquez? You've got class written all over you."

"That's because I'm from Chelmsford," Carmen agreed with a nod. "Say what you like about Essex girls, but class runs through us Chelmsford girls like letters through a stick of rock."

"Well, that's obvious," Cal agreed. "So tell me, what brought you to the back of beyond?"

"It was love that brought me here," Carmen said. "Love for a much younger and very-well-muscled man."

"Seems reasonable." Cal nodded, savoring the last forkful of his tart, which he had been delicately demolishing in the same way Artemis would polish off a bowl of tuna, slowly and carelessly, as if she were doing you a favor by taking it off your hands.

Cal always maintained that he didn't really like food, which was why he largely survived on anything that could be impaled on a cocktail stick or ordered in a restaurant where he would never consider either an appetizer or a dessert. All food meant to him, he would often say, was fuel.

But once, after Cal had had a particularly wonderful weekend with a man who then turned out to be married, he'd invited Sophie over to dinner to commiserate, telling her that her love life, which was even more sorrowful and emptier than his own, would cheer him up no end. Happy to oblige, because at that point in her life the nearest she had to a relationship was an occasional round-robin email from her ex-boyfriend Alex, Sophie had assumed that dinner would mean prepacked sandwiches, perhaps some minipizzas if she was lucky. When she arrived, however, not only had Cal cooked enough courses and quantities to feed twenty, he had baked as well: cakes, muffins, cookies, tarts, and more. It was like walking into a fine French patisserie. They had spent the weekend drinking wine and eating as much of the food as was humanly possible without actually rupturing their intestines and Sophie had let him hold forth on how terrible her life was because she knew that he didn't want to talk about his own.

"If you don't like food," Sophie had challenged him, forcing down one final slice of chocolate cheesecake, "then how come you're a better cook than Gordon Ramsay?"

"I do like food, and of course I can cook. I am very accomplished," Cal had replied. "What I don't like is that I only ever eat when I'm miserable. And I don't want to be miserable, so I don't eat."

Sophie had had to think about that for quite some time, during which she sampled a tiny slice of Cal's tarte tatin just to be polite and also because she thought the apples could feasibly represent one of her five fruits and vegetables a day.

"Wouldn't it be better to practice eating when you are happy so that you can have a healthy and happy relationship with food?" she'd asked him.

Cal had leaned back in his chair and narrowed his cornflower blue eyes as he looked down his impeccably chiseled nose at her.

"Well, obviously it would, but we all need a hang-up, Sophie, and this is mine. You, on the other hand, eat like a horse whatever the weather. I might be screwed up, but at least I'm thin and fashion loves me."

Sophie had never pressed him again on how he felt about food, because most of the time he did seem to be happy and thin, and as far as she knew, that ticked off at least two out of three boxes on his list for a perfect life. But she knew that much as he might be pretending to be eating Carmen's tart out of politeness only, he was finding it just as delicious as Sophie always did and she wondered if here, in the bosom of the coast, with the sea air in his lungs, he might stop thinking that eating food was equated with misery and just allow himself a little bit of happiness with a tart. Which under other circumstances was practically his personal mission statement.

"So tell me," Cal asked Sophie. "What am I going to do after Eve's fired me for being better at her job than she is? What will become of me?"

"You could always work for me," Sophie said, smiling as she remembered her wedding-planning idea.

"What, as a nanny? I thought you said that nannies who swore and drank weren't to be trusted."

"No, idiot. I know you think I gave up everything when I came down here, but the truth is, I've realized I don't have to. I'm starting my own wedding-services company, but different, you know. I'm going to offer exclusive quirky wedding venues, really special catering, and dress designers and everything else I can think of. It's going to be brilliant, and I am going to be brilliant at it."

"You will as well," Cal said, impressed. "It is the perfect job for you, starting your own business from scratch, Sophie—you'll love that. And if things go horribly wrong with you and Louis, at least you'll know you'll have *someone's* wedding to go to."

"Scrap that job offer," Sophie said mildly.

"You know I'm only joking, I want you and Louis to get married—how else am I going to be chief bridesmaid?"

"Hang on, sonny, I think you'll find that job's taken," Carmen protested.

"So far that position hasn't been filled," Sophie told them both. "I might compare and contrast how I feel about you tonight."

"So where are we going?" Cal asked Sophie as he sipped the double espresso that Carmen had made him with some aplomb, once he'd lusted after the outrageously expensive and rather beautiful Italian coffee machine she had invested in for the café, even though it was neither Olde nor had anything to do with Tea. "Where's the hot be-seen-there-or-die venue in this town? And where, more to the point, are the hens?"

"Um." Sophie looked at Carmen. "Well, to be honest, what with me not having lived here very long and spending most of my time with Louis and the girls, I was rather limited on hens. Carmen is it. Unless you count Mrs. Alexander, but she's babysitting, and I would have asked Grace if it wasn't for the fact that she's eighty-nine and quite likely to die if she gets too excited . . ."

Cal blinked at Sophie. "This is it? I've come eight hundred miles on a train without a buffet, and with a load of country people, for this, for *this*. Well, fine, I suppose I should have expected it, you've never exactly been popular. As long as the gin is flowing and the music's pumping, then I'm happy. So where are we going?"

"Well." Sophie tried to muster some enthusiasm for the night out she didn't really want. "There's a lovely art gallery on the harbor, with a bar that opens late sometimes . . ."

"Or a very nice fish place," Carmen said. "Very chic, and the chef once worked in the Dorchester Hotel."

"Chic?" Cal rolled his eyes. "I haven't come down here for chic, I've come down here for dancing, drinking, and wild sex in the surf."

"You've come down here for that?" Carmen asked him. "In September, you'll freeze your bits off."

"Also, don't forget, you've come down here to support me through Louis's love child debacle," Sophie told him, glancing at her watch again. It was just after six. Seth, if he was anything like his father, would be at least twenty minutes late. Wendy and Louis would be there right now in her front room. (Which for some reason Sophie pictured as garishly decorated, much like that of a low-rent hooker, although she accepted that the mental image could have a lot more to do with her personal feelings toward Wendy than Wendy's interior design tendencies.)

Wendy and Louis would be there waiting for the sound of the key in the lock, waiting for the moment Seth walked in through the living room door and found his father there. She felt her heart constrict with panic, not only on Louis's behalf but on his son's. She knew what it was like to live without a father and she also knew how shocking it was to discover that your whole life, everything you've believed to be unalterable and true, could be turned on its head in a second. Wendy had had twenty years to deal with what she knew, Louis only a few days, but Seth would have had no time at all, and she worried for him, because as confident and self-assured as he seemed, he really was still very young.

"It will all be happening any minute now," Sophie said, staring at her watch. "It feels wrong that I am here, thirty miles away, while Louis is meeting his son."

"Feels like an episode of *EastEnders* to me," Cal said. "But anyway, I am here now and I have come down to help you deal with the love child and in my considered opinion the best way for you to do that is to get me very, very drunk and find me a podium to dance on. So where are we going?"

"A podium you say . . . well, there's Isobar," Carmen suggested halfheartedly. "Although it's a very young crowd in there, and from what I remember they do tend to wear a lot of sombreros . . . but it is open until two tonight."

"And drinks are only a pound before ten," Sophie added.

"And?" Cal asked, seeming to be waiting for other options.

"That's pretty much it for late-night nightlife round here," Sophie admitted. "But there are many lovely pubs with local flavor. No podiums, mind you, but quite a few solid oak tables."

Cal thumped his head down onto Carmen's checked tablecloth.

"You're regretting coming to see me, aren't you?" Sophie asked him. "It seemed like a good idea to come down here and take my mind off my fiancé's illegitimate love child. You thought there'd be more excitement, didn't you? But now you've got here and all you've found is an off-season holiday town with one nightclub, you're wondering why you left your wonderful, vibrant, amazing city of London that loves you no matter what you do, aren't you?"

Cal looked up at her. "Frankly, yes," he said. "No . . . look, of course I'm not. I'm here for you, Sophie. I am just tired and I really need a nice, long, cool, and very alcoholic drink."

"We could always get in a cab and go somewhere bigger," Carmen suggested tentatively. "Penzance is only a fifteen-minute drive away, but I'm not sure it will be that much fun this time of year—

how about we go crazy and go to Newquay? There are loads of clubs in Newquay and, after all, this is your hen night, Soph. We need to find you some action."

"Newquay?" Sophie repeated. "That's where Louis is though. If I go to Newquay for my henless hen night, he'll think I'm following him around and that I don't trust him anywhere near his manipulative, scheming ex."

"Well, yes he would if you went to Newquay to go round to her house and invite yourself in," Carmen said, rolling her eyes at Cal. "But I'm not suggesting we do that."

"Oh, aren't you?" Sophie sounded a little disappointed.

"Cal's come a long way, and all of us need to have our minds taken off certain things, you off the love child . . ."

"Me off my nonexistent love life," Cal added.

"And me off . . . well, off of baking cakes for god's sake," Carmen said, looking around for something to blame. "If I sift another tablespoonful of icing sugar, I'm going to kill myself."

"I'm not wearing nearly the right thing for Newquay," Sophie said, looking down at her jeans and sneakers.

Cal said, "Look, let's go back to the B and B, I can have a shower, and then we'll bling up and blast off, whaddayasay?"

"Okay," Sophie said, but she knew even then, even before Cal had got back to the B & B and poured her into a pale blue silk shift dress and silver sling backs, that the evening was bound to end in a disaster of some kind. Except she could never have imagined exactly how disastrous it would be.

Ten

Sophie never remembered that she didn't like nightclubs until she was in one. And then she realized that she hadn't ever really enjoyed them, not even when she was twenty-two and actually knew the music that was playing. Now she felt rather inclined to say to anyone who might listen, if they could hear her over the din, that the music was too loud and the lyrics didn't make any sense. Besides, there seemed to be only two reasons that Sophie could discern to go to a large room full of men wearing tucked-in shirts and hearing bad music. One was to find a random person to have sex with, which she had never before been disposed to do and was certainly not interested in doing now, and the other was getting really, really drunk, which led to a subcategory of reasons that came under the general heading "Things I Want to Forget."

The really annoying thing was that as soon as Sophie was in possession of her large vodka and Red Bull, she didn't seem to want to drink it. Perhaps it was having one éclair too many at Ye Olde

Tea Shoppe earlier, but even one sip of the drink made her stomach churn. So not only was she rubbish at being in nightclubs, it seemed that she was also a failure at drinking to forget, which just about summed up her life at the moment. She was not even good at being bad.

Earlier, while he had been doing her makeup, Cal had said it seemed that loving Louis meant embracing his baggage too, and that she had to work out how and if she was able to do that.

"The trouble is," she'd told him, "sometimes I'll feel rather put out that I have almost zero baggage for Louis to embrace. If our emotional baggage was actual baggage, then all I'd have for him to deal with would be a half-empty wash bag, while he'd have me carting around a full set of three suitcases and a massive trunk, one of the ones you could probably fit a body in."

"Well, that's your own fault for living like a nun for so long," Cal had said. "My point is that if you love Louis, then you have to love his baggage. You have to embrace it, you have to at least try."

Sophie watched Carmen and Cal dancing together as if they were about to find some dingy corner and have mad, crazy sex and they both looked great. Carmen had popped home while she and Cal had gone to the B & B and had reappeared later in a black backless halter top and skinny jeans topped off by a lovely pair of stilettos. When Carmen and Cal had snaked onto the dance floor of the Tall Trees Club and Bar, all eyes had followed them for at least a few seconds, and many stayed to watch them dancing. They made a great couple, rippling to the alien-sounding music as if they'd been partners all their lives, and when Carmen did indeed haul Cal up onto one of the podiums, there had even been a small burst of applause.

Sophie sighed and twisted on her chrome bar stool so that her back was to the dance floor and concentrated on her drink. She really needed to get drunk; perhaps if she held her nose and downed it in one swallow. Her stomach churned at the thought of it.

"Buy you a drink?" Sophie dimly heard the offer being made as she stared at her glass wondering exactly what alcohol went well with an overindulgence in éclairs. A brandy perhaps? No, the thought of that actually made her want to vomit.

"Hey, you, I said can I buy you a drink?"

Belatedly Sophie realized that the offer was being made to her.

"Who, me?" she said, looking up at a blunt-faced young man leaning on the bar and staring at her rather hard, like a dog who hoped that it could will a piece of meat off the table and into its jaws.

"Don't see anyone else here," the man said. He smiled as he said it, but his smile lacked warmth. "It's off-season, slim pickings."

"You know how to make a girl feel wanted," Sophie said. She glanced back at the dance floor, where Carmen and Cal were nowhere to be seen. "Look, you don't want to buy me a drink. I'm engaged, and besides, I'm here with my friends."

"I don't care if you're engaged." The man shrugged. "And I can't see your friends. Look, all I want is a laugh and a bit of fun. So let me buy you a drink. You won't be sorry." He transferred his hungry gaze to her bust, which was burgeoning beneath the silk with much more gusto than the dress had been designed for.

"No thank you," Sophie said.

"Let me buy you a drink, I said." He straightened up, and although he wasn't much taller than Sophie was seated, he was stocky and his stance was threatening. "I only want to buy you a drink— where's the harm in that?"

"Don't be a wanker, mate. Leave her alone."

For a moment, as Sophie caught a glimpse of her rescuer from out of the corner of her eye, she thought that somehow Louis had found out where she was and had come to find her. But of course it wasn't Louis. Louis would never be seen dead in a place like this. It was Seth.

"And what the hell's it got to do with you?" The man poked Seth in the shoulder with a short, thick finger.

"I'll tell you what it's got to do with me." Seth leaned down until he was nose to nose with the man. "If you speak even one more word to either me or that woman, then I'm going to rip your head off, and if you don't believe me, then try me, because I swear to you I've had the worst night of my life tonight and right now killing you and going to prison for it doesn't seem like such a bad option."

Sophie gasped, her eyes wide, as she leaned back against the bar clutching her untouched drink, the condensation damp against the palm of her hand. She felt as if she should do something, say something, but as the two men faced each other she found herself glued to her chair by the gravity of Seth's fury.

The man stared hard, up into Seth's eyes, and then, shaking his head, stepped away, picking up his bottle of beer.

"She wasn't worth it anyway," he said, lumbering off into the darker recesses of the club.

"Oh, my." Sophie breathed out and reached to touch Seth's shoulder, which was rock hard with tension. "Seth . . . Seth, look at me. Are you okay?"

Seth turned to look at her and Sophie realized that he didn't remember who she was. He really had just turned up to pick a fight with a man who might have been shorter than he was but who could probably have put him in the hospital any day of the week if he'd wanted to.

"How do you know my . . . oh, you're the one from the wedding fair."

Sophie became anxious on discovering that the realization did not make him warm to her. The casual, flirty boy she had met then was gone, probably swimming around in the copious amounts of alcohol that it appeared Seth had consumed, no doubt hoping to forget that he'd just met his father for the first time.

"Sophie, my name's Sophie—I'm Louis's fiancée—your dad's—"

"Don't say it," Seth said, spreading his fingers wide as he attempted to sit down on the stool next to Sophie, only finding his center of gravity after swaying first one way and then the other.

"It must have been a shock," Sophie said as Seth picked up her drink and polished it off in one gulp before gesturing to the barman to bring him another.

"You could say that," he said, glancing sideways at her. "I mean, look at him! He looks like a lowlife. He turns up at my mum's house and just expects . . . I don't know what he expects. Where the bloody hell has he been for the last twenty years? Nowhere, that's where. I didn't need a dad when I was a kid and I certainly don't need one now that I'm a man. I don't know what she's playing at this time, I really don't . . ."

"Who do you mean—Wendy?" Sophie pressed him, as his eyes wandered back and forth without resting on any one thing. "What do you mean *this time?*"

"It's like I'm an adult now, right? So why does she still treat me like I'm a kid?" Seth asked her. "Springing that on me from out of nowhere when she could have talked to me, told me about him, maybe even asked me what I wanted for once—but no, it's all about her. It always is. And he . . . Louis . . . just turns up like he thinks it's going to be happy families. Screw that!"

"Look, I know it must seem weird, but it's not as if Louis knew anything about you before last week—"

"He's a wanker," Seth said, lurching a little closer to her. "Why are you marrying him? Marry me, I'm younger and the sex will be better."

"Seth, you're really drunk," Sophie said, pushing him ever so gently back into an upright position. "Are you supposed to be staying at your mum's tonight? Maybe you should get a cab back there."

"He'll still be there," Seth growled. "All over her. Bloody idiot."

Sophie felt herself tense with jealousy. Seth was drunk and angry, he didn't mean what he was saying, but she couldn't stop her body from reacting to it.

"I'll ring him if you like, see where he is. I just really think you need to go home, sleep this off, and give yourself a chance to think."

Seth looked at her for a long moment, his dark eyes searching hers. Sophie forced herself to continue meeting his gaze as he scrutinized her, feeling somehow that he was owed at least one person looking him in the eye.

"Okay," he said eventually. "But will you come outside with me? I'm not sure I'll make it to the taxi rank in one piece." His smile was sweet, youthful, and entirely his own. Louis had never smiled at her in that way. Perhaps he'd smiled at Wendy or even Carrie like that, but by the time she'd found him that expression had either faded or been worn away. Sophie guessed it must be the smile that had melted many a young woman's heart, but she relented anyway. This would be good, her helping Seth. This would be a way to insert herself into this family drama so that she could be there for Louis to help and support him. Although as Seth put his arm around her shoulders and leaned his body weight into hers, Sophie realized that this was a particularly heavy piece of baggage.

Outside, Seth leaned against a wall, his chin tipped up as he sucked in the cool night air. Keeping an eye on him, Sophie took a few steps over to the road to find a cab and ring Louis.

The phone rang three times and then went straight to voice mail, which meant that Louis had rejected her call. She stood for a second looking at the phone and thought about calling him again, but if he rejected her call twice in a row, then she would be angry with him, and she still hadn't had a chance to make things right after he'd left for Wendy's earlier that afternoon, distanced from her because of her inability to deal like an adult with what was happening. If she could help Seth, if she could calm him down and persuade him to talk to his father, then that would show Louis she was sticking by him, no matter what his past threw at her, that she loved him come what may.

One thing she could be certain of was that if Louis was rejecting her calls, then he was still with Wendy. And she didn't think she could send Seth home while Louis was there.

"Right," she said, going back to Seth. "Where do you live? In a dorm or something?"

"No," Seth said. "I've got a house with my mates. In Falmouth, I go to art college there." He peeled himself off the wall for a second and then, looking as if he were afraid he might fall, he pinned himself back against it.

"I don't feel so good," he said, looking around him warily.

Sophie thought for a moment. The way she looked at it, there were three options. She could put him in a cab back to Falmouth, but even if the cabdriver would take him the twenty-five or so miles, she wasn't at all sure Seth would be able to remember where he lived or get there without incurring some vomit-related cleaning costs. Or she could send him back home to his mum's anyway, even if seeing Louis again would make things much worse and more difficult for everyone. Briefly Sophie thought of accompanying Seth on this short journey to his mother's house, delivering Wendy's son back to her and reclaiming her fiancé at the same time, but as tempting as that was, she knew it wasn't a good idea.

The last thing Louis needed now was her turning up and demanding he come home with her. She had to give him space, and if while she was doing that she could somehow look after his son, then all the better.

The third option was that she *could* take Seth back to the B & B. After all, Mrs. Alexander was at Louis's house and Sophie knew there were quite a few rooms free. She *could* pay for a single room for Seth to sleep in, feed him coffee and Nurofen in the morning, and then once he'd sobered up try to talk to him about giving Louis another chance. For a few more moments Sophie thought hard about her plan, trying to detect any fatal flaws, but unable to see any she decided to take him back to the Avalon. After all, she was practically his stepmother. He was, in some small way, her responsibility, and by looking after him she was showing Louis that she cared.

Sophie dialed Cal's and then Carmen's number; neither of them answered, so she left a message on Carmen's phone telling her that she was going home and that she'd see them back at the B & B. She could have explained about taking Seth with her, but it would have taken a long time and he was gradually sliding down the wall, like one of those sticky little octopuses that used to be all the rage when she was at school.

"Come on, you," she said, hefting him up. "There's a cab."

"Where'm going?" Seth asked her in a blur. "Don't make me go back there, cos if he's there I'll—"

"No, you're coming back with me," Sophie said.

"Results," Seth said, grinning at her as she folded him into a cab.

"Not in *that* way. I live in a B and B. I'll put you in one of the free rooms so you can sleep it off, and if you want we can talk in the morning."

"Or we could just kiss now," Seth said, sliding his hand up her thigh as she got in the cab next to him. "I like older women, I like older women a lot."

"Seth." Sophie removed his hand from her thigh. "Just so we are clear, I am absolutely, categorically in no way going to kiss you, ever."

"We'll see," Seth said, that same sweet smile curling his lips. And then he passed out.

"That him?" Grace Tregowan asked Sophie as she deposited Seth with some difficulty and a minor back injury onto Mrs. Alexander's rose-printed sofa in the sitting room. "The love child. He's a looker, isn't he? Perfect opportunity for you to trade up."

"Mrs. Tregowan!" Sophie exclaimed. "He's barely more than a boy."

But still it was hard not to admire the sweep of his dark lashes as he lay there with his eyes closed, and the fullness of his lower lip, his mouth slightly open as he slept.

"I tell you," Grace said with a wink. "If I were sixty years younger, I'd teach him a thing or two . . ."

"What are you still doing up anyway?" Sophie whispered as Grace padded after her into the kitchen in her pink fluffy slippers. Sophie planned to risk Mrs. Alexander's disapproval by brewing a strong pot of coffee that was really only meant for the breakfast service (instant after 11 A.M. was the rule).

"The older you get, the less you sleep," Grace said. "I think it's because you know that death is getting closer, and the closer it is, and the less of life you have left, the less of it you want to miss dreaming about times gone by."

"You are going to live forever," Sophie said as Grace settled herself a little stiffly on one of Mrs. Alexander's kitchen chairs. "Hot chocolate?" Sophie offered.

"I shouldn't," Grace said, drawing her bed jacket a little tighter around her shoulders. "But that's never stopped me before, so go on then."

As Sophie switched on the coffee percolator, she took the tub of chocolate powder down from the shelf and heaped several large spoonfuls into two of Mrs. Alexander's mugs.

"How are your wedding plans going?" Grace asked her. "Are you coping with all of the love-child shenanigans and the other thing too?"

"The other thing?" Sophie asked as she took some milk out of the fridge.

"The wondering. Wondering if you're doing the right thing by marrying Louis. That thing."

"But I haven't been wondering about it, not at all," Sophie said as she heated a pan of milk. "If anything, I'm the one who wants to get married, most especially now . . ." Sophie trailed off and thought of the brochure for Fineston Manor, in the drawer with the unread bills. "The funny thing is," she said thoughtfully as she watched the milk, waiting for bubbles to break out on the peaceful surface, "that since all of this happened, I've felt that I might lose him."

"Well, that's obvious," Mrs. Tregowan said. "You met him in a stressful situation, you fell for him during difficult times. When everything seems settled and peaceful, when you have a chance to really listen to your heart, that's when you have doubts. Now everything is kicking off again, there's another drama and another woman to boot, you don't have time to listen or think, and that suits you because now all you have time to do is to try and fix things for him and try to keep him."

"I can't work out if you think that is a good thing or a bad thing," Sophie said, setting Mrs. Tregowan's chocolate on the windowsill to cool. Mrs. Alexander had told her that last year Grace had burned her stomach badly on a drink that had been too hot and too heavy for her arthritic hands. So Sophie and Mrs. Alexander always took care to fill her cups only halfway and wait for the beverage to cool before they gave it to her.

"Well, it's a good thing if you just want to marry him and hang the consequences," Grace said. "But then to feel happy, you'd have to create yourself a drama every few weeks just to drown out your real feelings, and you'd end up on morning telly with that bloody awful man shouting at you."

"That doesn't sound so good," Sophie said, sitting down opposite Grace with her own chocolate as she waited for the coffeepot to fill.

"Better to find a quiet place, away from all of this, and give yourself a chance to listen and feel, because the thing is, Sophie, I don't doubt that you love Louis—it's just that what with all this rushing and panic and drama I don't think you really believe it yet."

"Maybe you're right," Sophie said thoughtfully, tasting the thick chocolate that coated her tongue. "Maybe it would be a good idea for me to get away for a bit. But I don't want it to seem as if I'm running out on him, leaving him and the girls when they need me."

"It would only be for a few days, the girls would barely know you'd gone," Grace said. "And as for Louis, give him a chance to miss you. It never does them any harm. I left my third husband for three months, went to Morocco with this charming young man I met in the supermarket. Meat aisle, it was. I can tell you that Donald appreciated me more than ever when I got back. Every time he looked at me, he thought of me and that young man, which made him really jealous, which in turn made him want me even more. It worked wonders, I can tell you."

Sophie spent several seconds trying to think of something to say, but for once Grace had left her entirely speechless.

"So did you leave this Donald for your last husband then?" she asked, because Grace's love life seemed to cover every kind of marriage there could ever be and Sophie was finding it an invaluable resource when it came to working out what her own marriage would be like.

"No." Grace's smile was rueful. "He had a heart attack in bed one night. I missed him, the poor old bugger, but it was the way he would have wanted to go. I had ten wonderful, passionate years with him, so I can't complain."

"So you would say that you can base a marriage on passion alone?" Sophie asked, thinking that certainly the last few months of hers and Louis's relationship had been based on just that.

"Yes, as long as one of you dies before you stop fancying each other," Grace said. "Otherwise, once the passion wears off, you usually find you hate each other's guts and have nothing to talk about."

It wasn't exactly the answer Sophie was hoping for.

"I'm going to take this coffee to Seth," Sophie said, filling the largest mug she could find. "Want a hand getting to your room?"

"No thank you, love." Grace smiled. "I can get around perfectly well. But if you could hand me my hot chocolate before it goes stone cold that would be lovely."

Sophie paused and looked at Seth, sprawled on the sofa, his head tipped back, his mouth open; he looked disconcertingly like Bella when she was in a deep sleep, given over to unconsciousness with such abandon that you could almost believe she lived her real life in dreams.

"Seth." Sophie crouched down and shook his shoulder lightly. "Seth, I've got you some coffee."

His eyes flickered open and then fixed on her.

"Am I really at your place?" he asked her, his voice dry. "Or did I dream that?"

"You are at the B and B I stay in," Sophie said, setting down the coffee, taking his hand, and pulling him into a near sitting position. "I've booked you a room for the night. You can go and talk to your mum in the morning, when you've got a clear head."

Carefully she handed him the hot coffee. "I put sugar in it, I hope that's okay."

Seth took a sip of the coffee, his hand cupping the mug like Izzy's did when she was drinking hot chocolate. "That's perfect," he told her. "You are very nice, you know. You didn't have to rescue me. You could have left me in the gutter to sober up. I've done it plenty of times before."

"I couldn't do that," Sophie said, smiling, settling into a kneeling position on the floor, leaning her elbow on the seat of the sofa. She had seen two sides of Seth, flirtatious, then angry, and now she was seeing a third. He looked very young, like a blank page, and vulnerable, unprepared for what life might write on him. "Besides, can you imagine if Louis found out that I'd walked away and left you in that state? I'd be so chucked."

Seth sipped the coffee in silence for a moment, looking around at Mrs. Alexander's sitting room through half-closed eyes. Sophie guessed that it wasn't easy to embrace a hangover in a room decorated with flower prints and a menagerie of china animals.

"Why are you going to marry him then?" Seth asked. "I mean, you are a very beautiful, lovely, kind, proper woman. What did he do to get you?"

Sophie mused for a moment on what the phrase "proper woman" meant, but decided it probably had something to do with her age, so she decided not to ask.

"I was looking after his children, my best friend's children. Carrie—my friend—she died and I was the girls' guardian. Louis had been overseas in Peru—"

"Ran away from the kids then," Seth surmised.

"No, well, not exactly—it's a really long story, but the short version is that I thought that about him too. I thought he was a good-for-nothing, low-life loser who abandoned his wife and children and then just turned up years later, thinking everything was going to be all right because now he was ready to play daddy. But then I got to know him, and I found out about his story—his reasons for doing what he did. I realized that he is a great person, a wonderful person. And his daughters found that out too. I think the three of us fell in love with him at the same time."

"He's got you properly taken in," Seth said, shaking his head. "You look so clever too."

"Clever?" Sophie questioned him.

"I mean, you don't look like the sort of woman who'd end up in some backwater, living in a B and B, following a man around. You look like you're your own person."

"I *am* my own person," Sophie insisted. "I chose to come here. It's not like Louis hypnotized me to get me down here."

"That you know of," Seth said, his eyes widening. He and Sophie smiled at each other for a second.

"Let me ask you something," Sophie said. "Louis didn't leave you, he didn't even know about you—not until really recently, and as soon as he knew, he wanted to meet you, he wanted to work out how to be part of your life. So how can you hate him?"

Seth shrugged. "I've never had a dad, not really. Oh, there was Ted, the bloke who was stupid enough to marry my mum, but he didn't stick around for long. And I'm fine about it now, I actually don't give a toss. When I was a kid, that's when it was hard to cope with. You know, the fathers' race at sports day, or the other kids going off to a football game or on a camping trip with their dads? I had my granddad, and he did his best, but it wasn't the same—you know? Not the same as having your own dad around."

"I know," Sophie said, remembering her first Christmas without her dad. But at least she had known exactly what it was that

was missing from her life. Seth had never had a chance to understand that.

"Anyway, *that's* when it hurt, back then. But I got on with
things. Mum did her best, never let me go without, and Nan and
Granddad were always there. I got used to it, came to terms with it.
But I couldn't help but think about him, this man—my father who
Mum told me she had loved very much and who had loved her
back. I used to lie in bed at night and try and imagine him and
wonder why on earth he hadn't come to find Mum, the woman he
loved so much, and his son. I used to wish for him to turn up at the
school gates one day or be on the doorstep, out of the blue, on a
Christmas morning. And he'd fling his arms round Mum and kiss
her and he'd look at me and he'd say, 'Son, I'm never leaving you
again.' And I wondered and wondered if he was lying awake staring at his ceiling wondering about me too.

"But he never turned up at school or came round on Christmas, and as I got bigger I stopped thinking about him. I worked
out for myself how to be a man. And now I'm fine. I got my own
place, I got college, I got the band, my mates, and as many women
as I can get my hands on. I'm happy. And then suddenly there
he is, my dad. There he is suddenly turning up, just like I always
wanted him to." Seth's laugh was mirthless. "And it turns out that
not only has he not been thinking about me, or wondering about
me, it turns out that he didn't even know I existed until a few days
ago, and that all of those hours and days I spent wishing for him as
a kid meant nothing because I didn't even exist for him. You ask
me how I can hate him, and the answer is, I don't know what else
to feel about him, not now. All this, it's ten years too late—I don't
need a dad now and I'm not going to pretend that I do to make
him, my mum, or even you happy."

"I can understand that," Sophie said, resting her chin on her
hand as she looked up at him. "You're in shock, you haven't really

had time to take in what's happened. But you might change your mind if you think about it . . ."

"I don't want to," Seth said with a shrug.

"But you don't know anything about him, not really," Sophie said.

"I don't want to," Seth said, draining the last of his coffee.

"For example," Sophie pressed on, "when he was in Peru he was working for a children's charity—"

"So what if he couldn't be bothered to look after his own kids," Seth interjected.

"And he likes to surf, I bet you do too—"

"Hate it."

"Well, you're studying art, aren't you? Louis—your dad—is building up a photography business. Portraits, landscapes, weddings . . ."

"Weddings? Sellout."

"And he is a good dad . . . his daughters . . . your half sisters, really love him."

"They really love him now, after he comes back into their lives after years of leaving them on their own? They're kids, they don't know any different."

He looked at Sophie again, narrowing his eyes slightly as he examined her. "I bet you had a lot to do with that. I bet you got the kids to like him again, you fixed that mess for him and now you want to fix me, don't you?"

Sophie sat back on her heels and shook her head.

"I wanted his daughters to be happy because I love them, and they are happy now. And I love him, so yes I'd like to help him and you get through this and work out what to do, if you'll let me."

Seth put his empty cup of coffee down on one of Mrs. Alexander's lace doilies that she had told Sophie were there for decoration and were under no circumstances ever to be used. He sat up, and picked up one of her hands as she knelt before him.

"I like you," he said, looking into her eyes. "I'd like you to help me."

"Really?" Sophie was relieved and disconcerted at the same time. "That's great. Just say what you want me to do and I'll . . . oh."

Before she knew what was happening, Seth's fingers were in her hair, drawing her lips to his, and he was kissing her.

For a second, perhaps five, Sophie did not resist; the shock of what was happening disabled her fight-or-flight impulse momentarily. But it was also the heat of the vodka-soaked kiss that pinned her to the spot; it was a very good kiss. Perhaps it was five seconds, maybe ten, that she let Seth kiss her, but in any case it was several seconds too long because she was still a fraction of a second from pushing him away when Cal and Carmen came through the door.

"Oh my giddy aunt!" Carmen exclaimed as Sophie finally broke away. She pointed. "That's not Louis!"

"And when I told you to embrace Louis's baggage, this is not what I meant," Cal added.

Seth sprang out of his seat, still a little unsteady on his feet, and swayed out of the room, crashing into furniture as he lurched toward the door.

"Seth, wait," Sophie called after him. "What about the room?"

"The room?" Carmen repeated, scandalized. "The *room*?"

But Seth didn't speak, he simply found the front door and slammed it behind him, loud enough to dangerously rattle the Doulton figurines on the mantelpiece.

"Oh bloody hell!" Sophie said, sitting on the sofa and burying her face in her hands. "Bloody bloody hell—how did that happen?"

"What exactly *did* happen?" Carmen asked her. "Were you drunk and confused?"

"We were just talking and then he lunged; there was nothing I could do about it," Sophie attempted to explain, trying very hard to get the memory of Seth's fingers in her hair out of her mind.

"It didn't exactly look like there was anything you wanted to do about it," Carmen said.

"That's not true, he took me by surprise, that's all." Sophie looked at Cal, who was looking at her and shaking his head.

"Go on," she said wearily. "Say it."

"Only you," Cal said. "Only you could snog your dead best friend's husband's secret love child. Now what are you going to do?"

Eleven

Sophie had never been unfaithful to anyone in her life and she wasn't quite sure how to handle it. Technically, a kiss lasting only a few seconds, even if it was several seconds longer than it should have lasted, wasn't the worst crime one could commit against a loved one. But as Cal insisted on pointing out to her on several occasions, when that kiss was with your fiancé's son, it put a whole new spin on things.

She had run out after Seth, who had barged past Carmen and Cal and hailed a cab that was passing at the bottom of the street; before she could reach him, the car had pulled away, taking him god knew where. Wearily Sophie had turned on her heel, taking a deep breath of chilled sea air, before she slowly walked back to face her friends and try to explain to them what they had seen.

It had taken a lot of explaining. The three of them had sat up for what was left of the night, Cal and Carmen drinking Mrs. Alexander's Christmas sherry while Sophie made herself hot chocolate after hot chocolate, hoping the sugar rush would help her work out the best thing to do.

At just after 3:00 A.M., Mrs. Alexander came in and found them all in the sitting room, lounging on her best cushions, scattered on the floor, like teenagers who had been discovered having a party when they thought their parents were away.

"Still up?" she said, pressing her lips into a thin line, which meant that she had clocked the coffee ring on her best lace doily.

"Catching up, you know—you don't mind, do you?" Sophie asked her. "We thought it would be better down here than in one of our rooms. We don't want to disturb any other guests. We're being quiet and I'll replace the sherry and wash the . . . doily."

Mrs. Alexander nodded once, which was the nearest Sophie was going to get to an assent. "Well, Louis got back home about twenty minutes ago if you're interested."

Sophie was interested. In the midst of everything that had been happening, she'd forgotten that Mrs. Alexander wouldn't be coming back until Louis got home. He'd been at Wendy's by four thirty that afternoon, and she'd met Seth in the club just before eleven and left shortly afterward. Carmen and Cal had come in at two, and now it was after three. Louis had been on his own with Wendy for the best part of twelve hours. Why had he stayed there so long? Why hadn't he answered her phone call or at least called her back and asked her to relieve Mrs. Alexander? If he'd called her back, if he'd come and helped her with Seth, then her life would be a lot simpler at this point.

"Is he okay?" Sophie asked Mrs. Alexander.

"He was quiet," Mrs. Alexander replied. "Looked drained. Perhaps you should go over and see how he is."

"I've had too much to drink," Sophie lied, nodding at the sherry she hadn't touched. "I'll go in the morning."

"Right then," Mrs. Alexander said, looking disapprovingly at

Carmen and Cal, as if she suspected they might be guilty of a lot more than staying up late and drinking her sherry. "Clear up after yourselves."

"That's going to be harder to do than she knows," Cal said as they heard Mrs. Alexander go up the stairs.

"Just don't ever, ever tell anyone what happened," Carmen said. "It's simple."

"But what if Seth tells someone, what then?" Sophie said. "I'll look like a cradle snatcher, that's what."

"Deny it, deny everything forever," Carmen added. "It'll be your word against his. Besides, I'm the only cradle-snatching woman round here, I don't want you elbowing your way into my territory."

"Look, it won't come to that," Cal said. "The kid was really drunk, there's a good chance he won't even remember what happened, and even if he does, he's going to be so embarrassed he snogged an old bat like you he's never going to want anyone to know."

"Excuse me, but I think kissing an older woman is probably quite impressive," Sophie protested.

"And so does my James," Carmen added with a nod.

"It depends on the older woman, love," Cal said. "Anyway, in the great scheme of things, even though kissing your fiancé's son is potentially the worst thing you could have done, it's not that important. Just go home to Louis in a few hours and act like nothing's happened."

"Like I didn't have Seth here at all?" Sophie asked him.

"Probably for the best," Carmen agreed. "Think of it all as a nightmare . . . or maybe a dream, talking of which—how was that kiss, you looked like you were enjoying it."

"How many times do I have to say this! I was in shock, that's why I didn't pull away immediately." Sophie's voice rose sufficiently to cause her friends to shush her. "And anyway, you're not supposed to lie to your fiancé. If it was okay to lie to your fiancé, then I would never have told Louis about Seth in the first place."

"You do still want to be engaged to him," Cal said, "don't you?"

"Of course I do!" Sophie said. "I love him."

"Then go round later, act like nothing has happened, don't say anything, and play it by ear." Cal cocked one eyebrow. "And try not to snog any other of his relatives on the way."

Sophie paused outside Louis's front door, just as she had six months ago when she'd decided to come down here from London and see if she could make things with him work.

She had hesitated then, unsure of what her reception would be, unsure of how he felt about her. It was strange, given all that had happened and the ring on her finger, that she felt exactly the same way now, six months later.

Taking a breath, she slid her key into the lock and let herself in.

It was early, barely five A.M., and the house was dark and quiet.

Sophie had tried to stay at the B & B until later, to act as if this morning was a perfectly normal Saturday morning and that nothing untoward had happened last night, but she couldn't. After trying to fall asleep for over an hour and failing, spending several minutes instead tossing and turning and looking at the darkness where her ceiling ought to be, Sophie had got up and stood in the tiny shower in her bathroom, her forehead pressed to the textured tiles, the warm water running in rivulets over her shoulders and buttocks. When that didn't seem to calm her, she tried reading a book, even watching what little TV she could find on in the early hours of the morning for a bit, but nothing calmed her, she felt restless and anxious and desperate to see Louis. So she'd woken up Cal and told him where she was going.

"You didn't have to wake me up too," he complained, shoving his head under his pillow.

"I did just in case you wanted to talk me out of it," Sophie whispered to the pillow.

"Okay, don't go now. It's far too early, it will look weird, and anyway, I thought you weren't supposed to be there when the girls woke up until after you're married."

"No, I have to go," Sophie said. "I have to see him, I just have to. Everything is wrong and all pulled apart. If I wait until the sun comes up and it's officially another day, then everything that happened tonight will seem like a dream. It will seem unreal, only it is real. I need to be with him now. I need to be able to touch him and put my arms around him and hear his heart beating and know that we are still just as close as we've always been. I'll get up before the girls do, like I did the other morning. I have to go, Cal, I have . . . Cal?"

"Whatever," Cal mumbled. "Just please let me sleep."

Carefully Sophie set her bag and keys down on the hall table and crept up the stairs. Ever so carefully she pushed open Bella's bedroom door and peeped round to check on her. All she could see was a fluff of dark hair above the duvet, her small body curled up beneath it.

In Izzy's room all was quiet too, although Izzy had flung her covers off and lay there with her arms above her head, knees bent up, one toe pointed, as if she had fallen asleep mid dance step, which, knowing Izzy, was entirely possible.

Then ever so slowly Sophie crept into Louis's room. The room that would one day be their room. He was lying facedown. His clothes were strewn around the foot of the bed as if he had just climbed into bed and fallen right to sleep. Sophie watched him for a second or two in the half-light, sorting out his features from his son's. As she looked at him, her heart in her mouth for fear that he'd wake up and find her there, Sophie realized that the two men actually looked quite different.

Louis's jawline was square, his cheekbones were a little more pronounced, and he had a bump on the bridge of his nose that Sophie loved to run her forefinger over, tracing a path to his beautifully shaped mouth. Seth's face, in comparison, was soft, not yet fully formed, his face more heart shaped, like Wendy's, his nose straight and narrow. He did have his father's coloring though, and his father's beautifully shaped mouth. Sophie took a breath, running her hands through her hair, unsure of what to do next. Should she wake Louis up and try to talk to him? Explain what had happened with Seth? Or perhaps Cal was right. Perhaps she should just turn around and go back to the B & B and wait to see what the dawn would bring.

Then Louis moaned a little in his sleep, the flicker of a smile briefly lighting his face, and he rolled onto his back, exposing his torso. Sophie found she did not want to leave.

Slowly, quietly, she slipped out of her jeans and pulled her T-shirt over her head, shaking her hair out over her shoulders. After a second she unhooked her bra and slipped off her knickers.

In all the times she had been with Louis in this house she had only gotten into this bed with him once, although he'd begged her to join him several times. Sophie had always told herself and Louis that she was waiting for them to be married, waiting for the children to get used to the idea, but as she stood naked on the verge of getting into his bed, she realized that it had been about more than that. This place was a symbol, a final sign of commitment. And recently, when she should have been feeling so close to him and yet felt so far away, it was the only place where she knew how to reach him.

Sophie held her breath, uncertain of how he'd react, and then slowly, gingerly, as if there might be monsters lurking beneath the covers, she eased her way under the duvet, lying on her back next to him, the smooth sheet feeling cool against the heat of her body. Slowly she turned her head to look at his sleeping face, half obscured by the pillow. Wherever he was now he was probably far from the son who didn't want to know him and she wasn't sure he would thank her for taking him back to that world. Sophie bit her lip and looked at the ceiling. She'd never done this sort of thing before, woken a man up for sex. She wasn't exactly sure of the etiquette or procedure. Should she give him a quick prod, she wondered, and then pounce? The shock might give him a heart attack. Should she whisper sweet nothings in his ear until he opened his eyes and smiled at her? Except that despite her lack of experience in spending the whole night with him, Sophie knew that when Louis was out, he was out for the count. Once Bella and Izzy had treated him to an early morning serenade with their Barbie guitars and a set of drums made out of a tin that Bella had found in the garden shed. Louis hadn't turned a hair. He had snored through the whole of their hard-rock rendition of "Love in an Elevator." It had fallen to Bella to fill the toothbrush mug with cold water and tip it over her father's head in a bid to get her audience's attention.

The first thing Bella had said, Louis told her later, when he'd finally stemmed the shocked stream of expletives that had burst out of his mouth, was "Daddy, you are not supposed to swear in front of us."

Sophie tensed as Louis shifted his position again, rolling once more onto his stomach, one arm trapped awkwardly beneath him. At least if she pounced on him now, she'd save him from a terrible case of pins and needles.

There was nothing else for it, Sophie told herself sternly. After all, she was here now, literally naked and in his bed. The only alternative to trying to wake him up was to slip back out of bed and secretly put her clothes back on and leave; and although in the past

Sophie could have been fairly accused of being emotionally cowardly at many points in her life, she was determined that this was not going to be one of them. Sex was the thing that she and Louis were best at. It was the cornerstone of their love for each other. Here in his bed was the place where she would find the intimacy with him that had somehow slipped just ever so slightly out of kilter.

Sophie Mills braced herself for seduction.

Rolling onto her side she slid her hand down his back, stroking her palm gently over his buttocks. She watched his face as a frown flickered between his eyes and faded again. Sidling a little closer so that her breast brushed against his bicep, she repeated the action, stroking his back and bottom and this time softly kissing his shoulder and neck.

Louis's eyes flickered open.

"Wassat?" he murmured, hunching his shoulder against her kiss.

"It's me, Sophie," she whispered. "I missed you. I came to see how you were and whether or not you felt like having sex with me."

Sophie screwed her eyes tightly shut for a second. She really was going to have to work on her sexy-talk skills. Still, as hackneyed as they were, they were effective. Louis was now wide awake.

He rolled on his side to face Sophie, reaching out to trace the curve of her cheek with his fingers.

"Are you really here or is this just a very vivid dream?" he asked her, his voice low and hoarse.

"I don't know," Sophie said, hearing the smile in her voice. "Why don't you pinch yourself and see?"

Louis's arm encircled her waist and he pulled her body flush against his, moaning as her breasts crushed against his chest.

"I think I'll pinch you instead," he said into her neck, his hand cupping her bottom. "God, Sophie, it's so good to see you. How did you know I was missing you?"

"I didn't," Sophie said. "I just knew that I was missing you."

"I'm glad." Sophie felt Louis's mouth curl into a smile against her cheek. "Two nights in a row—does this finally mean you've declared a bed amnesty?" he whispered.

"Yes—and it's getting light, so you'd better make the most of it; I want to be downstairs and fully dressed before the girls wake up," Sophie replied before kissing him so hard that she pushed him onto his back and then she rolled on top of him.

"Oh, Soph," Louis said. "This is the best ever way to wake up."

Sophie smiled into his eyes as she moved on top of him. Here in his arms, in his bed, among his kisses and caresses, everything was perfect, nothing could touch them, they were safe from harm and could keep the outside world at bay for a few hours. As her hand traveled downward between his thighs, she briefly considered that perhaps passion wasn't the best basis for a serious relationship, but it was like Grace had said—as long as one of them died before they got bored with each other, everything would be fine.

"Aunty Sophie, you are in Daddy's bed." Sophie sat up with a jolt, drawing the covers over her breasts, to find Bella, in her pajamas, staring at her in shock.

"Oh god, I went back to sleep," Sophie moaned, more to herself than Bella. She looked at her watch. It was well past nine in the morning, which was the very latest that the girls ever slept.

"That is *Daddy's* bed," Bella repeated. "And you are not married yet—are you?"

Sophie struggled to compose herself and, even more crucially, form a coherent thought.

"No, no . . . um, *yes,* yes—I *am* in Daddy's bed because I was so jolly tired last night, I didn't think I could get back to the B and B without falling asleep on the way, and sooooo . . . Louis . . . Louis, wake up. Wake up *now*."

"What . . . again? Babe, you are amazing, but I am only a man—I need at least another half an hour . . . oh fu . . . flip—hello, Bellarina."

"Sophie is in your bed," Bella stated again, incredulous, as if she couldn't quite believe that no one else realized what was going on.

"Yes, I know," Louis said. "Sophie stayed for a sleepover."

"I'm sorry, Bella, it must be very strange for you to come in and find me here like this, but like Daddy said, I was very tired and decided to sleep over."

"A sleepover, but when?" Bella asked Louis. "Mrs. Alexander was still here when we went to bed and I heard you come in and Aunty Sophie wasn't here then. She wasn't even here when you went to sleep, and I know because when I went to the toilet, I checked on you and she wasn't here then."

Sophie trembled under Bella's concise interrogation technique, but Louis took it perfectly in stride, draping an arm around Sophie's shoulder and smiling at his daughter.

"No, she came for a late sleepover. Sometimes grown-ups have late sleepovers," Louis explained. "It was really more of a practice for when we are married and Sophie will be sleeping in this bed every night and we will get to see her every morning, which will be brilliant."

"Well, it was a bit of a shock," Bella said. "I wasn't expecting it."

"I'm sorry, Bella," Sophie told her. She reached out a hand, and to her relief Bella took it and climbed onto the bed, curling up against Sophie. "It must have been a bit of a shock to find me here this morning. I should have told you I was coming for a sleepover. I promise not to surprise you that way again. In fact, I won't be sleeping over again until after Daddy and I are married, I promise."

"Do you?" Bella and Louis asked at the same time, both looking equally perplexed.

"Apart from the surprise, I don't think I mind you sleeping over," Bella said. "I like it, and if you sleep over, then sometimes I can come and sleep with you like I did in London. Do you remember when we listened to the sound of the traffic and pretended it was waves?"

"I do," Sophie said, recalling how she and Bella had squeezed onto her two-seater sofa and curled up together whenever things got a bit too much for them.

Bella twisted around to look at her, a smile playing around her lips. "Did Daddy snore?"

"Yes." Sophie nodded. "All the time. I've never heard anything so loud in all my life."

"Then sometimes you can come and sleep in my room, because I don't snore. You snore, but only like a cat purring. Me and Izzy say that Dad's snore sounds like a wolf growling!"

"It does, or an elephant with a blocked-up nose," Sophie replied, sending Bella into fits of giggles.

"Hey, you two," Louis protested. "I do not snore."

"You do!" Sophie and Bella giggled together.

"So are you sure you don't mind me being here?" Sophie asked her. "That you're not upset or worried?"

"I like having you for a sleepover," Bella said, suddenly serious. "But it would be more fun if you were in my room. I've got a blow-up *High School Musical* bed, which is designed for the purpose of a sleepover. You wouldn't fit in it, but I would, and you could sleep in my bed, except that Artemis probably wouldn't want to share with you and if she got in my blow-up bed her claws might burst it, so we'd have to shut her in the kitchen with Tango."

"Don't you worry, I'm sure we'll work something out for my next sleepover," Sophie said, kissing the top of Bella's head.

"But for now," Louis said, his fingertip caressing Sophie's thigh under the covers, "how about you run downstairs and get the Coco Pops out—it is a Coco Pops day today, isn't it?"

"No, Daddy, it is a Shreddies day, which you know perfectly well. You don't have to worry. I don't need Coco Pops to make me feel better about Aunty Sophie having a sleepover."

"Right—well, good," Louis said, looking suitably chastened. "How about you run down and get the Shreddies out and I'll be down in a second."

Bella stayed on the bed, nestling into the crook of Sophie's shoulder.

"I'm glad I've got you, Aunty Sophie," Bella said.

"I'm glad I've got you," Sophie said, putting her arms around the little girl and hugging her gently.

"You are my BFF," Bella told her.

"And you're mine," Sophie said, utterly unclear as to what it was she had been told, only that whatever it was, it clearly meant a lot to the child.

"I know," Bella said. She cast a sideways glance at her father. "Daddy, can we just this once have Coco Pops today even though it is not, strictly speaking, a Coco Pops day?"

"Go for it," Louis told her.

She hopped off the bed and ran into the hallway yelling, "Izzy, get up! Aunty Sophie stayed for a sleepover and it's a Coco Pops day!"

"Yay!" Izzy shouted as she thundered down the stairs after her sister a few seconds later.

"That was tricky," Sophie said, lying back on the bed and examining the ceiling. "I was waiting for her to ask me where my pajamas were . . . we shouldn't have put her through that, or Izzy. I'm sorry, I wasn't thinking."

"I thought she was pretty cool about it," Louis said, sliding his hand up across her belly and resting it on her breast.

"I know she acts cool and together, but we shouldn't do this. She's only a little child, they both are. Children who have had a lot to deal with and precious little stability recently, they don't need any more surprises."

"Do you mean finding out you had a sleepover or do you mean Seth?" Louis sighed, withdrawing the warmth of his touch from her body as he flopped onto his back.

"Well . . ." Sophie hesitated. Until that moment the whole of last night had gone out of her head, except for the part where Louis's body had been wrapped around her. Play it by ear, Cal had said. See what happens.

"How did it go with Seth anyway?" she asked him tentatively.

"Badly." Louis rubbed his hands roughly over his face. "It went really badly. Wendy said we should come right out with it, no beating around the bush, she said. So he turned up to find me sitting in his living room—and when I saw him, Soph . . . it was so weird. I wasn't sure how I was going to feel, but I thought I'd feel something—like a spark of recognition, something in my chest, you know, that pulling feeling you get when you look at the girls. When I came back from Peru, I hadn't seen Bella for so long, or Izzy ever, but the second I set eyes on them, it was there, that ache that tells you you love them. But I sat there and I looked at this . . . this *man* and I . . . well, there was nothing there. And he must have seen that in my face, he must have known."

"So what happened?"

"It was like I said, he walked in, saw me sitting there, and Wendy said, 'Seth, this is Louis. Louis is your father,' just like that. For a second or two he was quiet, just looking at her and then me, and then he said, 'I don't have a father, I have never had a father, and I don't need one now. He's about twenty years too late.'

"And he walked out without a second glance. I met my son for less than ten minutes and we didn't speak two words to each other."

"It does seem a pretty brutal way to break the news to him," Sophie said. "It must have been a shock—like Bella finding me here this morning. I don't think I'd react much differently."

"Wendy said it was best," Louis said, shrugging. "She said he appreciated her being straight and open with him, and after all, she's the one who knows him, not me."

"So what happened after he left?"

"Well, Wendy had cooked, so I stayed and ate and we talked some more. Talked about the past, talked about Seth—tried to work out what to do."

Sophie tried not to imagine Louis and Wendy sitting across a table that was, of course, candlelit as they talked over that glorious summer of love they had spent in each other's arms. This wasn't about Louis and Wendy, this was about Seth, and she had to remember that or otherwise she'd drive herself mad.

"What are you going to do?" she asked.

"Wendy thinks I should go to his college in Falmouth, try to talk to him again, but I wonder if he needs a bit of space? Like he said, he's done without a dad for twenty years, and now I turn up and what have I got to offer him? It's not as if he needs anyone to teach him how to ride a bike or play football in the park." Sophie felt a pang as she thought of what Seth had told her last night before the kissing incident. Of how he'd longed for a father to do just that with him.

"Maybe I should just let him know I'd like to meet him again," Louis went on. "Let him know how to get in touch with me and then give him some space to get used to the idea—what do you think?"

"I really think that would be the best thing," Sophie said, thinking of the look on Seth's face last night. "I really think he'd appreciate knowing that you are thinking about him."

Louis looked uncertain. "But then again, Wendy is his mum, she should know best. If she thinks I should really go for it, really try and make a relationship with him now, then maybe I should do that . . . I don't want him to think I don't care even if—the fact is, Sophie, I haven't known him long enough to know if I do care about him. And if he's angry and resentful, then whose fault is that? It's mine. I've screwed up the life of a boy without ever knowing about it, and right now, right this moment, I'm finding it really hard to feel anything."

"You should do what you think is best," Sophie said, expressing her thoughts before she had a chance to censor them. "Maybe Wendy's got other reasons for wanting you to hang around so much, maybe she's not just thinking about Seth . . ."

"Like what?" Louis turned to look at her, impatience threaded in his tone.

"Like she likes having you in her life again, like she wants a reason to keep seeing you." Sophie was painfully aware of how irrational and foolish she sounded.

"Don't be ridiculous," Louis said, suddenly springing out of bed and scooping up his clothes from the floor. "I don't know why you have such a problem with Wendy. I thought you'd admire her, if anything. She's a single mother who's brought up her son, my son, on her own for twenty years and who just wants him to have the chance to know his father. What is your problem with that, Soph?"

Sophie wriggled awkwardly on the bed, suddenly feeling vulnerable in her nakedness and hurt that Louis was so quick to defend his ex against the woman he was going to marry. She knew what she should say, she should say that she didn't have a problem with Wendy, that she was just being silly, but she couldn't ignore her instincts.

"I just don't trust her," she told him despite herself.

"Why ever not?" Louis exclaimed, pulling up his jeans. "Last night, Wendy and I agreed to think things through and then talk again in a few days. Does that sound unreasonable to you? Does that sound like she's looking for excuses to get me to 'hang around'?"

"No, but . . . Louis, please don't be angry with me, I'm just trying to look out for you!"

"You know, if you stopped trying to 'look out for me,' then our lives would be a lot simpler right now," Louis said.

The two of them looked uncertainly at each other across the bed. Just then the doorbell sounded and the relief on Louis's face was clear.

"Girls, don't answer the—" Louis grabbed a T-shirt and ran to the stairs, but it was already too late. Bella had opened the front door.

"Dad," she called up the stairs. "That woman Aunty Sophie doesn't like is here."

Twelve

Hi, Wend." Sophie heard Louis greet his ex, all too aware that he was dressed in only his jeans, and was pulling his T-shirt on over his head as he headed down the stairs. "Hey, Bellarina, why don't you and Izzy watch your programs on the kitchen TV for a bit?"

"I don't want to," Bella replied. "I want to stay here and listen to you and find out about this strange woman."

"Well, this isn't a conversation for little girls, so go and watch TV please."

"Yes, but you see . . ." Sophie could hear from the tone in Bella's voice that she was in full negotiation mode. Normally Louis loved to engage her in her lengthy sometimes logically skewed but always entertaining debates about why she should be able to do whatever it was that he didn't want her to do. About 50 percent of the time she'd win him over. But Louis was not in the mood today and his tone was stern.

"Bella, do as I ask. *Now.*"

There was a pause and then Sophie heard Bella in the kitchen saying very loudly to Izzy, "We're going to watch cartoons even though they rot our brains."

Like Bella, Sophie was unable to resist the temptation to find out what was going on. But even though she didn't think Louis could send her away to watch cartoons, she was also fairly sure he'd want to talk with Wendy on his own. Quietly she crept out of bed, dragging the heavy duvet around her body and creeping to the edge of the stairs where she could just see the tops of Wendy's and Louis's heads without giving away her own position.

"So how is he?" Louis asked her, a reluctance in his voice, as if he didn't want to know the answer.

"I don't know, that's the problem." Wendy sounded upset, her voice shaky and strained. Sophie hazarded leaning over the banister, hoping to catch a glimpse of the other woman's face and try to discern if her expression matched her tone. But Wendy's head was bowed, her hair screening her features. Sophie could see Louis's hand on Wendy's shoulder. Only moments ago his long fingers had been caressing her thigh.

Sophie dropped the duvet at the top of the stairs and darted back into the bedroom, plucking her clothes off the floor where she had discarded them what now seemed like a lifetime ago. Hurriedly she slipped on her underwear, straining to hear the continuing conversation below, hurrying back to the banister in bare feet, the rest of her clothes tucked under her arm in a bid not to miss anything crucial.

"I haven't heard from him since he stormed off last night," Wendy was saying. "He's not answering his cell phone. None of his friends seems to know where he is. I thought he might have gone back to Falmouth, but no one there has heard from him. He gets . . . very emotional when he's upset." Sophie pulled on her jeans certain that the rasp of denim over her thighs could be heard in Penzance, never mind at the bottom of the stairs. "I don't know where he is, Louis. I'm really worried about him—anything could have happened."

Sophie held on to the banister as she pulled on first one sock and then the other. She knew; she knew where he had been at least up until two A.M. this morning, up until the point when he had kissed her.

"He'll be okay," Louis reassured Wendy. Sophie watched as he drew her into a hug, her chest tightening as she saw his arms around another woman. "It's not as if he's a kid. He can look after himself."

"I know." Wendy's voice was muffled by Louis's shoulder and Sophie knew exactly the scent that Wendy would be breathing in—a mixture of sweat and sex and the last traces of yesterday's aftershave. "It's just like I said, sometimes he can be a bit rash—acts before he thinks. He's got a temper on him, he gets really angry and self-destructive. When this girl he really liked broke up with him last summer, he went out on a bender and ended up in a fight with three other men. He got four broken ribs and a dislocated knee." Sophie heard Wendy take a ragged breath. "What if he's in some gutter somewhere?"

"Okay . . ." Louis hesitated and Sophie knew he was trying to work out exactly how worried he should be. "Have you rung the hospital? Police stations?"

"No. I couldn't bring myself to do it. That's why I came here." Sophie couldn't see her but she just knew that at that precise moment, Wendy was looking up at Louis with tear-stained blue eyes. "Perhaps I shouldn't be bothering you with this now, but I didn't know who else to turn to—I hoped we could do it together?"

Sophie's heart sank; she was going to have to tell them that she *had* seen Seth, and he *had* been very drunk and in a brawling mood. If it hadn't been for the fact that she had seen Seth and experienced his rash behavior with her own eyes, and even lips, then she would have thought Wendy was making the whole thing up, or at least exaggerating the situation just to get close to Louis. The hot, raw, and irrational part of herself still felt that way. But Wendy didn't need to make up complications to get to Louis, if that was what she wanted. She had his son, and that was reason enough.

Despite her mixed feelings toward Wendy, a mixture that consisted of one part hatred, two parts loathing, and one part irritation, she could not withhold information about a child from his mother, not even when the child was twenty years old and had recently made a pass at her. Sophie might have been new to motherhood, she might have experienced it only by proxy, but she knew how worrying about the children you loved could tear you to shreds and found she couldn't let Wendy go through that. As she thought about how she'd feel if Bella or Izzy was lost, she was all at once overwhelmed with an unexpected empathy for Wendy, an emotional upswell that tightened her chest and made tears spring to her eyes.

Brushing the tears away, she took a breath and descended the stairs.

"Oh, you're here," Wendy said when she saw Sophie.

"Yes—look, I couldn't help overhearing," Sophie said, fighting to keep her voice steady and free of emotion. "My friend Cal was down last night from London and he wanted to go clubbing, so he, Carmen, and I all caught a cab into Newquay for a bit of an early hen night, although there weren't any hens to speak of and—"

"And what's that got to do with anything?" Wendy asked impatiently.

Sophie fought hard to maintain her empathy for the world's most annoying woman.

"If you'll let me finish . . . We went to a nightclub and I saw Seth—"

"You *saw* him?" Louis asked her, his tone incredulous. "You saw Seth and you are only telling me this *now?*"

"I know, I was going to tell you, but I didn't exactly have time what with one thing and another . . ." Sophie hazarded a small smile. She knew that wasn't true. She could have, should have told him about seeing Seth as soon as she had woken him up this morning. "Anyway, the point is, I saw him and he was really drunk and pretty angry, so—"

"Why didn't you call me?" Louis challenged her, exasperated.

"I did, but you weren't picking up," Sophie snapped back, incredulous that suddenly she had to defend herself.

"You could have left a message," Louis countered.

"I would have, but I thought it was best to get your son out of the road before he got flattened by a taxi." Sophie felt cornered but took a breath and pressed on, determined to deliver the information she had, even if it was a little late. "Like I said, he was really drunk, angry—a bit punchy. He tried to pick a fight with this guy, and I thought it was best to get him out of there before he got into any trouble. But he refused to go back to Wendy's and I didn't think I'd find a cab that would take him all the way to Falmouth or that he'd be able to remember where he lived when he got there so . . . so I took him back to the B and B to sober up." Sophie rushed out the last part of the sentence in the vague hope that Louis and Wendy wouldn't hear and she'd be able to gloss over that.

"You did what?" Wendy asked her. "You took my son back to your B and B? What for?"

"To sober him up, what else?" Sophie replied, the memory of that foolish kiss weakening the conviction in her voice somewhat.

"Wait a minute." Louis ran his fingers through his hair, which was still tousled from sleep and sex. "I need a second to get my head around all of this. You knew all of this and you didn't tell me? I don't get it, Sophie. Why didn't you tell me?"

"I don't know," Sophie lied. "I suppose I was waiting for the right time. I'm sorry, okay? I should have told you sooner, but I'm telling you now."

"So is he there now?" Wendy demanded. "Is he still at the B and B?"

"Um, well, no . . ." Sophie felt her heart sink; not only had she withheld information from worried parents, she also now had to break the news that she had single-handedly lost Seth again. "He fell asleep on the sofa while I was making him coffee, but when I woke him up he seemed a lot better, a lot more together. He drank the coffee and we were having a bit of a chat about things when . . ." Play it by ear, Cal had said. He hadn't figured on two recently reunited, not to mention angry, parents hanging on her every word. It was definitely not a good idea to mention that Seth had kissed her and that she had been slow in breaking off the kiss. On the other hand, it was an excellent idea to never ever mention the kiss and to pray hard that Seth was either too drunk to remember it or too mortified to ever want to mention it again.

"When what?" Wendy asked.

"When he got angry again. He stormed off just as Carmen and Cal came back from the club. I went after him, but he'd got in a cab before I could reach him, and besides, I don't think he would have wanted to talk to me anymore." Not with the whole attempted snog thing, Sophie thought.

"And what time was this?" Louis had his hands on his hips the way they had been when Izzy had decided to paint his white Renault with her poster paints to cheer it up a bit.

"Just after two," Sophie told him reluctantly. "But at least we know he'd sobered up a bit and slept off some of what he'd drunk by then. I bet you the only reason he's not answering his phone is because he's sulking."

Louis looked as if he were about to say something that Sophie really didn't want to hear when there was a shriek from the kitchen and the clatter of cereal bowls on the kitchen tiles.

"Dadd*eeeeeeeee*," Izzy yelled in the tone that usually indicated she had sustained some minor injury that required rubbing or kissing immediately. "I've fallen off my stool *again*!"

"She has," Bella confirmed. "And a bowl is broken."

"I'm coming, poppet." Louis looked from Wendy to Sophie, his face strained and tense. "Go into the living room. I'll sort the girls and I'll be back in a second."

Sophie glanced warily at Wendy as she led her to the living room and indicated that she should sit on the sofa where not so long ago she and Louis had been having unbridled and carefree sex.

"Look, Wendy," Sophie began, attempting to build some kind of bridge. "I *should* have said something sooner about seeing Seth, but please believe me when I tell you I was only trying to help him."

"Trying to interfere more like," Wendy muttered, staring out of the window at the metallic gray day.

"No, not at all. The poor boy was really shocked—I just wanted to help him."

"Why?" Wendy's head snapped round and Sophie got the full benefit of her Medusa glare. "What has any of this got to do with you?"

Sophie was no longer able to prevent the exasperation that Wendy inspired in her from slipping into her voice. "If it wasn't for me, Louis still wouldn't know a thing about Seth, and besides, I am marrying him. This has got everything to do with me."

"Oh yes, that's right. I forgot," Wendy said, a mirthless smile on her lips.

"Forgot what?" Sophie asked her.

"Louis told me all about you last night, he told me everything.

How you moved in on your dead friend's life, like a vulture. Picking off her husband, her kids—even her home. What's your problem, Sophie? Can't you get a life on your own? Did you really have to wait for someone to die before you could get a man?"

"You *bitch*." Sophie growled the word, the full force of her fury boiling over in her guts. "How dare you judge me. You know nothing about me. Nothing about what Carrie and I meant to each other, and you certainly have no idea what Louis and I went through together and how much we love each other and those children."

"I know that barely more than a year has passed since your so-called best friend died and you're marrying her husband and taking her kids. Well, you can forget about trying to do the same thing with me. Seth is mine and Louis's, and our son hasn't got anything to do with you."

"Yours and Louis's?" Sophie's laugh was harsh. "Funny how now, after twenty years, he's suddenly yours and Louis's. What's changed, Wendy? Why so territorial now when only last week you were asking me not to tell Louis anything and forget I ever met Seth."

"But you did tell him, didn't you," Wendy hissed. "You did tell him even though I warned you that you would be sorry if you did."

"What do you mean?" Sophie asked impatiently. "How am I going to be sorry for telling Louis the truth?"

"I've been on my own for a long time now." Wendy's smile was icy cold. "I'm still young. And I was the first girl Louis ever loved; that's a powerful thing. Besides, unlike you, I actually am the mother of one of his children."

"What?" Sophie was aghast. "Wendy, wake up! Surely you don't think you can just waltz in here and break up Louis and me just to get back at me for telling him about Seth? A week ago you didn't want anything to do with him."

"But now I do," Wendy said. "And he wants something to do with me too, I can see it in his eyes."

Unaware that she had moved, Sophie found herself leaning over Wendy, her finger pointing millimeters from her face.

"Well, you can forget it," she threatened Wendy, her voice low and dark. "Because if you think that I am going to let a jumped-up, manipulative little tart like you anywhere near—"

Sophie crashed to a halt as Louis opened the door, his eyes blazing as he caught Sophie bent over Wendy, her face transformed by fury. Wendy's face crumpled. "Please stop attacking me, Sophie. I'm only trying to look out for my son."

"What's going on, Sophie?" Louis asked. "Leave her alone."

"But I . . ." Sophie straightened up, feeling her cheeks flushing. "Louis, this is ridiculous. You didn't hear what she was saying to me."

"All I want is to find out where our son is," Wendy sputtered. "I thought that as Sophie has already kept so much information from us, she might be able to tell us a bit more."

"Louis—that's not it, she was saying stuff about us, about Carrie!" Sophie looked at Louis, but his face was blank, shuttered off, as if he simply couldn't absorb any more information.

"Look, I think you'd better go," he said. "Let Wendy and me sort things out here."

"*Me?* I've got to go?" Sophie was incredulous.

"I think it's for the best," Louis said, looking at his shoes. "I'll call you later."

"Fine, if you want me to go, then I will go." Sophie heard the warning in her voice and wondered if Louis heard it too.

Suddenly the door slammed open and the girls appeared in the doorway looking around the room wide-eyed, hoping to find answers in the adults' faces.

"Why are you shouting?" Izzy asked, one or two Coco Pops still glued to her cheeks, her usually sunny disposition clouded. "Is this lady being mean to Aunty Sophie?"

"No, no, not at all," Sophie said as she held out her hand to Izzy, aware that she was countering her own story to calm the child. "No, we're not shouting, we're just worrying."

"Worrying?" Izzy asked, going to her.

Sophie sat down in the armchair that normally only the cats used and pulled Izzy into her lap. The child's eyes were filled with anxiety. "Is someone dead again?"

"No." Sophie pressed Izzy's tousled head into her shoulder and kissed her hair. "No one is dead and no one is going to die, I promise."

"You can't promise that," Bella told her, eyeing her father and Wendy warily as she went to join Sophie and Izzy, squeezing into the chair, next to Sophie.

"Bellarina, sweetheart, don't worry," Louis said, crouching down next to the armchair. He put one hand on Sophie's knee and brushed Bella's bangs out of her eyes with the other. "Everything is fine."

Bella tossed her head, brushing off his touch.

"You told Aunty Sophie to go," she stated bluntly. "We heard you."

"Only because I have some important things to talk to Wendy about," Louis said, trying to explain.

"What things?" Bella asked him.

"Things you don't have to worry about."

Bella and Izzy exchanged glances. Izzy leaned back against Sophie's shoulder and stuck her thumb in her mouth, her left-hand finger winding its way into her curls just as it always did when she was either worried or tired.

"We need to know things. Don't not tell us things," Bella said unhappily. "Is everything changing again?"

"No, no, nothing is changing," Louis assured her despite the look that Sophie gave him over Izzy's head. "Sophie is just going back to the B and B for a bit, aren't you, Soph?"

Even as she opened her mouth to affirm the statement, Sophie thought of the conversation she had had with Grace last night and her suggestion that Sophie take a break for a few days to clear her head. Feeling cornered by Louis and Wendy, Sophie suddenly couldn't think of anything she wanted more than to get away from all of this. She looked into Bella's eyes and shook her head, saying, "No."

"Yes you are, because Wendy and I have a few things to talk about, remember?"

"I know," Sophie said, careful to keep her tone even and calm. "Don't worry, I'll get out of your way. But I think I'll be going back to London with Cal for a few days. I've got a lot of things I need to sort out down there and now seems like a good time for me to go."

"Sophie, I didn't mean you had to . . . ," Louis began.

"No!" Izzy exclaimed, wrenching her thumb from her mouth. "No, you can't go, Aunty Sophie."

"I don't get it," Louis said. "That's not what I meant. You don't have to go back to London."

"Don't I?" Sophie asked him. "This is clearly something you need to sort out with Wendy on your own without me around interfering. I wanted to try and help but . . . you don't want me here. So I will get out of the way. And anyway, I need time to think."

"Think?" Louis and Bella said simultaneously.

"What about?" Louis asked her, his voice serrated with frustration. "Come on, Sophie, this is just silly, you're seriously overreacting—I mean seriously, you have to do this now?"

"Don't you love us today?" Izzy asked her unhappily. "Is that why you're going away?"

"No—I do, I do love you. I love all of you so much. But a lot has happened recently and it's all happened so fast that I haven't had time to think. I just need a little time to think. To breathe."

"But you are going to come back, aren't you?" Bella asked her. "You will definitely come back?"

Sophie looked into her eyes and felt the weight of a promise she'd made to her months earlier. She had promised Bella she would be there for her always, forever, whatever.

How everything had disintegrated so quickly from this morning in Louis's bed to this moment Sophie could not fathom, but that was exactly what had happened. All the rushing, she realized, all the excitement and the urgency to be married to Louis had been her attempt to prevent this, her desperate attempt to make their relationship into something solid and genuine before reality came crashing in and smashed their bubble to pieces, and suddenly the truth and strength of their feelings for each other would be tested. Now that they had real problems to deal with, she wasn't at all sure their relationship could stand it. Louis's asking her to leave didn't reassure her.

"Can you give us a minute please?" she asked Wendy without looking at her.

"But what about Seth—" Wendy began.

"Wendy, just wait in the kitchen," Louis told her without taking his eyes off Sophie.

Seeing that she no longer had Louis's attention, Wendy complied, closing the living room door softly after her.

Louis turned to his daughters. "Girls, please go upstairs so that Sophie and I can have a talk."

"But, Daddy—"

"Please, just go."

Bella whispered something in Izzy's ear and after a moment the pair left hand in hand, closing the door behind them.

"Sophie," Louis said, gently taking her hands in his. "You're angry with me and you've a right to be. I shouldn't have asked you to go. Look, nothing's changed. I still love you. All this—it's got nothing to do with you and me."

"It does, it has everything to do with you and me and how you see me in your life," Sophie told him. "I'm supposed to be your wife soon, the person who is always by your side and yet—Louis, you never talk to me, you never tell me anything about yourself unless I drag it out of you, and as soon as Wendy turns up on the scene, I might as well not exist . . ."

"Don't tell me you're jealous of Wendy?" Louis asked, incredulous. "For god's sake, Sophie, grow up! Wendy and I were over twenty years before I even met you. This isn't about her, it's about—"

"You might not think it's about her, but she certainly does," Sophie said bitterly. "And yes, I am jealous of Wendy, I am jealous of every second, every minute of your past that I don't know about, because it means that I don't know you. I really don't know you at all. And besides," Sophie went on, "you need to work out what to do about Seth . . . we both need some time."

"But you are coming back?" Louis asked her anxiously. "You are coming back to marry me on New Year's Eve?"

Sophie looked at him, removing the fingers of her right hand from his so that she could rest her palm against his cheek, feeling the stubble graze her tender skin.

"You haven't booked it yet," she said simply.

"I'll book it now, right now," Louis said. "I'll make the call now."

"There are more important things you need to do first," Sophie told him.

"I want to marry you, Sophie," Louis said. "You do still want to marry me, don't you?"

"I don't know," Sophie said very softly. "I know that I am so in love with you and that I love Bella and Izzy more than anything. But honestly? I don't know yet if the way we love each other is enough, if it's strong enough or real enough to make a marriage work."

"I can't believe this is happening," Louis said. "Only a few hours ago we were—"

"Please don't go, Aunty Sophie." Izzy spoke softly from the front hallway. Bella was standing next to her. "Please can we still get married? I want to wear my wings."

"I know," Sophie said, walking over to the girls. "And I'm so sorry, darling, but I have to go." She cupped Bella's cheek in the palm of her hand. "You understand, don't you, Bella?"

Bella looked at her for a long moment and then ever so slowly shook her head.

"This is all your fault," she said to Louis without a trace of anger or childish petulance. "You've ruined everything again."

She pulled away from Sophie and raced up the stairs, the pounding of her feet the only external clue to how she was feeling. Louis turned his back on Sophie.

"Right," Sophie said, a sense of unreality washing over her as she kissed Izzy on the head. "I'll see you really soon and you can call me anytime. Remember my number?"

Izzy automatically recited Sophie's cell phone number, which she had taught both girls during the summer when all the beaches were packed with holidaymakers and it would have been very easy for a small person to get lost.

"Good girl. I'll see you soon."

"How soon?" Izzy asked. "How long will you need to think? Do you think you will have finished thinking by Wednesday afternoon?"

"I don't know," Sophie said. "I'm not sure."

"But you will come back?"

"Of course."

"To live forever and be our . . . ," Izzy started, then stalled.

"What, sweetheart?" Sophie asked her, glancing at Louis, whose shoulders were hunched as he stared out the window.

"Be our sort of mummy," Izzy finished, looking anxious, as if she'd just asked for something she knew she was not allowed.

Sophie pressed Izzy's small body into hers and held her close until, as she always did, she wriggled to be free.

"I will always, always be there to look after you in every way that your mummy would have, I promise," Sophie told her.

"Yes, but . . . if you don't marry Daddy, then there won't be any rings and I won't be able to say it, will I?"

"Say what, sweetheart?" Sophie asked her.

"Say 'Mummy' to you," Izzy told her, unable to look her in the eye.

"I am coming back." Sophie felt her throat tighten. "I'll speak to you tonight. Now go and give Bella a hug from me and tell her I love her."

Sniffing and wiping her nose on the back of her hand, Izzy padded up the stairs.

"I'll call you tonight," Sophie said to Louis's back. He turned and crossed the room in one stride, catching her in his arms and pulling her to him.

"I love you, Sophie, and you love me. Please don't go."

It took Sophie a huge effort of will to take a step back from his arms.

"When you got back from Peru, you wanted everything to be okay again as quickly as you could make it happen. You wanted to win over the girls, you wanted a job, a home . . . and maybe you wanted me because I was the nearest thing to Carrie that the girls— that you—were ever going to get."

"No, that's not it at all," Louis told her. "I wanted you because you are strong and kind and the most beautiful woman I have ever seen. Because I fell for you, because you make me a better man. I want to marry you because I love you with all of my heart. But if you don't want to marry me, then . . . I don't think I could be with you knowing that you didn't feel the same way."

Sophie took a breath, feeling as if something inside her was tearing ever so slowly.

"Look, I know I shouldn't have let Wendy push you out—"

"No, you shouldn't have. Look, the last six months have been intense and wonderful and magical, but I don't know if they have been real. I think we both just need a bit of space to find out how we really feel."

"I know how I feel," Louis protested.

"I've got to go." Taking a step forward, Sophie kissed Louis on the cheek. "Please tell the girls about Seth, they need to know they can trust you; if they find out some other way, then I don't know how they will react."

"It feels like you're going forever," Louis said as she headed toward the door. "Are you going forever?"

Sophie didn't know what to say, so she closed the front door behind her without saying anything.

Thirteen

There is actually no good reason why I can't stay with you," Sophie said as she and Cal drove into London just after eight that evening.

"Yes there is; my flat is very small and you are very large," Cal said.

"I'd let you stay with me," Sophie said miserably. "God, I miss my flat. I wonder if the woman I let it to is in . . . maybe I could go round, you know, for an inspection or something, and then maybe we could become best friends and then maybe she would invite me to stay with her. I did leave her a very nice sofa . . ."

"I think legally that would be tenant harassment. Sophie, accept it, you don't really live anywhere and the one time I come miles and miles to visit you on a mission of highly uncharacteristic mercy, you end up kissing your dead best friend's ex-husband's secret love child by mistake and I have to go home again the very next day. Some holiday."

"Why do you have to do that?" Sophie complained as she pulled up at yet another set of red lights. "Why do you have to sum up my entire life like it's a tabloid headline? This is really hard for me, you know, to leave him and the girls behind like that—I didn't want to leave, but what else could I do? I couldn't just stay there feeling like an impostor in my own relationship, could I?"

"No, you couldn't," Cal said. "You did the right thing getting away for a bit. Louis loves you, he's just not used to loving you yet, if you know what I mean."

"I have no idea what you mean," Sophie said anxiously as she cut off an SUV to change lanes. "What *do* you mean?"

"I mean that for the last three years he has been his own man, he's had no one to answer to except himself. Then he comes back to the UK and before he knows it he's got two daughters and a fiancée to think about."

"Yes, but he's got us because he wanted us, because he fought for us," Sophie protested. "I didn't force him to propose to me."

"I know," Cal replied. "And that's not what I'm saying. What I'm saying is that when you're in a relationship, you have to adjust. You have to find different ways to live your life. After he left Carrie, before he found the girls and you, he dealt with everything alone. And he hasn't yet had a chance to get used to the fact that you are part of his life. That his problems are your problems and vice versa. He's still flying solo because that's what he's used to," Cal said.

"Do you really think that's what it is?" Sophie asked him. "That it is all just a bit too much too soon?"

"I think that's part of it, and I think with you out of the picture for a while he'll have a chance to miss you and think about things and I reckon you'll be back on for the wedding before you know it."

"But should we be?" Sophie asked him. "I wanted it all so badly, so quickly. I wanted to rush it . . . why? Why was it so urgent?"

"Because you didn't want to waste another second of your life without the love of your life by your side?" Cal ventured.

"Or because deep down I knew that none of this was real. What if I knew that it was nothing more than a glorified holiday romance?"

"Sophie, that's not how you feel. You love that man. That man loves you; you just need to work it out, okay?"

Sophie took her eyes off the road for a second to glance at Cal.

"Hang on a minute, where have all the witty one-liners and put-downs gone? Why are you so sincere all of a sudden?"

"I'm not, I just want you two to work out. There's got to be at least one couple on the planet destined for happiness, and if it's not me then I want it to be you."

"Cal, that's the nicest thing you've ever said to me."

"Unless it's me, then I don't care about you," Cal added with a smile.

When Sophie arrived at her mother's house, Iris welcomed her warmly. "If it helps, I think you've done the right thing, giving yourself some space," Iris said. "If you aren't sure about marrying Louis and you need to think about it, then why shouldn't you come home to your mother?" She paused and put her hand on Sophie's shoulder. "In fact, I'm glad it's me you've come home to."

Sophie felt glad too as she followed her mother up to her old room.

"Now, you'll need to find some clean sheets and shove Inky and Tipex off the mattress. They've been snuggling up in there for a while now, so it might need a brush down with a clothes brush and a squirt of Febreze."

"What's for dinner?" Sophie asked her, hearing the question echo from twenty years ago.

"Oh, darling, I'm sorry." Iris opened her bedroom door. "You'll have to fend for yourself, I've got to go out in a minute. I would cancel . . . it's just I've—well, I've got a date."

"A date?" Sophie said, testing the word on her tongue. It was unfamiliar in relation to her mother.

"Yes, dear, it's this man I met through the dog shelter. His name's Trevor. It's early days, you know, but he makes me smile. Is it awful for me to go out and leave you? It's just that this is only our second date and I thought if I canceled on him now he might think I've got cold feet and I haven't. My feet are decidedly warm."

"No, god no—you go, Mum," Sophie said. "Don't change your plans just because of me. I'll order in takeaway."

"We'll talk when I get back," Iris told her, kissing her on the forehead just like she had when Sophie was a very small girl.

Sophie's old room was not the comforting haven she had hoped for. Perhaps it would have been odd if it had still boasted the Manic Street Preachers poster and the black lace shawls that she had taken to hanging over the lamp shade in order to look a bit more Gothic, but still, she had hoped for the sense of sanctuary that the room had afforded her when she was a girl and needed a place to hide. After her father died her bedroom had suddenly become her whole world, a cocoon where she could plunge herself into the music she loved, curl up on her bed, and forget everything that hurt or confused her, which had seemed to be everything back then. She and Carrie had spent so many hours in this room talking about sex or what they thought they knew about sex in hushed voices, laughing over the problem pages in *Just Seventeen* magazine, and discussing every single boy they knew in exhaustive detail. It was here they had made promises to each other, here they had formed the bond that would one day lead Sophie into the path of Louis Gregory. It was in this twelve-by-eight-foot room with a window that Sophie's life had really begun.

Somehow it seemed an inauspicious place for a beginning, particularly as the room was cold—the radiator had obviously not been switched on in years—and smelled faintly of mildew and strongly of dog. With a heavy heart Sophie pulled on the same faded quilt decorated with pink and white hearts that she had used as a girl and wondered why she had insisted on coming back to London when she could just have gone back to the B & B where Mrs. Alexander would have made her hot chocolate and Mrs. Tregowan would have told her about her fourth husband and she could have watched TV until she'd fallen asleep.

Sophie never thought she'd feel nostalgic for her tiny B & B room, her twin beds and candlewick bedspread, but just at that moment she was homesick for the Avalon, for St. Ives and its constant cry of gulls. That room had felt like a place for a new beginning.

Carmen had told her not to leave.

Sophie had been throwing things into a suitcase while simultaneously brushing tears from her eyes, while Carmen and Cal sat side by side on her spare twin bed.

"I'm just saying," Carmen had pointed out. "If this Wendy is as crafty as you say she is, then why are you going now and leaving her an open field? You should be decking her. I'll deck her for you, if you like. You don't diss a Chelmsford girl or her mates and get away with it, not unless you don't like having teeth. Better still, give me her address, I'll send her a cake laced with rat poison."

"Can I just say," Cal interjected, "I'd still eat one of your éclairs even if I knew it was going to kill me."

"Thank you, darling." Cal and Carmen beamed at each other. "But anyway, even if you won't let me hurt her, I don't think you should run away, Sophie. You should stay and fight for your man!"

"It's not Wendy who's the problem, not really," Sophie said. "It's more about Louis. He's supposed to be marrying me, I am supposed to become his wife, and yet when one of the most serious and important things in his life happens, he doesn't want me around. I don't think he's thought past our wedding day. I don't think he's thought through what being married is really about."

"Have you?" Cal asked her.

"No," Sophie said thoughtfully. "I don't suppose I have. I suppose that I've been just as caught up in the drama and the romance as Louis, and I was looking for my fairy-tale ending. But that's not the ending, is it, getting married. It's only the beginning, and it's then that you have to work out what marriage is really about."

"I can tell you what marriage is really about," Carmen said. "I've been married, still am, technically, and let me tell you this. Marriage is about compromise. It's about accepting your choices and dealing with the consequences. It's about waking up every day and making the decision to try your best even if your hearts are not in it. That's what marriage is about and that's mainly why I left my husband for a younger man. That and the fact that he was terrible in bed."

"Hang on a minute," Sophie said as she jammed her suitcase shut. "A few weeks ago you couldn't wait for Louis and me to get married. You were practically dragging me up the aisle!"

"I know," Carmen said. "And that's because you two didn't look like you were settling for second best. You didn't look like you were getting married because you needed something to do. You looked— *look*—like you were in love."

"Love," Sophie sighed as she attempted to shove another pair of scarcely worn shoes into her suitcase because she knew that trainers and boots would not cut it in the capital. "What the bloody hell is love anyway? What does it mean? And you don't mean that about marriage. You'd marry James, wouldn't you?"

Carmen sighed and looked down at the perfectly polished tips of her boots.

"James wants to marry me," she said. "But I won't let him."

"Really?" Sophie asked, sitting down on the suitcase with a bump so that her clothes spilled out of the zipper like so many lace-trimmed guts. "Why, because you are still somehow married to your ex? James adores you!"

"Yes." Carmen nodded. "Yes he does, he loves me and he adores me and I'm his girlfriend, his babe, his woman. And I love him . . ." Carmen's smile was wistful. "I have never been happier than since I moved down here to be with him. All those years before this, all those flat, gray, married years seem like a dream, a life that happened to some other poor bugger. It's now and here that I'm awake and really living my life."

"So why not ditch your husband and marry your boy toy?" Cal asked her.

Carmen shrugged. "I'm fifteen years older than James, I'm still married, and I . . . well, I can't have children. Not without a lot of bother and injections and IVF and even then, at my age there's not much chance of it working. I've got fibroids, you see. I've known for years. It's never been in the cards. None of that matters to James now, he says all he wants is me and he doesn't care about kids. But he's only twenty-four. In another few years, two or three, he might feel differently. He might realize how much he wants to be a dad, he might meet a girl he can have children with. I can't tie him down to some old bird who might not be able to give him what he wants. So even though I'm the happiest I've ever been in my life, I don't ever think about us as permanent. I think of him as my bit of luck I have to enjoy and make the most of until one day it finally runs out."

"Oh, Carmen." Sophie reached across the narrow divide between the twin beds and picked up her hand. "It's just silly not to let yourself be happy. We're only on this planet once; if we don't take chances then what's the point . . ." Sophie trailed off as she listened to her own words. She had taken a chance, a huge chance in coming down to St. Ives to be with Louis. And now for the first time she wasn't sure if it was a chance that was going to work out.

"Look, I'm as happy as I need to be," Carmen stated, then changed the subject. "Are you sure you really have to go all the way to London to think? Are you sure you can't just give Louis a ring over there later and get things back on track between you?"

"No . . . I want to, but I just don't think I can," Sophie said.

"I'll keep an eye on the girls and that Wendy while you're away, but don't be gone too long."

Sophie sighed and looked at her watch; it was just after ten. She knew that she'd promised to phone Louis, but the girls were already in bed and she wasn't sure that she had anything new to say to him. Instead she texted him. "Got here safely, I love you. Speak tomorrow. xxxx"

Spread out on her bed were the fledgling plans for her wedding-planning service, ideas and notes she had stuffed hastily in her suitcase as she'd packed. Her rational brain, the part of her that longed for action and purpose and to make her idea into a reality, had thought she might go over this and finesse her ideas while she was staying in London, start researching possible venues or designers she might recruit. But with her own wedding still so unformed and suddenly seeming to hang in the balance, the idea had lost some of its shine. The rational part of her brain told her that a good business idea was a good business idea whether she was based in Cornwall or London, or wherever, and that whether or not things worked out with Louis, it was still a business she could make her own, start from scratch and build to success. But in her heart her plans were all tied up with Louis and her new life. Without him, they seemed, for now at least, irrelevant. What she needed was a sense of herself again.

She stood up and looked out her window, over the rooftops and at the sky that always glowed orange over London's thousands of streets, swamping any hope of starlight. This is home, Sophie thought, pressing her hot palm against the cool glass of the window. Just out there on the other side of the glass was the town that was always open for business. The city she'd grown up in, the streets she'd known like the back of her hand all her life, pounding down them in her three-inch heels, insulated by the layers of grime and fumes and indifference that years of London living had built up, cocooning her from anything that might startle her out of her routine. Always dressed to the nines, always ready for that last-minute conference call with the New York office, always ready to troubleshoot, to fix, and to achieve, Sophie had once been the only woman in the city who knew where to get, after 5 P.M., one hundred fairy lights within half an hour. She might not have been happy here, if happiness meant feeling and loving, but at least she had known where she stood, and she'd been the master of her own destiny.

Sophie tapped one short unvarnished nail against the glass. It was just after ten on a Saturday night in London, and she was holed up in her childhood bedroom like a refugee or a convict on the lam. What on earth was she thinking? She'd come back here to think, to feel like herself again, and the best way to do that wasn't to sit in her old room, entombed in the past. It was to be out there in the living, breathing, beating heart of the city.

Quickly Sophie picked up her phone and made a call.

"Christina? Hi, listen, I'm in town unexpectedly—what are you doing right now?"

It turned out that Christina was in the bar at the St. Martins Lane hotel at a private party, but as soon as Sophie had given her a brief synopsis of her situation, she'd pulled some strings and had Sophie's name added to the guest list. It had taken Sophie just over half an hour to shower, change into one of the dresses she'd barely worn since arriving in St. Ives, and slip on her cool and comfortingly uncomfortable designer shoes, shake out her long hair, and put on some lip gloss.

Opening her mother's front door, she stood on the doorstep and inhaled London. Gone was the constant cry of the gulls and the incessant poetic crashing of the waves. There was no magical light here that was supposed to lift the human sprit. You couldn't see a scrap of green, and if you breathed in too deeply you'd find yourself choking on traffic fumes.

Sophie smiled, she was very glad to be back.

"So what's the occasion?" Sophie asked as she settled herself into a booth with Christina and a luscious-looking mojito.

"It's my friend Alison's divorce party—do you remember her? You met her a while back, she was terribly impressed with your brave and impetuous decision to go to Cornwall in pursuit of a man. Anyway, her divorce came through and she's started a catering business that seems to be working out really well, so she's celebrating. That's her over there."

Sophie glanced over to a blond woman, around her age and groomed to within an inch of her life, who was laughing and talking to a tall red-haired woman. "She looks very happy to be divorced," Sophie observed. "It is slightly worrying, when you are on the brink of marrying someone, to see someone else who looks quite so happy to be getting out of it . . ."

"Yes, but you are marrying the man of your dreams, your fairy-tale romantic hero. She married a dyed-in-the-wool bastard, with barely any redeeming features. She told me she feels like her life is just starting now, which is pretty impressive seeing as she's got three kids to worry about."

"I've got three kids to worry about," Sophie mused, more to herself than to Christina. "And none of them is mine."

"Besides, Alison is very happy; she got the house in the settlement. Sold it, bought a business, Home Hearths Catering or some such artsy-fartsy organic country-type thing that ladies who lunch are into. And the moral of this tale is, never get married in a hurry to a man you barely know . . . oops, sorry."

"It's not the same!" Sophie exclaimed in horror. "Alison and I, we are nothing alike."

"No, no, I know, and I wasn't saying that you were," Christina reassured her hurriedly. "Divorce parties are quite the thing these days. But I've never heard of an end-of-the-engagement party. Especially not after only about five minutes. Come on, darling. Tell me all about it."

"I don't want to," Sophie said, watching Alison laughing, looking so happy and free. "I don't want to talk about it tonight, I just want to get drunk and have some fun." Sophie brought her drink to her lips with gusto, but for some reason the second she tasted it on her tongue she didn't want it anymore and suddenly she felt homesick for one of Mrs. Alexander's hot chocolates.

"Bloody hell, I'm even rubbish at drinking now," Sophie sighed. "And I used to be excellent at drinking, it was one of the things you could always rely on me to get right. Have you got any class-A drugs? I think that might be my only way to oblivion."

"You don't do class-A drugs," Christina said. "You are far too sensible. Oh, babe, come on. You look lovely, you've got on great shoes, and you're in the most exciting city in the world! Let your hair down and live a little. How about we cut this party? There're no single men here anyway, which, if you ask me, is a travesty at a divorce party, and go clubbing? We could catch a cab to that nightclub in Kensington where Prince William hangs out. We could see if we can cradle-snatch some royals."

"Not really in the mood for illicit aristocratic sex," Sophie said, stirring her cocktail without enthusiasm.

"Admit it—you're missing him, aren't you?" Christina sighed.

"Look, why don't you go outside and give him a call? He won't mind that it's late and I'm sure you'll feel better once you've spoken to him. Sounds to me like this is nothing more than a bit of bridal nerves complicated by the full-grown love child—is he single by the way? The love child?"

"You're right," Sophie said, choosing to ignore the last comment because, unlike herself, Christina had successfully managed to imbibe several mojitos. "I will call him. I'm sorry I'm being so lame. I think all that sea air must have sucked the party girl right out of me. I'll call Louis and come back and down that bloody cocktail if it kills me."

"And that's what I've always liked about you," Christina observed as Sophie slid from her seat. "Your natural joie de vivre."

As she headed out of the bar, Sophie passed a tall redheaded woman locked in the embrace of a long-haired man. They looked like newlyweds caught up in the first flush of romance, Sophie thought enviously. She could tell just by looking at them, the way they held each other, that they hadn't had to deal with any complications or problems; she closed her eyes just for a second, wishing ever so hard that she was back on the sofa in front of Louis's electric fire, not thinking about anything except being in his arms.

The lobby of the St. Martins Lane hotel was minimalist, decorated almost exclusively in white, with strange teeth-shaped chairs and a large and seemingly random chess set on the shiny tiled floor. Awkwardly Sophie perched on a tooth and took her phone out of her bag. Now that she had given herself permission to talk to Louis, she couldn't wait to hear the sound of his voice.

"Sophie?" The sound of her name in an unfamiliar accent stopped her in her tracks. She looked up and watched as Jake Flynn walked toward her. Slowly Sophie put her phone back in her bag. Jake Flynn, the man who could have been the love of her life.

"Sophie Mills, it really is you! You look fantastic—what are you doing here?"

"What are *you* doing here?" Sophie asked him. "You're not going to the divorce party too, are you?"

"The what? No, my fiancée is staying here. I've been out of town today, but I promised I'd take her to a late dinner when I got back." He gazed into her face. "You really look stunning. Sea air, love, and kids—it really suits you, you're glowing."

Sophie felt a hot flush sweep across her chest. Jake always did have a way of looking at her that made her feel desirable.

"I think that's probably just because it's a bit hot in there," she said, nodding in the direction of the bar. She beamed at Jake, surprised by how pleased she was to see his familiar face in this familiar place. For a second it felt as if the wheel of time had turned backward and she was where she had been a year ago, working on an unrequited crush on Jake and desperate to get the promotion that would take her to the top of her profession. It felt almost as if her old life had been waiting in suspended animation, holding its breath until she returned, ready for her to pick up where she had left off in such a hurry. But she knew that wasn't true. Jake might have wanted her once but that was many moons ago and now he was getting married, and so—she reminded herself a little belatedly—was she.

"So what are you doing now?" Jake asked.

"Oh, well, I'll probably go back to the party for a bit."

"Come to dinner with me," Jake pressed her.

"But what about your fiancée?" Sophie asked him. "I don't suppose she's expecting a threesome, unless there's something you're not telling me."

"Sophie Mills, are you flirting with me?" Jake chuckled.

"I don't know, am I?" Sophie asked, surprised. One thing her life with Louis had changed for sure was how she felt about herself.

Now she felt beautiful and desirable. Even if Jake had fallen for another woman, she was sure he could see that in her.

"So how long are you in town?" Jake asked her.

"I'm not sure, I'm visiting my mum so—"

"Have lunch with me then? Before you go back. Promise?" Jake's smile was a perfect balance of boyish and dashing.

"Yes, yes I will—that would be lovely," she said.

"God, you look great," Jake said again as he slowly seemed to take in every millimeter of her face. "Stunning."

"Stop it, you'll give me a complex," Sophie said and grinned. "Another one!"

For a second the two of them stood there smiling at each other.

"Jake, I thought you were going to come up to my room to pick me up!" a woman called out across the foyer.

"Oh, there's my girl," Jake said, his smile dimming just a fraction. "That's my fiancée, Stephanie."

Sophie watched as an immaculate chestnut brunette with hair a little shorter and a little thicker and a lot more styled than Sophie's marched over to them on a pair of very high heels. She was wearing a gray pencil skirt topped off with a high-necked cream satin blouse that emphasized the shape of her bountiful breasts. As she approached she smiled warmly at Sophie and extended a perfectly manicured hand that Sophie took rather self-consciously, suddenly aware that her fingertips had been nowhere near nail polish in months.

"Hi, I'm Stephanie Corollo. Delighted to meet you . . . ?"

"This is Sophie Mills," Jake said, kissing Stephanie on either cheek. "A former associate and good friend I just bumped into."

"Sophie, how lovely to meet you," Stephanie said. "And may I say what fabulous shoes? Manolo, 1980s, am I right? You and I have a lot in common. Will you be joining us for dinner?"

"Oh no," Sophie said. "I'm supposed to be at a divorce party, and besides, three's a crowd and all that . . ."

"Nonsense, Jake and I practically live in each other's pockets as it is, and I don't have any girlfriends on this side of the Atlantic. I'm dying for someone to talk to about things with frills. Come to dinner with us? I'm sure Jake would love a reason not to talk about wedding plans for a few hours." Stephanie's plea was charming and sweet and Sophie found her quite hard to resist, but the fact that she had been, on more than one occasion, in a rather compromising position with her fiancé made Sophie feel that she had to.

"I would love to, but I can't. A friend went out of her way to get me into that party and I can't run out on her. But it's been lovely to meet you, Stephanie. You and Jake make a fabulous couple."

"We do, don't we?" Stephanie said, slotting her hand into Jake's and smiling at him. "Well, come on then, darling, they said they'd hold our reservation until eleven thirty, and after the day I've had, I need at least two glasses of wine. Make that bottles."

"I'll call you," Jake said, interestingly not making any mention of their proposed lunch date.

"Do that," Sophie said, nodding, watching for a while as Stephanie strode out of the foyer and into the night, trailing Jake in her wake.

Sophie took her phone out of her bag to call Louis, but the urge to speak to him had waned and it didn't seem like such a good idea anymore.

Fourteen

The morning after her night out with Christina and her surprise encounter with Jake Flynn, Sophie found a text message from Louis on her phone: "Glad you got there okay. We're all fine." There was nothing else, not a hint that he missed her, that he was worried about her, or that he even wanted to talk to her. Sophie's thumb hovered over the Call button for a long moment, but she resisted the urge to call him.

She spent the rest of Sunday in bed, or in her pajamas sitting on her mother's sofa, eating cereal and watching TV.

"It's just like summer holidays all over again," Iris told her, drawing back the living room curtains to let in some late-September sun that made Sophie blink and rub her eyes. "You never used to want to go out and get fresh air back then either. I practically had to kick you and Carrie out of the door and tell you to enjoy yourselves. The last thing you need is to be sitting around in the dark moping. Why don't you go out for a walk? Take a dog or two. If you take Scooby he'll pull you along and you'll hardly have to put in any effort at all. You need some fresh air to blow away those cobwebs, that's what you need," Iris assured her.

"What I need is a new brain," Sophie told her mother. "A new brain, one that knows how to process rational thought, and I need a new heart, a hard as stone heart, not one that falls in love with the world's most inappropriate man at the drop of a hat, and most of all I need not to think, and sitting here watching whatever is on the telly is exactly the best way to do that. I need all of those things and nothing that has anything to do with fresh air. I've had more fresh air recently than any sensible pair of lungs can deal with and just look where that's gotten me."

On Monday Sophie was awakened just after nine by her cell phone.

"I miss you," she'd breathed into it, answering it while still half asleep and hopeful that it was Louis.

"Really? I haven't given you a second thought." Cal's voice exploded in her tender ear. "Look, I think you should come and take me to lunch today. Eve hates me, and even though I've never done better at work, I have the distinct feeling she's looking for a way to take credit for all of my ideas and shove me out. I need to fight fire with fire—I need your Machiavellian backstabbing skills."

"I don't know, Cal," Sophie said, yawning, stretching so that her feet dangled over the end of the bed. "I was thinking about having a duvet day. I've discovered that I like lounging around in my pajamas watching daytime TV. And anyway, my body's just realized that I haven't slept late in six months and it's demanding I catch up with the deficit."

"Oh no, you don't," Cal warned her. "You don't get to stay in bed moping. You need to be up and about and telling me how to oust Eve permanently without incurring a criminal record, while I commit artery suicide with a double bacon cheeseburger. You owe me, Sophie. I've lost hours of my life listening to you twittering on about Louis, debating if he is or is not the love of your life, blah, blah, blah, and I've never complained."

"Er, excuse me—" Sophie began to protest.

"Barely ever complained. And now it's your turn."

"Okay, fine, you're right," Sophie conceded. "You are a good friend to me and I should be a better one to you even if I am in the middle of my own personal crisis. I'll get up and get dressed and come and meet you for lunch."

"Great, come and pick me up at my office at one," Cal instructed her.

"Well, I would, but I don't really know if I want to deal with all the fuss of going back to the office . . ." But Cal had hung up.

After a shower Sophie spent much longer than she'd anticipated in deciding what to wear for her first visit back to the offices of Mc-Carthy Hughes, which had once been such a huge part of her life. She had to get her look exactly right and she had to do that with the haphazard collection of clothes she had thrown into her suitcase. Somehow she had to find a look that said she was happy to have given up her hard-earned and well-paid career for a man she barely knew, but that, given the need, she could step back into it at a moment's notice because her finger was still firmly on the corporate-event-planning pulse. Sophie found herself thinking of Jake Flynn's fiancée Stephanie Corollo as she dressed, in the end picking a smart cream shirt to top off her pencil skirt, and finishing with a neat vest that nipped just under her breasts. It took her an age to dry her hair with her mother's weak and dangerous-looking hair dryer, the very same one Iris had been using to blow-dry various animals since the seventies. When she came to putting her makeup on, she found that half of it was missing, probably having found its way into Bella and Izzy's play makeup set. Eventually though, Sophie was able to stand in front of the mirror and give herself a once-over. She looked good. She looked like a woman in control, even if she wasn't entirely sure that some of the long blond hairs that had strayed onto her shoulders didn't belong to an afghan hound called Marilyn.

Just as she was leaving, her phone rang. Sophie looked at the name that flashed onto the screen as she picked up her jacket and bag, expecting it to be Cal. But it was Louis's name that came up on the screen. He was calling her at last. He was missing her at last, and most important, he was making the first move.

"Hello," she said tentatively, an edge of uncertainty in her voice.

"Is this Aunty Sophie?" Bella's voice boomed out. Whenever she was on the phone, she always had a tendency to talk twice as loudly as normal, which Sophie put down to the several months she'd lived with her grandmother.

"Bella? Yes, it's me," Sophie said, a rush of warmth sweeping through her. "Why aren't you at school, are you feeling poorly?"

"I am at school," Bella bellowed. "Me and Izzy borrowed Daddy's phone out of his jacket pocket this morning and took it to school so we could talk to you. We put it in Izzy's book bag because nursery children hardly ever get searched."

"I'm here too!" Sophie winced as Izzy's high-pitched shriek came through.

"Shush or else we will be discovered!" Bella urged her sister, who collapsed into a fit of giggles, giving Sophie a mental image of Bella swooping the phone out of her sister's reach as Izzy tried to grab it.

"Bella? You've taken Daddy's phone without him knowing and smuggled it into school?" Sophie asked her anxiously.

"Yes," Bella said. "We wanted to talk to you and Daddy said

not to phone you until you phoned us, because you needed to think. We were going to call you on the phone box outside school because we know your number, but we needed money or a credit card so I borrowed Daddy's phone instead."

"You were going to leave the school grounds on your own to try and phone me?" Sophie asked, trying to quell the alarm that heightened her tone. "Wouldn't your teachers have noticed?"

"Not at pickup time, it's easy to sneak past the teachers with all those people in the playground," Bella said proudly, which didn't exactly reassure Sophie, but right now she knew the last thing Bella needed to hear from her was a scolding, not if she was prepared to go to those lengths to talk to her.

"And where are you now?"

"We are in the playground, behind the scooter rack—it's lunchtime," Bella told her a touch impatiently.

"And are you okay?" Sophie asked her.

"We're not bad," Bella said. "Daddy seems quite cross most of the time. And that Wendy woman keeps coming around. They keep talking without us being able to hear them, but I know they are talking about Seth. Who is Seth?"

"He's Wendy's son," Sophie said uneasily, hating the position that Louis was unwittingly putting her in, forcing her to tell half-truths to the children.

"Well, I don't know why Daddy's so worried about him. Anyway, I miss you a lot."

"And me, and me too!" Sophie heard Izzy in the background.

"I miss both of you too," Sophie reassured them. "I really do. But you know Daddy's going to be worried when he finds out his phone is missing. He needs it for work."

"Except he's not working this week," Bella told her. "He's stopped all of his work to help that Wendy woman find that Seth person."

"Has he?" Sophie asked, taken aback. She hadn't quite expected Louis to alter his life so radically the moment she left the scene. What did it mean that he'd turned down or called off work right at the moment when his business was gaining a reputation? Did it mean he was willing to give up, for his son, for Wendy, everything he'd been building over the last few months?

"When are you coming back, Aunty Sophie?" It was Izzy who spoke this time, having successfully wrested the phone from her sister.

"Um, well . . . soon I expect." Sophie glanced at her watch. She was going to be late for Cal.

"Tomorrow?" Izzy asked. "Tomorrow is soon."

"It might not be exactly tomorrow," Sophie told her, feeling her chest tighten. "But it will be soon."

"Do you promise?" Izzy asked her solemnly.

"I do promise that I will see you soon," Sophie said, hating to be vague, but knowing that with Izzy at least, an open promise would be sufficient.

"Hey . . ." Izzy yelped a protest as Bella came back on the phone.

"We have to go, there are teachers coming," Bella hissed.

"Oh . . . right, but, Bella, listen—give your phone back to Daddy as soon as you see him, okay? I want to talk to him tonight. And promise me that you will not ever go off the school grounds unless it's with a relative or someone else you know, okay?"

"Okay," Bella hissed. "Got to terminate connection. Roger, over and out."

Once the connection was severed, Sophie thought for a moment, feeling uneasy about the lengths Bella had gone to to talk to her. Nothing really bad had happened, but still, if the seven-year-old was prepared to consider sneaking out of school to make a call to Sophie, then what else might she do if she felt under pressure? Sophie felt angry with Louis, who surely must know she would always have time to talk to the girls. He was being petulant, punishing her for leaving, and it was the children who were suffering. Sophie would have called him right then if he'd had his phone and told him exactly what she thought of him banning the girls from speaking to her, and of canceling his work to follow Wendy. But she didn't, and all in all that was probably a good thing.

Sophie looked up at the skyscraper where McCarthy Hughes was located and felt her heartbeat quicken. There had been something about her journey over here, the rumble of the Tube train as it carried her into the heart of the city, the smell of the damp autumn air as she emerged a short walk from her former offices, that had sent adrenaline surging through her body, reminding her of the thrill she used to get from her job.

Not so long ago, the building she stood in front of had been her entire universe and she had been at the hub of it. And now she was back.

"Sophie!" Nick Parkin spotted Sophie first when she walked into the open-plan office. "What are you doing back?" He greeted Sophie with a hug, whispering into her ear, "Please tell me that your romantic dream didn't work out and that you've come to rescue us from the Evil Queen and bring spring back to Narnia again. It hasn't been the same since you left."

"I'm sorry, Nick, but coming back here is the last thing on my mind," Sophie lied, wondering uncomfortably if the feeling she was experiencing in her gut was the feeling of being at home. She stopped by Clara Hodgkin's desk to say hi.

"Sophie, how are you?" Clara exclaimed. "What's life like on the outside?"

"It's great, thanks," Sophie told her.

"Well, I don't need to tell you how difficult things are here. No one's got any money. No one's getting new accounts. The only one who's doing okay is your protégé, and Eve doesn't like it one bit. I know you ran away to a better life, but I miss you, Soph. Any chance you might come back?"

"No," Sophie told her. "I don't think so, Clara. Look, the experts say that things won't be that bad for long."

"Are they experts on Eve getting a personality transplant?" Clara joked bleakly.

Sophie slowed as she approached the office that had once been hers and was now Cal's. Leaning over his desk in a tight black dress that showed every single one of her ribs was Eve, examining something on Cal's computer screen.

Sophie stood in the doorway and looked around at what had been her domain for so long. It was the place where she had tried so hard to be secretly in love with Jake Flynn and where she had first heard the news that Carrie had died and left two small children in need of a guardian. Cal had changed it completely, as Sophie knew he would. It had been painted a fresh white, he had moved in a sofa, there was a vase of ostentatious flowers, there were new blinds, and artwork was hanging on the wall.

"A-hem," Sophie coughed to make her presence known, even though she was fairly sure that both Eve and Cal knew she was standing there.

"Sophie Mills!" Eve said slowly, a second or two before she looked up from the screen at Sophie. She treated Sophie to a thin red-lipped smile. "You look like you're enjoying country life. At least the food."

"And you look more and more like a Disney villain every time I see you," Sophie commented back sweetly. "Are you hoping to get a film role this year?"

"Well, you're the expert—after all, your entire life is make-believe." Eve raised an eyebrow. "Tell me, how is life with your off-the-shelf family? Everything you hoped it would be?"

"And more," Sophie said, shooting a look at Cal that warned him he better not have told Eve anything about her current issues.

"Yes, well, I suppose a twenty-year-old stepson probably is more than any new bride would ask for." Eve smirked as she shook her head.

"And how are you?" Sophie asked her. "Still totally and utterly alone?"

"Only on the nights I want to be." Eve walked over to Sophie and held out a hand. "It's good to see you, Sophie. We miss you around here. Total pain in the arse you might have been, but you were quite good at your job."

"I was good at your job too," Sophie reminded her. "Which reminds me, how's Gillian dealing with stepping down?" Sophie was interested to find out how her former boss was getting on. The die-hard career woman had withdrawn from her executive position at McCarthy Hughes, deciding to make spending time with her children her top priority, just before Sophie had made her own decision to leave. Sophie wanted to hear that Gillian was happy, that she had made the right choice. Somehow it seemed terribly relevant just then.

"Gillian was a pain in the arse after you left," Eve sighed. "Even though they brought her in only as a consultant, she was on my back every minute, as if I might not fill her matronly shoes every bit as well as you did! But then she got pregnant, a swan-song baby or something. Went on and on about leaving for good, taking time to enjoy her pregnancy for once, and I've hardly heard from her since. Obviously, I don't need her help or advice . . . but to just wind up your whole life to gestate. Who does that?"

Sophie shrugged. "Mothers?" Gillian had left to be with her own children. To most people, those who weren't raised by wolves anyway, that made perfect sense. But Sophie had left her life behind for someone else's children and a man she barely knew. Until recently it couldn't have seemed simpler, but now suddenly Sophie was seeing it through someone else's eyes and she found that she was doubting herself.

"Well, listen, I have to get on, top job to do and all that, but just so you know . . ." Eve paused in the doorway as she was about to leave. "Look, Sophie, we need all the good people we can get right now. And you were—are—one of the best. If you ever do need a job, then please come and ask me. You could have your old job back like a shot, anytime; I really mean that."

"Isn't my old job your current job?" Sophie asked Eve.

"Your old, old job. Anytime. I'd love to have you come work for me."

"Um, isn't her old job my new job?" Cal sounded alarmed.

"Well, like I said, we need good people." Eve narrowed her eyes at Cal. "But actually, Sophie, I miss your input. If you thought you could come back, I'd have a word with the board. Create a post for you—something appropriate, flexible—something that could suit you."

Sophie nodded, trying hard not to let the inner smugness she felt show on her face. Eve still needed her, *wanted* her. McCarthy Hughes did miss her after all, and just then, when she was unsure as to exactly how much she was wanted elsewhere, that was hard to resist.

"I'll bear it in mind," Sophie said as Eve slinked out of the office and across the floor like a black mamba in heels. She turned to Cal, who suddenly looked anxious.

"I want to have a word with you," she said.

"You never said not to tell anyone," Cal said a little later as they sat over a mixed meat grill with onion rings and relish.

"I assumed that as my best friend you wouldn't tell anyone, because generally friends keep each other's secrets," Sophie chided him. "I've always kept your secrets."

"I never have any secrets," Cal protested. "And anyway, you can't have a go at me. I need your help. You heard Eve, she wants me out and you in!"

Sophie's expression softened and she pushed the bowl of fries they were sharing over to Cal. "It's not that bad. Eve wants you on your toes, she wants you to feel anxious, as if your job might be on the line—that's her management style. But you heard her, she needs good people, and even if you rub her the wrong way, results show that you are doing well. If she tried to get rid of you, she'd be shooting herself in the foot and she knows it."

"So you're saying I just have to put up with her hating me?" Cal asked miserably before stuffing a fistful of fries into his mouth.

"Endure," Sophie advised. "If I know Eve, some other poor soul will fall under her Medusa gaze soon enough. And this time it might be someone she could actually get rid of. So what if she makes your life a misery? As long as you keep on doing your job as well as you are, she can't touch you."

"Oh god." Cal's head thumped down on the tabletop. "I'm not made to endure life. I'm made to enjoy it! I don't know if I can take it. I never thought I'd say this—but I miss the days when I was your secretary and the most work I ever did was reading *Hello!* magazine."

"You don't mean that, Cal." Sophie smiled. "This is your career, your job—the thing that defines you and your future. Success doesn't come easy. You need to pay with blood, sweat, and pain."

Cal's forehead found its place on the tabletop once more.

That night Sophie shut herself away in her old room and resolved to call Louis. After all, now she had a reason to phone him, a solid,

concrete, and rational reason that wasn't purely about her wanting
to hear the sound of his voice and hoping that he missed her. She
wanted to talk to him about Bella's threatening to sneak out of
school and secretly taking Louis's phone to call her. She steeled
herself as she listened to the dial tone, which rang for longer than
the normal four it took to get Louis to pick up. When the phone
was finally answered, it wasn't Louis's voice Sophie heard.

"Hello?" Wendy said. Sophie resisted the urge to instantly hang
up. Knowing that her name would have come up on Louis's phone,
she didn't want Wendy to know that her answering Louis's phone
had rattled her in any way.

"Hi, Wendy," Sophie said in an even tone, using the other
woman's name to show that she wasn't remotely bothered. "Can
you get Louis for me please?"

"Sorry, he's . . . a bit tied up at the moment," Wendy said, de-
liberately vague. Sophie glanced at her watch. In all likelihood
Louis was with the girls, probably giving them a bath or reading
them a story. It was just Wendy's tone and her own imagination
that led her to picture him tied naked to the radiator in the living
room while Wendy toyed with him. "I'll tell him you called."

"Thank you," Sophie said. "And please tell him it's important."

"Of course it is," Wendy said before disconnecting the call.

Sophie waited until midnight for Louis to phone back, but the
call never came. Which either meant he didn't want to talk to her
or Wendy hadn't given him her message. Sophie considered ringing him again, but the thought of hearing Wendy's voice kept her
from doing so. It looked like she'd have to wait for him to contact
her after all.

For the rest of the week Sophie lived her old life, except that it
now included sleeping late because she didn't go to work every day,
although she did meet Cal at the office for lunch. She shopped for

clothes that were entirely inappropriate for a seaside town in winter, taking her neglected credit card out for a spree around the West End. She went with Cal to a poetry reading in a bookstore on Charing Cross Road. She spent ninety pounds in her favorite Covent Garden salon having her hair shaped and styled, leaving the stylist a ten-pound tip even though she'd just paid ninety pounds for her hair to basically look the same. And in a fit of nostalgia for her much missed flat, she made an impromptu call to check on her tenant.

She called in the middle of the day hoping that the new occupant would be out and that she could just let herself in with the keys she still had, have a nose around, perhaps make herself a cup of tea, sit on the sofa, listen to the traffic stream by, and remember when her life was a flat horizon with nothing on it at all.

The tenant, a Miss Mary Harding, had the day off. She was not pleased to see Sophie at all, reminding her that she was supposed to give twenty-four hours' notice if she wanted to visit and letting her in the front door barely long enough for Sophie to see that her living room had been painted a dark plum color and that a green throw now obscured her lovely sofa before Mary Harding all but threw her out again, telling her she was expecting visitors. Back outside, Sophie sat on the very step where she had found Louis waiting for her all those months ago. She had never dreamed that that moment would lead to this one.

As Friday approached, she noticed two things acutely. Jake had not called her and asked her out to lunch as he had promised and she had heard nothing at all from her fiancé.

Sophie wondered how it was possible to go from feeling like the most wanted and loved woman in the world to feeling like an incidental irritation in the life of someone she had almost given up everything for. She knew that her old life, her comfortable, closed-off city life, was still here for her, that she could even have her old job back if Eve was really serious. But the problem was, now that she'd had her space and time to think things over, Sophie discovered she didn't want it anymore.

"Coffee?" Iris asked Sophie as she emerged from her bedroom just past eleven, almost a week after she'd arrived in London. "Come on, you need to get something hot inside you or else you'll waste away."

Sophie shook her head; she had been grateful for the opportunity to sleep late over the past week but found it was taking her much longer to wake up than usual. Her head felt fuzzy and she felt more tired and muddled now than she had when she went to bed. It didn't help having her mother fussing over her and forcing her to eat breakfast for fear she might become anorexic, unless, of course, she asked for a bacon sandwich, in which case her mother's concern would turn to the dangers of obesity while several smelly dogs milled about her legs. This morning though, the merest thought of bacon turned Sophie's stomach. In fact, the idea of breakfast in general turned her off completely, which was most unlike her.

Iris waved a coffeepot under Sophie's nose as she entered the kitchen, which was exactly the same as it had been when she'd left home, the walls lined with pine tongue and groove except for one that was covered with pearlescent wallpaper that shimmered in the morning sun and hurt Sophie's eyes. Sophie backed away from it and slumped into a chair.

"Got any decaf, Mum?" She yawned, burying her head in her hands.

"Decaf?" Iris asked her bowed head. "You always said decaf was for losers who wanted to pay for coffee-flavored water. I thought you'd want the real stuff after another night out. What was it you and Cal went to see, some Russian play? I never had Cal down as a Russian-play fan."

"He's not, but he is the fan of a Russian-play fan," Sophie said, wondering exactly how she had let Cal persuade her to be the third wheel on his first date with an existential poet just in case it turned out that dark curls and brooding eyes weren't enough to keep him amused and he had to make a quick escape.

"And yes, I did hear you come in, thank you very much."

"Well, it wasn't as if I was singing at the top of my voice or crashing around," Sophie said petulantly. "I was as sober as a judge. All this stress has made me go off drinking, and it's not bloody ironic, it's bloody inconvenient. I mean, that's what we British do when things don't go well. We drink ourselves into oblivion and make ill-advised choices. Now I'm being forced, against my will, I might add, to think things through with a clear and rational mind. Although I'm not so sure about the rational bit . . ."

"You weren't drinking and you haven't had coffee once this week?" Iris asked thoughtfully, still holding the coffeepot.

"No, Mum." Sophie sighed wearily, feeling as if she was seventeen again. "But you don't have to worry. Neither of those things is a classic sign of an eating disorder. If anything, they show that I am super healthy. Apart from my cream tea and choux pastry addiction, and frankly, when you live in the West Country, that's practically a requirement." Sophie looked around the kitchen that was mutt free, except for Tripod, her mother's three-legged Spaniel cross who'd been injured in a collision with a bus, and was now happily grazing from a buffet of dog bowls left unguarded for a few blissful moments.

"Where are all the dogs anyway?"

"The ones that can be trusted not to dig up next door's dead gerbil are in the garden and I corralled Scooby and the others in the living room," Iris said. "I thought we should talk alone."

"I might be mistaken, but I think talking in front of dumb animals does qualify as talking alone," Sophie said.

"Those dogs understand every word I say and some of them are very sensitive. Little Miss Pickles knows immediately if there's something amiss, and her hair falls out. I will not be responsible for a bald Pekingese. Besides, you talk to that cat of yours."

"Yes, but Artemis is not a dumb animal," Sophie said. "And anyway, what about Tripod?"

"Tripod is deaf," Iris replied as she searched her cupboards until she pulled out a packet of herbal tea. "I've got peppermint tea." She squinted at the box over the top of her glasses. "It was best before 2002, but I shouldn't think it will kill you. Do you fancy that?"

"Peppermint tea; do you know, that's exactly what I fancy," Sophie said, brightening up. "I didn't know I liked peppermint tea."

Iris pursed her lips and put the kettle on.

"How about poached eggs for breakfast?" she offered her daughter.

"Poached eggs? No thanks, the thought of egg yolks makes me feel like throwing up. I'll just have some toast, thanks . . ."

Iris set a mug of steaming peppermint tea down in front of Sophie and sat opposite her at the table.

"Listen, Sophie," she said. "I haven't really had a chance to talk to you properly since you got here, what with me getting to know Trevor and you shopping for England. You and I need some mother-daughter time, but you hardly ever seem to be at home and when you are you're usually asleep. Still, I want you to know that I am here for you and I know you wouldn't have come back unless it was really serious."

"It's okay, Mum." Sophie smiled at her as she embraced her mug of tea, cupping it with both hands. "I didn't come here expecting you to fix all my problems. It's just really good to know that I've got a place to come to if I need it. And I think it's great that you are seeing this Trevor fellow . . ." Sophie trailed off, feeling slightly nauseous again. "Anyway, I'm really glad you're happy. I'm really glad you've found someone. He sounds like a lovely man."

"And he's dishy too," Iris assured her, a youthful bloom coloring her cheeks. "So talk to me, darling. I'm all ears."

Sophie studied her mother's Formica tabletop, an array of seventies-style flowers spiraling in various shades of orange across its surface. When she was a little girl, she had sat at this very table, discovering faces, creatures, and sometimes entire other worlds in that pattern while her parents talked over her head. Her dad used to say she was always away with the fairies. Her dad also used to make a smiling face out of bacon and tomatoes and put the plate under her nose, making her laugh out loud. For a second, sitting in this kitchen, at this relic of her youth, the memory of her father was so strong that it almost felt as if he were standing beside her; Sophie suddenly missed him with a strength she hadn't experienced in the longest time, tears tracking down her cheeks.

"Oh, sweetheart, is it really that bad?" her mother asked her, rubbing her shoulders vigorously.

"I don't know—it's not even that I'm crying about. I just thought about Dad and that set me off. I'm just a mess at the moment, Mum, it's like someone peeled away a layer of my skin and I'm feeling everything just a bit more than I used to. I'm bursting into tears at the drop of a hat, making life-changing decisions without thinking about them. I'm very confused."

"Well, this thing with Louis's son and his mother must have made you feel unsure," Iris told her. "Any woman would feel odd about her prospective husband's secret child turning up out of the blue even if he is twenty years old, didn't you say?"

Sophie nodded, thinking of Seth, distraught on Mrs. Alexander's sofa. She had failed him instead of helping him. All she'd done was make a difficult situation even more confusing and difficult for him. She barely knew him, it was true, but somehow Sophie felt he'd spent a lot of his life covering up for how lost and confused he was really feeling. It was something in his eyes that she recognized. Something she used to see in her own eyes whenever she looked in the mirror.

"And from what you've said, this Wendy doesn't seem like the most sensible of women, trying to come between you and Louis when she should be worrying about her son."

"She just hates me, that's what it is," Sophie explained. "She's got it into her head that she hates me and that she wants to take Louis from me and it is crazy. It's even crazier that she thinks I feel threatened by her. Louis likes her, I can see that—she was really important to him once. And he's trying to work out the best way to deal with discovering that he's got a son, but he wouldn't just drop everything we have for her, would he?"

"No. No, I can't believe that he would. He is sure, isn't he?" Iris asked her.

"Sure about what?"

"That this Seth is his son. He knows that for sure?"

"Well, he hasn't done a DNA test or anything, but you should see Seth, Mum. He looks almost exactly like Louis. A little smoother, a touch rounder in the face—but other than that . . . well, they have to be related."

"All I'm saying is that it might be a good idea to verify the facts before the lives of so many people get seriously complicated," Iris said. "Louis is tall, dark, and handsome, and from the sound of it, this Seth is tall, dark, and handsome. All that means is that the boy's mother likes tall, dark, and handsome men."

"No, Seth is Louis's son, I'm sure of it. He has exactly the same expression when he's angry, the same smile, he even kisses like . . ." Sophie trailed off suddenly, finding Tripod's attempt to get her to stroke him terribly endearing.

"How do you know how he kisses?" Iris asked as Sophie scratched Tripod under one ear, so that the poor hound leaned rather too far to the left and toppled over onto the floor.

"Okay . . . I'll tell you, as you clearly insist on dragging it out of me with your vicious interrogation techniques." Iris raised an eyebrow. "He tried to kiss me, okay, he actually did kiss me, but he was very drunk and angry and I was very surprised, so I didn't react as quickly as I probably should have. It's not as if I fancy him or anything . . ."

"No, dear, because with your track record that would be a bad idea," Iris said mildly.

"My track record?" Sophie exclaimed. "What do you mean, Mother? I was practically a virgin until I met Louis."

"I know, darling, I'm just saying. When it comes to forming relationships, you seem to always pick the rather complicated route. On paper Louis was the last man you should have fallen for. Or the second from the last anyway; I'd say his son would definitely be the last."

"I have not, am not, and do not at any point intend to fall for Seth. I was caught off guard and he is so like Louis, or like Louis would have been once, fresh and young and untouched by life. Just for a second I wondered what it would have been like to meet him then, when he was young and carefree and without a personal history to rival Henry the Eighth's . . ."

"From what you've told me, it doesn't sound like Seth is very carefree to me," Iris said. "Sounds to me like he's a rather troubled young man with a mother who puts her own interests before his."

"I don't know . . . I don't really know what Wendy's like. All I know is that she really hates me for rocking her boat and seems quite keen to get her own back, no matter what happens."

Iris watched her daughter thoughtfully in the September sun.

"Well, leaving all of that to one side, you still love Louis, don't you?"

"I do," Sophie said hesitantly.

"You don't sound so sure," Iris said, pouring herself another cup of coffee and watching Sophie's face closely as the aroma caused her to unconsciously wrinkle her nose for the briefest second.

"Mum, the thing is, how do you know the difference between love and just really, really, really amazing sex and fun and laughing and getting on really well? Because before Louis, I'd never had really amazing sex, I'd never really even *liked* sex. But now with Louis I can't get enough of it. And I know he feels the same way about me. I mean it feels like we can't be alone in a room together for more than five seconds without having to rip each other's clothes off . . ."

"Okay." Iris held up the flat of her hand. "I'm delighted you feel that you can talk to me openly about this, darling, but you are still my little girl and that is a bit more information than I need to have. Thank god Tripod is deaf."

"Well, anyway, I'm head over heels with Louis. I'm infatuated with him. I can't think of a single thing about him that I don't love with a passion. I even like the way he snores, Mum. I even like his *snoring*. And I know that won't last, I know it's not real—so what if in a year, or two years' time, I wake up to him snoring and I realize that I hate it, and I hate him, and the infatuation has worn off and all I'm left with is this man I don't really know and who doesn't really know me and all we have in common are his children, who deserve so much better than another failed relationship. That's what I'm worried about."

Iris studied her coffee thoughtfully, bending over to scratch Tripod's tummy.

"You always were far too sensible," she said eventually.

"What do you mean?" Sophie asked her impatiently. "How is it even possible to be too sensible?"

"I met your dad when I was sixteen and he was eighteen," Iris said, ignoring her question. "It was at this Christmas party at the old youth club on Seven Sisters Road; it's not there now, of course, there's never anything for young people to do these days. No wonder they're all stabbing and shooting each other—"

"Mum, stick to the point, if you have one, that is," Sophie prompted her.

"Sorry—I saw him playing snooker with his mates, full mod outfit, the suit, the tie, the hair, and I melted on the spot. I fell for him so hard that I couldn't look at him, let alone talk to him. Whenever he was around I had trouble breathing, and the only way I could deal with it was to ignore him. This went on for about two years. He went out with every single one of my friends but never me, he never asked me out. I'd lock myself up in my bedroom at night and play my records and cry my eyes out."

"Why didn't you tell him you fancied him?"

"I don't know. Why didn't you ever engage in a proper relationship until you were in your thirties? I was shy and a bit repressed, I suppose, and a child, which is a pretty good excuse," Iris explained. "Besides, he was the best-looking, most popular boy in our group and I was a skinny kid with lank hair and no breasts. I protected myself by staying away from him."

"You and Dad got married when you were twenty-three, didn't you? What happened?"

"Well, for one thing I got breasts—but anyway, at eighteen Dad went off to university and I stayed in London, working in my mother's dress shop. You know, you don't get shops like that anymore, little boutiques. My mum running up patterns in the back room, me out front talking fashion with the girls . . . those were happy times."

"Okay, get to the bit where you met Dad again," Sophie urged her. Remarkably, her mother had never told her this story. Perhaps she hadn't been interested when she was a child, and after her father died it was probably too hard for Iris to talk about it.

"So one day—years later, when I was, let me see, twenty-two—I was at the cinema, can't remember the film, some piece of rubbish, black-and-white northern kitchen-sink type thing—I love a good musical, you don't get enough musicals anymore—"

"*Mum.*" Sophie tapped the tips of her fingers on the tabletop.

"I was there with this other boy, Justin Parker, I think his name was, when I saw your dad in the foyer and all those feelings I used to have for him, the stomach churning and the chest tightening and the butterflies and the goose bumps, all just whooshed back and I felt like that silly skinny little kid again. He had his back to me and his arm around another girl. I don't know why, but he turned around and looked right into my eyes and he smiled, and I realized that he knew who I was—he remembered me. And in that second I knew that I was going to marry him. I knew it right then."

"So how did you get together then?" Sophie asked her, enthralled. "What happened next?"

"He left his date standing there and came over, said hello like we'd always been old friends, and because I wasn't young or scared or shy anymore, and because a lot of lads used to ask me out back then and I knew I wasn't bad looking, I suddenly found I could talk to him. We stood there just talking and laughing about old times until the foyer of the cinema was empty, his date had walked off, and I had to tell mine to go."

"What a scandal!" Sophie laughed.

"We went to this little coffee place behind Upper Street, open all night, full of cabbies and truckers and kids in black turtlenecks with too much eyeliner who thought they were cool. You don't get places like that anymore." Iris caught Sophie's expression and rolled her eyes at Tripod, who seemed to be listening intently despite his deafness.

"Your dad bought me a lot of coffee—espresso, because I wanted him to think I was sophisticated—so it might have been the caffeine that was making my heart race, except that it only happened when I looked at him. We'd been in there about an hour, laughing and joking, when he suddenly reached out and touched my hand and I felt this surge of electricity go through my body. It was so strong that I thought I should have been jolted across the room and sitting in some cabbie's lap with my hair standing on end! I'd never ever felt anything like that before. He looked into my eyes and he said, 'Why did you never talk to me back then? I was crazy about you, but you always ignored me. I went out with all your friends to try and get your attention, but you never once looked my way.' I just laughed and told him about my crush on him and we couldn't believe it, we couldn't believe that the pair of us had felt like that all those years ago and had never managed to do anything about it." Iris trailed off, a tiny smile playing around her lips as she relived that night.

"He had a little flat on Balls Pond Road. Bloody horrible place it was, cold and a bit damp, but he took me there that night and I stayed out until the morning for the first time ever. My mother had my guts for garters, I can tell you—but it was worth it." She smiled at Sophie. "That was the night I found out I liked sex. We were engaged four months later, married within the year."

"That's so romantic," Sophie said, feeling those all-too-familiar tears building behind her eyes again. "So when did that bit wear off?"

"I felt about him then exactly the way you feel about Louis now, even though you're quite a bit older than I was when I met your father. I adored him, I couldn't think of a single thing about him that I didn't love. I even loved his hairy shoulders . . ."

"And so . . . did it go off once you were married for a few years?"

"Of course it did," Iris said.

"See, I told you!" Sophie said, panicked.

"Well no—'go off' is the wrong way of putting it—it changed, it *evolved*." Iris nodded, pleased with the word she'd found. "Life, money, children, work—that's all the stuff that can get in the way of love, the stuff that can push it to the back burner, make you forget that you are more than just coparents and housemates until one day the flame burns out and dies. The thing is, if you're worried about how to pay the mortgage or you've been up all night with the baby, if you can remember that love, that passion that brought you together and allow yourself to feel it, no matter what else is going on—then it grows, it deepens and becomes your strength, your fortress against whatever life throws at you."

Iris leaned across the table and stroked Sophie's face with the back of her hand. "Sweetheart, it's so rare to be able to look at another person and say that's the one for me, and to know it with all your heart. And sometimes I think that these days people are more afraid than ever to think about how they really feel. You all get married later, you all have children late, all so worried about living your lives before any of that happens, and that's crazy because loving someone, loving children—that *is* life. All the rest of it is just 'stuff.' You only get the kind of deep, strong, wonderful love that your father and I shared if you're brave enough to ride the waves that take you there. Your love for Louis will change and evolve—but if you believe in your heart that you do love him, and you never let anything make you forget that, then it can only change for the better."

"Mum," Sophie said softly. "That was really profound."

"I know," Iris said, nodding sagely. "You see, I do know some things, you'd be surprised by how many things I know if you ever took the trouble to ask me."

"I know." Sophie's smile was rueful. "So what about Trevor? Do you feel that way about Trevor?"

Iris grinned and Sophie couldn't help but mirror her expression when she saw the twinkle in her mother's eyes.

"He makes me very happy," she said, nodding. "But your father was the love of my life. I still regret those six years between the ages of sixteen and twenty-two that we were apart, and I just thank my lucky stars I had him for as long as I did and that he gave me you."

"So you don't think I'm bonkers if I marry Louis on New Year's Eve, not that we'll ever get the venue now."

"I don't think you're bonkers if you marry Louis at whatever time. Especially not now."

"Why not now?" Sophie asked her, finishing the last of her tea.

"Especially not now that you're pregnant."

At that precise second Sophie's phone burst to life in the pocket of her dressing gown.

Staring at her mother openmouthed, she reached for it and answered. It was Jake.

"Hey, Sophie, sorry I haven't called before now—Stephanie has had me all over town running around doing wedding stuff. This morning she feels it is necessary to buy out the whole of Heal's. I left her haggling over a pod of designer tables—whatever that is. I don't suppose you could make lunch today, could you?"

"Oh yes," Sophie said, perhaps a touch too eagerly to be seemly when talking to another woman's fiancé. "Yes, Jake—fantastic. When and where?"

"How about a late lunch, say two? At J Sheekey's, do you know it?"

"Great, I'll see you there," Sophie said, checking her watch and mentally calculating the exact number of minutes she had to turn herself from aged teenage throwback to foxy girl about town. "Look forward to it."

"Me too, honey," Jake said before hanging up. "Me too."

Sophie set her phone down on the table and looked at her mother.

"I am not pregnant," she stated, reinforcing her point with a slash of her hands. "Mother? What on earth makes you think I'm pregnant?"

"You've gone off alcohol . . ."

"I'm stressed and my stomach's all churny, that's all it is."

"And the smell of coffee turns your stomach."

"I've never really liked coffee *that* much . . ." Sophie slowed as she remembered that until very recently she'd downed two cups of the black stuff before even opening her eyes. "Anyway, that's probably living by the sea and not having to get up at five every morning to be in the office by six. I don't need caffeine anymore, my body has weaned itself off it."

"I thought you said you were stressed."

"I am stressed *now,* but I wasn't stressed when I went off . . . gave up coffee."

"And you keep crying . . ."

"That'll be the stress and PMS probably," Sophie said, shrugging.

"And, darling," Iris added timidly. "You've gained a little weight."

"Ah well, yes, I know that," Sophie said. "I have a lot of cream teas, Mum. Besides, you don't put weight on in pregnancy until you're quite far along so . . ."

"So when *was* your last period?" Iris asked her carefully, accepting Tripod's paw that batted at her knee and shaking it as if they had only just been introduced.

"Well, it was . . ." Sophie trailed off as she thought. She had never been especially in tune with her body's biological rhythm, her cycle had never been that regular. "I don't know, a few weeks ago. Three, or so I expect. Like I said, I'm premenstrual probably, that's why I'm doing all the crying and stuff."

"Sophie." Iris looked serious. "Think of a thing you were doing the last time you had your period. An event, something you were doing with the girls maybe."

Sophie crossed her arms and huffed out a sigh, exactly as she had when Iris used to tell her to tidy her room.

"Fine," she said. "I was at the roller disco with Bella and Izzy in the guildhall. I remember because it hadn't stopped raining even though it was July and those two were whizzing around like maniacs and all I wanted was a hot water bottle and a good book."

"July," Iris stated. "When in July?"

"It was summer holiday obviously, Louis was doing this big wedding out of town, it was a really big deal, his first large commission, and that was July seventh, which was . . ." Sophie stopped talking.

"Over two months ago," Iris finished for her.

"Oh god," Sophie said very quietly. "I'm having an early menopause."

"No, you're having a lot of sex. Darling, I think you need to get a test."

"I just . . . I don't feel pregnant and we are always very careful . . ."

"Do you have any idea what it feels like to be pregnant? And how careful? Were you on the pill?" Iris asked.

"No," Sophie confessed. "But we always use a condom . . . more or less."

"More or less?" Iris asked.

"Well, maybe once or twice we got a bit carried away and . . . well, we went for the Catholic method instead—oh god, Mother, I thought you said no details."

"Darling, you need to go and buy a pregnancy test today," Iris told her. "Babies come when you least expect them. Look at Tripod here. He was supposed to have had the snip but he still managed to get Miss Pickles pregnant. The vet said it was a modern miracle. Either that or Miss Pickles has been playing around with another black-and-tan spaniel."

"I can't go and buy a test. I'm going out for lunch," Sophie told her. "In fact, I have to go and get ready now, so, sorry, can't discuss this anymore."

"Sophie, I know that you like to push things to the back of your mind rather than face them full on but . . ." Iris stalled as Sophie glared at her. "Get a test on the way back," Iris advised Sophie as she dashed upstairs. "And stay away from raw fish!"

Fifteen

As Sophie entered the wood-paneled finery of J Sheekey's, she pushed her mother's crackpot theory to the back of her mind. She was not pregnant. She would know if she was pregnant. There would be a feeling, a prescient knowledge that she was about to become an actual full-blown biological mother to another human being. Something that profound, something that life changing couldn't just creep up on you when you weren't looking, surely? It would have to announce itself in your psyche with some sort of intuitive fanfare, otherwise it simply wasn't fair play. It was true that Sophie had not been especially clear on a lot of things that had been happening in her life recently. She wasn't clear about love and what that meant exactly about marriage or commitment. But one thing she was totally, completely, and utterly clear about was that she was not ready to have a baby. And so she dealt with it in the way she had always dealt with worries or problems that had overwhelmed her since she was a child. She decided not to think about it.

The concierge took her coat and led her to a table in a corner booth where Jake was waiting for her, wearing his weekend uniform of light blue button-down shirt topping a pair of chinos.

"You look radiant," he said, half rising to kiss her on the cheek as she slid into the booth next to him. Sophie had to admit that she did look good. She looked like her old self, only a bit hippier and with a new and improved cleavage. After her mother had aired her preposterous theory, which probably had a lot more to do with Iris's longing for a grandchild and her HRT, Sophie had made a special effort to dress like a woman who was certainly not pregnant. She had slipped on her loyal and steadfast black Dolce & Gabbana heels, which she teamed with a black knit dress that set off her pale complexion and blond hair, her cake-enhanced curves filling out the dress much more satisfyingly now. She'd never have the cleavage of Miss Stephanie Corollo, but she was more than pleased with how she filled out the dress. The absolute truth was that she had tried on another skirt she'd brought with her, only she hadn't quite been able to zip it up, and even if she had, it would have made her newly round tummy look even bigger than it was. But even so, here she was, a modern, stylish woman. A woman who was most definitely free of any sort of reproductive type of condition of any kind.

"Hope you don't mind," Jake said. "I've ordered champagne and I thought we'd start with some Colchester oysters; a dozen are on their way, is that okay?"

"Um." Sophie wanted to say, "Yes, fine, oysters, I love them," but a little nagging part of her wouldn't allow it. "The only thing is, I've become allergic to shellfish."

"No! Not now that you live right by the sea where you can practically scoop up crustaceans with your bare hands?" Jake commiserated. "You should have mentioned it when I suggested we come here!"

"I know, but I'm still getting used to the idea," Sophie told him. "It's come as a bit of a shock."

"No problem, I shouldn't have been so presumptuous." He called over a waiter. "I'll change the order—how about their deep-fried white bait, it's to die for. And you can enjoy the champagne."

When Sophie thought about champagne, all she could think about was the taste of sweaty socks. Bile rose in her throat.

"Except that I'm on antibiotics," Sophie said. "I can't drink. I mean I literally can't drink. I keep trying, but nothing seems to go down." Jake laughed and Sophie wondered what chemical outlets were available to potentially gestating people and decided that probably there were none. Except that she wasn't a potentially gestating person. She was sure of it. Almost.

"So you're back in London visiting your mother?" Jake said.

"Yes, duty calls." Sophie smiled. They were almost sitting side by side in the booth, his thigh barely six inches from hers. J Sheekey's was a busy, exclusive place, this had to be a table Jake had specifically requested and he would have had to have some considerable clout with the management to get it on such short notice. Which meant that not only did he want to impress her, he wanted to sit as close to her as possible, a fact Sophie found intriguing.

"No trouble in paradise then?" Jake asked, with just the merest hint of hope in his voice. He picked up her left hand and looked at her ring finger. "Wow, you're engaged too—congratulations. You should have said the other night."

"Oh well," Sophie said, dropping her lashes coyly. "I didn't want to steal your thunder. Congratulations to you—Stephanie is lovely."

"Yes, she is, isn't she?" Jake smiled fondly. "She's pretty stunning in every respect."

"Why doesn't she stay with you at your apartment while she's in London?" Sophie asked.

"Appearances. She's from a very old New York Italian family. She's got a great-grandmother, who's about a hundred or something and who sets a lot of store in appearances, that's filtered down to Stephanie. She's an old-fashioned girl at heart. We spend pretty much every night together, but we need to do it at two separate addresses."

"I think that's sweet," Sophie said. "I've started to think that no sex before marriage is probably an excellent idea."

"Really? You surprise me, you don't look like a woman who's not . . ." Jake stopped himself, blushing. "You look very happy."

"So will you buy a house when you're married?" Sophie asked, mildly disconcerted by the way he was looking at her while talking about his fiancée.

"Stephanie's got this amazing penthouse overlooking Central Park. We'll live there."

"What, you mean you'll go back to the States at weekends or something?" Sophie was surprised.

"No, I mean I'll go back to New York for good. Stephanie didn't want to live in the UK. She'd miss her family too much, and I couldn't think of anything to stay here for, much as I love this town and its people . . . especially some of them." He paused to smile at her and Sophie found herself smiling back at him. Despite gorgeous, successful, and independently wealthy Stephanie, despite the ring on Stephanie's finger and her own, Jake still found her attractive and she found that, in this instance, what with the late-period debacle and Louis's overly complicated personal life, she liked it. She liked it very much.

"She seems like a woman worth moving to another continent for," Sophie said softly as Jake slid a few millimeters closer to her.

"She is," he told her, leaning toward her a little, as if he were breathing her in. "She's the perfect match for me . . . which makes me wonder why . . ."

"Why what?" Sophie asked him in what she thought would widely be considered a seductive tone. She felt inordinately proud of herself. Until very recently a seductive anything would have been well out of her reach.

"Why I've never quite been able to get you out of my head," Jake said. "You never really wanted me, we barely did more than kiss a couple of times, yet here you are sitting in front of me and all I can think about is how much I'd like to kiss you."

"Well, I've got to say I'm not surprised," Sophie said, making Jake sputter out a mouthful of champagne.

"No?" he asked her.

"Well, you know, there's this place, this table—oysters, champagne. This is not a lunch that one friend throws for another. It's a seduction lunch, Jake, whether you realized it or not. You planned to get me here for one last little spin before you marry Stephanie. Next you'll be telling me you booked a hotel room so that we can have coffee in private."

Jake stared at her openmouthed for a second, as if he were about to protest, and then he laughed.

"You're right," he said. "I think that in the back of my mind I was hoping for something . . . but I promise you, I didn't plan it— there is no hotel room. It's just that you look stunning, Sophie. Being in love really agrees with you, and when I saw you it reminded me of how much I liked you. How different things would have been if you'd liked me back, and that got me wondering, I guess. I'm sorry."

"Don't be sorry," Sophie told him, reassured that he still found her attractive despite herself because it meant there was no way on earth she could have any kind of bun in her oven. Pregnant women couldn't be beguiling and seductive. Mother Nature wouldn't allow ladies to go round flirting when they had an actual baby inside them, that would just be *wrong*. Sophie was certain that being knocked up meant sexiness went out the window. And she was definitely sexy, she was on fire with desirability. If only her so-called fiancé found her as hard to resist as Jake did.

"I think it's because you've changed." Jake's voice was low. "It's as if something or someone has switched you on, you look alight with life. You look incredible."

"Thank you," Sophie said. "It's the same for me, seeing you, you know. I think that if things had been different, if we'd met at another time, then maybe we would have rubbed along pretty well together. But I don't think we would ever have really been in love. Not like you are with Stephanie . . . not like I am with Louis."

"Stephanie is amazing," Jake said. "And I do love her. It's just . . . I really like kissing you, Sophie."

"You know, it could be useful," Sophie said thoughtfully. "To kiss someone other than our fiancés just to be able to compare and contrast. You know, to make sure that the feelings we think we are feeling for our significant others are real."

Sophie raised her eyebrows, surprised by what she had half suggested.

"Are you suggesting we kiss each other purely for scientific research?" Jake asked her.

"Am I suggesting that?" Sophie hedged.

"I think you are." Without warning Jake grabbed her hand and all but dragged her out of the booth and through the restaurant, turning heads as he went.

"We have to make a call," he told the waiter, who looked astounded as Jake rushed past. "Back in a minute."

Sophie followed Jake, not absolutely certain of what was going on until they emerged into the alleyway that ran behind Tottenham Court Road.

Without pausing to take a breath, Jake put his hands on her shoulders and backed her against a graffiti-covered wall. For a second he looked at her, breathing hard, and then he kissed her. And Sophie kissed him back in a way she never would have before, her body hungry for intimacy, responding to Jake long before her mind could process what was happening. For several seconds everything about the kiss felt wonderful, incredible. And then Sophie realized—the lips that sought out her neck were not Louis's, the hands that had traveled down from her shoulders and across her breasts weren't the ones her body longed to be touched by, and, most of all, she was standing in an alleyway kissing a man who wasn't the father of her baby. Not that she was pregnant, but if she were, then that would have been bad.

Sophie pushed Jake away.

"Wow," Jake said. "Not exactly sure the results of that experiment went the way they were supposed to."

"Aren't you?" Sophie asked him.

"Not if I was supposed to discover that I don't like kissing you, because I do. A lot."

"No you don't," Sophie told him, despite the evidence to the contrary that was quite clearly visible in his chinos. "And neither do I. You love Stephanie, I could see it all over your face when you talked about her, and I love Louis. I really do, and I don't know what I'm doing kissing you in a back alley, because kissing you only made me miss him more."

"Ouch." Jake sighed, picking up her hand and kissing it. "You know, it kills me to say it, but I don't think I would ever have been the right man for you, even if Louis hadn't come along."

"Maybe not—but judging from that kiss, Stephanie's a very lucky lady," Sophie said, smiling tentatively.

"So can we still have lunch?" Jake asked hopefully, holding her hand. "We can swap wedding plans."

"I'd love to have lunch with you. But I don't actually have any wedding plans yet," Sophie told him as she followed him back into the restaurant.

"Really? You're not like any bride I know. Listen, if it's not too awkward you should talk it through with Stephanie. That woman is a wedding-planning machine."

"Is she . . . ?" Sophie suddenly had visions of a transatlantic wedding-planning empire as they settled back into the booth. "Jake?"

"Yep?" Jake asked her, considerably more relaxed than he had been when they'd left.

"Thank you. It's so good to have you as a friend."

His smile was perhaps a little sad as he kissed her on the cheek and then said, "Sophie, I was always going to be your friend."

Sixteen

Sophie stood in the pharmacy on the corner of Highbury Grove for a long time, looking at its meager selection of nail polish. She thought of Stephanie Corollo's long, glossy red nails and then examined her own broken plain ones, still a little Cornish sand collected in their corners, and she picked up a bottle of Scarlet Woman from a little basket of bargain items located next to the copper arthritis bracelets.

The woman behind the counter watched Sophie closely, her facial expression set in mistrust and disapproval. Perhaps it was because she wasn't used to lengthy browsing in the tiny pharmacy where people probably usually knew exactly what they wanted when they dashed in on their way home from work or while rushing the kids off to school. Perhaps, in her designer black knit dress and Dolce & Gabbana shoes, Sophie looked the type to try and run off with a bottle of nail polish worth fifty-nine pence. Most likely though, Sophie concluded, it was because the woman knew that Sophie had not come in to buy nail polish, or an emery board, or indeed any of the other miscellaneous items she was clutching in her hands, but the pregnancy-testing kit she kept looking at, sitting on the shelf, which she hadn't yet had the courage to pick up.

It was foolish, Sophie knew, for a woman her age and in her circumstances to feel embarrassed about buying the item she needed. She was not some irresponsible teen or some good-time girl who'd end up on a morning chat show waiting for the results of a paternity test. She was a woman in her thirties, and an engaged woman to boot, with a ring to prove it, even if she wasn't entirely sure how she'd left things with her fiancé. By almost anyone's standard in the modern world, she was probably perfectly entitled to be buying a pregnancy test without anyone judging her.

The trouble was that Sophie judged herself. If her mother was right about her condition, she hadn't noticed any difference in herself for over two months. She was on the brink of motherhood and had taken about as much care in approaching that responsibility as a lemming careering over a cliff—and what kind of mother would that make her? Once, when the girls had first come into her life, she had moaned to Iris about her lack of any kind of maternal feeling, not to mention a total absence of the women's intuition that people, mostly other women, harped on incessantly, hinting that the female of the human species was ever so slightly psychic when it came to her offspring. Iris had told her that she had just as much maternal instinct as the next woman and that all she had to do was listen. Yet for possibly two months she had been potentially pregnant, and she hadn't experienced the merest flicker in her subconscious to alert her to what would be the most pivotal, life-changing moment in her existence on planet earth.

At that second her phone burst into life in her pocket, causing her to drop the merchandise she was holding onto the floor. The woman behind the counter sighed and folded her arms under her breasts.

"Sorry," Sophie said to the woman as she fished the phone out of her bag and saw Louis's name on the display. The sight of his name set her heart racing, but she was prepared for it to be anyone on the phone but him, including Bella and Wendy.

"Hello?" she answered.

"It's me," Louis said. Sophie tensed; his voice sounded flat, distant even as it nestled in her ear.

"I know," Sophie told him, picking up the items she'd dropped.

"It is okay for me to call you, isn't it?" Louis asked her edgily. "You said you'd call and you haven't."

"I have called," Sophie said, surprised by the chill in her voice. "Wendy answered, and I left a message for you to call me back but you didn't."

Louis was silent for a long moment. "You didn't try again though," he said, not leaving Sophie any wiser as to whether or not Wendy had passed on the message.

"Neither did you," Sophie said. She wanted to talk to him about her call from Bella, but she knew that would be the worst possible thing she could bring up now. He had called her at last and she didn't want to overwhelm this fragile contact with a rush of information.

"I'm really glad to hear the sound of your voice," she said softly, desperate to draw them a little closer together, even over so many miles. "I've missed you."

"Have you?" Louis sounded uncertain, defensive, but perhaps just a fraction warmer. "It's just that I wasn't sure if you'd walked out on me and the girls or not."

"I would never do that," Sophie promised him.

"So you've just walked out on marrying me?" Louis asked her tightly.

"Look, Louis—"

"Yes, I know—you need space. You don't need to explain anything to me, that's not why I'm ringing you. We've been looking for Seth all week, but he's nowhere. One of his flatmates says he met this girl in Tottenham at a gig the other day, and apparently he really liked her. She lives in London. Wendy's really worried about him. He hasn't answered his phone all week or tried to contact her—she says he can be a bit rash if he's upset about something. She's really worried, so we've got the girl's address and we're coming up to see if he's there. We'll be leaving in an hour or so. The roads should be pretty clear, so we'll make good time. I thought I'd let you know in case we bumped into you."

"Right," Sophie said, fighting both the irritation that rose in her chest at the very mention of Wendy's name and the urge to point out that the chances of Louis "bumping into" her anywhere in the capital city of several million were slim to nil. But she didn't want to sound facetious and unreasonable.

"What about the girls?" she asked.

"Mrs. Alexander's said she'll mind them; hopefully we'll get back by Sunday, otherwise I'm not sure about school on Monday . . ." Louis trailed off.

"Look, Mum's house is sort of on the way to Tottenham," Sophie said. "Bring them to me. Mum would love to see them, I'd love to see them, they'd love to see the dogs. They can stay the night while you go and see Seth and then perhaps tomorrow I could take them to see their grandma." Sophie was referring to Carrie's mother, who lived in an assisted-living home a short drive from her mother's house. "And if they miss one day of school it won't be the end of the world. If you and Wendy need to stay in London longer, I'll take them back home."

As Sophie said the last word of her sentence, she felt a pull in her chest and pictured Louis's living room, lit only by the electric fire. She felt homesick for a place where she didn't fully belong yet.

"And perhaps we could have a few minutes to talk things over?" Sophie added.

Sophie again eyed the selection of pregnancy tests on the shelf. She wasn't exactly sure how Louis would take the news of yet another surprise child at the moment, and suddenly she felt very sad. If she was pregnant, if her body could possibly be playing host to a fledgling human life without having the common decency to drop her a line and let her know she was expecting company, then it should be an occasion for joy, delight, and wonder. A special time for both herself and Louis. But, as it was, the news would have to be juggled with another new arrival, even if he was six foot two. Louis seemed to have a surplus of children right now. And after what he'd said about not wanting any more children, she wasn't sure that news of another one would give him any kind of joy at all.

"It's a long way to bring them for a couple of nights, but they would much rather be with you than Mrs. Alexander," Louis said thoughtfully. "Are you sure?"

"Of course I'm sure—and if you and . . . Wendy need a place to stay, you could stay at my mum's too. Wendy could have the sofa—although she would have to share it with Scooby and he can get a bit frisky at night."

Louis did not laugh, and too late Sophie realized that she had managed to sound flippant again.

"Thanks for the offer," Louis told her. "But I'm not sure what we're doing."

Sophie swallowed her irritation at his use of "we" without her being included in it.

She gave him her mother's address and said, "So I'll see you at Mum's then? Call me when you're nearly here."

"Thanks, Sophie," Louis said.

"No problem, and, Louis—I love you," Sophie said. A beat of silence passed before she realized that Louis had already hung up.

"Right," Sophie said, turning to look the shop assistant in the eye. "This is ridiculous. I am a grown woman." She dumped the items she had collected on a display of cough medicine and turned around and picked up the first pregnancy kit she could lay her hands on.

Iris and Sophie stood outside the bathroom while they were waiting for the results of the test.

Iris had suggested Sophie bring the test out of the bathroom with her, but Sophie said that, pregnant or not, she had not yet reached the point in her life where she felt comfortable about walking around with a plastic stick she had recently urinated on. Besides, knowing her mother's dogs, the odds were high that one of them would make off with it and bury it in the back garden at the first opportunity. "All right then," Iris had said. "Let's go downstairs and make tea while we wait."

"No, I've only got to wait three minutes, less than that now," Sophie said, peering in through the crack she had left open in the bathroom door. She could see the test kit glinting innocuously in the September light. It just didn't look like it had the power to change your life completely, she thought. The manufacturer should endow them with more gravitas, perhaps a chrome trim and a red flashing light, something that said "Your life will never be the same again." White plastic didn't seem to do it.

"Three minutes minimum," Iris said. "We could have tea and then come and look. Another five minutes won't make you any more or less pregnant."

"No, Mum, I'm standing here until the three minutes are up and then I'm going in."

"I'll cover you," Iris said, her smile fading when Sophie didn't laugh. She crossed her arms and leaned against the textured wallpaper. Miss Pickles trotted up the stairs and eyed Iris for a moment before walking past, no doubt intending to catch a nap on Sophie's bed.

"I know," Iris sighed, rolling her eyes as if she and the animal had just had a conversation.

There were several beats of silence, punctuated only by hearing Miss Pickles throwing any unwanted items of Sophie's off the bed as she prepared for her nap, and then Iris piped up, "Is it time now?"

Sophie glanced at her watch.

"Twenty more seconds," she said, continuing to study the watch face. "Ten."

The two women watched each other, reflections of their pasts and their futures, and silently counted down the last ten seconds remaining between Sophie and her fate.

"This is it," Sophie said and she pushed the bathroom door open.

"I'm not sure you should have out-of-date peppermint tea now that I know you definitely are pregnant," Iris said, putting the kettle on the stove, which was her stock response to most of life's ups and downs. On the day her dad had died, Iris must have made a hundred cups of tea. Sophie remembered being sent out to the grocer to get another box of eighty tea bags.

"I'll just pop out to the corner shop now and get some fresh," Iris offered, picking up her purse.

"No, just give me a glass of water," Sophie said. "Don't go out, please."

Iris put her bag down and filled a glass, setting it in front of Sophie.

"Isn't it funny how things can change just like that," Iris said conversationally, snapping her fingers to illustrate the point.

"I'll say," Sophie replied absently.

"Listen, sweetheart, I know it's a shock—but you know you love Louis and you're going to marry him. Perhaps a baby now is a little sooner than you might have planned, but I promise you that once you've had a chance to get used to the idea, it will be fantastic. It will be wonderful."

"It's just so final," Sophie said slowly. "It's just so definite."

"Yes, babies do tend to be quite definite." Iris looked perplexed. "What do you mean?"

"I meant that up until this point I still had choices. I could still have come back to London, got my old job back or one like it. I could still have flown off to New York and disrupted Jake's wedding. I could still have told Louis that I've had enough of him and his crazy ex and his secret son. In fact, up until this point I could have cut the last year out of my life and never looked back, but I can't do any of that now. I definitely can't, because I am that thing. The *p* word. Pregnant. That is me, I am it. Knocked up."

"Yes you are," Iris said, sitting next to her. "And I can see how it seems as if the world is suddenly closing in on you. But ask yourself—if you weren't pregnant, would you really have done any of those things? Would you have come back to London and worked in an office job that took over your life? Would you really have flown to America to break up the marriage of some man I've never heard of, but who I suspect is probably who you went to lunch with today? Would you really have left Louis because he's got an annoying ex or would you have helped him sort things out with Seth and stood by him because even though it scares you to death you love him? And most of all, Sophie, would you, could you, ever cut those little girls out of your life? Baby or no, I don't think you would have done any of that. Because that's not you, that's not my daughter who I am so proud of."

"Are you really proud of me?" Sophie asked, surprised.

"Of course I am," Iris told her, draping her arms around her daughter's shoulders. "I didn't understand you when you were working all those hours at McCarthy Hughes, never taking a breath to enjoy life, but I was always proud of you. And now I've seen how very brave you were in taking on those girls and how much you fought for them. And how you risked everything to be happy . . . I thought it would be impossible for me to be more proud of you, but here you are about to give me my first grandchild. Things couldn't get much better."

Sophie nodded. "I know," she said. "It's just that I'm pregnant. And it probably really hurts having a baby, and if I couldn't work out I was pregnant in the first place, how in god's name am I going to deal with it when it arrives?"

"You did know you were pregnant, you just didn't know you knew," Iris told her. "You went off alcohol and caffeine, you put on a little weight. Your body was protecting your baby even if it took your brain a little while to catch up with the signs. And it will be the same when the baby's here. You'll be amazed by what you know without knowing you knew it. You'll learn the rest and you'll cope and you will be brilliant at it. Look at how you coped when you took in Bella and Izzy. Look at how much love you gave them and how they trusted and respected and loved you back, and you'd had nothing to do with any children before then." Iris kissed the top of Sophie's head. "Look, darling, you won't be a perfect mother because there's no such thing. But you'll be a brilliant, loyal, loving, fun, and fair mother, and do you know how I know that?"

Sophie shook her head. "Is it because you've been on the dog tranquilizers again?"

"Because you already are, you already are a mother to those two little girls."

Suddenly Sophie pictured Carrie, with Bella in her arms, her lips pressed lightly to her firstborn's forehead, the look in her eyes one of shining contentment and joy. Sophie knew that whatever she had learned about love and trust from Carrie's daughters had been at her best friend's and Bella and Izzy's expense. Precious stolen minutes, memories that the three of them would never be able to share together, snuffed out in a few minutes of arbitrary destruction. And as she thought about the tiny spark of life that had begun to burn inside her, she felt overwhelmed with all that Carrie and her children had lost.

"I'm not their mother," she said. "I never will be."

"But you're the next best thing, and you love them every bit as much as you will love your own. And if Carrie could be here now she'd thank you for giving them the love she can't any longer."

Suddenly weary and indescribably sad, Sophie rested her head on the table and wept.

"That's it," Iris said, rubbing Sophie's back the way she used to when Sophie was a little girl. "You let it out, you'll feel better for it. And you wait and see; once you've told Louis, you'll feel so much better. I bet you he'll be overjoyed."

"I am very pleased to see you, Aunty Sophie!" Izzy said into Sophie's hair as she flung her arms around Sophie, who was attempting to fend off a small pack of overexcited dogs as she bent to embrace the four-year-old. Louis must have stopped at some point on the way to change them into their pajamas. Izzy was wearing her favorite pink fluffy pony pajamas with feet and Bella had on the dark red flannel she'd chosen herself, all bundled up underneath a red-and-green-tartan dressing gown that somehow succeeded in giving her the air of a Victorian amateur detective rather than a seven-year-old girl.

"Come here, Bella," Sophie said, kissing her a little haphazardly on the bangs as Scooby shouldered Bella to one side hoping it was him Sophie was inviting for a hug rather than the child. "Oh, I've missed you two!"

"This is Wendy," Bella said to Iris, screwing up her eyes as Scooby gave her an inquisitive lick on the cheek, pointing at Wendy, who was standing in the living room doorway peering over Louis's shoulder as if she were using him as a human shield. Louis looked a little awkward standing in the hallway; he had never been to Iris's house before. And he looked as if he didn't know what to do or where to stand. "Wendy is Daddy's friend who used to go to school with him. They did do kissing once but not anymore because now Daddy loves Aunty Sophie. Wendy has a grown-up son who has run away, although he is grown up, so . . ." Bella shrugged, as if to say "What's the big deal?" "Daddy has brought us to London because he is going to help Wendy look for Seth. So that is why we are here. And to see you, Aunty Sophie, not to visit you, because you only visit people you don't see very often, but we are still going to see you very often, aren't we? Because you are only visiting your mummy, aren't you? And then you are coming back to St. Ives to be with us."

"Yes I am," Sophie said, looking up at Louis and hoping to catch his eye, but he seemed to be studying the floor. Taking a breath, Sophie smiled, hugging both girls to her chest amid a forest of wagging tails. "It's been years since I've seen you!"

"It's been a week," Bella informed her, smiling all the same. Sophie dragged her bundle of girls onto the sofa, out of the worst attention of the dogs, and cuddled them to her. Apart from her need to know exactly where she stood with Sophie, Bella seemed quite calm about their unscheduled trip and Sophie knew that was because she thought she understood what was going on. Yet it was clear that Louis had still seen fit to give her only an edited version of the truth and that worried Sophie. Eventually he would have to tell his daughters exactly who Seth was, and Sophie knew that Bella would feel hurt and betrayed, and Sophie was afraid of how she would react. If only she could have a chance to tell Louis all her worries and fears.

"Hello, you two." Iris appeared with a plate of pink-iced cookies that immediately attracted the attention of all the dogs and the children in the room, so much so that she had to hold them above her head.

"Now I know it's late, but I thought just this once it would be okay for you to have a cookie and some hot chocolate before bed. Not you, Scooby." The girls giggled as Scooby made an attempt to balance on his back legs to reach the cookies and Iris smiled sweetly at Louis. "That's okay, isn't it, Louis?"

"Of course, Iris." Louis advanced into the room for the first time, stepping over dogs to reach Sophie's mother and plant a kiss on her cheek. Sophie tried not to notice that he had kissed her mother before he'd come anywhere near her, but his apparent disinterest in her stung as badly as if he'd slapped her in the face. She dipped her head, burying her face in Izzy's hair and closing her eyes until the threat of tears had passed. "Thanks so much for having them to stay. They'd much rather be here with Soph and you than anywhere else."

"It's no trouble," Iris said, smiling fondly at the girls. "You know I think of you as family, and you two lovelies are the best little girls I know, yes you are!" Iris chucked Izzy under the chin as if she were one of her pet dogs, which in fairness she did bear a striking resemblance to because as soon as the cookies had appeared, she climbed down from the sofa and stood perfectly still at Scooby's side, her head not quite level with his, both pairs of eyes fixed firmly on the prize.

"Well, you come with me then," Iris said. "And you, Bella. We'll go in the kitchen and let Daddy and Sophie have a few words." She looked at Wendy and sniffed.

"Come through and have some tea, Wendy," she all but commanded.

Sophie looked at Louis's companion. She looked like she hadn't slept much, as did Louis. His stubble had grown halfway to a beard and he looked a little lost, like he had the first time Sophie met him, on the night he'd flown back from Peru after finding out that Carrie had been killed. He'd been waiting for her outside her flat because he'd been desperate to find the children he had abandoned, one of whom hadn't even been born when he'd left, and make amends. That night Sophie had mistaken him for a tramp. Tonight though, no matter how disheveled and tired he looked, there was no doubt that he was the man she loved; suddenly she was exhausted by all the thinking and the striving to be certain. All she knew was that she loved him and wanted to do whatever it took to make him happy. And if that meant waiting for him to resolve things with Wendy and Seth, then she would.

"We haven't got long," Wendy said, glancing at Louis as she followed Iris toward the kitchen. "I really want to try and see Seth tonight."

"Won't be long," Louis said, smiling reassuringly at Wendy as Sophie herded the last of the dogs out behind the other woman, shutting the door behind her. Finally they were alone.

"I've missed you," Sophie said, standing an awkward three feet from him.

"Really?" Louis asked her. "I wasn't sure if you would."

"Yes." Sophie smiled cautiously. "I know I shouldn't have just rushed off like that, I was tired and Wendy really did make things difficult and well . . . Louis, it turns out I was very hormonal." She paused, desperate to ask him if he had missed her too, but terrified by what he might say.

"It's okay," Louis said, shrugging, directing his attention to the mantelpiece where her mother kept an array of her school photos, from cute and ponytailed five-year-old to awkward teen. "It's all right that you want some space to think about us. I didn't want you to go, but I've had a chance to think about it and maybe it's the right thing."

"The right thing?" Sophie felt a cool wash of fear sweep through her. "What's the right thing?"

"That we take a breather, have some time apart. Put the engagement on hold."

"On hold?" Sophie asked him.

"Yes." Louis redirected his gaze to the ceiling, and then to the toes of his boots, seeming to prefer looking anywhere but at her. "It's like Wendy said, the timing's not great. I need to get things sorted with Seth, I need to work out what's happening there and get it on an even keel. So maybe it is best for you to move in with your mum while I'm doing that."

"Out of the way," Sophie confirmed, her tone nudging at anger.

"No, that's not what I mean." Louis frowned. "Look, it was you who packed a bag and left without a moment's notice. All I'm saying is that maybe it is a good idea after all."

"Because Wendy says so?" Sophie was desperate to bring things back to the point where she felt she could reach out and touch and kiss him and tell him about the baby, but the more she wanted that, the more she seemed to say the very thing that would push him away.

"No, not because of Wendy, because of Seth and because it's what you want."

"And what you want too," Sophie said, struggling to contain the tears that came so quickly these days. "When you say put the engagement on hold . . . what do you mean?"

"I mean exactly that," Louis told her. "I'm a man, I mean what I say. There aren't any double or triple hidden meanings with me."

"And then?" Sophie asked him, bewildered by how quickly it had come to this between them.

"I don't know, you answer that one," Louis told her. "You're the one who left."

Sophie struggled with the hundreds of things she wanted to say, but they somehow wouldn't form themselves into a sentence.

"I think you should go and find Seth," she said instead, feeling somehow as if she was breaking for good an invisible bond. "It's late."

"Okay," Louis said and nodded. "We'll probably be all night, so I'll ring you in the morning."

"Fine," Sophie said and bowed her head.

"Right, I'll get Wendy."

As Louis strode past her, Sophie grabbed his arm. It was the first time they had touched each other since he'd arrived.

"Louis, I have to tell you something." Sophie swallowed. She simply could not find the words to tell him she was pregnant. Not now, not when things were like this between them and she was sure that the news would serve only to drive them further apart. "I really think you should tell the girls who Seth is and why you are looking for him so hard."

"I know you do," Louis said.

"If Bella finds out another way, she'll be so hurt and angry. I'm worried about how she'll react, especially after she took your phone—"

"She what?"

Sophie realized belatedly that Louis probably still didn't know about that. "She borrowed your phone to call me one day. They wanted to speak to me and they didn't understand why you wouldn't let them call me. Neither do I, for that matter. You know how much I love Bella and Izzy; no matter what happens between us I will always be there for them."

"They are my daughters and I know them. I know what's best for them."

Sophie nodded, realizing that he was in no mood to listen to her, and let go of his arm. "I hope you find him."

"Me too," Louis said, opening the door and unleashing a cacophony of canines into the room, excited all over again to find people there. "Me too."

As Sophie lay in the middle of the double bed in the nicely appointed guest room where the girls were to sleep, she wondered vaguely why her mother had insisted on putting her in her old bedroom despite the fact that it was now used more as a kennel and storeroom and came complete with an extra layer of dog hair and no heating. It had to be habit, she supposed. Her mother couldn't imagine her sleeping anywhere but in the room she had grown up in. Still, she was glad the girls had this nice, cozy room to stay in that was relatively free from pet invasion, unless you counted Tripod, who Iris let sleep in here, and he was really only three-quarters of a dog.

"So then," she said, finishing that night's story, "Petal the Princess Fairy Pony got on the boat and sailed off into the sunset looking for the World of the Mermaids."

"No, it's the *Land* of the Mermaids," Bella, the principal author of the story, reminded her.

"Sorry, the Land of the Mermaids, and tomorrow we will follow her wonderful adventures in the Town Under the Sea."

Sophie looked down to where Izzy was already fast asleep in the crook of her arm, her thumb plugging her mouth, her long, dark lashes sweeping the tops of her cheeks. Just to look at her, already so lost to her dreams, made Sophie feel very, very tired.

"Aunty Sophie," Bella said, drawing Sophie's attention to her large, dark, and very wide-awake eyes.

"Yes, darling?" Sophie stifled a yawn.

"Who is Seth really?" Bella asked her. "Why is Daddy helping that Wendy woman, who you don't like and neither do I?"

"I wouldn't say I don't like Wendy," Sophie said cautiously. "I don't really know her that well. It's just that sometimes you meet someone and you don't really get on with them. I'm sure Wendy is a nice person really to . . . to some people."

"But why is Daddy bringing us all up to London to find Seth if he's got nothing to do with us? He is a grown-up, he probably doesn't need finding."

"Well, sometimes grown-ups need looking after too," Sophie said, noting Bella's thoughtful expression with weary dismay. It meant that, unlike her sister, the child was not at all sleepy. She was in a questioning mood. And that in turn meant Sophie was either going to have to go against Louis and tell Bella the truth about Seth or lie to Bella and risk losing her trust forever.

"But why is Daddy helping Wendy, because they weren't even friends before a week ago and you and Daddy were doing the wedding and now no one is talking about the wedding and Daddy is helping that Wendy woman and I don't understand why."

Sophie closed her eyes; it was warm and cozy in the double bed, snuggled in between the two children. It would be so easy to simply close her eyes and drift off to sleep with her girls in her arms, but she had to find a way to answer Bella, otherwise she knew the little girl would be staring at the ceiling in the lamplight, keeping herself awake with wondering.

"Well, you know my mummy," Sophie began a little uncertainly.

"*Yes.*" Bella seemed equally skeptical about the direction the conversation was taking.

"She loves me and worries about me a lot, even though I am properly grown up. And Wendy is Seth's mum and she worries about him too even though he's an adult, because mummys never stop worrying about their children, not ever. And poor Seth is feeling angry and worried and upset and Wendy hasn't really had a chance to talk to him, and see if he's okay. And sometimes when you're worried you need another person, a friend, to help you get through it. I know Daddy and Wendy haven't been friends for a long time, but really good friendships never fade away, they last for years and years even if you never see the person, because you know how much you care about them, come what may. Like your mummy was . . . is still my best friend, because even though I'll never see her again, I won't forget how much I love her."

"So does Daddy love that Wendy woman?" Bella asked, looking alarmed.

"No, no, he cares about her and that's why he's helping her." Sophie hoped she was right about that. "He's being kind."

"And that's the only reason?" Bella scrutinized her, her dark eyes quizzical.

"Yes," Sophie confirmed uncomfortably.

She watched the frown between Bella's eyebrows relax as she turned her body toward Sophie and rested her head on Sophie's shoulder. Bella trusted whatever Sophie told her.

"Can you stay here and sleep with us tonight?" Bella asked. "Like I sometimes used to sleep with you on the sofa in your flat and we'd listen to the sound of the traffic and pretend it was the sea, remember?"

"Yes, I remember," Sophie said, feeling guilty that it was her half-truths that had soothed Bella at last. "And yes, I'll sleep here with you two tonight. There's nowhere else I'd rather be."

Seventeen

Sophie knew she was doing the right thing by taking Bella and Izzy to see their grandmother when they were up in London, but she had been glad to leave Mrs. Stiles's flat, even though she suspected this might be the last time the girls would see her. Mrs. Stiles had deteriorated since the last time Sophie had seen her.

Although the children loved their grandmother and were always delighted to see her, Sophie noticed that they changed whenever they were around her. Subtle differences. Izzy's natural ebullience ebbed away, and the bright, curious spark that was always present in Bella's eyes dimmed. They instinctively adjusted their behavior to fit in with the kind of woman she was, a woman who, Carrie always said, thought that enjoying life too much was a sin. Mrs. Stiles was always very sweet with the girls, pouring them the ancient lemon-barley water she kept just for their visits and giving them boiled sweets.

As Sophie watched her give each child two sweets, she tried to reconcile this thin, fragile woman with her bold and beautiful daughter. Carrie had fought almost all of her life against the emotionally repressive atmosphere her mother had brought her up in, determined that her daughters should have the childhood that she didn't, one full of laughter, fun, and freedom. And so although it was Sophie's duty to take the children to visit Mrs. Stiles as often as possible, there was something about the sound of the ticking clock in the silent living room and the dustless china figurines that paraded along the mantelpiece, Victorian dancing ladies swirling to music only they could hear, that made her think of Carrie's longing to be free.

To the delight of the children, Mrs. Stiles brought out her tin of vintage buttons, which she had been collecting since she was a girl, and put it on the table for the girls to play with. They would make pictures with the buttons, or host button balls, picking out the finest and glitteriest buttons and naming them princes and princesses.

"And how is he?" Mrs. Stiles asked her, referring to Louis as she and Sophie watched the girls from the small kitchenette.

"He's well, thank you," Sophie said. It was all she ever said. Carrie's mother had always disapproved of Louis, even before he'd found out about Carrie's affair and run away to Peru. But after that point she had him down as a weakling and a coward and barely bothered curbing her tongue for the sake of the children. If she found out about Seth, their engagement, or the baby, Sophie wasn't sure how she'd react. Carrie used to tell dark, Gothic tales of her mother losing her temper, shouting and screaming and locking Carrie in her room for hours on end, but Sophie was never sure how much of that was Carrie's love of a good tale and how much was based on fact.

"And you and he still . . . ?" Mrs. Stiles never liked to refer to Sophie's relationship with Louis directly either.

Sophie nodded, suspecting that now was not the ideal time to discuss their ups and downs, not that she'd dream of talking them over with Mrs. Stiles anyway. She watched as Carrie's mother warmed the pot before pouring boiling water onto loose tea leaves, and compared her to Grace Tregowan. Mrs. Stiles had to be at least fifteen or even twenty years younger than Grace, but Sophie could no more imagine Mrs. Stiles having four husbands than she could imagine Mrs. Tregowan ever bothering to warm a teapot when one-cup tea bags were so much quicker. Old age is not a great leveler, Sophie realized. It doesn't gently usher you into an age of peace and reflection when somehow your heart and mind are cocooned from the world, at least not unless you let it.

For Mrs. Tregowan old age meant living in hopes of husband number five. For Mrs. Stiles there was only quiet respectability, waiting out the last of her days without a hope of a final swan song, or any last railing against the fate that took her daughter from her before she ever really knew her.

"Still working, is he?" Mrs. Stiles asked as she stirred the tea leaves around in the pot.

Sophie nodded. "Yes, the photography business is doing really well now."

"He did well out of Carrie," Mrs. Stiles observed bitterly. "Her death set him up nicely."

"The girls got the security of a home and he got to set up a business that meant he'd be able to look after them. It's no more than Carrie would have wanted," Sophie said, lowering her voice, keeping an eye on the girls in case they were listening. Fortunately they both seemed entirely absorbed in the world of buttons. She watched Mrs. Stiles's hand tremble as she poured a cup of pale-looking tea into a fine bone china cup.

"And how are you?" Sophie asked her, forcibly brightening her voice as she took the cup and saucer. "Are you keeping well?"

"I'll be gone soon," Mrs. Stiles said, looking into the living room where the girls were chattering, their heads bent together over the mosaic of buttons.

"All I want to know is that those two are properly settled, properly cared for by someone I can trust not to disappear." Mrs. Stiles turned to look Sophie up and down and gestured at the ring that Sophie hadn't thought to hide. "You marry him, you'll be a mother to them like Carrie was. And you promise me that even when that one comes along, you will treat them exactly the same way that you do now, that you will never make them feel left out in the cold or alone?" Mrs. Stiles nodded at Sophie's stomach, lowering her voice as she spoke.

"That one? You mean? Oh no, I'm not . . ." Sophie stopped, caught under Mrs. Stiles's steady gaze. "No one knows," she whispered. "No one."

Mrs. Stiles nodded. "It's not as if I'm going to tell anyone, so you've no worries there."

"Thank you," Sophie said, briefly pressing the palm of her hand against her belly, an unconscious protective gesture.

"I've had a lot of time to think since Carrie went." Mrs. Stiles kept her voice low. "I wasn't a good mother, perhaps I was never supposed to be either a mother or a wife. I drove her father away because I was never content, and after he'd gone I constantly tried to pin Carrie down, to trap her like a butterfly—but what for? I'm glad she fought me and had the life she wanted, even if it was difficult sometimes, and I'm glad she gave those girls all the spirit and fire and imagination that she got from somewhere, though God knows it wasn't me. She's gone now, and soon I will be, and as far as I'm concerned you are the only person those girls can rely on—"

"Mrs. Stiles, really, Louis is not like that—"

"No, let me finish. I don't know what he's like or what he's not like and I don't want to know. But what I do know is that at the first sign of trouble, he ran out on Carrie and the children. Perhaps she deserved it, but those girls didn't. And if he can do it once, he can do it again. So you marry him, you have that . . ." Mrs. Stiles nodded once more at her stomach. "But you look after my grandchildren, you swear to me that you will always look after them."

"I swear," Sophie said, reaching out to touch Mrs. Stiles's brittle shoulder. "I swear to you, the same way I swore to them, they will always have me. Always, forever, whatever."

Mrs. Stiles inclined her head. "Thank you," she said. "That comforts me."

Sophie placed her hand gently over her abdomen. "How did you know about this?"

"Just being old," Mrs. Stiles said, treating Sophie to a rare smile. "You get to my age and there's not much gets past you. Besides, you've got that look about you, you look like a mother."

Sophie pressed her lips together hard, determined not to cry now before the very person who would appreciate it the least. It was the only tribute she knew she could pay to this woman she understood so very little.

"Just make sure he looks after you the way he never looked after my Carrie," Mrs. Stiles said, patting Sophie on the back of her hand, fully appreciative of her determination not to let her emotions show. "Don't let him run out on you."

When it was time to go, Mrs. Stiles delighted the girls by allowing them to take the ancient tin of buttons away with them. "When I was your age, I used to play with these for hours and hours with your great-aunty Evie, just like you two do. And your mother used to play with them too when she was little," she said as she solemnly gave the tin to Bella, whose expression was wide-eyed as she received the treasure. "Some buttons in here belonged to my grandma, which makes them a hundred years old."

"That's as old as God, nearly!" Izzy breathed in wonderment.

"Well, not quite, but anyway, you promise me that you will take care of them and that you will never lose them, and that when you see or find a very interesting or special button that you will add it to the tin. And then one day you will be able to pass it on to your children."

"I'm not having children, I'm having cats," Izzy told her.

"We will look after them," Bella told her grandmother, sensing the gravity of the situation a little better than her sister. "Mostly I will."

Mrs. Stiles nodded and with some difficulty bent to kiss both girls, holding them close to her until they wriggled to be free. "Good-bye, my beautiful girls," she said with a finality that made Sophie uncomfortable.

"Good-bye, Grandma, see you next time," Izzy said, hopping off toward the car.

"Good-bye, Grandma, thank you for the buttons . . ." Bella paused. "I love you."

"Sophie," Mrs. Stiles said as Bella raced off to join her sister. "Keep Carrie's memory alive for those two, won't you?"

"Always," Sophie said. "I'll see you in a month or so."

"Perhaps," Mrs. Stiles said, kissing Sophie briefly on the cheek.

As Sophie climbed into the car, she looked at her phone. It was almost lunchtime and she still hadn't heard from Louis. She wondered about calling him, but then decided against it. He'd said he'd call if he had anything to tell her. If she called him now, it would look like she was pestering him, that she felt about him the same way Mrs. Stiles did, that she expected him to run away at the first sign of trouble. Sophie did not believe that. So she had no choice, she just had to sit it out and wait for him to get in touch.

· · ·

It was almost five and getting dark when Sophie finally got the girls back to her mother's. She still hadn't heard from Louis. He had been out of contact for nearly twenty-four hours, and most of that overnight. She had no idea what had happened to him, if he'd found Seth or even if he was okay. For the first time since she'd known him, she found herself worrying that he was dead in a ditch somewhere, but at least the worrying masked the hurt, the pain it caused her to realize that he could so easily shut her out of his life. That the hours and days could go by without him needing to talk to her or be near her, especially when she longed to spend every waking moment with him.

Taking her phone out of her bag, Sophie looked at it, willing it to ring. She knew she shouldn't phone him, but when it came down to it, she couldn't wait any longer. After all, she loved him and she was having his baby. If that didn't give her the right to call him whenever she wanted, then she didn't know what did.

The phone rang for a long time and Sophie was on the verge of hanging up when Louis finally answered.

"Hi," he said, sounding tired.

"Are you okay? What's happening? Where *are* you?"

"I'm . . ." Louis paused, probably while he looked around. "I'm in a café in Tottenham. I've been here for hours, just waiting."

"Waiting? What for? Did you find Seth?"

"Yes, we tracked him down late last night."

"So what happened? Did you sort anything out?" There was a long silence on the other end of the line and for a while Sophie thought Louis had hung up.

"Are you still there?" she asked.

"Yes." Louis sighed. "It was pretty bad. Seth was drunk and on something when we found him, and he was very agitated. He got angry with Wendy for springing this—me—on him. He kept asking her what she was playing at, what she wanted this time . . . I don't really know what he meant by that . . ." Louis paused as he collected his thoughts. "And he's angry with me for existing, for even trying to be part of his life. There was a lot of shouting and then he . . . well, he tried to punch me. The last thing I wanted was a fistfight with my own kid, so I left Wendy with him to try and talk to him, calm him down. I told her I'd wait for her to call me, and I've been hanging around in Tottenham all day waiting, but I haven't heard. I'm knackered, Soph, and I miss you and the girls."

Sophie caught her breath. It was the first time he had said anything to indicate that he'd thought about her since she left St. Ives. She clung to the throwaway sentence like a life raft.

"Well then, get on a bus or in a cab and come over here," Sophie pleaded with him. "It's barely half an hour away, and if Wendy calls and she needs you, you can be back there in no time." Louis was silent. "Please, Louis, come back here, have a hot bath and some food and a hug from all your girls, because it sounds as if you need it."

"Can I include you in that description?" he asked her. "Are you still one of my girls?"

Sophie paused as she struggled to suppress the sob that suddenly constricted her throat.

"Of course I am. Of course I am your girl. Come over here and let me hold you, please."

"I'm on my way," Louis told her.

Sophie had to wait for several minutes while Louis was overwhelmed by a pile of happy girls and welcoming dogs, all keen to get a piece of him, quite literally in some of the dogs' cases.

"Daddy, we missed you!" Izzy cried. "I'm glad you're back even though you smell funny. Where have you been?"

"Did you find him?" Bella asked. "Did you find Seth? Is he okay?"

"Yes, we found him and he's okay," Louis said as Sophie dragged Scooby off him and then ushered the big dog, plus a few others, out into the hallway.

"So can we go home now?" Bella asked. "Because it's fun in London, but I don't want to miss school. We are studying the past. I like the past, especially the Romans."

"Um . . ." Louis looked at Sophie.

"I'll take you back home tomorrow, okay, girls?" she said. "I think Daddy might need to stay and help Wendy for a bit longer."

"Ohhh," Bella moaned. "Daddy, I wish you would hurry up and stop helping that Wendy woman—we're never going to get married in time if you don't *focus*."

"I know, I know, darling, I'm sorry." Louis hugged her. "That's what I want more than anything too." He looked at Sophie over the tops of the girls' heads, his eyes asking a silent question.

Sophie sat down next to him and found his hand among the tangle of children.

"It's what we all want," she said, feeling the tears of relief sting her eyes as he squeezed her fingers in return.

It seemed to take an age to get the girls to bed and settled. There had to be the Petal the Fairy Pony Princess and her Adventures in the Land of the Mermaids story from Sophie, then another story from Louis, then a brief discussion as to why the adults didn't go to bed at the same time as the children, and then a certain amount of to-ing and fro-ing concerning glasses of water, lights to be left on, and the exact way that the bedroom door should be left ajar.

Finally, when they were settled, Sophie and Louis waited downstairs, sitting on opposite armchairs as Iris did her makeup in the mirror over the mantelpiece.

"Sorry," she said to both of them through lips puckered to receive a second coat of red lipstick. "It's just that the light in the bathroom is terrible and I want to look nice for Trevor." She spun round. "Will I do?"

"You look great, Mum," Sophie said, having to concede that despite what she considered to be a rather inappropriate shade of red lipstick for a woman of a certain age, which she included herself in, Iris did look good. Trevor had certainly set her glowing.

"Are you sure you don't mind me going out?" Iris asked.

"We're sure," Louis and Sophie said together, catching each other's eyes and smiling as they spoke.

"It's nice to know when you're wanted," Iris said and smiled at them, turning to Louis. "And I am very, very glad to see you here, young man. Don't go dashing off now for a bit until you and Sophie have talked properly. You've got a lot to talk about. A lot of very important things—"

"Good-bye, Mum," Sophie said firmly.

"Right, yes, well, good-bye. And good luck."

Once Iris was gone they sat for a few moments just looking at each other.

"Are you okay?" Sophie asked him eventually.

He nodded. "I'm a bit shell shocked I suppose. I don't know what I expected when I found out about Seth. So much has happened so quickly that I still haven't really had time to think about what it means. Maybe I expected some big reunion and some sort of father-and-son bonding. Perhaps I thought I'd take him down to the pub and we'd have a few beers and get to know each other. But I didn't expect him to hate me simply for existing. And I didn't expect my turning up to send him off the rails quite so spectacularly."

"Don't forget, you don't know him, you don't really know Wendy anymore," Sophie said softly, tentatively. "I haven't had much to do with Seth, but from what I can tell I think he's had a pretty hard time of it, he seems fragile and unsure. Yes, he's a great, big, hulking man, but he's still very young," Sophie said. "Did you know who you were or what you wanted when you were twenty? It's a lot for him to deal with, a father figure in his life just when he's working out for himself what it means to be a man."

"You know what, you're probably right." Louis looked at his hand for a moment. "I don't know why I haven't talked this through with you more—I've cut you out of everything that's been happening, and I don't really understand why—maybe it's because I can't get used to having someone who will always be by my side. But I do know that it was stupid of me. I need you." Louis's eyes met hers. "Please can I come over there, I really want to hold you."

"Please do," Sophie said, holding out her arms, and then once Louis was beside her Sophie was exactly where she wanted to be—in his arms, inhaling his smells, listening to the sound of his heartbeat slowing and relaxing.

"This has been the most stupid, awful week of my life," Louis whispered into her hair. "Remind me to never, ever let you go again. Nothing is right when you aren't around. I can't think, I can't do anything without you. I don't want to do anything without you, ever again."

He bent his head, searching out Sophie's mouth and kissing her as she wound her arms around his neck, pressing her body into his, sighing as she felt the heat rise in her veins. And then she remembered that she had something really quite important to tell him.

"God, Sophie, I love you," Louis told her, his hands finding their way under her top as he ran them down her back, reaching for her bra strap.

"Hang on," Sophie said, pushing him away from her a few millimeters with the palm of her hand.

"Am I going too fast?" Louis asked her, his finger stroking her back. "I'm sorry, I just want you so much. And we're together, alone . . . on a sofa. It seemed like old times."

"No, it's not that, I want you too, but there are things we still haven't talked about, things I need to say—"

"Everything you've said to me since this happened is right." Louis sat back, pushing the hair out of his eyes. "I'm so sorry if I've let this business with Seth get in the way of us getting married. I've been talking utter rubbish and Bella's right, I need to focus. I don't want a break from you, I need you. You're the person who can help me get through this and, more than that, you're the person I long to be with. I just need you, babe. I just need you."

"I know." Sophie smiled. "I don't need a break from you either; if anything, I need you more now than I ever have. I love you. I want to marry you. So who cares if we don't know what the future holds? It doesn't matter because I can't wait to be married to you and living with you and the girls."

"You don't know how happy that makes me," Louis whispered, brushing back a strand of hair from her face.

"I'm glad," Sophie said. "Because, Louis, there's something else I need to tell you . . ."

Sophie paused; now was the moment, now was the time for her news and she wanted to make sure she chose exactly the right words to convey it.

"I know what you're going to say and I think you're right," Louis said, stopping Sophie in her tracks.

"Really?" she asked him, catching her breath. "What about?"

"About telling the girls the whole truth about Seth. I need to talk to them. I need to explain that he's not just some random boy I'm helping. I need to tell them that I'm his father and he's their half brother."

There was an audible gasp from the other side of the living room door and the sound of glass smashing on the hall tiles.

"Oh no," Sophie whispered as the living room door slammed open, sending Scooby scrambling to his feet and racing up the stairs.

"You LIAR!" Bella shouted at the top of her voice, broken glass all around her bare feet, her face red with rage, her eyes molten with fury and betrayal. "You liar, you liar, you liar—you said Seth was just a lost, grown-up boy. You liar!"

"Bella, darling, don't move," Sophie said, but it was too late, Bella ran into the room across the glass without seeming to feel anything. Louis jumped to his feet and tried to catch her, but she flew at him, beating him with her balled-up fists, causing both of them to sink to the floor.

"Why didn't you tell us, why?" Bella howled as she attacked him. "Are you going to leave us again? Are you going to live with that Wendy woman and Seth now? Are you going to leave us again, like you did before?"

Bella screamed, kicking and hitting as Louis tried to restrain her. Seeing that the soles of the child's feet were bleeding, Sophie knelt down, trying to reach out to soothe her, but the child's blows caught her arms and chest.

"Come on now," Sophie said softly. "Come on, baby, calm down. Come to me and let me look at your feet. I think you may have cut them."

Her fury burning out as suddenly as it had flared up, Bella turned to Sophie, flinging her arms around her neck and sobbing, her expression as she watched Louis one of pure hurt and disbelief.

Carefully Sophie lifted her off the floor and carried her over to the sofa. It had been a long time since she had seen Bella like this, months ago, when Bella was first readjusting to having her father back in her life. Sophie and Louis had taken them to the London Zoo and Bella had got mad at Izzy because Izzy had naively looked forward to their daddy taking care of them now that their mummy was gone. Bella's hurt and fury had shocked Sophie then, it had been a terrifying glimpse into how the little girl was really handling her grief and the upheaval in her life. In the intervening months Sophie had hoped that Bella had come to feel safe and secure, certain in the knowledge that she was cared for and loved. She knew how obsessed the seven-year-old was with knowing all the facts and she understood why. But even she was stunned by how insecure and precarious Bella must still feel. At how much pain and fear she had been hiding all this time. The poor child still wasn't certain that her world was a safe place, and perhaps after losing her mother so suddenly, she would never feel certain of that.

As Sophie stroked her back, Bella stopped trembling, her breathing evening out into regular sobs. Sophie met Louis's eyes over Bella's head as he knelt on the floor looking at his daughter in despair.

"I knew it, I knew it," Bella said, turning from Louis and weeping into Sophie's hair. "I knew he was going to go again. I knew he'd leave us again."

"I'm not, Bellarina, I'm not leaving you—I'd never leave you."

"You did before," Bella said accusingly, half turning her head to look at him. "And now you're going again, and I don't want you to. It's not fair, Daddy!"

"No, no, sweetheart—it's not that way. I'm not leaving. I'm going to marry Sophie and we're going to all live together forever."

"Don't lie," Bella shrieked at him. "I don't care. I don't want you. And Izzy doesn't want you. You . . . you don't care that we were on our own in places we didn't like for weeks until Aunty Sophie found us, and you didn't care that you left us with Mummy, and you didn't care that Mummy was dead, and there was no one . . . and you're a liar and I don't want you. I want . . . I want my *mummy*. I want my mummy back."

"Oh, darling," Sophie whispered into her hair, rocking her against her shoulder. "Poor, poor baby."

"I want to go home," Bella sobbed, the words broken up on each ragged breath. "Please take me home."

"Of course I will, first thing tomorrow we'll go straight back home."

"Bella, listen," Louis tried again. "Let me explain."

Bella burrowed even deeper into Sophie's body as Louis gingerly sat down next to her. "I didn't know anything about Seth. I didn't know I had another child, a grown-up son, until just a little while ago. The only reason I didn't tell you about him was because I was finding out about him myself. Not because I wanted to leave you or live with him or anything like that. I love you and Izzy and Sophie. I'm never going to leave you."

Bella was unresponsive, her face hidden in Sophie's hair. Sophie looked at Louis and shook her head, signaling that he should wait before he said anything else. Louis nodded and sat back on the sofa, looking shell shocked.

"Come on, my baby," Sophie said, lifting Bella slowly up in her arms, a little unsteady under her weight. "I'll carry you back up to bed and we'll take care of those feet. You need to sleep, and in the morning I'll drive you all home, okay?"

Before Bella could respond, Louis's phone rang. Woman and child watched as he checked the name, hesitating for a fraction of a second before answering.

"Hi, you okay?" he asked. "Yep, yep, okay."

He put down the phone and looked at Sophie. "I have to stay on in London a bit longer."

"I knew it," Bella sobbed. "You like that Seth and that Wendy woman better than us."

"No, no, darling. I've just got to stay for one more day—"

"Stay forever!" Bella told him, weary with anger. "I don't care. I hate you!"

"Just wait," Sophie said to Louis. Carefully she walked over the broken glass and carried Bella to the bedroom, where Izzy was still blissfully asleep. She lay Bella gently down on the bed and went to the bathroom to search out antiseptic spray and Band-Aids.

"It's not too bad," she said as she gently examined Bella's feet. "No glass, just a few little cuts. These Band-Aids can come off in the morning."

"Want to keep them on," Bella grumbled as Sophie tucked her back into bed.

"Okay then, keep them on," Sophie said, smoothing the child's hair back from her face so that she could plant a kiss on her seldom-seen forehead.

"Bella—you trust me, don't you?"

Bella nodded.

"I promise you that Daddy isn't going to leave you," she told Bella. "He didn't mean to keep the truth about Seth from you. He thought he was protecting you and Izzy until you were ready to find out about Seth. Perhaps he was wrong, but I know one thing. He loves you and your sister with all his heart. And the biggest regret—the thing that makes him saddest in all the world—is that he ever left you before. I know now that he would never ever leave you or Izzy or me again. I promise you."

"Do you?" Bella asked, her lids swollen and heavy. "Do you promise?"

"I do, sweetheart."

"And you won't go anywhere, will you, because you said always, forever, whatever and that's the rule, isn't it? You can't leave us now you've said that, can you?"

"No," Sophie said. "And I never will, come what may."

"Want to go to sleep," Bella mumbled, her cheeks still wet with tears as she drifted off, with the sudden release only a child can have.

Sophie took a deep breath as she walked back down the stairs, preparing what to say to Louis, how to help him deal with what had just happened and work out what to say to Bella. It meant that she'd have to wait at least another day before telling him she was pregnant, but as long as she could get things between him and Bella on an even keel again that didn't matter. She stepped over the broken glass and pushed the living room door open and her heart sank.

Louis had made a liar out of both of them.

He'd left.

Eighteen

*I*t was just after four on Sunday afternoon when they finally drove into St. Ives and Sophie decided they should head to Ye Olde Tea Shoppe before they did anything else. As taking up smoking again was definitely not an option and gin was off the table, even if she could stomach it, she decided that a cream tea for two all to herself was the *only* option.

She hadn't seen the point in waiting in London for Louis to get in touch. For one thing, she'd tried his cell phone the moment she'd realized he'd gone and found it ringing behind a cushion on the sofa. And he had not called her since he'd left without saying good-bye.

It had still been dark when she packed up the car that morning, the chill in the air seeping through her coat and sweater. As she slammed the door of the car shut, she stood perfectly still for a second, watching the rising sun streak the dirty sky with gold over the chimney tops and trying to work out exactly what had happened last night.

Everything had been going so well, everything had been almost perfect, and then before she could tell him about the baby, Bella's whole life, and even Sophie's estimation of Louis, who she thought she knew so well, had shattered all around her, just like the glass smashed on her mother's hall tiles. What she couldn't understand was that Louis hadn't even stayed to see that Bella had gone to sleep, to check that her feet weren't too badly cut, to tell her where he was going and when he'd be back. He'd just left, without his phone, and Sophie had no idea why.

Suddenly afraid, she had sat down in the chair and wept. She was frightened for Bella and Izzy, scared of the loss that was still damaging and that she barely understood. And she was fearful for herself and her baby, the tiny life inside her that had to have been battered by the torrents of emotions that had wracked her body recently. But the thought that made her most afraid was that Mrs. Stiles was right about Louis. He would run away from trouble when the going got hard, just like he had when he found out about Carrie's affair. Sophie thought back to the night when he'd described how he'd felt and why he'd left, the night they'd first slept together. He'd seemed so genuine, so plausible—a vulnerable man who'd made a mistake and bitterly regretted it. But what if he'd said what he knew she wanted to hear in order to get her into bed? What if he'd just run out on Bella because he couldn't cope, just as he'd given up on Carrie because he didn't have the guts to fight for her? Sophie shook her head; that wasn't her Louis—that wasn't the man she loved, the man she knew—it couldn't be. She was tired and upset and hormonal and Mrs. Stiles's warning was echoing around in her head like a siren, tempting sailors onto dangerous shores.

Sophie had picked up Louis's phone, her thumb hovering over the keypad as she contemplated reading his texts and checking his messages, perhaps trying to find something that might tell her where he was, and then before she knew what she had done she'd thrown it hard against the wrought-iron fireplace, smashing its fragile plastic casing to pieces.

And on that cold September morning Sophie realized that for the first time since she'd met Louis, she was angry with him. She was blood-boiling, heart-pumping, teeth-grindingly furious with him and she knew that if he turned up on the street at that moment she would happily have punched out his lights.

Even so, on the drive back down to Cornwall, she had kept her phone by her side, and her hands-free plugged in, convinced that he would find a way to call her eventually, full of apologies for dashing off, with news of a genuine emergency and wondering what had happened to the phone he'd so stupidly left behind. But as the journey wore on and the girls' enthusiasm and collection of songs wore out, Sophie's phone remained silent. She stared at it furiously, willing it to make a noise, but still it didn't ring, and that made her angrier still.

She was too old and too pregnant to be waiting for her boyfriend to call her at this stage in her life. Now was the very time she should be feeling secure and happy, not wondering if she even still had a relationship. But the fact was that Louis was gone and he'd left her to pick up the pieces of his daughters again.

"When is Daddy coming home again?" Izzy asked just as they hit Devon. It was a question that Sophie had endeavored to answer several times on her journey down, but her trite answers of "Soon, sweetie" and "Before you know it" had not satisfied the four-year-old and had succeeded only in drawing sighs from Bella.

"He'll be back when he's finished helping Wendy with Seth," Sophie told her hesitantly. It was the grain of truth that Bella had been waiting to pounce on.

"Because Daddy is Seth's daddy and Seth is our half brother," Bella informed her little sister without ceremony. Sophie had tried to persuade Bella not to tell Izzy about Seth until after they got back, but she knew it was unfair to ask a child for such restraint and she counted herself lucky that they'd made it this far before Bella blew the story wide open.

In the driver's seat Sophie braced herself for Izzy's reaction.

"Oh," Izzy said, thinking for a moment. "But isn't Seth a grown-up man? And Daddy's a grown-up man, so he can't be Seth's daddy—that's just silly! Grown-up men can't be grown-up men's daddies!" The idea seemed to tickle Izzy, making her giggle. It wasn't quite the reaction Sophie had been expecting.

"That Wendy woman is Seth's mummy," Bella went on, determined to make her sister understand. "Daddy and that Wendy woman used to do kissing when they were young. So even though Seth is a grown-up man, he is still Daddy's son and our half brother."

"How can he be half a brother?" Izzy quizzed her, her giggling rubbing Bella exactly the wrong way. "Hasn't he got any arms or legs?" She doubled over in her car seat with laughter, finding herself utterly hilarious.

"He's our half brother because he's only . . . ," Bella trailed off, at a loss as to how to explain. Sophie decided it was time for her to step in.

"Half brother means you have the same mummy or daddy. You and Bella have the same daddy as Seth, but there are two different mummies. Your mummy and Seth's mummy, who is that Wendy woman," Sophie explained, using Bella's phrase for Wendy without thinking and gaining some small satisfaction from it.

"So we really have half a brother then?" Izzy asked, perplexed.

"Yes, and that's where Daddy is," Bella added darkly. "With him."

"And when is he coming back?" Izzy inquired, her voice suddenly trembling.

"We don't know," Bella said, scowling out the window. "He might not come back at all, not if he prefers them to us."

"Bella . . . ," Sophie warned as she caught sight of Izzy's face in the rearview mirror, on the brink of crumbling into tears.

"Of course Daddy's coming back." Sophie glanced at her dark and silent phone and added through gritted teeth, "Eventually."

"So tell me all about it then," Carmen asked her as soon as she had the girls settled at a table by the window with a pile of pens, a coloring book, and a plate of sandwiches.

"I don't really know where to start," Sophie said bleakly, spreading jam on her second scone. "The long and the short of it is that Bella overheard us talking about Seth when she came down for a glass of water and she found out that he's their brother. She went ballistic—it was so frightening, Carmen. I thought the girls were settled, that they were moving on with their lives, coping without Carrie. But I was a fool to think that it could be so simple. I lost a parent and I'm still not over it, and I was much older than them when it happened. Bella is terrified that her whole world is going to get pulled out from under her again, and as for Izzy, she's always laughing and chuckling away, but sometimes I look at her and I still don't think she really understands that Carrie isn't coming back one day."

"Poor little mites," Carmen said, glancing over at the girls, who were frantically drawing picture after picture of mermaids and fairy ponies. "They've had it harder than most, but they're lucky too. Lucky that they've got you and Louis there for them."

"But have they? I mean, I panicked and went off to London and left them more or less at the drop of a hat and now Louis has disappeared into the night. I have no idea where he's gone, who he's with, or if he's even coming back. I don't know anything and that means I have nothing to tell the girls. And add that to the fact that he hasn't called me and I've wrecked his cell phone, not to mention that I'm pregnant, and then you've got a right old mess."

"You're pregnant!" Carmen gasped, clapping her hand over her mouth just in time to stifle the salient word before the girls heard it. "You're *pregnant*?" she asked again in a whisper.

"Yes," Sophie said and nodded. "It came as something of a shock to me too."

"Well, I don't know why, what with all that shagging you've been doing. One of the little buggers was bound to get through eventually. After all, if there's one thing we know about Louis it's that he's fertile."

"Thanks for that," Sophie said through a mouthful of cream and jam. "Anyway, what do I do now?"

"Stop eating cakes for a start," Carmen said. "I've heard that pregnancy pounds are the hardest to lose. I can't believe that knowing you're pregnant he left you in the lurch! That just doesn't seem like Louis at all."

"No—he doesn't know. I haven't had a chance to tell him yet. But please feel free to beat him up on the grounds that he has generally left me high and dry with his two angry and confused daughters. He definitely deserves a slap or two for that."

"You're pregnant," Carmen repeated, her eyes wide with wonderment. She reached out a hand to cover Sophie's. "Oh my god, babe—that's immense."

"I know!" Sophie said. "It's taking me a while to get my head round it, but I think that I am, or at least I will be, really pleased. Me pregnant with an actual child, who'd have thought it?"

"At least now you have a reason to eat for two," Carmen joked, but there were tears in her eyes.

"Oh, Carmen, I'm so sorry. I'm being completely tactless," Sophie said, remembering only then what Carmen had told her just before she left St. Ives.

"Don't be so silly," Carmen said, shrugging off with one shoulder any pain she might be feeling. "If I tried to avoid every pregnant woman around here, I'd never go out. Thank god I'm not still in Chelmsford—the place is crawling with them. Besides, I've had a lot of time to get used to the idea and I'm fine with it. Really I am."

"And how are things between you and James?" Sophie asked her. "Is that still all okay?"

"Yes, of course it is, me and James are as tight as a drum," Carmen said, smiling. "For now at least. What you and I need is a plan, a plan to find Louis and get him back down here looking after his girls and wife-to-be like he should be."

"Short of hiring a private detective to find him again, I honestly don't know how to do that," Sophie told her. "Chances are he didn't know my phone number by heart, because it was stored in his cell, which is now well and truly dead. And I don't know Wendy's number. I think the only thing I can do is wait for him to get in touch . . . and I bloody hate it."

"I know!" Carmen said. "He'll have left a message for you on the phone at his house. He knows that number."

"You're right," Sophie said, sitting up. "That's probably what he's done."

"Well then, go home and check it now and then phone me and tell me exactly what he said."

Sophie glanced at the girls, who were still eating.

"I'd better wait for them," she said, tapping her fingernails on the gingham tablecloth.

"Leave them here with me, they'll be fine," Carmen offered. "They can help me close up and then I'll take them out the back for a bit of telly."

"No," Sophie said. "Thanks, Carmen, but no—I promised I wouldn't leave them, and for today at least I think that means not even for five minutes."

• • •

The girls were tired and irritable when Sophie finally let herself into Louis's house. She made herself wait to check the phone for messages until she got them undressed and washed and into bed.

"I'm glad I'm home," Bella told her as she kissed her good night. "And I'm so glad we've got you."

"Always," Sophie promised her.

Downstairs she stared at the phone, hopeful that it would contain some news of Louis and his whereabouts. She picked it up and heard the altered dial tone that signified there was a message. Sophie found her heart was racing as she dialed 1571 and waited to hear the one new message.

"Hello Mr. Gregory, this is Mrs. Tallen from St. Ives First School, calling on Friday afternoon. Bella's teacher informed us you took her out of school early for a weekend trip to London. We are calling to remind you that early departures are against school policy. We'd be very grateful if you would call back and confirm you understand this policy."

"You have no further messages," the automated female voice told Sophie primly.

She hung up the receiver and sat down on the bottom stair with a bump. Her mum had promised to call her if she heard anything from him, so he couldn't have been there. Where was he?

Suddenly exhausted, weary to the bone, Sophie climbed up the stairs and fell, fully dressed, onto Louis's bed. She dragged the covers over herself and hugged her arms around her shoulders. Dimly she became aware of another presence on the bed and, opening one eye, saw Artemis turning in three circles before settling down next to Sophie, her back pressed against Sophie's belly. It was so odd, so uncharacteristic of the cat to ever seek Sophie out for any kind of companionship, Sophie worried the cat was sick. Hesitantly she reached out a hand and ran it along the cat's sleek back, expecting a tooth-and-claw protest any second. But Artemis remained still, her breathing steady and sedate beneath Sophie's hand, and far from seeming ill, Sophie noticed that she looked better than she ever had; her natural, always hungry feral thinness seemed to have disappeared and her rib cage had filled out to pleasant house-pet plumpness. Sophie smiled to herself as she let her heavy-lidded eyes close once again. There were four mixed-up females in this house and somehow they had all found a place in the world with each other.

Sophie's shattered brain had been halfway through forming yet another question when she fell asleep, all her worries and fears still unanswered as she drifted into fretful dreams.

"Sophie . . . Sophie*eeeeeee* . . . Aunty Sophie, wake up! It's a school day!"

Slowly, painfully, Sophie opened her eyes to find Izzy's face looming millimeters from hers, her big eyes looking out of focus as she peered at Sophie.

"Oh god," Sophie moaned, rolling onto her back and rubbing her eyes. "What time is it?"

"Eight forty-five," she heard Bella say somewhere in the periphery of her vision. "It's a really good job you went to bed with your clothes on, otherwise we'd be *really* late for school."

Sophie sat upright too quickly, the blood rushing from her head and leaving her dizzy, the corners of the room wheeling around her as she put her heavy head in her hands.

"Right," she said, waving her arms at the girls, her eyes still closed. "Go and find cereal and I'll get you some clothes together . . . we'll be late but we can blame your father—"

"But we've had breakfast already," Bella informed her. "We had Coco Pops and a cornetto each from the freezer for dessert, because we were thinking that breakfast is the only meal without dessert and we didn't think that was fair. Plus, we've been dressed for hours."

"And hours and hours," Izzy reiterated.

Sophie blinked her eyes open and looked at the girls. Sure enough, they had cobbled together an approximation of their school uniform, with a few customized touches gleaned from the dressing-up box. Izzy was wearing one of Bella's school sweaters pulled over a yellow sundress, which she'd accessorized with her gray school tights and topped off rather optimistically with play high heels that Sophie wasn't keen on her wearing in the house, never mind out of it. Bella had done a little better, squeezing herself into one of Izzy's school sweaters, the sleeves of which ended just below her elbows. She wore it over a blue-and-white-checked summer school dress with pink socks and her sneakers that flashed lights every time she jumped up and down.

Sophie looked at her watch and weighed the pros and cons of delivering the girls in their own versions of the school uniform on time, or getting them changed and scrubbed and taking them in an hour late. Trying once more to shake the sleep out of her head, she stretched her arms above her head and looked at Bella and Izzy.

"You'll do," she said. Painfully Sophie hauled her body out of bed, briefly running her fingers through her tangled hair.

"You know, Bella, you're right, it *is* lucky that I'm already dressed."

If Sophie had not been exhausted, angry, confused, and pregnant when she dropped the girls off at school, she might have felt a little paranoid about the looks that some of the mothers and guardians gave her as she shepherded them through the sea of shiny, newly washed hair and perfectly turned-out uniforms.

But for once she was too preoccupied with her own thoughts to care what other parents might think of her, the interloper, the girl-friend. Besides, Bella and Izzy were the toast of the school, drawing crowds of admirers around them as they showed off their unique styling. As Sophie headed out of the gate, still rubbing last night's sleep from her eyes, she knew there would be a message left on Louis's phone detailing the unsuitability of the high-heeled shoes and asking for a replacement pair to be brought in. And no doubt when she picked them up this afternoon there would be a letter in their book bags reminding Louis of the school's dress code and their policy on glitter-gel eye makeup, but Sophie didn't care.

Louis had gone, he had walked out on her in the middle of the night to help his first love, not to mention getting her pregnant without her full permission. He'd made her fall in love with him, enticed her away from the life she knew and understood, and then left her, the selfish bastard. And if getting him into trouble with St. Ives First School was the only way she could strike back at him for all he had done to her, then she was damn well going to take it; she wasn't proud.

Desperately in need of some clarity, Sophie decided to walk, leaving her car parked outside the school gate as she headed toward the B & B where she could find some sanctuary in her twin room, a place where she could think and look in the mirror and try and see her own reflection once again.

It was a brilliant chilly morning as Sophie walked into the heart of the town. The sky dazzled her, reflecting light off the flat and glassy ocean that ricocheted in turn off the whitewashed houses. This was the light that Carrie had loved so much, Sophie thought as she headed instinctively for the shoreline, the magical radiance that seemed to bend over the coastline throwing even the smallest rock into sharp relief, making it seem possible to see every blade of grass or grain of sand from miles and miles away. Sophie had lived with the St. Ives light for a while, but it was only now, when her head was so muddled and brimming with confusion, that she really felt that particular atmosphere, that sensation that you were just a little closer to the sky here than anywhere else in the world. She paused, taking a moment to breathe in deeply, feeling the cold air numbing her from the inside.

The tourists were almost completely gone, and the cobbled streets were largely empty, so Sophie decided to take the long way round to the B & B, walking through the town and around the harbor, stopping briefly at the tacky gift shop, its entrance garlanded by pirate hats and slogan T-shirts. This was where Izzy had been pestering her father to buy a life-size inflatable dolphin for weeks.

She paused in the crook of the harbor, looking out at the boats that were currently bobbing on the high tide. In a few hours the tide would be out and the boats would be stranded on the soft golden sand, beached on their sides, many of them, their fat bellies billowing skyward, waiting for the water to come back and make them beautiful again. Only a month ago she and Bella and Izzy had walked in among the boats almost every day, when the tide was out, collecting rocks and interesting shells. The girls had liked to imagine that they were mermaids swimming beneath the surf, in and out and under the hulls looking for treasure. That had been only a few weeks ago, but it seemed like centuries, so much had changed since then.

"Where are you?" Sophie whispered into the wind, absently hoping that it would carry her words to wherever Louis was. "Please, Louis, don't do this to me. Don't disappear on me now that I finally know how much I need you."

Nineteen

You never know, he might be lying in a hospital bed somewhere," Mrs. Alexander said, patting Sophie gently on the shoulder, offering her own unique brand of comfort as she set an extra-large cooked breakfast down in front of her. "From the sound of things, I wouldn't say he's really left you, love. It'll be something to do with the boy and that Wendy woman."

"Of course he hasn't left you," Grace Tregowan affirmed. "Not for good anyway. He might be having a final fling before he settles down with you, that's not uncommon. You can't move at the Wednesday-afternoon tea dances for fellers feeling you up in the hopes of getting their way one last time before they pop their clogs. It might be a bit like that for your young man—although in his case he has sown a fair bit of his wild oats already."

"Oh great," Sophie said, poking at her scrambled eggs with her fork, feeling her stomach turn at the thought of it. "So he's either dead or groping some woman under a mirror ball. What on earth am I worrying about?"

"I didn't say dead," Mrs. Alexander reminded her, refilling the salt and pepper cellars. "I said lying in a hospital bed. He doesn't necessarily have to be dead."

"He doesn't necessarily have to be anywhere!" Sophie's anger flared like a lit match. "He should be here with me, looking after his *daughters,* looking after his *pregnant fiancée,* that's what he should be doing."

"Pregnant?" Mrs. Alexander gasped.

"He's got you up the duff, has he?" Grace asked her. Sophie nodded, pushing the plate of bacon and eggs away.

"I knew it wasn't like you wanting the decaffeinated tea," Mrs. Alexander said. "Pregnant. Well, I'll say one thing for Louis. If there was a sperm Olympics, that man's stuff would win the gold."

"You poor love," Grace said, covering Sophie's hand with her own, her palm feeling tight and cold against Sophie's boiling skin. "But he won't have walked out on you."

"Won't he?" Sophie asked her in dismay. "After all, he's done it before. He did it to Carrie."

"Well yes, that was a scandal," Mrs. Alexander said thoughtfully.

"You knew about that when we first met you?" Sophie asked her. "You've never mentioned it before."

"Didn't really seem appropriate to mention it before, and besides, it was gossip and you know I'm not one for gossip," Mrs. Alexander said, pursing her lips. "And you were my guests here then and now you're my friends. I know Louis and I know that he's not the sort of man who'd just run off and leave his little girls and pregnant wife."

"Oh, he's left a pregnant wife before, has he?" Mrs. Tregowan said. "That doesn't look good."

"Yes, but this is different, totally different," Sophie said desperately. "Carrie told Louis to go. She told him she wanted to start a life with another man. He was hurt and shocked and overreacted by going halfway around the world and not coming back for three years. But he didn't run out on her because she was pregnant. And anyway, he doesn't even know I'm pregnant. In fact, Louis is probably the only person in the entire world who doesn't know I'm pregnant. I was just about to tell him when he walked out on me. And now I don't know what to think. What if by himself he worked out I'm pregnant and did run a mile? He was saying only the other day that he didn't want any more kids."

"Don't be so silly. You two are getting married, of course he was going to want kids," Mrs. Alexander told her. "You're a family. A little unit. Louis wouldn't mess that up; he's been through too much to get you."

"Don't you worry, he'll turn up," Grace said. "Mr. Tregowan always turned up in the end. Well, except for the last time . . ."

"So what was he up to then?" Sophie asked her, a little hysterically. "Was he an international spy or an octogenarian Casanova or both? What was he getting up to when he disappeared?"

"Alzheimer's," Grace Tregowan said, nodding once. "He'd go out and forget where he was."

"Oh god, I'm sorry," Sophie said, aghast at her thoughtlessness.

"Don't be," Grace told her, rubbing her hand. "I'm not sorry. I had the happiest years of my life with my William."

Mrs. Alexander pushed Sophie's plate toward her. "Come on, Sophie. Have a bite of toast."

"I've not a single regret in my life," Grace assured Sophie. "Not a one. Maybe I could have had a safer life, a more stable one. Married some nice, safe, steady man and stayed with him, ticking all the moments of my life away. Maybe that's what being alive is about for some. But it's not for me. It's never been that way for me. William was my swan song, my last great love. I'm not sorry I found him, and if it's one thing that I know because of him it's that love doesn't waver through the hard times. It sticks fast and it grows stronger than ever. And I know your love for Louis will stick fast too. Even through all of this, just like that baby in your belly, it will grow and will flourish."

"Especially if you eat the toast," Mrs. Alexander reminded her gently.

"But what if his love doesn't stick fast for me?" Sophie asked, chewing the bread that tasted like burnt cardboard in her mouth. "How will I cope with a baby on my own? I mean, I've got this business idea that I think will really work, but how do I start that up and have a baby, and what about the girls? I need to be near them; how will it be, my living here with Louis's baby and Louis and the girls living in their house? Oh god, how did I get in this mess, how will I cope?"

"Well, you've coped perfectly well so far," Mrs. Alexander pointed out. "People do cope, women cope—better than that, we make it right. That's what we're good at. Men are good at general knowledge and parking. Women are good at life—you've shown that already."

"It's just that starting my own international wedding-services company will have some of the shine taken off it if I've just been left at the altar, knocked up."

"You haven't been left at the altar," Mrs. Alexander said. "He'll be back."

"And when he gets back," Grace told her, "you can bloody kick his arse, the insensitive fool."

Sophie wasn't sure if it was the pregnancy itself, or simply the fact that now that she knew about it, she was suddenly exhausted. There didn't seem to be enough hours in the day or night for her to sleep sufficiently as her body labored over making another human life and her head and heart tried to reconcile everything that had happened to her since that moment almost a year ago when she'd found out that Carrie was dead and she was responsible for her two little girls. Telling her she was far too pale for her liking, Mrs. Alexander had sent Sophie up to her room for a nap after she'd finally eaten her toast and Sophie had fallen asleep before she'd even had a chance to think of taking a shower.

"I'll call you when it's time to pick up the girls, okay? You and that baby get some rest."

She had been deep in a dreamless sleep when Mrs. Alexander came to wake her, having to resort to gently shaking her shoulder to get her to open her eyes.

"Sophie, it's time to fetch the girls."

Sophie sat up and rubbed her eyes. "Really? Is it one o'clock already?"

"No, love," Mrs. Alexander said slowly. "It's just before three. I thought I'd leave you to the last minute, you looked like you needed it."

Sophie had to think hard for a moment about why that was a bad thing and then it hit her. Izzy finished school at one o'clock, not three. She was more than two hours late to pick her up.

"Oh god," Sophie said, pulling on her shoes. "The school is going to kill me. They must have tried phoning Louis's house and his cell phone and not had any luck, and they don't have my number! How am I ever going to cope with a baby when I can't even get them to school and pick them up on time?"

"I'm sorry, I didn't think," Mrs. Alexander said as Sophie raced past her and out to her car.

"It's not your fault," Sophie called back. "I should have remembered." But when she reached the curb, she realized her car wasn't there, that she had left it outside the school, and now she had less than five minutes to cover a twenty-minute walk.

"Oh no, no, no, no, no!" Sophie cried, stamping her feet on the pavement in despair. "No car!"

"Calm down," Mrs. Alexander said, hurrying down the path in her slippers. "I'll call you a taxi."

"Thanks, but no, a taxi will take twenty minutes just to get here. I'll run up there—you call the school, tell them I'm on my way."

This time Sophie took the most direct route to the school, which was all uphill. She felt the sweat trickling down her back on the chilly afternoon even as her breath misted in the air. The sharp jab of a stitch lodged in her side and her heart pounded as she powered up the hill, forcing the deadweight of exhaustion to the back of her mind. She was still perhaps ten minutes away when children from the school started filtering past her, in ones and twos at first and then a steady stream of excited children chattering about their day to mothers, some of them scooting down the hill a little too fast for a mother's comfort. As the hill steepened, and the downward flow of children thickened, Sophie's progress slowed even further and it seemed it took an age for her to make the last five hundred yards. But as weary and worn out as she was, once she was in the playground she ran to the school entrance where she was sure she would find the girls waiting for her and a cross-looking teacher with her arms folded.

"I'm here," she announced breathlessly as she skidded to a halt on the parquet tiles. But the reception area was empty except for the school secretary doing some photocopying and one of the cleaners.

"Oh, sorry, excuse me," Sophie asked the secretary. "I'm Sophie Mills? I'm late to pick up my . . . my fiancé's daughters. Izzy and Bella Gregory? I'm really late to pick up Izzy, and I'm so, so sorry. I'm pregnant, you see, and I've lost their father and apparently the ability to stop talking when it's inappropriate. And now you're another person who knows about the baby when he doesn't."

The school secretary blinked at her.

"Anyway, if you could just tell me where they're waiting?"

"They haven't been brought here," the secretary told Sophie hesitantly. "I haven't heard about any late parents or . . . helpers today. And I would have been the one to make the calls if Izzy had still been here at one. Are you sure their father didn't fetch them today? After all, if you've lost him . . ."

"I . . . I don't know," Sophie said, battling the rising wave of nausea and frustration surging through her.

"Try their classrooms," the secretary suggested. "But really, don't worry, I'm sure it's nothing to worry about. We're very careful here. We don't let our children run off onto the streets on their own, you know. I bet their daddy's got them and he just forgot to tell you. Men, hey? They never tell you anything."

Could Louis have come back without letting her know and picked up the girls? Sophie wondered as she turned on her heel and headed toward the classrooms. That had to be what had happened. The secretary was right. The school wouldn't just let Izzy wander off with no one to look after her. It had to mean that Louis was back, a thought that flooded Sophie with a sense of relief and fury in equal measure. What was he playing at, not letting her know he was back in town?

Sophie knew the nursery would be long empty, so she went to find Bella's classroom where her teacher, Mrs. Sinclair, was pinning some artwork to the walls.

"Hello," Sophie called out, breathless.

"Hello," Mrs. Sinclair said, looking up, not pleased by the interruption.

"I just wanted to confirm that it was Louis Gregory who picked up Bella today, wasn't it?"

"No." Mrs. Sinclair spoke to her as if she were ever so slightly stupid.

"No?" Sophie's heart stopped beating for a few terrifying seconds. "Then who was it?"

"It was her big brother."

Twenty

*H*e came at lunchtime and took Izzy," Mrs. Sinclair explained. "I know because young Miss Aster was quite flustered by him. When they came back at three to pick up Bella, they had a huge inflatable dolphin in tow. I asked Bella about him and who he was and she told me he was her brother and that he was picking her up today. It came as a surprise to me, I didn't know she had a big brother, but she seemed very excited about going with him. All three of them went off together."

"Her brother picked her up," Sophie repeated, wide-eyed with horror and a million other half-formed thoughts running through her head that she didn't quite understand yet.

"Yes," Mrs. Sinclair said slowly. "Is there some kind of problem?"

"Yes, yes," Sophie said. "There is the rather large problem that she has never met her brother before," Sophie said. "She doesn't know anything about him. I don't know anything about him. The last thing I knew, he was in a dive in London, off his head on drugs and alcohol, and you just let her go with him?"

Mrs. Sinclair stood frozen to the spot. "But Bella told me he was her brother, and she's such a sensible girl, not at all the sort to go off with a stranger." Sophie thought of Bella's plan to sneak out of school and make a phone call. She had been worried about how Bella would react if Louis pushed her too far, and now she knew. Izzy was tiny and trusting. Seth probably charmed her out of the young and inexperienced nursery teacher's arms as easily as he would have charmed birds from a tree, and Izzy would not have denied that he was her brother or said she didn't want to go with him. If anything, she would have been delighted to meet him. Bella, on the other hand, would know that Seth was not supposed to pick them up from school. Perhaps she wanted to be the one to solve the mystery and find him, or perhaps she just wanted all of her own questions and fears answered. Maybe she saw that he already had Izzy and decided she had to go with him to protect her little sister, but either way, she had decided to go with him. Whether she knew it consciously or not, Bella had made the decision to show her daddy what happened when he walked out on her. Sophie found that she had stopped breathing.

"I had no reason to be suspicious. Izzy had already been with him all afternoon. He didn't look like he was drunk or on drugs, he was smart and clean. He looked fine."

"No adult told you that they were going to be picked up by their brother. You shouldn't have let them go with anyone but me or their father!" Sophie shouted at her.

"But Bella told me he was her brother, and she wanted to go."

"She's seven years old and Izzy is four. They don't know when or where they should be going. Oh god." Sophie turned away from Mrs. Sinclair as the enormity of what had happened finally hit her. "Oh god, I don't know what to do."

"I would never have let her go—but he already had Izzy and

she looked so happy with her dolphin. And Bella told me it was fine, she said, 'He's my brother' . . ."

"Oh god . . ." Sophie struggled with the fact that she couldn't get through to Louis, that she didn't know Wendy's number, and that she had no idea what Seth was like other than angry and confused and possibly on drugs and he had her two girls.

"I've got to find them," she said. "I've got to. I've got to find them."

She turned on her heel, suddenly desperate to be out and looking for them, even if she didn't have the faintest idea where to start.

"I'll call the police . . . ," Mrs. Sinclair said after her. "I'm so sorry! Bella said he was her brother . . . I thought it would be fine."

Sophie ran to her car, pulling the ticket off the window and screeching when she saw that it had been clamped for a parking violation.

"No, no, no!" she shouted, kicking the car and immediately feeling it kick back through her toe and spine.

Where was Seth? Where had he taken them?

Sophie knew nothing about Seth except that his mum lived in Newquay and he went to college in Falmouth. She didn't know if he could drive, or if he had a car. And she had no idea what he wanted with her girls. She had to think, she had to get her body and her brain moving. She had to get to them as soon as she possibly could.

Grabbing her phone she dialed Carmen's number and held her breath while she waited for her to pick up.

"Ye Olde Tea Shoppe," Carmen said as she picked up.

"Carmen, I'm at the school and . . . and Seth's back, he's—he's got the girls, my car's clamped. I don't know where they are, I don't know anything, or what to do . . ."

"Stay there," Carmen said. "I'll be with you in five."

• • •

True to her word, Carmen walked out of the tea shop leaving a regular customer in charge and was at Sophie's side in minutes.

"Right, let's think," Carmen said as Sophie scrambled into her car. "Now, we know he's not a nut or a pervert. He's not going to hurt them. He's just a messed-up kid who's done something stupid."

"Do we know that?" Sophie asked Carmen, her heart gripped with icy fear as the car pulled away from the roadside. "Do we know he's not going to hurt them? Because if anything happened to them because of me, I'd never . . . how would I? I couldn't . . ."

"Shush," Carmen told her. "The police are already looking, they were already asking around when I left the tea shop. I've told all my customers to keep an eye out. He won't take them out of St. Ives, I'm sure of it. Bella wouldn't let him; she's done stranger danger, she knows what to do."

"But he's not a stranger, he's her brother and she'll be trying to find out about him, get to know everything—you know what she's like."

"No, I'm sure he'll have taken them somewhere they know. What about the park? Let's try the park."

Sophie hadn't known that the passing of time could be so agonizing. As Carmen drove her to the park, each second that passed without her being certain of the exact whereabouts of her girls dragged over her, rasping every inch of her skin as she battled with the fear of the unknown, and every moment passed too quickly, too much time slipping by between the last time she had known they were safe and now, as if they were gradually falling out of her reach.

The park was empty except for some bored teenagers leaning against the swings and spinning slowly around on the merry-go-round as if they were gang members in L.A. and not a bunch of kids in Cornwall.

"Excuse me," Sophie said, marching over to them, aware that the tone and pitch of her voice would instantly alienate them, high and angry as it was. "Have you seen a man, tall and dark, with longish hair, and two little girls in here this afternoon?"

"Why?" one of the boys asked her as he kicked one more revolution out of the merry-go-round. "He a pervert or something?"

"No . . . no, they're my . . . I'm looking after them and I need to find them, please," Sophie pleaded. "If you've seen them . . ."

"Pigs have already been round here asking," another kid spoke up, from the top of the climbing frame. "We've been here since four and we've not seen them."

"Really?"

"What, you saying I'm lying?" the boy challenged her.

"Sophie, come on," Carmen called from across the park.

"Yeah, Sophie, go on," one of the boys said.

"Hey, Sophie, got any smokes?" another one called as Sophie hurried back to Carmen.

"What else you got under that jacket, Sophie?" she heard as she shut the car door.

"Take no notice of them," Carmen said. "They're just idiot kids, they don't know anything. I was thinking we should go and check the house, you never know—and Bella knows the neighbor's got a key."

But when they got back to the house, it was standing quiet in the twilight, no lights on in any room, no outward sign of life. Just to be certain Carmen waited in her car with the engine switched on as Sophie raced through the house checking every room, pausing in the girls' bedrooms, looking at the clothes strewn thoughtlessly across the floor, the school shoes discarded in a corner. The house had never seemed more empty. She picked up the phone and listened to the single monotonous ring tone; there were no messages waiting.

As she scrambled back into Carmen's car, the sun was already low in the sky.

"Seth hasn't thought this through, he doesn't know what he's doing," Sophie said anxiously. "It will be dark before long—and then what? He's never been to Louis's house, he doesn't know where they live. What's he going to do then? What if he panics and realizes how much trouble he's in . . . ? Then what's he going to do? Wendy said he was impulsive. The last time Louis saw him he was agitated, on some sort of drugs, he's sometimes violent . . . oh god, Carmen."

"There's no point in thinking about that now, he's just a kid, a boy. He's not going to do anything stupid. All we have to do is think . . . where else might they go? Would he take them to one of the beaches? Maybe they're at one of those having an ice cream or something. Think about it, he's doing it to find out about Louis, to find out about being a big brother. He'll want them to like him, to be impressed by him. He'll have taken them out for ice cream somewhere, I bet you. He won't have thought about all of this pain, he's just a kid himself. He'll have thought he was doing a good thing."

"The beaches," Sophie said quietly, willing herself to believe in Carmen's logic even though it was cold and getting dark and the likelihood of a cone of Mr. Whippy on the beach seemed ever diminishing, like the beaches themselves as the tide came in. But it was something to do and she had to do something. "Let's check them."

They drove from beach to beach as the sun sank into the sea. They stopped to talk to dog walkers and hard-core swimmers in wet suits, most of whom said that the police had already asked the same questions. All of them said they hadn't seen the girls or Seth.

They'd been walking along the wall of the harbor when Sophie sighted her first woman police constable speaking to some die-hard tourists sitting huddled on benches, warming themselves over fresh pastries.

"I'm Sophie Mills," she told them. "The girls' guardian while their father's away. Has anyone seen them?" The constable was very young, her face smooth and round. She didn't look older than Seth himself, and her discomfort in talking to a distraught woman was palpable.

"It would help if you had a photo to give us." She offered the advice apologetically.

"No," Sophie said, shaking her head and glancing at her watch as moment after moment separated her further from the children.

"Yes, madam, it really does help to have a photo," the young woman told her. "Hold on here and I'll radio through to the station, get the sarge to come and have a word with you about protocol."

"*No!*" Sophie found herself shouting. "No, because . . . it's not that bad, it's not that serious. They haven't been abducted. They're just somewhere around here. We just need to *look*."

"A photo would help," the policewoman told her, unable to look her in the eye. "Seriously, it's only something to help jog people's memories. It doesn't make it any more serious. It will help."

"This is a waste of my time," Sophie gasped as she dragged her wallet out of her bag and handed the constable the school photo that she kept in the clear plastic part, the first photo of anyone that she had ever carried anywhere. It had been taken at the end of last term, Izzy with her hair sticking up vertically because she'd insisted on styling it herself that day and had a very individual idea on how a headband should be worn, and Bella, sitting alongside her, her smile prim and proper, her shoulders straight as she posed for the camera.

"It's my only one," Sophie said reluctantly as she handed it over.

"We'll find them," the policewoman told her.

"So he's not taken them for ice cream," Carmen said as soon as Sophie shut the car door. She kept her eyes ahead, on the road, determined not to let Sophie pause for thought as she pulled away and headed out of the town center. "And he wants to get to know them, he wants to find out about them. He'll ask them about Carrie, about what it was like when Louis came back. Where would Bella take him? Where would she take him to explain everything? Maybe Carrie's grave?"

"Carrie doesn't have a grave, she was scattered over the . . . oh my god." Sophie looked at the cliffs that rose up behind the town.

"They could be up there, they could have taken him to meet their mummy."

Carmen pulled the car up as close as she could to the footpath that led up to the cliff edge, driving her SUV much farther over the rough terrain than was strictly allowed, but the rest of the way had to be walked; once again Sophie found herself laboring uphill, against the clock, her heart pounding in her chest as she strove for the crest. As she finally reached it, she expected to see nothing but the empty expanse of the jagged edge of the land as it jutted into the sea, and the faint embers of the day dying in the sky.

She caught her breath as she saw the silhouette of people on the horizon. They were sitting on the rough grass, and she couldn't be sure how many there were or how old they were. They could as easily have been a courting couple or a pair of bird-watchers as two small girls and their confused older brother.

Slowly, quietly—fearful of the sound of her own heart hammering in her chest—Sophie crept toward the group, holding her breath as the small huddle of humanity finally fell into focus. She stopped by an outcropping of rock about fifteen feet behind them, standing in the shadows, and let out a long, silent, sigh of relief. It was Seth. Seth and her girls, sitting at a safe, but still frighteningly close, distance from the cliff's edge.

Sophie edged carefully around the rock until she could make out what they were saying. She had to pick her moment, she had to make sure he couldn't hurt them before she let him know she was there.

"Mummy's out there, somewhere," Izzy was explaining. "And she's in the trees and the sky and the lampposts and the bushes and the . . . sea and the boats and stuff. She's everywhere, Aunty Sophie says, keeping an eye on us and loving us. But this is our best place to talk to her, here because this is her most favoritest place."

"Man, you must miss her a lot," Sophie heard Seth say as she crept closer to him. He didn't sound like a crazed loon who'd just kidnapped two children in order to hurt them. He didn't even sound angry, just tired and, somehow, relaxed.

"I've always had my mum," he explained. "Mum's always been around, but I never had a dad, except for a bit, and that turned out to be rubbish."

"We didn't have our dad for a bit," Bella told him. "He left us when I was little and Izzy wasn't even born. I don't think he meant to, but he went and . . . then it was just us and Mummy for ages."

"But he's back now, yeah?" Seth asked her. "And that's cool, right?"

Sophie squinted into the gloom, afraid to move any closer. She could see evidence of sandwich wrappers and a Styrofoam cup lying on its side on the grass. Hot chocolate probably if Izzy had anything to do with it.

"He was back until he found out about you," Bella said, her

tone darkening. "And then he went away again to find you. He kept going away and leaving us and now we don't know where he is. Because he's not with you."

"He was, babe," Seth said, ruffling her hair. "Bloody hell, I'm sorry I messed you up. I didn't really think about you lot. I was just angry with him and Mum, you know? For thinking it was cool to drop that on me from out of nowhere. I went off, acted like a fool. My mum and your dad have been chasing me round the bloody country and they haven't finished yet. I never told them I was coming back down here today. I just had to get away from her, always telling me how it's going to be. I'm not a kid anymore. I don't need anyone to tell me how anything is going to be. I'll decide that for myself."

"You're not supposed to go anywhere without telling your mummy," Bella chided him. "They told us that in stranger danger."

"And does your mummy know where you are?" Seth asked her uncomfortably.

"Yes, 'cause we just told her," Izzy said, pointing at the darkening sky. There was a moment's silence.

"I've never had a big brother before," Izzy said. "Is there hugging? Hope so because I'm a bit chilly."

Seth was quiet for a moment, Sophie unable to see his expression as he looked out to sea.

"I don't know," he said eventually. "I've never had really little kid sisters and stuff before. I don't even know *any* kids. But I guess a quick hug should be all right." Sophie watched as he put his arm around his four-year-old half sister and rubbed her shoulder briskly.

"I should get you back, really," he said. "I've caused enough trouble."

"But why? You're our big brother," Izzy said. "That's allowed."

"Suzanne Dean's big brother picks her up every Thursday for football practice," Bella added.

"Yeah, but she probably lives with her brother, she probably knows all about him. You'd never met me before today."

"You look a lot like Daddy," Izzy said. "Only smoother."

"You don't look much like that Wendy woman at all," Bella added.

Seth chuckled. "Is that what you call her?" he asked. " 'That Wendy woman'—it suits her."

"Are you cross with your mummy?" Izzy asked him, just as Sophie was about to make herself known. She paused, waiting to hear Seth's answer.

"She does my head in a lot of the time," Seth said. "It's like, I know she went through hell having me so young and on her own. And she's done a bloody lot with her life considering. Got her own business, got her own place, pays her own bills, and got me to art college. She's always done her best for me. But sometimes it feels like she thinks that because she's done all of that, she owns me, you know? And this thing with your dad, my dad . . . It's not like it's the first time she's tried to spring a bloke on me and told me this is the way it's going to be. She was married once to this decent enough bloke when I was a bit older than you. She told me he was my dad, she told me to think about him like my dad and love him. I didn't want to at first, but I did want to make her happy, you know, and she said that if I could love him, then I would make her happy. So I tried, and I got to like him. Love him even. It was a big deal for me, to have this bloke in my life, to share him with her and to trust him . . . and then it didn't work out with her and he was gone. We never heard from him again because that wasn't what she wanted. And I was supposed to forget all that stuff I felt about him, supposed to forget he was my dad and act like it never happened. And now she's trying the same bloody story on me again. It's like, I'm an adult—I don't need a dad now. I don't need anyone telling me what to do. Do you know what I mean?"

"Not really," Bella said carefully. "Not exactly. But also she is four and I am seven. You're not supposed to swear in front of us."

"Sorry," Seth said. "I forgot you are such little dudes."

"I loved Daddy and then he went away," Bella told him. "I was little, littler than her, but I remembered him and I missed him even though I was really small. Then Mummy *died*." She spoke the word carefully, as if she was aware of how important it was, how that single word and its meaning had altered the course of her life. "We were very, very sad and Aunty Sophie came and got us from Grandma's and took us home and looked after us."

"And let us eat nuggets," Izzy remembered fondly.

"And then Daddy came back," Bella added.

"I didn't even know he was my daddy." Izzy giggled. "That was a bit funny."

"But I did, I knew," Bella said. "I didn't like him very much. Because he'd been away so long and I felt funny and angry and shy."

"You shouted at him," Izzy reminded her. "And do you remember when we made that tent out of Aunty Sophie's coat and I got stuck in the toilet!"

Seth chuckled as Izzy collapsed into giggles against his shoulder.

"She does that," Bella explained. "She laughs about things when she's worried. I'm the only person who knows that. And now you."

"Cool," Seth told her. "I think that's a cool thing to do if you're worried. Like whistling in the dark."

"'Cept I can't whistle," Izzy said.

"Man, I'm totally tops at whistling," Seth said, grinning at her. "I'll teach you, babe."

He turned to Bella. "So what happened to make things cool with your dad then?"

"Aunty Sophie said that sometimes grown-ups are stupid, and do stupid things too, and that him not being there didn't mean he didn't love us, it just meant he was stupid. And we came back here, and when we got here he looked like my daddy again," Bella said.

"Until you were invented," Izzy told Seth matter-of-factly. "Then he went off with that Wendy woman."

"It's a bloody mess for all of us then, isn't it?" Seth said, shaking his head. "Sorry, forgot not to swear again. She's cool then, is she, Sophie?"

"She goes to sleep in her clothes." Izzy giggled.

"She made a special promise to look after us," Bella told him. "She's not used to being a mummy, but she's tried really hard to be our mummy even though she doesn't know it, and even though we have a mummy we love, we love Aunty Sophy like she's a mummy. An extra one who's here to do us teas and give us hugs."

"And she talks to us about Mummy whenever we like," Izzy said, suddenly thoughtful. "Daddy never really talks to us about Mummy, but Aunty Sophie does all the time and it helps us to remember her."

Sophie pressed her hand against her chest, desperate to run up to the girls and hug them and tell them how grateful and glad she was to have the chance to love them. But they had never spoken to her this way, and she was beginning to realize that there was so much about how they thought and felt that she didn't know about. For some reason they could talk to this brother they barely knew and she wanted to hear more.

"And she loves Daddy a lot, they do a lot of kissing," Bella added.

"So before I rocked up, it was all pretty cool for you kids then," Seth said.

"Yes," Izzy said. "We're getting married to Aunty Sophie and there will be wings."

"So you don't really need me around screwing it all up for you, do you?" Seth said, standing up suddenly, making Sophie's body tense as she stood in the shadows. Bella and Izzy stood up too, the safe distance between them and the cliff edge shrinking as Seth strode nearer it, the girls in his wake. "What would be best for you little dudes is for me to get out of here and let you get on with your lives."

"No! Stay!" Izzy ran full tilt toward Seth and the thin air just behind him, catching hold of his hand at the last second and breaking her speed against his weight.

"Yes, stay," Sophie said finally, raising her voice just enough for it to be heard above the sea breeze that whipped through the grass, keeping it calm and friendly. Keeping all the fear and anger and shock at bay. "Stay there, Seth, and don't go any closer to the edge, please."

"Aunty Sophie!" As she had hoped, Izzy let go of Seth's hand and raced toward her, followed closely by Bella. She clasped them in her arms, pressing their small bodies against hers as if she could somehow fold them into her flesh and keep them safe from harm forever.

"We've been with Seth," Izzy said. "We had chocolate for tea."

"You came for us. Are we in trouble?" Bella asked her, her arms wrapped tightly around Sophie's body.

"No, no . . . no one's in trouble," Sophie said carefully, aware of the distant sound of police sirens growing ever louder; she wondered if Carmen, worried about how long she'd been gone, had alerted the police. "I was very worried about you, but you're not in trouble."

"I'm sorry," Seth said, his back to the sea, his hands in his trouser pockets. He looked like a little boy who'd been caught with his hands in the sweets jar.

"You bloody stupid boy," Sophie said, her voice angry and low as she clung to the girls. "You should be sorry. You can't just run rampant through people's lives because you're having a hard time. No matter how difficult or messed up you think your life is, you have no right to drag two small children into it and put them in danger."

"Was there danger?" Izzy asked her, suddenly alarmed. "What, monsters?"

"Leave Seth alone," Bella said indignantly. "He's been kind to us, not bad. Not a monster."

"I know, darling, but he shouldn't have taken you away without asking. I was so, so worried."

"I'm sorry, Sophie, about everything . . ." Seth took a step closer to her. "But I would never hurt them. I wanted to meet them without Mum and Louis on my back. Louis said I should meet them, so I decided I would. Today. I didn't think, I didn't get how much you'd worry. I thought you'd be cool once you knew they were with me."

"You brought them here, to the top of a cliff, and you're standing there talking about disappearing for good!" Sophie exclaimed. "How on earth would that make me feel cool?"

"What, you think I'd . . ." Seth shook his head. "I meant like transferring courses to Manchester or something, not topping myself. Those two are proper cool. I don't want to wreck things for them. Or you, you seem like a decent kind of woman, taking them on when they had no one. Looking after me when I'd got a bit out of control. I want you to get your wedding with your wings and be happy before me and my bloody mother mess it all up for you. Look, I'm stupid. I'm really bloody stupid, but I'd never . . ." He paused, the trouble he'd caused just registering on his face. "Oh god, I'm so sorry."

"Sorry?" Sophie let out a ragged, rage-filled breath. "You bloody, bloody idiot, Louis," she sobbed, collapsing on the cold, wet grass, the girls still in her arms.

"Aunty Sophie!" Izzy's giggles echoed in her ears. "Don't be silly."

"I can't breathe," Sophie gasped. "I can't . . ."

"But it's okay, we're okay now," Bella said, placing her palms on either side of Sophie's face as she lay on the ground, dimly aware of the wet grass on the back of her neck.

"I feel . . . I can't . . ." Sophie felt the heat of the girls' bodies in her arms as she pulled them closer to her, determined never to let them go again. And then she felt nothing.

Then there was nothing.

Twenty-one

Someone was holding Sophie's hand as she came round in the back of the ambulance, its rocking motion as they headed toward the hospital bringing her back to the world. She tried to sit up, but her head spun and her vision blurred whenever she tried to move. She could see the drip in her arm though and feel its cool fluid circulating through her veins.

"I'm pregnant," she blurted out. "Please, don't give me anything that's going to hurt my baby."

"You're pregnant?" a male voice spoke. "Like with a baby?"

"Yes, Seth, I'm pregnant, and your antics with my children haven't exactly helped matters, thank you very bloody much, so just get the hell out of my ambulance . . . oh, Louis, it's you."

Sophie concentrated very hard, forcing her eyes to focus on Louis's face. "But how . . . when did you arrive . . . have I been out for weeks or something? Is the baby born and I didn't notice? Where are the girls, are the girls okay—are they here?"

"Hello," Louis said, staring at her. "Hello, Sophie. The girls are fine, they are safe, Mrs. Alexander and Carmen are with them at home. The police had a word with Seth, but after I talked to him they let him go home with his mum. You've been out for about half an hour, but the paramedic says you're going to be fine. I got back just a little while ago. Seth had gotten himself into trouble, gotten himself arrested for being drunk and disorderly—trying to pick fights in a part of town where every other kid carries a weapon. He got drunk again and told Wendy he didn't care what happened to him. Wendy was so frightened for him that she called the police and they kept him in a cell overnight to sober up. We went back the next day to pick him up, but they'd already let him go. I never thought he'd come back down here. Bloody student-rail discount cards, I blame them." Louis attempted a smile, but Sophie just stared at him, somehow detached from what he was telling her, from everything except the lull and sway of the ambulance, as if she were still unconscious and dreaming, only with her eyes open.

"Seth called Wendy this morning, told her he was coming back to Cornwall to meet his family. We followed him down, as quickly as we could. But when I got back, the house was empty. Mrs. Alexander said you'd rushed off to find the girls, the school said their brother had them. I didn't have my bloody phone. But I found James at the lifeboat house. He told me you were with Carmen, and I rang her. I came straight to you, Soph."

"You came too late," Sophie told him, coming around ever so slowly as everything he said to her began to sink in. "Where were you, Louis? You walked out on us!"

"I know . . . I know . . ." Louis closed his eyes, on his face an expression of pain. "When you took Bella upstairs to clean her feet, Wendy phoned back. She said she was really worried about Seth. Said he'd gone off into the night and she didn't know what he might do . . . she said she thought he might hurt himself. She begged me to come and help her find him. I kept thinking that it was all my fault, and I knew the girls would be safe with you. I just went. I didn't know I'd left my phone. I didn't think you'd be gone before I had a chance to speak to you. I didn't think and . . . Sophie, did I imagine it or did you just say you're pregnant?"

Sophie turned her face away from him.

"Listen, mate," the paramedic told Louis. "We'll be in Penzance in a minute. The girl's just fainted. Give her a bit of space, okay?"

"I'm sorry." Louis kissed the back of Sophie's hand. "I'm really, really sorry. We can talk about it whenever you want. But, Sophie, please tell me, are you really pregnant?"

Sophie nodded slowly, biting her lip fearfully.

"I'm just over two months gone," Sophie told him wearily. "I'm sorry."

"You're sorry?" Louis asked her. "Why in god's name are you sorry?"

"Because you've already got three children. And you said you didn't want any more. And I didn't realize I was pregnant until my mum told me when I was in London. You'll have another child with a useless mother who can't get children to school on time and leaves them to be kidnapped by their unhinged brother."

"Listen, that was scary, but it wasn't your fault," Louis said. "And the girls weren't ever really in any danger."

"I didn't know that, and neither did you until you got here," Sophie said, swallowing as she remembered the fear that had consumed her. She turned to look at him. "And you got here too late, you bastard!" Without warning she punched Louis hard in the arm, making him yelp and the paramedic whistle through his teeth. "You should have been there, you should have been there to look after your daughters and take care of me. That's what you're supposed to do, but you left, you bloody left again. Because that's what you do, isn't it?"

"It's not . . . honestly it's not. I know that's the way it looks, but it's not how it is," Louis said. He glanced at the paramedic then unstrapped his seat belt so that he could kneel on the floor next to the trolley she was strapped to.

"Sophie, you're pregnant. You, Sophie Mills, are pregnant with my baby—that's . . . that's amazing, it's incredible. It's the best, most brilliant news I've heard in a long time. I know I've screwed up, I've screwed up badly, and I'm sorry. I didn't know how to handle things with Seth and Wendy, and instead of talking to you about it, relying on you like I should have, I shut you out. I let you down, and I let my daughters down—something I swore I'd never ever do again. You don't have much reason to believe me right now, but I promise that I will look after you and Bella and Izzy and our baby. And Seth, if he'll let me. And I know I don't deserve it, but the only news you could give me now that would make me any happier is that you will still marry me despite what a bloody fool I've been."

Sophie stared at him, chewing her lip.

"Seth kissed me," she told him. "That night when he came back to the B and B he kissed me and I let him. It was only a few seconds, but it probably wasn't appropriate under the circumstances. I'm telling you because I'm trying to think of all the skeletons that could possibly be in my closet before we go any further."

"Okay," Louis said. "That's a bit weird, but it doesn't matter. Nothing matters as long as you'll still have me."

"And when I was in London, I had lunch with Jake and he told me I was incredibly sexy and beautiful and he kissed me too, which was wrong, I know, but it helped me realize that I don't want to be kissed by anyone but you. Not even a younger version of you."

Louis breathed out a long, slow breath.

"Okay," he said. "I'm pretty ticked off about Jake and I may have to track him down and kill him, but I get it. I wasn't around. I wasn't there for you and you were confused. And as for Seth, well, if there is one thing I've learned about him it's that he's impulsive, he acts first and thinks later. Plus, I'd try to kiss you if I were him. You're the most beautiful girl in the world. So it's okay, none of that matters. I forgive you."

"Oh, mate," the paramedic said as they pulled to a halt in the hospital parking lot. "You were doing so well right up until that moment."

Sophie stared at the murky mass of shadows on the monitor. Amid the gray, like the churning clouds of a stormy night, lay a small black pearl, perfectly round, a serene, dark world, the world her baby inhabited.

"It's too early to see much," the nurse told her. "But everything looks good so far, and if you squint really hard . . . you can just about see the heartbeat. See that little flicker there?"

Sophie peered at the image, feeling as if she were attempting to divine her own future, and then suddenly she saw it, just as images of animals and faces had emerged from the pattern on her mother's Formica kitchen tabletop, it was there. Just a scrap of life, the merest flicker of a candle that might be snuffed out at any second except that it kept on burning.

"Wow," Louis said from the doorway, where Sophie had told him to stand unless he wanted another thump. "Look at that, Sophie, that's amazing."

He edged a little closer and bent over so that he could get a better look.

"Can we have a photo?" Louis asked the technician.

"You won't see much, but you can have one," the nurse said, smiling at him. Tentatively Louis reached out and picked up Sophie's hand; she withdrew it immediately.

"I'm sorry," he told her. "It just sort of came out. You're the one who should be forgiving me, not the other way round. I know that now, especially after you slapped me. You slap hard for a recently unconscious pregnant lady."

Louis rubbed his jaw gingerly.

"The thing is . . ." Sophie stopped and looked at the nurse.

"Don't mind me," the nurse said, handing Sophie a wad of tissues to rub the gel from her stomach. "I'll just pop out and let the doctors know the results. You two have a few minutes to get straight."

"The thing is," Sophie said once they were alone, "if we were solid, if we were the kind of couple who should get married, then things wouldn't have happened this way, would they? You wouldn't have cut me out of what was happening with you and Seth and that bloody Wendy woman. I wouldn't have run away to London at the first possible opportunity and thought about kissing Jake . . ."

"And actually kissed Jake," Louis added, a little darkly.

"And if we hadn't been so wrapped up in this bubble of us, and being in love, and thinking that the whole world would just fall into step with us because we wanted it to, then maybe I wouldn't have gotten accidentally pregnant."

"You're not the first woman in the world this has happened to," Louis told her. "It's not as if you're some kid, on your own without a father on the scene . . ." Louis trailed off, obviously thinking about Wendy, a fact that caused Sophie's jealousy to spike. At this moment in time, she didn't want his thoughts to stray from her for one second.

"Actually, since the moment I found out I was pregnant there has been no father on the scene," she told him sharply. "I've been coping with this alone, Louis. We've all been coping alone because you weren't there."

"I know . . . I know, and that was wrong, but I've been stretched so thin recently. I've been trying to do the right thing and ending up getting it wrong all of the time. I should have listened to you about Seth, especially about telling the girls, and I shouldn't have shut you out of what was happening. But I couldn't ignore him and Wendy either, could I? You were the one who told me that. You said I had to find out about my son and you were right. You have to see that all the mistakes I've made weren't because I was being a coward and running away. I made them because I wanted to get things right. I want everything right before you and I start our married life together. And anyway," Louis went on, "so what if we were wrapped up in a bubble of love, that's what being in love is about, isn't it? Being happy, experiencing the joy of being with someone who is so perfect and so right for you." Louis caught Sophie's wrist as she stood up to button her jeans. He pulled her close to him, entwining the fingers of his other hand in her hair.

"You make me so happy, happier than I've ever been," he told her. "I thought I made you happy too."

"You did, you do," Sophie insisted. "Most of the time. I've never felt so happy, but it shouldn't be at the expense of everyone else."

"What do you mean?" Louis asked her.

"We thought that because we were happy, everyone else was too—but they're not. The girls aren't happy; yes, from day to day they're okay, but deep down they aren't over losing Carrie or the trauma they went through, of course they're not. Their mother died. How could we let Carrie down so badly? You saw Bella when she thought you were going to leave her. She still doesn't feel safe or secure, Louis. She still thinks you might abandon her at any moment. And did you know that if Izzy is frightened or worried, she hides it by laughing and being silly? I didn't know that, I didn't know it until Bella told Seth, someone she barely knows, about it on the cliff top. She told him, not you or me, and now that I think about it, it makes perfect sense. Little sunny Izzy, always so full of fun even in her darkest hour, but that's not true. All she was trying to do was keep the shadows at bay. Neither one of us noticed that. Because we didn't want to. We didn't want reality crashing in and spoiling things for us."

Sophie shook herself free from Louis's grip and went to the door. "And now this, now a baby. What's that going to do to them? You want me to say that everything's going to be fine. That I'll marry you and we'll have our baby and we'll all live happily ever after. But I just don't know if that is possible anymore."

"What are you saying, you're saying you'd consider . . ." Louis went to Sophie and put his hand on her belly.

"No, god no—of course not," Sophie said.

"Then what?" Louis asked her.

"I'm just not sure that I can marry you," she said. "That's what I'm saying."

"Okay, so the idea of marriage freaks you out, I get that, I think. And if you really don't want to do it, we don't have to. We can live together—you, me, the girls, the baby—like one big happy family."

"I love you," Sophie said. "But I don't know. I don't know if we are ready to do that yet. It would be easy to say that we are because of the baby, but I don't want Bella or Izzy or our child to have to go through any more upheaval, any more confusion or loss, because you and I aren't as strong or as close as we need to be to really make this family work."

"Are you saying that you'll stay in the B and B forever with our baby?" Louis asked.

"I don't know," Sophie said. "Maybe I am."

They were silent on the way home, Sophie staring bleakly out the window as Louis drove her car.

"Well, I'm telling you one thing, you're not going back to the B and B tonight," he'd said as they climbed into the car. "I want you with me and the girls where we can keep an eye on you."

"You heard what the doctor said—I'm fine. My blood pressure is fine, the baby is fine. I don't need keeping an eye on."

"Sophie, you are having my baby. Bella and Izzy's and Seth's half brother or sister. Whatever you decide about marrying me, we are a family no matter where you live, and I love you. I know you're upset with me and you're worried about the girls, but for tonight you are coming home with me and that's that."

"I'm coming because I want to see the girls," Sophie told him. "Not because you said so."

Carmen opened the door and Sophie found herself engulfed in a mass of hugs.

"You're alive!" Bella cried, burying her head in Sophie's stomach.

"I told them you were going to be fine," Carmen said. "But they got themselves in a right state, especially Izzy." Carmen nodded toward the front room, where Izzy was sitting on the sofa sucking on the sleeves of her pajamas as she watched *The Little Mermaid*. She didn't even look up at Sophie standing in the doorway.

"It was the ambulance that scared her," Bella said, her voice muffled somewhere in Sophie's middle.

"The ambulance?" Sophie hugged Bella to her ever so tightly and then released her.

"There was an ambulance after the car accident," Bella said slowly, entwining her fingers in Sophie's. She looked up at her father.

"I see you are back," she told Louis as she made her way into the living room.

"I am. And I'm back for good now, I promise," Louis told her.

Bella said nothing, following Sophie into the living room to find Izzy, leaving Louis and Carmen standing in the hallway.

"Come in the kitchen," Sophie heard Carmen say gently to Louis. "Mrs. Alexander is making us all bacon sandwiches. It was the girls' special request."

Followed closely by Bella, Sophie walked into the living room where Izzy stared doggedly at the screen, her knees tucked up under her chin, her toes curled in on themselves as if she were hanging on for dear life.

"Hello, sweetheart," Sophie said softly as she sat down carefully next to her, Bella sitting on her other side. Izzy didn't waver.

"Are you okay?" Sophie asked her, brushing a curl from her forehead. "You've had a very long and busy day, you must be ever so tired."

Izzy shook her head from side to side once.

"Did you have a nice time with Seth?" Sophie asked. Izzy nodded.

"You must have been worried up on the cliff when silly Sophie fainted. Were you worried, Izzy?"

Izzy kept her eyes on the screen, but she took her thumb out of her mouth. "They took Mummy in an ambulance. I was in the car still when they took her. I was left behind with the other lady, and Mummy went in the ambulance and she didn't ever come back. I was frightened."

Sophie nodded.

"I remember. You must have been very scared when I went in the ambulance, but I was fine. I was just a bit silly and forgot to eat and I fainted. They had to take me to the hospital to check me out, but I was okay. Ambulances help people."

Izzy turned to look at her, her face still and serious, just like Carrie's in the few precious moments when Carrie was quiet and thoughtful.

"We've got a new older brother," Izzy explained. "His name is Seth. He came to get me from school and I went with him, and I shouldn't have, but I did. He bought me a giant inflatable dolphin, but I think I left it on the cliff . . . he's going to teach me to whistle."

"Is he?" Sophie asked. "That's good. It will be fun to get to know him, won't it? And I expect that once you know him a bit better, you'll do all sorts of fun things with him."

"I would probably like to go to a circus with him," Izzy said thoughtfully. Then without warning she hurled herself at Sophie, wrapping her arms around her neck.

"You must stay now," Izzy told her. "And not faint again."

"I promise not to faint again," Sophie said.

"Or go away in an ambulance."

"I won't."

"At the circus will there be an elephant like Dumbo with huge enormous ears?" Izzy asked her, quite tickled at the thought.

"An elephant that can fly?" Sophie asked. "With huge enormous floppy ears?"

Izzy giggled. "Yes, I'd like to go for a ride on one of those."

"Well, you never know," Sophie said.

Sophie sat on the edge of Louis's bed, fully dressed, and looked around the room. This would be only the third time she had slept a whole night here. The first time she had crept in and taken her clothes off before seducing Louis, the second time she had crashed fully clothed and confused. Now as she sat on the edge of the bed, Louis took off his clothes, set his watch down, and went off to brush his teeth in only his boxers. It was like being part of a couple. A proper grown-up couple, and it felt strange.

Sophie sat perfectly still, fully dressed, looking around the room, the wardrobe that was half empty, the wall devoid of pictures, only the faint ghost of the last owner's artwork where the wallpaper had faded in the sun, leaving an impression of the past.

"Are you getting in?" Louis asked her, dropping his boxers in front of her. Inexplicably Sophie blushed and looked away.

"Are you shy?" Louis asked her, smiling a little as he knelt down in front of her. "Are you scared seeing me naked? I mean I know that I have an impressive physique, but it's probably a little too late to be scared of it now." He put a hand on either side of her on the bed.

"Sophie," he said softly. "We are okay, aren't we? I mean, you're angry with me and I deserve it, and you've been through hell all alone these past few days, but we are okay? Aren't we? Because if I think I've messed this up when it's all almost so perfect, then I'd never forgive myself. I know you said you didn't want to marry me and you wanted to live in the B and B with our baby and just visit every now and then, but that was crazy talk, wasn't it? You didn't mean it, did you?"

Sophie looked up into Louis's eyes.

"I love you," she told him. "I want to marry you. I just don't know if I can. Bella and Izzy are so afraid that something bad is going to happen again. And Seth, he barely knows who he is or who you are, and just as you're getting to know him, then a baby comes along."

"Listen," Louis said, sitting back on his heels. "If Bella and Izzy are afraid that something bad is going to happen, then we have to make them see that a baby is one of the best things that can happen. And the very best thing we can possibly do for them is to give them the stability they need. Get married and live all together here as a family and prove to them that nothing bad is going to happen. And as for Seth, well . . . I'll find a path with him. Maybe now is the perfect time for him to join the family, because he won't be the newest one for very long. Soon there will be this one." Louis nodded at her belly. "Our baby, yours and mine."

As he looked at her, his eyes lit up and Sophie felt her heart quicken.

"You really are pleased about the baby, aren't you?" she asked him.

"Pleased? Sophie, I'm over the moon. You're having my baby. You, the love of my life."

He leaned toward her and kissed her.

"Now listen, you've had a very long and difficult day and you need to rest." He lifted the hem of her T-shirt, pulling it over her head, pushing her gently back onto the bed. Sophie did not resist. "You just lie there and I'll put you to bed," Louis whispered, unbuttoning her jeans and pulling them off her hips and legs. Gently he lifted her legs onto the bed, running his hand lightly over her belly and the tops of her thighs as he looked at her.

"You are incredibly beautiful, you know," he told her, rolling her onto her side so that he could unhook her bra. Gently he slid the straps off her shoulders, the tips of his fingers running over her breasts as he removed the garment.

"The most perfect being I have ever seen," he said, kissing her stomach as he eased her underwear off.

Naked in his arms, Sophie looked into his eyes. "I love that you see me that way," she whispered.

"Well of course I do," he whispered back. "It's the way you are."

Twenty-two

"Aunty Sophie, Aunty Sophie, quickly, wake up, it's an emergency!"

Sophie prized open her eyes to find Bella staring at her, her big brown eyes shining in the half-light, brimming with tears. "Come quickly," Bella half-whispered, half-sobbed.

"What's happened?" Sophie sat bolt upright. "What is it? Is it Izzy?"

"No," Bella said, dragging Sophie out of bed where Louis was still asleep. "It's Artemis, I think Artemis is dying."

Sophie grabbed a dressing gown from the back of the door and wrapped it hastily around herself as she followed Bella into her bedroom.

"Dying? Bella, what do you mean—where is she?" Sophie asked her, the last dregs of sleep trickling slowly away.

"She's under my bed." Bella knelt on her carpet and pointed underneath her bed, her face stricken with fear. "I knew it was strange because she doesn't usually come in at night, she's usually out killing things. I was just going off to sleep when I heard her coming in, but she didn't say hello, she just went right under my bed. I heard her scrabbling about in my spare blanket, she must have dragged it under there, and then she went quiet and I must have gone to sleep but I shouldn't have because . . . because I woke up and she was crying . . . I looked under the bed with my Barbie flashlight and I thought I could see blood. So I tried to fetch her out and see where she was hurt but she scratched me." Bella offered Sophie the back of her hand where four long and painful-looking red welts were forming. "I think she must be dying because she's never ever hurt me before." Bella let out a sob. "She can't die, Aunty Sophie, please don't let her die. I need her."

Sophie put her hand over her mouth and took a breath to compose herself. In her head she had visions of Artemis hit by a car or a truck, crawling in and up the stairs in the night to find a safe place to lick her wounds. Just as fearful as Bella of how badly hurt her precious cat might be, she braced herself and, taking Bella's flashlight, knelt down on the carpet and peered under the bed. Artemis was breathing heavily, lying on her side, her head toward Sophie, so Sophie could not see the bulk of her body.

"Hello, girl," Sophie said. "You're not looking too good there, are you? I'm just going to see if I can get you out and we can have a look . . ." But the second Sophie's hand approached Artemis, the cat lashed out, her panting and distress apparently increasing.

"What shall we do?" Bella asked Sophie, gripping her dressing gown with clenched fists. "What shall we do to save her?"

Sophie fought to control the tremble that shook her voice, desperate not to show Bella just how afraid and upset she was. "I'll just see if I can feel anything one more time, so we know where she's hurt, and then we'd better call the vet. Go get my phone from the bedside table. Go on, quickly."

Carefully Sophie took the flashlight and on her hands and knees peered under the bed, but this time instead of approaching Artemis directly she tried to look at her from a different angle. She blinked, trying to make sense of what she was seeing amid the rucked-up blanket that Artemis had ensconced herself in.

"Hang on a second," she said as Bella arrived back with the phone book and phone. "Something's happening, she's . . . what is that?"

Sophie stared wide-eyed as Artemis half sat up and began licking something soft and slimy. At first Sophie thought it might be a dead mouse or a bird, but she had never seen her cat be so gentle with another living thing. And then as Artemis licked away the slime and gunk from the tiny creature, Sophie realized it was furry and orange. For a second she thought the injured animal had taken comfort from Izzy's toy cat, but then the tiny creature stirred, wriggling closer to the cat. Sophie stared at Artemis as she continued to lick the little creature, tenderly, lovingly, washing its face clean of any muck as it took its first breath.

Sophie gasped, clasping her hand over her mouth, tears springing to her eyes. She sat back on her heels and handed the flashlight to Bella.

"It's okay," she told Bella, grinning from ear to ear. "It's fine, Artemis isn't dying. Oh look, Bella." She hugged the little girl hard. "Artemis is having kittens!"

"Right," Sophie said, coming back into the room armed with supplies. "The vet says we should have towels in case she needs a bit of help with rubbing them awake, dental floss in case Artemis doesn't cut the cords properly, and some yogurt. He says she might fancy a spoonful of yogurt to keep her going. Oh, and a big box to put them all in once she's finished. I thought that old packing box in the shed would do. We have to line it with shredded newspaper."

"There are two now!" Izzy said, as she lay on her tummy in front of the bed. Louis had taken Bella's bedside lamp and laid it on its side next to the bed so that they could all get a clearer view without using the bright flashlight. "The second one looks gray to me . . . oh, they are soooo cute. We can keep them all, can't we?"

"What I don't understand," Louis said, keen to gloss over that subject as he hunkered down next to Izzy, "is how Tango ever got near enough to make this happen, the old dog. The old cat dog. Artemis has hated him from day one, and he's always avoided her."

"I told you I saw them hugging," Izzy said triumphantly. "They are in love!"

"What I don't understand is that Artemis is a rescue cat," Sophie said. "She's supposed to be spayed. I'd never have let her move in with an unneutered tom, even one as soppy and hopeless as Tango, if I hadn't thought that."

"Well, someone, somewhere, made a mistake," Louis said. "Because that cat is most definitely fertile."

"And now they are married!" Izzy said, clasping her hands together happily and rolling onto her back for a moment. "Married and having babies. Just like you and Daddy are going to, Aunty Sophie."

Sophie's and Louis's eyes met above the girls.

"How many kittens do you think she will have?" Bella asked. "I'm hoping for about twenty."

"The vet said four or five, most likely," Sophie said. "He said if she's still in labor in another few hours, then he'll come over and check her out, but he expects she'll be able to manage perfectly well on her own."

"Look at her, look, Aunty Sophie." Bella dragged Sophie back down onto the carpet to peer under the bed again. "Look, she loves her kittens."

Sophie watched as Artemis licked the two kittens that already nestled at her nipples. She looked so gentle and so tender with them, like an entirely different cat from the one Sophie knew and loved. This Artemis knew exactly how to be a mother, how to break the membrane sac so her kittens could breathe, how to lick them clean and bite off the umbilical cord. The fierce, angry loner cat had been transformed into a mother, all of her natural instincts flooding in just when she needed them.

"She's going to make a wonderful mother," Sophie said, wincing slightly as she straightened up, her body still stiff and aching from lack of sleep.

"And so are you," Louis told her, his cooling hand on the back of her neck.

Bella looked up at him sharply.

"What do you mean?" she asked him.

Sophie and Louis looked at each other and Sophie nodded. She didn't want to keep any more secrets from the girls.

"I mean," Louis said, reaching out to hold Sophie's hand, "that Sophie is going to have a baby. And I'm the baby's daddy and you and Izzy are going to be big sisters."

"That's awful!" Izzy cried out, horrified. "You're not even married yet."

Sophie watched Bella's face very closely as she took in the news.

"It's okay, Izzy—you don't have to be married to have a baby."

"You don't?" Izzy said. "Tango and Artemis are married. How long will it take for the baby to get here? Will it take longer than the wedding? If I am a big sister, will I get to boss the baby around, like Bella bosses me around? Will I get a bigger bedroom? I want a bigger bedroom if I am going to be a big sister and my own Nintendo DS. Is that why your tummy is so fat, Sophie, because there's a baby in it? How big is the baby in it now?"

"Just hold on for a second." Sophie laughed, holding her hand up to stave off any more questions as she kept an eye on Bella, whose gaze was fixated under the bed.

"The baby is going to be here in April," Sophie told Izzy. "It's not very big at the moment, hardly anything to see at all, really, although I have got a picture I can show you later if you like. So I'm afraid that all of this"—she patted her tummy—"is mainly cream teas and jam."

"Can I name the baby?" Izzy asked her. "I would call it Petunia."

"Oh well . . . maybe," Sophie said.

"What if it's a boy, dummy?" Bella said, her eyes still fixed on Artemis.

"If it's a boy then I would call it Rufus," Izzy said. "Like the dog next door, that way when we take it to the park we can call after it, 'Here, boy, here, Rufus.'"

Izzy giggled, which Sophie would once have found reassuring, but now she wondered if Izzy was really expressing shock and anxiety with her jokes.

"Bella?" Sophie said, easing herself up onto the bed. "What do you think about me having a baby?"

Bella sat back on her heels and looked at Sophie.

"I'm not sure," she said slowly. "I like things how they are. With just us. I like you looking after us."

"I like it too, but that won't change," Sophie told her. "I'll still look after you. I'll still always be here for you. I promise."

"But that baby will be your baby," Bella said, pointing at Sophie's middle. "You will love it more than us." She glanced at Louis. "He will love it more than us because it's your baby."

"You are all my children," Louis said. "I'll love you all the same."

"Even Seth?" Bella challenged him.

"Eventually," Louis said. "Given the chance, then yes. I'll love him too."

Izzy sat up, watching Bella, her face still and thoughtful as she listened.

"And as for me," Sophie told both the girls, "it's not possible for me to love anyone more than I love you."

"Isn't it?" Bella looked uncertain.

"Mitchell Lambert in my class has four brothers and a sister and their mum loves all of them the same," Izzy said.

"Yes, but Aunty Sophie isn't our mum, is she?" Bella said. "She'll be the baby's mum, but she won't be ours."

"Oh, I forgot that," Izzy said sadly.

Sophie rubbed her hand over her face and looked at Louis, who reached out and stroked Bella's hair.

"The thing is," she said slowly, "I know I am not your mum, but I *feel* like you're my daughters. I feel like you are *my* girls. Carrie was your mummy, and she always will be—but when you were gone and missing and I didn't know where you were, all I could think about was *my* girls, my daughters. About getting you back and keeping you safe. Artemis is lucky, she's got an animal instinct to tell her how to be a mummy, the second that her first kitten was born. But I realize that I've been even luckier. I've had you two to show me what being a mummy is really about. So that when this baby comes, when your little sister or brother arrives, then I'll be able to do nearly as good a job at it as Artemis."

"Will you bite off its cord with your teeth?" Izzy asked her, in awe.

"Probably not," Sophie said. "But apart from that, I think I'll be better at looking after this baby because I've got you two. You're my daughters and I love you and nothing, nothing on earth, will change that. I promise you."

Bella peered under the bed again. "Now there are three!" she exclaimed. "This one looks tortoiseshell."

"Anyway, I've been thinking," Sophie went on, treading ever so carefully. "The last thing on earth I want for you and Izzy is to worry about anything, so if this is all happening too quickly for you, if you feel that everything is changing too fast, then Daddy and I don't have to get married. I can stay in the B and B with the baby and things can go on as they are."

Louis dropped his head.

"But if you do get married, then what?" Bella asked her.

"Well, then I'd come and live here, and the baby would live here too eventually, and we would all be together every single day."

"And Seth would sometimes visit too," Izzy added. "To teach us to whistle."

Bella got up and sat next to Sophie on the bed.

"I don't want you to move in after you've got married," she said, and Sophie felt her heart sink with a disappointment that she hadn't fully appreciated until she heard Bella's verdict. "I don't want to wait that long. I want you to move in now. After all, Artemis will need help with the kittens, and you'll need extra looking after, and if you're here then . . ."

"Then?" Sophie asked her with bated breath.

"Then we'll be a family," Bella said.

"And you're happy for me and Sophie to get married?" Louis asked both of the girls.

"We are," Bella and Izzy said together.

Louis looked at Sophie. "And what have you got to say?" he asked her.

"I have this to say." Sophie's smile was radiant. "Louis, Bella, and Izzy—will you marry me?"

• • •

Soon after Artemis's fourth and final kitten was born, Louis sent Sophie and the girls back to bed, just before 8:00 A.M.

"You need rest," he said, kissing Sophie on the forehead. "And you two could do with at least one day off from school what with all the excitement you've had. I'll sort out Artemis, get her box ready and all that business."

Sophie and the two girls curled up in Louis's bed and drifted off to sleep the moment their heads touched the pillows.

It was midday when Sophie finally woke, feeling refreshed for the first time in ages. The girls had already gone, as she found them down in the kitchen, cooing over Artemis and her kittens, who Louis had put in a box next to the boiler.

"Good morning, Sophie," Louis said, encircling her with his arms. "Good morning, beautiful woman and bride and mother-to-be. The vet popped in to take a quick look at Artemis and he says she is fighting fit. Tango even turned up for breakfast and tried to have a look at his offspring but Artemis sent him away with his tail between his legs, which is pretty much all he will have there soon. The vet says we have to have them both done really soon if we don't want a repeat performance."

"That's great that she's doing so well," Sophie said as she sat at the table and looked into the box at Artemis with her kittens. "That's really, really wonderful."

"Well, probably not for Tango, the poor fellow," Louis said, wincing. "But I have got more good news. We have been busy, haven't we, girls?"

"Yes!" Bella jumped up excitedly, resting her palms on Sophie's knees. "We have got surprises," she said, wriggling her fingers in what Sophie assumed was an indication of mystery.

"Really?" Sophie asked her, a little cautiously. "Not entirely sure that I'm up to surprises."

"I called Fineston Manor this morning and they still have New Year's Eve free," Louis told her.

"They don't!" Sophie exclaimed delightedly before her brow furrowed. "But why do they? Is it a rubbish place where no one wants to get married?"

"No, it's a wonderful place where lots of people want to get married. It just seems that very few people have a ceremony a mere three months after they decide to get married, and no one else has booked it. They're thrilled we still want it, they've promised me candlelight and music and they'll do all the catering—we just need to look at menus and give them numbers."

"That's a fantastic surprise—but New Year's Eve—it's only a couple of months away—there's so much to do. I need to find a dress that won't make me look like a house."

"Or a horse," Izzy interjected.

"Ah well, that's our other surprise," Louis said, grinning at Bella. "I phoned Carmen earlier to tell her about the kittens and Fineston Manor and to ask her about the cake and all that and I asked her if she knew of any dressmakers in the area who might help us."

"Did she?" Sophie asked.

"She did better than that. She knows *the* dressmaker, the one who designed the dress you saw and loved at the fair? Apparently, after it all kicked off, Carmen decided to phone the organizer and find out about the designer, got her number, address—everything. She said she would have mentioned it sooner but everything seemed a bit up in the air."

"A long way up in the air," Izzy commented as she gazed happily at the kittens.

"Anyway, they're a small outfit based in Plymouth. I called them today and Ellen, that's the designer, said if you go in tomorrow they can fit it for you extra loose and then just before the wedding, take it in or let it out so that it flows perfectly over all of your curves. I tried to get her to tell me what it would look like, but she refused."

"Quite right too," Sophie said, and then, "Oh my god, I'm so happy."

"I should have known it would be a fashion item that would make you happy," Louis said, smiling.

"But what about invitations?" Sophie said suddenly. "We need to invite people in a couple of weeks, which means we need invites now."

"I know," Louis said. "And I've got the perfect idea for them. I'll take a photo of all of us, the whole family. I'll get my mate Steve down at the printer's to print us up the invites with the photo on the front. We'll be telling everyone that this is a new start, not just for you and for me, but for all of us. That we're a family now and that's the way it's going to stay forever."

"I love that idea," Sophie said, reaching out to touch his face.

"I'm glad, because the girls and I have been talking. And there is one more person we'd like to ask to be in the photo."

Sophie nodded. "Seth."

Wendy's house was remarkably unlike the bawdy bordello that Sophie had imagined. It was a modest duplex in a suburban part of Newquay, tastefully decorated in pastels and white. Her kitchen, where Sophie sat opposite Wendy as she sipped a cup of tea, was largely painted lemon yellow, with glittering white units. Wendy might be an evil old relationship wrecker, but it turned out that she liked to keep a clean home.

"Thanks for inviting me in," Sophie said, keen to break the silence that hung in the air between them. "Louis would have come in too, but we thought that under the circumstances he and the girls had better stay in the car."

Wendy nodded. "I can see why. I was going to call today anyway, to say thank you to you and Louis for helping sort things out with the police. When I got Seth home and he realized just exactly what he'd done, all the thoughts that must have been going through your head and how frightened you must have been, he was gutted. He is gutted. He knows he's blown it."

"Blown it?" Sophie asked her. "What do you mean?"

"Blown getting to know Louis and his sisters; he knows that after yesterday there is no way you will want him anywhere near them."

"But that's not true," Sophie said. "Yes it was stupid and frightening and if I'd had the chance to get my hands on him yesterday, then I probably would have killed him. But nothing has changed. He's still Louis's son, he's still the girls' brother. They—we—want him in our lives."

"I see," Wendy said, pursing her lips briefly. "Did Louis tell you?" she asked Sophie. "Only I think if we're going to move on from this, then you should know."

"Know what?" Sophie asked uneasily.

"In London, that second night, the night that he left you and came to help me. After the police had Seth, it was god knows what time, really late. Louis took me back to my B and B. I tried to get him to stay with me, tried to get him to come to bed with me. Threw myself at him really, made a right fool of myself. But he didn't want anything to do with me, not even for a second. He told me he loved you, he told me he'd sleep in a chair downstairs, and he did, all night. I got into my bed and I thought about Seth in a police cell and Louis downstairs on the chair and it hit me, what a bloody stupid selfish cow I'd been, putting Seth and Louis and you through a lot of pain. I'm sorry, Sophie."

Sophie sat back a little and glanced down at her lukewarm tea wondering if this was all some sort of evil mastermind confession and that in a second Wendy would announce she'd sweetened the tea with cyanide.

"You're sorry?" Sophie felt it was best to check.

"I got angry and jealous and insecure. Angry that suddenly my nice stable little life was going to be turned on its head, jealous that you seemed to have everything I never had without even having to try, and furious that Louis was about to waltz into my son's life, and get to be his dad without having to do any of the hard stuff, without having to go through the years and years of struggling that I did. It didn't seem fair, and I blamed it all on you. It's me Seth gets his rash and angry side from."

"Oh, right," Sophie said, cautiously. "I'm sorry, Wendy. I don't know exactly what to say. I mean I know this must have been hard on you. But you're the one who turned it into a fight over Louis; I still don't really get that. Why?"

Wendy sighed. "Look, my life's been what it's been and I can live with that. It's my choices that have brought me here. I chose not to tell Louis about Seth, although I think my dad probably had a lot to do with that. I chose to keep him when I could have had him adopted. And it's been tough. Mum and Dad were there for me, but I never had those years of being young that everyone else had. No nights out down at the pub, no real boyfriends to speak of. It's really hard to get a boyfriend when you've got a baby to look after. Never went to college. I loved Seth, with all of my heart. But I never felt like I lived my life. I didn't realize it until I saw Louis again."

"You've been through a lot," Sophie agreed. "Seth told me how much he admires you, how much you've done for him. I don't know if that quite gives you the right to try and steal my fiancé."

"I know that now," Wendy said and shrugged. "When I saw Louis that day, all of those carefree teenage feelings came back to me, the way I felt with him, how happy I was, and I suddenly realized that I had his son. I didn't want those feelings coming up and dragging me down again. I'd gotten used to my life, I was content. But then you saw us at the fair and put two and two together and I realized I didn't have a choice anymore. I'd have to face the way I used to feel about him. And I thought I wanted those feelings back, I thought I wanted him back. I used this whole thing with Seth to try and get him back. I thought the more time he spent with me and worried about Seth, the more likely it was that he'd start to feel about me the way he used to. But that was never going to happen. He was never going to leave you. I'm sorry."

Sophie nodded. "Well, for what it's worth, I'm sorry too for turning your life upside down when you asked me not to."

"I don't suppose you had a choice," Wendy said.

Sophie shrugged. "I probably didn't have to do it quite so abruptly. I'm the one who started this whole roller coaster. I'm sorry for that."

The two women sat in silence for a moment and Sophie looked toward the front door, thinking of Louis and the girls waiting in the car.

"What about Seth?" Sophie said. "Will he come down? I'd really like to talk to him."

Wendy went to the foot of the stairs and called up them.

"Seth, come down and talk to Sophie, love. Come on, she's not angry."

Sophie waited for the heavy footfall on the stairs and finally Seth emerged into the bright kitchen, the sleeves of his sweater pulled down over his fingers. His eyes looked red rimmed and swollen; he looked pale, scared, and very, very young.

"Hello," he said, unable to look Sophie in the eye as he sat down at the breakfast bar. Wendy put the kettle on.

"Are you okay?" Sophie asked him gently.

"I am," he said. "I'm fine—are *you* okay? I'm so sorry about what happened. No one at the school said I couldn't take the girls. I mean I thought if it was a problem, they would have stopped me. But no one did."

"I know," Sophie said. "Look, I'm not going to pretend that yesterday wasn't the most horrible, stressful, and sickening two hours of my life ever, but I understand why you did it, I think. And Louis understands too. We just want to put it behind us all and move on."

"I know," Seth said. "And you don't have to worry. I won't be hanging around anymore. I'll stay away, I promise."

"No . . . we don't want you to stay away. We want to get to know you . . . if that's okay with you. I know it will be really strange to begin with, but Louis is a good man and a great dad and . . ." Sophie glanced at Wendy. "I'm going to marry him on New Year's Eve."

"That's quick," Wendy said. "You pregnant?"

"Yes I am, actually," Sophie said, making Wendy spit out her tea. "But that's not why we're getting married. We're getting married because we love each other."

Seth grinned and then his face fell. "God, you're pregnant and I put you through all that; I'm such a sod."

"Well, it wasn't your finest moment, but I'm fine and the baby's fine and now we all want to move on. Focus on the wedding and the baby. Focus on this strange and wonderful new family that we're creating and which will hopefully include you." She looked at Wendy. "Both of you."

Seth and Wendy exchanged glances, the meaning of which Sophie couldn't quite determine.

"I came here to ask both of you to the wedding, and Seth— Louis and I would love it if you would be in our wedding-invitation photo along with me and Louis and his other children. Would you think about it at least?"

"Where is he?" Seth asked her.

"He's in the car with the girls," Sophie said. "We didn't want to rush you or crowd you. I think you've had a bit much of that recently."

"They can come in for a bit if you like, can't they, Mum?" Seth asked Wendy. "Have a cup of tea?"

Wendy nodded. "Of course," she said. "Of course they can."

"I said I'd teach the girls to whistle," Seth explained. "Got to start somewhere. It's a complicated business, whistling."

"I'll go and get them," Sophie said with a smile. Glancing at his mother, Seth followed her into the hallway and stopped her at the door.

"Listen, Sophie, this person you've seen, the person who kisses his dad's fiancée, gets drunk, gets into brawls, and wanders off with his kid sisters, that's not me. That's not all of me, anyway. It is a part of me, but it's a part I'm sorting out, you know, getting under control."

"I know you are," Sophie said.

"Being a big brother is going to be cool," Seth told her. "Having little kid sisters to be there for and another one too, maybe it'll be a boy and me and Louis will be able to take it fishing and stuff."

"Do you like fishing?" Sophie asked him in surprise.

"Can't stand it, but that's big brother territory, isn't it?" Seth replied with a smile.

"I don't know," Sophie said. "This is new for me too, you know. Brothers, fathers, being a mother. I think the best thing you and I can do is take one step at a time and see how we go."

"I'm up for that," Seth said as he opened the door and waved at Louis and the girls in the car. "I'm definitely up for that."

Epilogue

I've seen worse, I suppose," Cal said as Sophie stepped out from behind the screen in her wedding gown.

"What? Shut up," Carmen cried, crossing the bridal suite to take Sophie's hand in hers. "Oh, darling, you look beautiful. That dress is so perfect. You'd hardly know you were five months gone."

"I don't care if they do," Sophie said, turning to look at herself in the mirror and smoothing the cream silk over her bump. "I want the whole world to know."

"You look like a princess." Izzy oohed as she ran into the room, followed closely by her sister, both of them wearing dresses made out of yards and yards of dusky rose net, each with a pair of specially made beaded wings attached to their backs.

"No, like a queen," Bella said. "And we're your princesses and we especially like the buttons."

It had been Bella's idea to sew some of the buttons from Mrs. Stiles's box onto Sophie's and her and Izzy's dresses. She had come to Sophie about a week earlier and opened her cupped hands to reveal a treasure trove of mismatched cream, ivory, silver, pink, and pale blue buttons that together looked like a Cornish sky at sunset.

"I had a thought," Bella had said carefully. "These buttons used to be Mummy's and now they are ours, and I thought if we put them on your dress, then it would be like Mummy was there with us too, wouldn't it? And it would be something borrowed—like you're supposed to have at a wedding. And some of the buttons are old and some of them are new and there are two blue ones, so it would be awfully lucky as well as nice. I could stick them on with glue if you like."

Sophie had been so touched that she had called the dress designer immediately and taken the girls down there that afternoon. Although she'd drawn the line at letting the girls loose with glue anywhere near her cream silk, they had worked with the designer to adorn their dresses with the buttons, and the effect was a beautiful, original, and unique design.

As Sophie ran her hands over them, she felt for a second as if her old friend was in the room with her, holding her hand.

"And how do I look?" Cal asked, gesturing to his suit, which had been dyed to exactly match the bridesmaids' dresses.

"You look nice too," Bella told him. "Even if I'm not sure about a boy as a bridesmaid."

Christina handed Sophie a glass of water. "I'd like to offer you champagne, but, well, what with the bump, water will have to do."

There was a knock at the door, which Carmen went to answer.

She picked up Sophie's bouquet of pink winter roses and handed it to her.

"They are all ready for you out there. Are you ready, darling?" she asked. "Ready for a new year, a new life, a new baby, a new husband?"

"I am," Sophie said, looking at the door. "I am so very ready."

• • •

The candlelight was reflected in the chandeliers, making the room glitter and sparkle as Sophie slowly walked down the aisle on her mother's arm. Izzy and Bella walked in front of her, supposedly to scatter rose petals but actually waving at people, and in Izzy's case stopping for a chat when she saw Grace Tregowan and holding everything up for a few seconds.

Then finally Sophie found herself standing opposite Louis, Bella and Izzy on either side of her, and a rather nervous Seth at Louis's shoulder, clutching the rings.

"I didn't think you could look more beautiful," Louis said. "I was wrong."

"We're here," Sophie whispered as the celebrant prepared to start the ceremony. "We're doing this at last. You and I are getting married!"

And it seemed like a dream to Sophie as she stood in the candlelight with all her family and friends around her, Izzy's hand tucked into hers as Louis made his wedding vows, Bella standing by her side, her arm around Sophie's waist. She saw Grace Tregowan and Mrs. Alexander sitting in the front, Grace resplendent in red and Mrs. Alexander plowing her way through a box of tissues. She saw her mother standing behind her, determined not to cry, and Trevor waiting for her a few rows back with what Sophie happened to know was an engagement ring in a box in his pocket, because earlier that morning he'd come and asked her if she would mind if he proposed to her mother while they were down in Cornwall.

Best of all she saw the man she loved; she saw Louis telling her and the whole world that he was going to be by her side forever. That he was her husband.

"And do you, Sophie Mills, take this man to be your husband?" the celebrant asked her. Sophie smiled at Louis and hugged his two daughters close.

"I do," Sophie said. "Always, forever, whatever."

Acknowledgments

Thank you to Maggie Crawford who is always such a pleasure to work with and who brings so many fresh ideas and creativity to my writing. And also to all of the team at Simon & Schuster/Pocket Books for their continued dedication and commitment to my work. I can't believe how fortunate I am to have found such a fantastic publisher.

I would also like to thank my agents Lizzy Kremer in the United Kingdom and Jill Grinberg in the United States for all the work they do on my behalf.

It has been such a pleasure to be back with Sophie, Louis, Bella, and Izzy again that I have to thank my wonderful readers on both sides of the Atlantic who inspired me to write this new installment in Sophie Mills's life. I hope they enjoy it as much as I have.

Readers Club Guide

Introduction

About a year ago, Sophie Mills's life was turned upside down when her childhood best friend died and left Sophie in charge of her two young daughters. A true city girl, Sophie surprised everyone, including herself, when she moved to the country to be with the girls and their father, Louis—her best friend's widower.

But adjusting to life as a semi-permanent mother in a small town isn't as easy as Sophie imagined. She can't quite make that final commitment to move in with Louis and the girls—she's on her way to becoming the longest-paying guest of the local bed-and-breakfast.

Just as Sophie starts to feel secure, Louis's first love resurfaces with some shocking news. Now Sophie can't help but wonder: Can Louis take responsibility for his past as well as his present? And can she fulfill her solemn promise to be there for two frightened little girls "always, forever, whatever"?

Discussion Questions

1. The prologue to *The Accidental Family* takes place six hours after Sophie shows up at Louis's door in Cornwall, and the first chapter begins six months later. What has changed over those six months? How has Sophie and Louis's relationship evolved, and how has it remained the same?

2. The night that Louis proposes, why does Sophie insist that he is asking her permission to go on a surfing trip to Hawaii? What other miscommunications does this scene foreshadow?

3. Sophie complains to Cal, "Why do you have to sum up my entire life like it's a tabloid headline" (page 210)? What are some of the more tabloid-worthy moments of *The Accidental Family*? Which plot twist shocked you the most?

4. What were your first impressions of Wendy Churchill, Louis's first love? Did she meet your expectations in the end? Why or why not?

5. With four husbands in her past, eighty-nine-year-old Grace Tregowan has plenty of stories about love and loss. Which stories and pieces of advice seem to affect Sophie the most, and why?

6. Consider how Bella and Izzy handle the turmoil in their family. How does each girl cope with fear and uncertainty? How are their reactions similar, and how are they different?

7. Sophie feels she can relate to Seth's sense of loss and confusion: "She knew what it was like to live without a father and

she also knew how shocking it was to discover that your whole life, everything you've believed to be unalterable and true, could be turned on its head in a second" (page 156). Why doesn't Seth seem to respond to Sophie's sympathy? Could Sophie have done more to help Seth? If so, what?

8. Discuss the reappearance of Jake Flynn, Sophie's former love interest. Does Jake seem happy with his fiancée? Is his kiss with Sophie purely for "scientific research," as he says, or does he really want Sophie back? Explain your answer.

9. Iris shares the story of how she and Sophie's father met and fell in love. Compare this story to Sophie and Louis's. What do these romances have in common? How are they different?

10. Sophie has a broad support network, from sensible Iris to irreverent but loyal Cal to sexy, practical Carmen. Among Sophie's friends and family, which character is your favorite, and why?

Enhance Your Book Club

1. Plan a dream vacation to Cornwall, England! Pretend you and your book club will be spending a long weekend in this coastal region. Where would you stay, and what would you want to see? You can research Cornwall tourism at www.visitcornwall .com.

2. Treat your book club to a proper English tea! If there is a tea shop in your town, hold your book club meeting there. Or if you're hosting at home, you can find recipes for scones, cakes, and other Sophie-approved delights at www.joyofbaking.com/ EnglishTeaParty.html.

3. Follow the example of Iris, Sophie's mother, and volunteer at your local animal shelter. You can search for a shelter that needs help by entering your zip code on this website: www.pets911 .com/organizations/volunteer.php.

4. Take a peek into Rowan Coleman's world by reading her blog at www.rowancoleman.blogspot.com.

Questions for the Author

1. You open *The Accidental Family* with a bedtime story recounting the adventures of Princess Sophie, Prince Louis, Bella, and Izzy. Why did you choose this fairy-tale format to bring readers up to speed on the events of the previous novel, *The Accidental Mother?*

I wanted new readers to be able to pick up *The Accidental Family* and read it as a stand-alone book, but I was aware that at least some of Sophie and Louis's life from *The Accidental Mother* was really pertinent to this book. At first I tried to weave the events of the past into the main text, but most of the time I found that it slowed the book down and got in the way of the narrative flow. I had the idea for the bedtime story one evening while telling my daughter a made-up bedtime story in which she was the heroine. I realized how much children love to hear about themselves and that this is exactly what Sophie would do, not only to help the children understand what had happened but to help her understand it too.

2. The promise "Always, forever, whatever" plays a central role in *The Accidental Family*. How did you come up with this key phrase?

I have known my best friend, Jenny, since we were children, and during the course of our friendship we made each other many promises of loyalty that we have kept. We have always been there for each other through all of life's ups and downs. Although we never used the "Always, forever, whatever," when I thought about how to sum up the kind of friendship we had, that was the phrase that kept coming to mind. Best of all, I get a lot of mail from readers who tell me they have adopted it as their very own friendship motto.

3. Wendy is a complicated character; Sophie sometimes struggles to hate "that Wendy woman" when she considers the hardships of a single mother. Was it hard to resist creating a truly evil rival for your heroine? Why did you make Wendy's motivations so complex?

Life is complicated and I feel that the majority of people try their best to get it right, even if they don't always achieve it. Wendy makes life very difficult for Sophie; she manipulates Louis and her son—but only because she is looking at Louis and Sophie and the life she might have had if she had made different choices. Jealousy and regret are powerful emotions, and all of us have been overpowered by irrational feelings at some point in our lives. Apart from anything else, I try to write characters that are identifiable and realistic, and things are rarely ever as simple as "good" and "evil."

4. The cliffs and breezes of Cornwall really come alive in this novel. How does this part of the world inspire you?

I love Cornwall with a passion. I first visited as a child and have fond memories of roaming its sandy beaches, climbing over rocks, and fishing for crabs in rock pools. Over the years I have become more and more attached to it, particularly St. Ives when I discovered the artist colony that grew up there and I found out more about the artists' lives and work. During the summer it's so packed full of tourists that you can barely move, and in the winter it's wild and empty and full of untold stories—but all year round it never loses its charm for me. If you can visit, do!

5. Sophie takes quite a few romantic risks in this novel, from accepting Louis's proposal to kissing two other men. Do you think risk is necessary for romance—or at least for a good love story?

I think in Sophie's case the risks she takes are due to her uncertainty about the way her life is heading. Everything has changed very quickly, as she hasn't had a moment to catch her breath and think about it. Although she loves Louis and the children, she is still testing her own sense of commitment. From a wider point of view, when it comes to writing a romance or a love story, risk and complication are definitely necessities. I really hate putting my characters through some of the things I do. Part of me would like them to have a nice life, meet a nice partner, and settle down—but that doesn't make for very compelling reading!

6. Sophie and Carmen experience the madness of a wedding fair, overwhelmed by the cake samples and dress exhibits. Have you experienced this kind of wedding fever firsthand? Do you think it takes an event planner and a pastry chef—like Sophie and Carmen—to navigate the chaos?

I have been a bride, so I understand the fever that takes hold of wives-to-be! It can become the sole focus of a woman's attention in the months leading up to her wedding, and everything else fades in comparison. Unfortunately, I think the obsessive side of wedding planning can detract from the joy and pleasure of the actual day. Do you need a wedding planner? Probably not—but hiring one might help everyone stay sane.

7. Iris is able to guess almost instantly that her daughter Sophie is pregnant. Do you believe in a mother's intuition? Do

you think many women worry that they lack this instinct, like Sophie does?

As a mother, I have to say I do believe in mother's intuition. Often it is a mother who knows first if her child is ill or unhappy—sometimes even before they do. And I don't think that changes as the child grows into an adult. No one knows me better than my mum. She guessed I was pregnant before I knew about it. Before the birth of my first child I worried and worried that I wouldn't be a natural mother, that I wouldn't be able to get it right. I realized eventually that there is no such thing. All of us learn from page one starting on day one—there is no shortcut to learning how to bring up a child, and I don't think you ever stop learning. I do think that you gradually develop the kind of knowledge of your child and the depth of love for your child that becomes intuition.

8. Sophie seems to be in limbo between high-heeled shoes and wellies—glamorous London life and muddy coastal life. Are you more likely to step out in heels or boots, yourself?

I love a pair of high heels, I love to be glamorous, period. Like Sophie, I am an occasion dresser. But I also have a dog and very beautiful woods near my house, so muddy wellies come out of the closet regularly too.

9. Which book did you find more challenging to write: *The Accidental Mother* or its sequel, *The Accidental Family*? Why?

It's hard to say. Both books had their challenges. With *The Accidental Mother* I was starting from scratch with new characters and I had to work hard to give the story credibility and an edge of reality. But on balance I'd say that writing *The Accidental Family* was harder because I knew that so many readers really loved *The Accidental Mother* and had been waiting a long time to find out what happened next, and I didn't want to let them down.

10. The story of this "accidental family" seems far from over, as Seth joins the family and Sophie looks forward to her first baby. Can readers look forward to another book in this series? What does the future hold for Sophie and her family?

I honestly don't know. I always like to finish a book without all the loose ends tied and an unknown future laid out for my characters to inhabit, but I don't always feel the urge to write about it. *The Accidental Family* came about because so many readers asked me what happened next to Sophie and Louis and because once I started thinking about it I couldn't stop! I might very well revisit them in the future, but for now I have new characters and new ideas that I am working on.